NIGHTMARE GIRL

GENAVIE CASTLE

CASTLE PUBLISHING

COPYRIGHT

ISBN - 978-1-962047-12-8 Ebook

ISBN - 978-1-962047-13-5 Print Paperback

Cover design by: Genavie Castle

Edited by: EPONA Author Solutions

Printed in the United States of America

ABOUT THIS BOOK
CONTENT / TRIGGER WARNINGS

Everything about this book is entirely fictional. This is a stalker romance novel suitable for mature audiences only. There are dark elements within these pages. Please consider these potential trigger warnings before moving forward.

Graphic sexual content
    Explicit language
    Stalking
    Violence
    Un-aliving
    Date rape references
    Mass shooting references
    Childhood abuse
    Breaking and entering

Lastly, if you have a daddy kink, virgin kink or somnophilia kink, this book will probably ruin it for you. Consider yourself warned.

Oneiromancy - noun -
the interpretation of dreams in order to foretell the future.

PROLOGUE

THE LOUD MUSIC combined with the hundreds of voices speaking simultaneously was deafening; I could barely hear myself think. I moved past the revelers, doing my best to avoid the bodies bumping and grinding on the dance floor or the couples getting frisky on the sofas pushed to the side to make room for the crowded space. The bass thumped in my chest, and the smell of stale beer permeated the air. I walked through the party, moved through the living area, and froze. The world around me faded into the background as she maneuvered through the room, seemingly in slow motion. Her hips swayed with each graceful step. She tossed a stray strand of silky dark hair over her shoulder; a playful smile spread across her plump pink lips. Mesmerized, I followed her as she strolled through the party. My steps were slow, calculated as though I were stalking prey.

A handsy male grabbed her elbow, and she elegantly brushed him away and moved past him. The way she rejected him made me smile. She rounded a corner, and I lost sight of her. My heart rate galloped in my chest. I searched the crowd, and a drunken frat boy bumped into my chest, sloshing his beer. He gave me a slurred apology, then stumbled away from me. I continued searching for her, room by room, until I caught a glimpse of dark hair. Please be her. A slow smile graced my lips as I saw her mount a barstool at the makeshift bar. I beelined straight toward her and then stopped in my tracks. She was . . . captivating.

She leaned over the bar counter, picked up a red solo cup, and filled it with liquor. Her cropped sweater rode up her torso, revealing smooth porcelain skin. A short skirt skimmed her upper thighs, and the sight of her flesh made my heart stutter in my chest. I reminded myself to breathe and took another step. The dark-haired beauty eased back onto a barstool and swiveled in my direction. She raised her cup to her lips and peered at me through long, thick lashes. Our eyes locked. She lowered the cup, her tongue ran across her lower lip, and she slowly uncrossed her legs. My jeans became uncomfortably tight as my blood rushed to my cock. I needed her. I wanted her. I had to have her. Her piercing blue gaze traveled the length of my body as I approached her. My feet couldn't move fast enough. With each step, I memorized every inch of her perfect features, marveling over the way the lights surrounded her like a golden halo, making her look every bit the innocent angel and the seductive temptress. My hands were clammy, my pulse raced in my chest, and my skin buzzed with electrical jolts. Almost there.

An annoying buzz muted the sounds of chaos reigned around me. Shattered glass and fallen bodies surrounded me. I shook off the fuzziness in my head and searched for her. My body felt sluggish, and I struggled to get to my feet. Anxiety gripped my chest, and then there she was on the floor. Not moving. I rushed to her side. My stomach lurched. Blood covered half of her face, and her blue eyes were vacant. I pressed two fingers to the delicate spot on her neck and realized she was gone.

I bolted upright, breathing hard. Sweat covered my body, and my heart raced.

Fuck me. Not again.

CHAPTER 1
LAZARUS

I HARDLY RECOGNIZED the man staring back at me. My gray eyes were tinged with red, and their dark circles and scruff on my jaw made me look ten years older than I was. I turned off the faucet and dunked my face in the water-filled basin. The cold water stung and chased the sleep deprivation that had plagued me for the past several nights.

Fucking nightmares. They'd been happening for weeks and had gotten more vivid every time. Who was she? And why was I dreaming about her?

As much as I hated to admit it, I knew exactly why I was dreaming about her. I didn't want to face it. I didn't want to come to terms with the fucked up reality of my life . . . my heritage. It had been years. Why now? The woman, whoever she was, was important —that much I could admit. I needed to save her. Why? Mine. The answer came loud and clear.

I pulled my head out of the sink and depressed the stopper, allowing the water to drain. I dried off my face, went into the closet, and pulled on a pair of joggers and a T-shirt; the dream, no, the nightmare, played on repeat in my head. The dark-haired beauty's lifeless body flashed into my mind, making my stomach clench. I scrubbed my hand down my face, knowing I had to find her . . . but how? Put out a wanted ad on the internet? Hire a sketch artist and hand out flyers. All of those options screamed psycho, and I'd had enough of being called a psycho for ten lifetimes.

A queasy feeling of unease rolled through me. Talking about it would help, and I'd put off the visit for too long.

I left my room, bypassed the guest room, and did a double-take. Shit. I had . . . guests. Annoyed, I turned on the lights and crossed the length of the room in a few long strides.

"Wake up! Time to go!!" I shouted, shaking a slender arm.

The females groaned.

"Sorry ladies, I have an emergency I need to tend to." I grabbed the women's clothing from the floor and threw them on the bed.

"What time is it?" one of the women asked, rubbing her eyes.

"Time to go." I was being a dick, and I knew it. But I didn't want to deal with these women. I wanted them gone. Why'd I let them fall asleep in the first place? That wasn't like me. I usually was a hit-it-and-quit-it kind of guy. And then I remembered, I wanted to fuck myself into oblivion in hopes the damn nightmare wouldn't return. My brilliant plan had almost worked. I'd been exhausted after our little romp but had enough sense to go to my room and fall asleep. Guess I'd forgotten to throw them out beforehand. *You're getting sloppy, Laz.*

"Geez, you're pleasant in the morning," another woman complained while tugging a dress over her body.

"Like I said, emergency." I stalked out of the room and waited by the front door, calling downstairs. "Hey, Mike. I have two . . . guests who need a cab or ride-share. Can you take care of that?"

Mike gave me an affirmative, and I was ready to head back to the guest room to hurry the girls along when they came plodding through the apartment, still drowsy or maybe drunk. Maybe both.

I motioned toward the door. "The security at the front desk will arrange a ride," I said.

"Can we see you again?" The blonde woman traced her fingernails down my arm. I cringed.

"Uh . . . no." I stepped out of reach. "Emergency. I'm not sure when I'll be back."

"Can we at least get your number?" the other woman asked.

"No, but um . . . thanks." I shut the door behind them. Yes, I was truly an asshole. But I didn't give a shit. It's not like I'd made promises I had no intention of keeping. I was upfront about what I wanted. Every. Single. Time. If the woman wanted to read into the situation in hopes of making herself a permanent fixture in my life. Well, that was her problem. Not mine.

The smell of their perfume lingered and made me grimace. I stalked back to the guest room, which was a second primary suite used for entertaining guests and tore off the sheets. Everything smelled like them—the sheets, the room. It was nauseating. I thought of throwing the used sheets in the washing machine, but I decided to forgo the hassle and went into the hall to toss them in the trash chute. I passed the elevator just as the doors were closing.

"Is he throwing out the sheets we just slept on?" a female voice said.

I chuckled. Yes, I was being a total asshole and I wasn't sorry about it at all.

———

The drive to Montpellier Gardens was three hours, giving me the time to clear my head. I'd avoided this visit for too long and needed to get right with myself. The nightmares were fucking with my head, and it was a state of mind that wasn't conducive for someone in my line of work. A paid assassin couldn't afford to be distracted. And I had a big job lined up, which I hadn't taken seriously since the nightmares had started. I worked with my brother, Ezekiel, and our uncle, Josiah. They'd been asking for updates, which I couldn't give. It was a family-owned business, and my specialty was executing hits. So it wasn't like they were going to replace me. Still, there were only so many excuses I could dish out.

It'd be much easier if I could have just called her instead of making the three-hour drive. Hell, it would have been easier if I could have talked to anyone about the shit going on in my head half of the time. Growing up thinking I'd been damaged in the brain will do that to a kid. I wasn't damaged, Aunt Pol had taught me. I was just different. Gifted. I pushed the thoughts aside and pulled into a diner to grab breakfast. Twenty minutes later, I arrived in Montpellier.

"Good morning!" a mousy-haired girl chirped in greeting.

Jesus, she was just too cheerful for this early in the morning.

"Yeah, I'm here to see Polly Frasier," I said gruffly.

"And you are?" she asked, her focus on the computer screen in front of her.

"Her nephew, Lazarus."

"Oh, well, aren't you sweet, visiting your aunt and bringing her what smells like breakfast? If you could sign into the login sheet there." She pointed with her chin at the clipboard on the far end of the counter. "Ms. Polly is scheduled to be in the gardens. I'll let her attendant know to expect you. Do you know your way around?"

I nodded, signed the sheet, and walked to the terrace overlooking the gardens.

Montpellier Gardens was an assisted living facility. The best money could buy. Aunt Pol was Mom's sister and had been looking out for me since my mother had passed. She understood my affliction. The women in my family had said it was a gift passed down through the generations. Psychologists and a stint in the looney bin said differently. According to the professionals at Bright Haven Behavioral Institute for Teens, I had an overactive imagination. The men in white coats and cheap ties had diagnosed my prophetic dreams as delusions. I called bullshit on all of it. The damn dreams weren't a gift, but they were real, and no amount of medication would make them go away.

Memories of my time spent at Bright Haven came crashing back to me.

"You're going to stay here for a while," my stepmother had said. "And I want you to be on your best behavior."

"Why? Why am I staying here?" I asked.

"They'll help you with your condition," she replied curtly.

"I don't have a condition! It was a dream!! Just a silly dream we'd been joking about," I argued.

"Making up lies and telling jokes are two different things!"

"It wasn't a lie!"

"Fine, you were hallucinating. That's worse! Maybe your stay should be longer." She stomped away.

"Wait 'til my father finds out!" I shouted as she walked away.

My stay at Bright Haven had lasted weeks. I didn't belong there. None of the kids did.

I had been eleven, and even then, I had a stubborn streak a mile long. I refused to take the medications they'd tried to shove down my throat. I bit an orderly's fingers more than once and kicked one in the nose. I was small then, but fierce, and determined to fight them. I'd taken my beatings and vowed to make those men pay.

Six weeks in that damned facility robbed me of my innocence, and I emerged irrevocably changed, and not in a good way. By the time my father rescued me from Bright Haven, so much damage had already been done. The remedial punishments I'd received left more than physical scars. Those I could handle. It was the psychological ones that had done the most damage.

Ultimately, I'd gotten my revenge and enjoyed every minute of it.

CHAPTER 2
LAZARUS

FINGERS SNAPPED in front of my face and brought me back to the present.

Blinking my eyes, I nodded at the attendant, who my aunt was shooing away.

"I almost had to smack you in the face, son." Aunt Pol's brows scrunched with concern.

"Now, now, that's no way to greet your favorite nephew. Especially one who drove three hours to see you and brought you breakfast and your favorite cream puffs from Gabi's Diner." I dangled the white paper bag in front of her.

She narrowed her eyes at me and then held her hand out for the goodies. I chuckled, then leaned to peck her cheek.

"How are you doing, Pol? Is everyone treating you well?" I sipped the last dregs of my coffee.

"Like royalty." She withdrew the breakfast sandwich, set it aside on the table in front of her, then dug back into the bag and pulled out a clear plastic container holding a pastry. Aunt Polly had a weakness for sweets. She didn't waste time; she popped open the lid and practically inhaled the chocolate cream puff. I watched with mild fascination.

"This is so good. I cannot believe you brought only one." She licked the cream off her thin lips.

"The last time I brought a box, you ate the entire container. So that would be a no," I said.

She waved a chocolate-covered hand in the air. "I'm not in the mood for your lectures, son. Out with it. What's got your panties twisted into knots?"

"What do you mean? I'm not . . . twisted. And I don't wear panties," I scoffed.

"Sure. We almost called the paramedics while you were sitting there, staring off into space for forty minutes straight."

"I wasn't staring into space," I retorted. "Not for forty minutes. Maybe like twenty seconds."

She frowned, then licked the chocolate off her fingers. Once thoroughly satisfied that she'd gotten every trace of chocolate and cream, she sipped her tea, folded her hands neatly in her lap, and gave me her full attention.

"I'm listening." She smiled.

"Is it safe to have a proper visit now?" I chided. Aunt Pol was serious about her cream puffs, and I knew talking to her while she was enjoying the treat would get me nothing more than scornful looks and curt conversation.

She laughed. "It's good to see you, Laz. I would ask if you're okay, but if you're here, that means you're not. Tell me everything. It's been too long."

I proceeded to tell Aunt Pol about my dreams. She listened intently and asked the usual. When did they start? How often? Did the dreams change in any significant way?

I answered her as best as I could. They had started a month ago. I remembered it succinctly because the first time I dreamed of beauty, the dream had stopped when our eyes locked, and I'd awakened with a heavy boner.

It happened again a week later, and a few days later, the dreams escalated to her death. That shook me to my core. And the worst part of it all, I had the same dream continuously. Every night for the last several days I dreamed of her death. I'd wake with my heart hammering in my chest as though I couldn't breathe.

Aunt Pol regarded me with a curious look, and then a smile broke on her face.

I wrung my hands together, willing my irritation with my aunt to disappear. *This is Aunt Pol, you like her.* I reminded myself.

She chuckled, and my irritation grew.

"Are you serious with the laughing right now?" I scowled.

She clapped her hands together and let her laughter free. "Oh, my dear boy." She cupped my cheeks. "There is hope for you after all."

That was it. I was going to punch my sixty-eight-year-old aunt in the fucking face.

"Don't you see? You've found the one. Your one true love. And here I was, worried that you'd die alone and become a priest."

I chuckled at the thought of me being a priest. Celibate? Me? Never going to happen. The whole idea of giving up sex was . . . unnatural. But the conversation with my aunt wasn't going as I had hoped. I'd turned to my wise old aunt because she understood me. She knew me, and she was like me. Or so I thought.

"Aunt Pol, this isn't helping at all." I crossed my arms over my chest.

"You're such a grumpy butt," she replied.

"I am not a grumpy butt," I snarled for added effect.

"Okay, you're a grumpy old man," she teased. "How about you take me for a stroll in the gardens? Old man."

"I'm not old either." I rose and moved behind her wheelchair.

"Well, quit acting like it."

"I just told you about my nightmare, and you're acting like I just met the love of my life on *The Bachelor*."

"I used to love those shows!! Too much drama, and everything about it is so staged. You'd be good at it. But then again, you're too grumpy. Those high-maintenance bitches wouldn't know how to deal with you."

I laughed. "Just because a woman knows what she wants doesn't mean she's high maintenance."

"Please. Have you watched that show?" She turned her head to look at me. "No, of course you haven't. So, no lectures from the peanut gallery."

I just laughed because I knew this discussion wasn't going anywhere. I wouldn't get the answers I sought, so we strolled through the gardens, talking about unimportant things, and for the first time in the last few weeks, the weight of my nightmare didn't feel as heavy.

My aunt was somewhat of a celebrity in Montpellier. It was an assisted care facility for people with disabilities. My aunt had an aggressive case of rheumatoid arthritis. It had started when she was young and gotten progressively worse as soon as she hit sixty. I had offered to hire a live-in nurse, but we'd had difficulty finding reliable care. I found this place for her, and she and I agreed one week, if she hated it, we'd go back to finding a live-in. One week was all it took for her to love it here.

They had an excellent medical team on staff. Whatever treatment plan they had her on helped slow the progression of the disease. The rest of the people who worked there doted on the residents. They had an excellent meal plan created by a former Michelin-star chef. The accommodations were more posh than my penthouse flat. And they had plenty of activities to keep her busy. It cost me a small fortune every month, but her health had improved, and to see her live out her remaining days happy and smiling was worth every penny.

"This is my nephew," Aunt Polly told one of the staff members. A new girl. Cute. Doable. I smiled at the woman, and she smiled back. I'd be down for a quickie in the storage closet. My posture straightened, and I drew my shoulders back.

"But he's not for you," Aunt Pol continued. "He has a serious girlfriend whom he will marry soon."

The girl looked at me with a pinched, sour face. She was probably disgusted that I'd been unabashedly flirting while having a girlfriend at home.

God damn it, Auntie. My ego deflated like a popped balloon. She'd just cock blocked me.

The girl scurried off faster than I could say boo.

"Was that necessary?" I muttered and pushed her chair down the garden path.

"Oh Lord! Your face!!" She cackled.

"It's not that funny."

"Get used to it, sonny boy. I can't wait to meet my new daughter-in-law." She clapped her hands with glee.

"It's like you didn't even hear a word I said. Maybe we need to have your ears checked."

"What are you going on about, grumpster? I swear it's like you should be the one stuck in an old folks home."

"This is not an old folks home."

"Right. Just a home for those who cannot care for themselves. So much better. Rub salt in the wound, why don't you?"

"That's not what I meant. God!"

"There he is, the grumpiest of all bears, folks." She waved her arms around as though introducing me to a crowd of no one.

Her antics made me laugh. We continued through the gardens with her making jokes at my expense. I had to admit I loved her sense of humor. Only my aunt could call me out on my shit. And having to defend myself had helped me to forget all my worries. It was a morning well spent.

I brought her back to her room for her mid-morning *siesta*; before leaving, she patted the side of her bed.

"Lazarus, my dear boy. My son. I am happy for you. This . . . woman, in your dreams."

"Nightmares," I corrected.

"Dreams." She scowled. "It's only a nightmare if you cannot

protect her. Find her. Only you can protect her from her early demise."

"How do you know that? And where do I start?" I ran my fingers through my hair.

"You know how I know. Our dreams are our gifts." Then she held up her hand. "No. Don't say it, Lazarus Ford. Do not mention those quacks who think they know us and can diagnose our gifts because they read many books. No."

I zipped my mouth shut for a moment. After a long pause, I broke the silence.

"How do I find her?"

"Our dreams are meant to lead us to where we need to be. You've done this before. I am not sure why you are resisting so hard right now," she explained with a derisive tone.

"I haven't had a prophetic dream in years," I admitted to her.

"That means this one is important," she replied immediately. "Write it down, if you must. Every last detail. You said it was a college dorm party. Perhaps you need to start there."

"I'm not in college," I grumped.

"As if you can't figure out how to get to a college dorm party. Jaysus wept. Grumpy old butt. Off with you before you infect me with your grumpiness. Or oldness. Or butt-ness."

"That's not a word." I stood.

"It is now. Thank you for coming. And keep me posted. I want to know the minute you find her."

I kissed her cheek and left, wondering where I might find my nightmare girl.

CHAPTER 3
LAZARUS

FOUR DAYS after visiting Aunt Pol, I hadn't found my nightmare girl, and the lack of sleep turned me into an ornery fellow. Maybe my aunt was right. I was a grumpy old ass like Shrek. That made me laugh. I at least still had my looks. And money. I laughed harder and realized I was laughing at myself alone in my multi-million-dollar penthouse . . . like a deranged lunatic. Oh fuck, I was turning into Howard Hughes.

I pulled on my running gear and went for a run in the park near my building. Sex with random chicks hadn't kept the nightmares away, and I'd hoped running and weight training was the answer. Maybe I needed to work more.

Working with family had many benefits. I was paid well and didn't need to deal with admin bullshit. Paper pushing and dealing with people was not my forte, but firing off a high-powered weapon gave me a slight high that made me almost euphoric. Yeah, I got off on killing. It was my thing and the only thing that had kept the damn dreams away. Yet, handling a dangerous weapon in my current state hadn't seemed like a good idea either. I shrugged off the thought of dreams and picked up the pace.

Thanks to Uncle Josiah, we had the reputation of being fast, efficient, and selective. Our services were expensive but well worth the price tag. I could offer my services independently without my family's assistance if I wanted to. Why not? I'd been offered jobs more times than I could count. It was a small niche business. If you weren't in the know, you wouldn't know. Mercenaries were an odd bunch. We operated clandestinely. The shadows were our friends. I was speaking for myself as I'd only met a few like me. It was a life of solitude which hadn't bothered me until the nightmare girl who wouldn't stop fucking with my sleep and my focus. Yeah, I was full-on blaming the nameless beauty as though it were all her fault.

I let out a frustrated growl and pushed my body faster.

Dark hair and ice-blue eyes swam in my vision. Fuck me sideways. Nightmare girl was now haunting me during waking hours. I pushed harder, nearly sprinting. Where would I find her?

I hadn't heeded Aunt Polly's advice; perhaps that should change. I needed to be proactive and start trolling the local campus. There was only one university in the area, so that wasn't too hard to do. And I was an alumnus. My college experience had been different than most. I went, studied, and then worked on more important things, like weaponry, fighting skills, and physical combat. Chicks thought I was an athlete with my six-two-frame and solid muscle. But . . . fuck no. Team sports weren't my thing, and neither were crowds. And there it was, my reluctance to venture into some stupid college dorm party. I'd crashed a few while in school, which hadn't been all that long ago, even though Pol liked to tease me about being old. I'd just turned thirty. Okay, maybe that was too old compared to the kids running amok in college. The age factor wouldn't stop me from saving the girl and getting some sleep.

I reached the five-mile mark and slowed until I was at a brisk jog, then began walking. My body was tired, and my mind clear for the moment. I decided then that coffee would be an added boost and keep me awake while I puzzled out what to do about my nightmare girl.

My penthouse was in the middle of town, with plenty of bars, restaurants, and coffee houses within walking distance, but I chose one I hadn't been to in a long while. I liked the vibe and ambiance. It was understated and not your usual corporate chain. They catered to a specific crowd of misfits—which was kind of my people, except their menu was geared toward the dietarily snobbish, aka fucking vegans.

Buzzy's didn't serve animal byproducts, so I got my coffee black, like my mood.

The coffee house was busy, so I took my drink to-go and sat outside in the courtyard area. The cool fall breeze brushed against my nape, and despite the caffeine, I began to feel the pull of exhaustion. I tipped my head up to the sun. It didn't take long for my nightmare to make an appearance. Damn it. I didn't push away her image as was usually the case. Instead, I memorized it; her eyes were big and round and a pale blue that made me want to swim in them, and her sultry voice filled my ears.

I blinked rapidly. That was a first. I'd never heard her voice in my dreams. How long had I been out? I looked at my phone, and only two minutes had passed. The same sultry voice caught my attention, and I whipped my head left and right, searching for the sound.

A few feet away from me, a dark-haired woman approached Buzzy's. The tall man beside her completely obstructed my view of her, yet I knew it was her . . . my nightmare girl.

I leaned forward in my chair, straining to hear their conversation.

"Do you want anything?" she asked him as he held the door open for her. My heart stopped in my chest.

"Nah, I'm good. Strict diet of an athlete, babe."

What a douche.

"I'm gonna wait out here for ya. I gotta make a call."

She walked in, and he sauntered to the seating area and sat at a nearby table. The guy was built like an athlete, tall, lean, corded muscle. Football player, if I had to guess. He was taller than me by an inch or so, not that that mattered. My bullets had a non-discrimination policy when it came to wank stains like this guy. I sized him up for another second, then asked, "Hey, man, you mind watching my stuff? I gotta grab something from inside?"

"Sure, no problem." The guy nodded.

Sucker.

I left my hat and armband for my phone on the table and went in to check out the girl I knew was mine.

I approached the counter and stood behind her while the barista handed her items.

"What can I get you?" the cashier asked me.

"Umm . . . just water." I picked up the bottle, tapped my phone on the payment terminal, and turned just as she made her way to the front door.

My heart stuttered in my chest. The nightmares I'd had didn't do her justice—she was fucking beautiful. And mine.

I followed her. Before I could say anything, her friend stood and greeted her with a boyish grin most women would find charming.

"Aww, you didn't have to get me anything," he said, reaching for one of the coffees she held.

She swerved out of his reach. "I didn't. This is not for you."

I placed my cap on my head and sat down as my nightmare girl walked over to a woman sitting on the ground several feet away.

"Hi Elaine, it's been a while," she called out to the woman.

"How you been, girl?!" the toothless woman asked.

"Can't complain. Just studying all the time. I got you a little something." She handed over the cup of coffee and a pastry bag.

"Bless you, my beautiful Leigh. Always so generous."

"No problem. How've you been?"

"All good." The woman's hands shook as she pressed the cup to her lips. "Still at the shelter most days. Sometimes, I need to be free."

My girl chuckled. "Glad to hear it. Can I get you anything else?"

"No, girl. It's good to see you."

"You too, Elaine. I'll see you again soon." She patted the woman's hands and walked back toward me with a haunted look in her eyes.

Her act of kindness astounded me. She had a big heart, my night-mare girl.

"You are too sweet!" The blond man wrapped her in his arms in a brutish way.

She pulled away from him and glanced back at the woman. "Yeah, well, I wish I could do more."

"Oh, listen to you, you bleeding heart. We can't save every lost soul. You know that, right?"

"We? 'We' didn't do anything," she retorted.

"Right, right, it's all about you. How can I forget?" He draped an arm over her shoulders.

"You're such an ass." She shoved him away and walked by me.

"Come on, I'm joking. Let's go back to my dorm, and I'll make it up to you." He pulled her close to him again.

He just topped my kill list.

"I have to study." She wiggled out of his embrace.

"Special girl, that one," a gravelly voice said.

I flinched. I didn't startle easily, but this woman—Elaine, my nightmare girl had called her, with the half dozen shopping bags and a hitch in her step—snuck up on me.

"What are you?" I asked, while keeping my eyes trained on my girl walking away with that brute.

"Shouldn't you be askin' about your nightmare girl?"

I didn't need to see my reflection to know my face had gone pale white. "What the? How the??" I shook my head, knowing how she knew what was going on in my head was the least of my worries.

"What's her name?" I finally asked.

The older woman laughed. "Too late for questions. I must be off. But it's not too late for your nightmare girl. Use your wits, boy. Save her."

And then she ambled off faster than I thought she was capable of.

CHAPTER 4
LAZARUS

THE FIRST TIME I laid eyes on my nightmare girl, I was so mesmerized; she made me speechless. I didn't even speak to the woman, which was a grievous error on my part.

To make up for my mistake, I'd become a regular at Buzzy's, hoping she'd return. I sat at the same table, at the same time, in hopes she was a creature of habit, but she hadn't been back. Neither had Elaine—the woman who somehow knew my secrets. Elaine called my nightmare girl Leigh, which could have been a nickname.

I'd searched online and the university's database and got a dozen hits. Out of those, I had been unable to find a photo match. There were a couple that didn't have photos, which wasn't helpful. It was frustrating as fuck. And thus, I found myself frequenting the coffee house like an addict.

My nightmare resumed, so I wasn't about to give up on my quest. On my third visit to Buzzy's, my heart stopped a few feet from the door. A gusty wind blew dark hair around her pretty face—my nightmare girl.

I hurried toward the door, but a man wearing too much cologne was already there and held the door for her. She thanked him politely, placed a large bag on a table, and stood in line. She hadn't noticed me as I waited behind her. She stood so close her perfume filled my senses. I inhaled, deeply embedding her scent in my memory.

She wore baggy jeans, an oversized sweater, and sneakers like the last time I'd seen her. She dressed for comfort and practicality instead of fashion, although her loose clothing did nothing to hide her curves. My gaze roamed over the rounds of her ass as she stood in front of me. Her glossy hair fell like raven feathers down her back, and I imagined wrapping the silky strands around my fist while taking her from behind. Yep, it didn't take long for my thoughts to nosedive into the gutter.

I leaned in closer and took a particular interest in the sound of her voice. It was kind of low and husky. I wanted to hear her moan my name. Christ, shoot me dead. I'd never been so turned on by the sound of a woman's voice before. What the hell was wrong with me? I was so enthralled with taking her in, I hadn't been paying attention to her conversation. A conversation she was having with the man who used too much cologne. Fucker just landed the second spot on my kill list.

I pumped the brakes on my lustful imagination and paid closer attention to the conversation. Their discussion was harmless enough, but there was no denying what number two on my list was vying for. I ground my teeth. Too much cologne wearer had good game. He paid her compliments and made her laugh. I clenched and unclenched my hands. It'd be so easy to snap his neck.

He paid for her coffee, and her body posture went rigid. Either she didn't want to accept his offer or wasn't impressed. Interesting. She politely accepted, and they stepped off to the side.

"What can I get you?" the barista asked. "Sir?"

"Coffee, black," I said.

Robotically, I handed over my card to the barista, tapped a few prompts on the credit card terminal, and then moved to the end of the counter where Cologne Guy was talking Nightmare Girl's ear off.

She seemed disinterested, so I watched, listened, and waited.

The cologne guy followed my nightmare girl to her table. I grabbed my coffee and took a seat directly behind hers. I pulled my phone off my armband and pretended to fiddle with it while the suit guy made moves on my girl.

The fucker was working it. He wanted her, and he was a smooth motherfucker.

The barista delivered their drinks and a paper bag, and I caught sight of her name—Leighton. I smiled and then frowned. My focus flitted over to the barista. Medium-build with big brown puppy dog eyes that were glued to my girl. Well, shit. He seemed harmless enough, but the way he had doodled her name surrounded by hearts all over the cup told me he had other ideas.

"I haven't seen you in a long while. You must be busy with school. We need to put up a sign over your table that reads "Do not disturb" so that you can get all that studying done right here while sipping the best latte." The barista's gaze roamed all over her chest.

Yep, welcome to the list, Number Three.

Cologne Guy asked her to dinner and left his card. My knee bounced restlessly under the table. I wanted to steal the card from her, but my nightmare girl simply left it on the table under her many books. I breathed in deeply, trying to calm myself before approaching her.

My phone rang. Montpellier Gardens. I answered, knowing whatever it was, was important.

The facility needed to make some changes that took too long to review. My nightmare girl sat in front of me, studiously poring through books, so I sat sipping the caffeine, answering their questions, and watching my girl.

Suddenly, a loud, boisterous blonde stormed through the door, and immediately my hackles raised. She went straight toward my girl.

"This has taken much longer than anticipated, and something urgent requires my attention. If you'd be so kind as to email me the necessary paperwork, I'll respond as soon as I return to my office." I hung up the phone without waiting for an answer and listened to the conversation happening in front of me.

Pretending to be occupied with my phone, I focused on my girl, and the person who I'd assumed was a close friend. Leighton called her Hallie. They were complete opposites, not only in looks, though both were pretty women. But Leighton downplayed her beauty. She didn't wear much makeup. Her long, dark eyelashes framed her piercing blue eyes, and she had a natural pinkish glow on her cheeks, likely from the cold. Hallie wore full-on warpaint and skin-tight clothing like she was going to a nightclub at eleven-thirty in the morning.

If their appearance wasn't enough to highlight their differences, their discussion was. Keeping my head down, I leaned forward in my seat and listened, gathering intel on my girl.

A few moments later, the two women left. I could have shot myself in the head for not speaking to her sooner, but the conversation she'd just had with her friend was most enlightening. I grinned and mulled over the few things I'd just learned about my nightmare girl. One, Leighton was the most intriguing woman I'd ever seen. Two, I was not too fond of her slag of a friend. Three, I learned where she'd be later in the week.

CHAPTER 5
LEIGHTON

I HEFTED my book bag over my shoulder and exited my apartment, leaving behind the sounds of moans and grunts coming from my neighbor's place. I smiled inwardly, thinking how lucky my best friend was to be so carefree with her sexuality.

I'd had my share of flings over the years. That's what college was for, wasn't it? I hadn't been as carefree as Hallie; hell, I didn't know anyone, male or female, that was like her. Hallie's longest relationship had been a whole three-day weekend, and the longest she'd gone without a relationship was maybe half that. In some ways, I was envious. I wasn't going to lie. She was confident with her sexuality and didn't bother with modesty.

I was more comfortable hiding behind loose clothes and waiting for the man to make the first move. Maybe that needed to change. I'd been single for nearly six months and hadn't been on one date. I'd been content living vicariously through Hallie, which, I had to admit, was pretty pathetic of me.

I switched my heavy ass bag to my other shoulder and continued to Buzzy's. It was a small eclectic coffee house and bookstore—just my vibe. Most students preferred the hipster joints closer to campus, but this place was me. I'd been coming to Buzzy's since I'd transferred to Ashmore University—a smallish school in the Pacific Northwest. In my opinion, it was the country's best-kept secret, hidden amongst a thousand miles of verdant pine trees and bordering the moody Pacific Ocean. Yes, it rained a lot, but today was a warm, sunny day.

The wind blew my hair in every direction as I struggled to open the door to the cafe. A strong arm reached around me and held the door open.

"Thank you!" I said to the stranger. I couldn't see, thanks to the hair impeding my vision, but I smelled him. The strength of his cologne nearly made my eyes water.

Safe from the wind, I eyed my favorite table near the fireplace, and plopped my book bag on the tabletop to reserve my space. My book bag thudded on the wooden surface, and I almost apologized for the disruption, but there was no one to disrupt. It was mid-morning, and I had just missed the breakfast rush.

There was a short line at the counter, which gave me an opportunity to eye the pastry case.

"Smart move," a male voice said.

I gave him a bewildered look.

"Reserving your table before placing your order," he added.

"Oh, yeah. My shoulders needed the break," I replied, taking a step back to put some distance between my olfactory senses and his cologne. It wasn't a horrible smell. It was just . . . too much.

"What are you studying?" The man, impeccably dressed in a blue pinstriped suit, asked. He fidgeted with his pink tie and flashed me a genuine smile, showing off perfectly straight, recently whitened teeth.

He was kind of cute. And a well-off businessman if his gold Rolex was any judge.

"Umm . . . psychology."

"Psychology. Uh oh. Smart and beautiful. I should probably stop talking to you now."

"Hey, now. Be nice."

He laughed. "How much longer do you have?"

"This is my last semester," I replied.

"Winter semester grad. That's cool."

I shrugged. "I took some time off a few years back."

He laughed again. "What can I get you?"

My body stiffened. "Oh, um . . . that's nice of you, but I can pay for my coffee."

"It's no bother. Maybe one day you'll pay me back with some of my psychological issues."

"Oh my. That might take a while."

He cracked up laughing, which made me smile. Any man who could laugh at a joke made at his expense was genuinely okay in my book. He placed his order and told Henry behind the counter that he'd be paying for my drink and whatever else I wanted.

I sighed inwardly. I wasn't one to take handouts. And I hated feeling like I owed him something because he bought me a cup of coffee.

"Hi, Leighton! Your usual, right?" Henry, the barista, asked me.

"Yes, please, and thank you." I turned to the cologne guy. "Thanks, that's generous of you."

"You're welcome, Leighton." He smiled.

Oh, he was smooth. Red flags went up in my brain. If it's too good to be true, it probably was. I tempered the warning and plastered a sweet smile on my face as we scooted to the end of the counter until our drinks were ready.

"I'm Nick. Nick Hanford." He extended his hand.

"Leighton. Nice to meet you."

"I put in your order for the breakfast wrap, Leigh. Your drink will take a minute, and I'll bring it to you. For now, here's your drink, sir." Henry slid over a drink and gave me a wink. I'd already had breakfast, but I suppose I could save it for later if someone were buying. I was a starving student. Sort of.

Nick followed me to my table, and we chatted for a bit.

"I hate to leave, but I have a business meeting," he told me.

I nodded. "Of course. It is Monday, after all."

"I'd rather stay here and get to know you," Nick smiled.

This guy knew all the right things to say. The warning bells in my head sounded like a Tibetan gong driving off evil spirits.

Henry approached my table with a drink and paper bag in hand. "I haven't seen you in a long while. You must be busy with school. We need to put up a sign over your table that reads "Do not disturb" so that you can get all that studying done right here while sipping the best latte."

"Thank you, Henry." I smiled at the barista.

"Well, I better get to it," Nick said as Henry returned to the counter.

"Thank you for the coffee and breakfast." I smiled politely.

"My pleasure, but . . . I'd like to buy you a real meal. Dinner?"

Yeah, this guy had all the ladies eating out of his palm. Handsome, wealthy, polite. Those weren't bad things, but something about him was off.

"Um . . . sure," I replied despite the warning bells going off in my head. He was just too perfect. That always creeped me out. Or maybe I was reading into things too much.

At least I didn't respond with a resounding *fuck no*. I almost patted myself on the back for not choosing my typical no response. Usually, I wore my "don't ask me out" sign on my forehead. I guess my warning sign was on the fritz. But seriously, what was the harm in having one dinner? A girl has to eat.

"You seem like a smart girl with steadfast morals, so I won't push. But here's my card. I'd really like to see you again, Leighton." He handed me a card with his contact info and a cheesy picture. "Your move, sexy." He winked.

I almost burst out laughing before he exited Buzzy's.

Grateful to be alone at my table, I sat, took out my books and laptop, and got to work.

I was eyeballs high in the intricacies of human behavior when a storm of blonde hair blew through the door.

"There you are! I've been looking everywhere." The familiar voice of my neighbor and best friend cut through the room. "Are you hiding from me on purpose?" she accused, her voice shrill.

Did we have plans I'd forgotten about? I tilted my head to the side and waited for her to continue. She didn't. She leaned over my table and hugged me.

"It's an emergency. I need you."

No, it wasn't an emergency. And no, she didn't need me. Hallie liked to make mountains out of molehills. She had a plethora of first-world problems.

Despite her dramatics, I asked, "What's wrong?"

"I need you to come shopping with me. I need to look hot for this interview. And I need your help."

I looked down at my baggy jeans and oversized sweater. "Fashion advice? From me?"

"Yes, you. You're . . . you. The hottest nerdy girl on the planet. You can make honest and professional look hot without being trashy or too . . . boring."

"And you call that an emergency?" I began putting my books away, knowing arguing with her when she was in one of her moods was pointless.

"Well, yeah. I really need this gig, Leigh. My daddy will cut me off if I don't get a job. Like . . . really cut me off."

I smirked. "Ah, I see. More money. More problems."

"Go ahead and laugh. But it won't be funny when I have to start paying my own bills."

I giggled.

"Seriously, Leighton, this is important. I'm scared." Her eyes watered.

Damn, she was good. And serious. She would not know what to do if her father pumped the brakes on the money train. I, on the other hand, was the exact opposite. Perhaps that was what made our friendship work.

"Hallie, sweet cheeks, you have unprotected sex with random

dudes. If unplanned pregnancy and STDs don't scare you, you ain't afraid of shit," I told her.

She gave me a devilish smile.

"I do love me some cream pie." A look of pure bliss washed over her gorgeous face.

"I'll take your word for it," I told her.

"What? You don't ride bareback? Like ever?!!" she shrieked. Buzzy patrons glanced our way.

"Seriously? Announce it to the world?" I waved my arms around.

She laughed. "You haven't lived until you're overflowing with cream."

"You're nasty." I packed up my things.

"Who's Nick Hanford?" She picked up the business card. "Oh, he's cute. And an investment banker." She fanned herself with the card.

"He bought me coffee." I shrugged.

"And he wants to go out with you," she said.

"Yeah, and I'm thinking not." I stepped away to throw out my empty coffee cup.

"Oh, don't be a prude," she replied.

"Thanks, Henry!" I waved at the barista.

"Anytime, Leighton. Don't stay away for too long, or I'll have to start stalking you." He waved back.

That was an odd thing to say. I shrugged off the comment and returned to my table to find Hallie grinning from ear to ear.

"What?" I asked. "What did you do, Hallie?"

"Someone has a dinner date this Saturday," she said in a sing-song voice.

"You didn't." I glared at her.

"I did. From your phone," she said. "And girl . . . he is eager." My phone chimed.

"And you need to learn to stay out of people's business. As your future therapist, that is the first thing we will work on."

She laughed.

"And if he turns out to be a psycho, I will never forgive you," I added as I slung my book bag over my shoulder.

"I can't believe you haven't let a guy shoot his load in you," she said, completely dismissing my comment.

I shook my head. "Breeding kinks are all you, Hallie."

"But it's so freaking good!" She humped the air as we exited the coffee shop.

CHAPTER 6
LAZARUS

AFTER LEIGHTON LEFT with her friend, I hurried home to change into proper business attire and went to my office—the one I never used.

The receptionist's eyes widened, and she muttered something under her breath as I stepped off the elevator. I growled at her for good measure, and she nearly ducked under her desk to hide. Proud of myself, I smiled inwardly and stomped toward my designated office, glowering at anyone who dared to glance my way.

The Sentinels was a division of Ford Limited—not the car manufacturer, that was another family. Solomon Ford, my father, started a private air charter service. It had grown over the years from one private jet to having nearly a dozen jets in every major city in the US and across the globe. As his son, I'd learned about the business and had been granted all the perks that came with it, including a seat on the board of directors, but the airline business wasn't my calling. My stay at Bright Haven had set me on a different path. One my father had been reluctant to set me on, but I wasn't complaining. I liked being the family hitman.

My father, and Uncle Josiah—Dad's only brother—started The Sentinels as a side project. Josiah and I shared the workload and occasionally worked together on jobs. But mostly, Uncle Jo worked in the office alongside Ezekiel.

Zeke was two years older than me and better at running the business. He'd studied computer coding and had a particular proclivity for cyber security. I suppose he was the brains, and I was the muscle. But I wasn't worthless when it came to sleuthing. I could hold my own when it came to cyberstalking. Zeke and Josiah were excellent at their respective jobs, and I did trust them, but I did my own research on the contracts every so often. I didn't like going in blind if I could help it. Leighton was a private matter. I wasn't going to hand this particular job over to anyone, not even my brother, who, although we didn't speak to one another much outside of work, was my oldest and only friend.

My presence at the moment was causing a stir, and I couldn't give a rat's ass as long as no one bothered me with trivial shit. I had a critical mission to do.

At my desk, I fired up my computer and logged on. I ran Leighton's name through our database. While the system sorted her info, I made a mental note to research Henry, the barista, and Nick Hanford, the investment banker. I didn't have a name for number one on my kill list, the blond dude, so I also decided to hack into Buzzy's online security system. It hadn't taken long to get into their antiquated system. It was a small business, and it wasn't like they were dealing in espionage. It was a vegan-friendly coffee house, for fuck's sake.

I hacked into their digital surveillance archives and found the date I sought. I scrolled through hours of footage and found a perfect shot of my nightmare girl. I paused on the pixelated photo, downloaded the pic, and did the same with number one on my kill list. I'd run his image through our facial recognition software.

Pleased with myself and the information I'd gathered, I felt calmer. I was getting closer to claiming her, which hopefully meant I'd get a decent night's sleep.

A knock on my door had me turning from the screen with a scowl. Zeke entered my office with a wary look.

"This is a surprise." He sauntered to my desk and sat in the chair opposite me. "And you're wearing a suit. What's the occasion? Is there a meeting we were supposed to have?"

"No. I work here too, you know."

"I know that, asshole. I sign your fucking paychecks. You're just never here. What are you working on?"

"Fuck off. Just because you have the authority to sign your name on a piece of paper doesn't mean you control my life. I don't have to tell you about everything I do."

He held up his hands defensively. "Whoa! Ceasefire. I was curious, is all."

I grunted an acknowledgment.

Zeke was the spitting image of our father. So was I, for that matter. Dark hair, gray eyes, and the same cleft in our chin. It was uncanny, considering we'd had different mothers. My father was quite the philanderer. Solomon Ford had three sons from three different women. All two years apart. Margaret, his wife, and Zeke's mother, hated me with all the firepower of the sun. I didn't blame her, not really. My father wasn't an easy man to live with. Neither was I, for that matter. Zeke and I used to joke that he probably had more illegitimate children out there.

My older brother rubbed his chin and said, "Laz, you're my brother, and I would do anything for you. If you need me, all you have to do is ask."

He was right, and I'd known it all my life. Our father had taken me away from my mother at a very young age. My six-year-old self couldn't understand why she wouldn't allow me to stay with her forever, but she was defenseless against him and all his shady friends and piles of money. Zeke's mother hated my guts. I was proof of her husband's infidelity. I couldn't blame her, and her insistence on having me out of her hair every weekend was a blessing in disguise as I had gotten the chance to spend time with my mother and Aunt

Polly. I learned about my family's history and the legacy of prophetic dreams. My mother always told me, "Your father will give you a life I couldn't imagine. Learn all you can from his connections, Laz. Use his position to make a life for yourself." She was right. It had been a hard road during my teenage years, but worth it overall.

"Thanks, man." I finally said to Ezekiel. "I know you mean well, but this has nothing to do with you or the company."

He quirked his eyebrow at me. "Fair enough. We should . . ." he paused. "We should get together sometime. We haven't done that since you were in school."

I shrugged. I didn't need bonding time. That wasn't my style.

"Don't do it for me or us. Do it to make the other one jealous."

I grinned. Yeah, it'd be worth it just to make that fucker jealous.

Davis, our father's third son, had been a thorn in my backside since we were kids. It was his blabbering mouth that had gotten me thrown in Bright Haven. In hindsight, it worked out well for me; although, I could have gone without the scars. And if that was his only offense, I probably could have forgiven the schmuck. But he was a pathological liar, constant meddler, kiss-ass and know-it-all. It was better to steer clear of him, or I just might lose my mind and shoot him in the face.

Zeke felt the same. My oldest brother had always wanted to become a professional hockey player. He trained hard, and he was good. He'd even received a full scholarship. Zeke had taken Davis to his mother's house one morning. Davis and his mother had insisted Zeke take Davis skating at a rink near her house. Zeke had been a good skater, and somehow, he ended up with a broken knee that had ended his career. He was lucky he could walk. No one knew the full extent of the accident except the three present that day. Davis and his mother had the same story; Zeke hadn't said a word, but ever since then, he hadn't wanted Davis or his mother anywhere near him.

I had been at my mother's that weekend, and the night before, I'd had a dream about an ice skating accident. Ezekiel was the only skater in the family, so I'd called the house, and Margaret refused to let me talk to her son before he left to drop off Davis. By the time I'd gotten hold of him, he was in the hospital. I suspected it hadn't been an innocent accident. But I was young when it had happened and already pegged as the family psychopath. At age fourteen, I had my demons to bear.

"He is here, by the way," Ezekiel added. "I thought you might be here specifically to annoy him."

A low growl emanated from my chest. I sounded like a beast, and at that moment, I was ready to hunt that asshole and tear him apart with my bare hands. The trip down memory lane sparked a rage in me that would never go away.

"Easy," Ezekiel said. "He's in a meeting, and although I hate the fucker as much as you do, it's better to ignore the runt. Don't let him get under your skin. He hates it when he's not included."

My brother was right, and I remembered to calm my breathing.

"Alright, then," I logged off my computer and stood. "I've done everything I came to do. Thanks, man."

Ezekiel walked me to the elevator, no questions asked.

The door opened, and out stepped Davis. Ezekiel was an arrogant ass but tolerable prick. I was a bonafide asshole who glared more than smiled. Davis had shifty eyes and was always scheming. The man didn't look anything like us. We used to say that he wasn't a Ford. He didn't even have the same last name, something his mother had insisted upon, but Solomon protected him. And that was the only reason he was still alive.

Ezekiel gave me a slight shake of his head, telling me not to engage. I rolled my eyes. My unofficial title with The Sentinels was The Fixer. I eliminated issues . . . ahem . . . people who caused problems. It was a bit ironic that I could destroy assholes that had nothing to do with me, and the one asshole that had effectively ruined my childhood was standing before me, still breathing. God, I wanted to break his fucking neck.

"What are you doing here?" Davis asked.

"None of your fucking business." I stepped around him, then turned to face Zeke. "See you this weekend. Saturday, six-ish, right?"

"Yep, I wouldn't miss our weekly brotherly bonding time for the world." Ezekiel played along.

It was a juvenile dig, but the look of envy on Davis's face had me all but glowing with selfish pride.

CHAPTER 7
LAZARUS

LEIGHTON RAE PARKER was a psychology major with a three-point-eight GPA. Her choice of major made me grimace. Psychologists were my least favorite people. I hoped it was a passing fascination rather than a real passion. And if it was . . . maybe I could convince her to choose another career path or none at all. I had plenty of money. She'd never have to work again. Yeah, I was getting way ahead of myself.

She worked part-time in the university library, and when she wasn't working, she was there studying. Leighton kept to herself for the most part. She didn't have a substantial following on social media and wasn't much of a partier, which was somewhat surprising because Hallie, the blonde woman she was with at the coffee shop, was quite popular.

Hallie's social feeds taught me that Leighton had recently broken up with Keith Maynard, number one on my kill list and all-star quarterback. According to the info I'd been able to piece together, they'd called it off last spring, and he'd been seeing someone else. Now that school was in session, he wanted her back. From what I could tell, he was sleeping with anyone wearing a skirt, and she must've known that, too, because she continued to push him away.

Leighton lived off-campus in a pricey, single-story townhome, which I learned was owned by her stepfather. As lovely and expensive as it was, it was severely lacking in the security department. Using only my credit card, I jimmied my way into her front door during broad daylight.

The townhome had a simple layout, which opened into a small dining room and kitchen combo to the right and a tidy and a cozy living room to the left. The far wall of the living room was lined with bookshelves. I glanced at the books, taking note of the titles. She had numerous textbooks, mostly about psychology and human behavior, and a vast collection of smut, judging by all the half-naked men gracing the covers.

I moved down a small corridor, passing a utility closet containing a washer and dryer and more storage space. Her bedroom was on the left, directly behind the living area, and the bathroom on the right.

Another door at the end of the hallway led to a patio area. I tested the lock and frowned at the flimsy mechanism. A small concrete slab was directly behind the back door, barely large enough for the wrought iron two-seater garden table.

A solid brick wall enclosed the patio, and spruce trees had been artfully planted alongside it, effectively hiding the dismal concrete.

A patch of dirt with copper plant markers bordered the concrete wall to the right, dividing her property from its neighbor, who just happened to be Hallie.

On the opposite end, the brick wall continued down a narrow alleyway to a gate that allowed her to enter her own backyard without going through the house. A deep scowl formed on my forehead when I noticed the broken latch on the gate.

This place was so unsafe I'd wanted to kidnap her and force her to live with me.

I returned to Leighton's bedroom, which, unlike the organized living area, looked like a tornado had come through. Clothes were strewn all over the neutral travertine flooring, and her bed was unmade. I flopped down on the queen-sized mattress, rubbing her scent all over me. Rolling over, I smooshed my face in her pillow and inhaled her delicate floral scent. Blood rushed to my groin as I imagined her sleeping . . . naked . . . on this bed. Out of curiosity, I reached over and opened the nightstand drawer and smirked as I pulled out a fucking vibrator. Leighton, you naughty little girl. The dildo wasn't shaped like a penis, it was curved, and the other end had a piece I couldn't quite figure out. I brought the device to my nose and caught the barest feminine scent. I imagined Leighton pleasuring herself, wet and writhing. My cock swelled in my jeans. My tongue flicked the tip. The faintest taste of her arousal tickled my taste buds, causing me to adjust myself. I turned on the device. It vibrated, and the piece on the other end caused a gentle suction and massage. Oh, hell no. The device was slender, lacking the girth and length I'd always been proud of. And I'd like to think I was a good fuck. But there wasn't a man in the world who could compete with something that penetrated, sucked, and vibrated at the same time. Irritated, I stabbed the power button shutting it off, and tucked the damn thing in my pocket. She was not using this again.

Reluctantly, I got off the bed and thoroughly searched her apartment while making special notes of what made my girl tick. After my perusal, I pulled out my phone and listed items I needed for my next clandestine visit. I left her place, satisfied with my findings, and threw the fucking vibrator in the nearest trashcan.

CHAPTER 8
LEIGHTON

I ROLLED the cart of books and meandered through the aisles, shelving tomes in their proper places. It was mindless work and paid shit, but I loved being around the books, and it gave me something to do.

In the middle of the political science section, a meaty paw covered my nose and mouth while an arm wrapped around my torso, fastening my arms to my sides. My heart lurched as panic surged through my veins. I stomped my boot on the assailant's foot. He released me with a high-pitched screech.

"Fuck! Leigh! It's just me." Keith hopped up and down on one leg.

"Leighton? Is there a problem?" Tracy, the head librarian, scowled.

"No, sorry. It's a misunderstanding," I told her.

"Damn you, Keith! You scared the shit out of me," I whisper-shouted at my ex and smacked his arm.

"I wanted to surprise you," he said. He glanced at his foot. "Fuck, I have a game this weekend."

"Creeping up on a girl is not cute, Keith. For fuck's sake, I thought you were attacking me."

"Sorry. I thought . . . I don't know what I thought. I just wanted to see you."

I rolled my eyes. "Come here, have a seat." I drew him away from the students studying nearby and guided him to a chair.

He sat, slid off his shoes and socks, and wiggled his toes. His toe was red but not swollen.

"I'm no expert, but it looks fine," I told him.

"Yeah, it should be. It still kind of hurts, though. Do I least get a kiss?" He leaned toward me.

"You never quit, do you?" I glared at him.

He flashed me his pearly whites. Damn it, he was handsome. And he had those gorgeous, tanned muscles. Despite my heart's protest and my brain screaming reminders that he was a cheater, my body was leaning in for those lips.

A resounding thud snapped me out of my lust haze. I rose, searched behind me for the sound, and noticed a textbook on the floor several feet away.

"Leighton?!" Tracy frowned at me. "What is going on with you today?"

"Sorry! It wasn't me," I replied.

Keith snaked his arms around my waist. "Guess I should leave you to your books."

I untangled myself from his embrace. "Yes, you should. And get your foot looked at. Just to be safe."

"I'm glad you still care about me." He smiled.

"Keith, what are you doing? This is over," I said.

"It doesn't have to be. I apologized a million times for my one mistake, which happened while we were apart. I want us to be together. Is there someone else?" His gaze searched my face.

"No one special, but I am dating again," I said, thinking about the date Hallie had set into motion.

"That doesn't make me happy. I'm not going to lie. But . . . fuck. I deserve it, I guess." He pulled me close, crushing me to his chest. "Leigh. Don't give up on me. I won't ask you to stop seeing other men, but will you at least consider coming to the Halloween party? With me?"

I frowned into his chest.

"You don't have to answer right this minute but think about it. Please," he said into my hair.

He kissed my forehead and left me feeling confused.

Hours later, I trudged to my apartment. Keith's visit had occupied too much space in my brain. I hated it, and worse yet, I didn't have a solution. Not even a potential one. Fuck.

Men were so complicated. Or was it me? Keith and I decided to take a break while he went home for the summer. It had been my idea. An idea I came up with because I didn't want to spend the entire spring break with his parents. I'd met them a time or two; they were lovely people. Staying at their home for months seemed like a heavy commitment. I wasn't ready for that then or now. My brilliant plan, however, didn't include the reality that he'd start dating someone else so quickly. His new relationship came at me like a tidal wave, and I should have prepared myself for it because Keith was an attention whore. He took that summer fling and posted it all over social media. And that hurt like a motherfucker. So maybe it was my fault. And perhaps I should be more forgiving. Nah. It was never the woman's fault.

An uncomfortable sinking sensation in my gut chased the silly thought away. I glanced around me, not noticing anything other than shadows.

My apartment was a short fifteen-minute walk from campus. Although I had a car, I never used it. Parking was a nightmare, and I enjoyed walking even during rainy weather. Usually, there were more people out. The hair on my arms stood on end, and I picked up the pace. My building came into view. *Almost there.*

A few minutes later, I was back in my apartment. The warmth and security of my haven welcomed me. I locked the door and sighed in relief as the creepiness that had slithered over my skin slipped away.

Fucking, Keith. I blamed my ex's surprise visit for the unease I'd felt walking home. Or maybe it was him. No, couldn't be. That wasn't his style. Keith was an all-eyes-on-me kind of guy. He wouldn't skulk in the shadows.

I opened my fridge door and frowned at its emptiness—it was time to place a grocery delivery order. I popped open a can of Truly Lemonade and took a swig while searching my pantry for a little more kick. Bubbles filled my belly as I pulled a bottle of tequila, three-quarters empty. Tequila and lemonade? I shrugged. Why not? I mixed the concoction in a tumbler, then moved through my house, undressing as I went down the short hallway. Passing the kitchen, I slipped off my jeans and sweater, placed them in the washer, and then went to my room.

I went straight to my nightstand and picked up the television remote. I preferred reading to watching television, but tonight, it was all about the noise. The quiet in my apartment and the uneasy feeling from earlier had me feeling more wary than usual. And my tequila-hard lemonade concoction hadn't kicked in. I randomly selected a channel and decided to calm my nerves with a hot bath.

As I crossed the short distance between my room and the bath-room, I noticed a dark silhouette at my window. I dropped to the ground, and my heart thundered in my chest. What the fuck? The silhouette had a medium build and was flat-chested. It had to be male, I thought. My breath came in short gasps. I crawled forward toward the entry where I'd left my phone.

My tiny apartment had a bay window next to the front door that let in plenty of light during the day through a gauzy curtain. The lights were off, so whoever it was couldn't see into the apartment clearly, but I imagined it wasn't enough to conceal my near naked-ness. The bubbles in my belly felt like acid.

From the floor, I glanced up and noticed a faint red glow near his face. My nostrils flared, detecting the sour stench of nicotine seeping through the seams of the door—definitely not the all-star quarterback, then.

Staying out of sight, I stood slowly and smacked the window. The dark figure disappeared. I reached for my cell phone, which had been in my purse, and dialed 911. While speaking with the operator, I got dressed and waited until the police arrived.

I remained on the phone with the 911 operator until the police showed. It took them seven minutes. Not horribly long, but long enough for my stalker to kill me. I rubbed my arms over my hoodie.

Hallie, who lived next door, arrived home as the police left.

"Leighton, are you okay? What's going on?" She embraced me.

"I'm fine," I told her. "Some creep was spying on me when I came home."

"Shit. Did they catch the guy?"

"No, apparently, they looked around and found nothing. And, of course, none of the neighbors saw anything either. It's . . . violating. The guy was standing right here outside of my window looking in." I gestured to my window.

"Do you think it's the same guy? The one that was leaving notes on your car?" she asked.

I hadn't even thought about that. A year ago, some freak had been leaving weird notes and roses on my car at school. The stalker had broken into my vehicle a couple of times. I got a new car which still didn't make me feel safe, so I started walking. I never had contact with the creep again. Now that I was single again, it could be the same person. But now the asshole knew where I lived. That made me sick.

"I hadn't thought about that." I massaged my forehead. "Maybe? I guess it's possible. I almost thought it was Keith. He stopped by the library earlier tonight."

"No, it wasn't him." She shook her head. "I mean, I'm sure it wasn't. Wait? He stopped by the library. Tonight?"

"Uh, yeah. He appeared out of nowhere while I was working and scared me half to death. If it weren't for the cigarette the creeper had in his mouth, he would have been my first suspect," I replied.

"I'm sorry, I should've been here. Why didn't you call me?" Hallie said with a sympathetic frown.

"Don't be. There wasn't anything you could have done. It happened so fast, and the police are doing what they can." The stress of the day pulled at me.

"You must be freaked. Do you want me to stay? Hang out for a little while?" she asked.

"Thanks, but I'm exhausted. I need to sleep," I told her.

We said our goodbyes, and I got into the shower. The heat of the water wasn't enough to alleviate the ickiness of being watched. I scrubbed until my skin felt raw and then slumped to the shower floor in tears. Did I do something wrong? Why was someone stalking me again?

I began berating myself with a barrage of questions. Was I leading someone on? Did I make someone angry? Was I dressing too provocatively? Was it that guy who bought me coffee? No, his cologne would've been a dead giveaway. Who would do this and why?

The water ran cold, and my skin was wrinkly, forcing me to pick myself up from the shower floor. I crawled into my bed, emotionally exhausted.

Seeking comfort, I smooshed my face into my pillows, which smelled different. Masculine. I sat upright with a start, my heart rate clamoring in my chest for the third time in one night. Was he in here? I sniffed my pillows and blankets—the faintest hint of spice and leather. I walked through the house, sniffing around, then returned to my bed and inhaled. The diffused scent was so minimal it was probably my imagination running wild. I glanced at the empty bottle of tequila on my nightstand, then shook my head. Maybe it was me. I settled my thoughts, and then I realized something significant. There wasn't the slightest hint of smoke. Okay then, just my imagination.

I placed my phone on the pillow beside me and snuggled under the covers, pretending a strong man, smelling of leather and spice, was holding me protectively in his arms.

CHAPTER 9
LAZARUS

WATCHING Leighton work at the library should have been boring, but it wasn't in the least. Contentment filled me as I observed her from afar. She stocked shelves and worked behind the desk, helping other students find books. All was going well until number one on my list showed up. The fucker snuck up behind her, and I was ready to tear his throat out. Leighton surprised me by defending herself. It wasn't a lethal move, but it had been effective. He leaned in for a kiss, and she almost met him halfway. I tempered my rage by knocking a heavy tome off the shelf. That was enough to get him out of the library and away from her. Number One was a nuisance, and I'd have to deal with him soon.

An hour later, I followed Leighton home after she'd finished her shift, shaking my head the entire time. Her apartment wasn't far from campus, but walking alone in the dark was a big no in my book for all women, especially the one that was mine.

The sun had gone down hours ago, and although there were students milling about, I'd counted three deserted areas on her way home that would make it so easy for someone to abduct her off the streets. Couldn't she have taken a ride share or driven? According to my research, she had a driver's license and an electric car sitting in front of her apartment, paid for, once again, by her stepfather. At least she wore sensible shoes. If she'd been wearing heels, I'd throw her over my shoulders and spank her ass for not being more cautious with her life.

Her apartment complex came into view thirteen minutes later. I remained in the shadows as she made her way to the front door and waited. Hidden by the darkness, I watched from across the street as she unlocked the door and entered her apartment. The sheer curtains did little to conceal the inside of her home. I moved to position myself directly in front of the bay window and was pleased she hadn't turned on all the lights. From the twenty feet distance, I could barely make out her silhouette.

I was about to leave when the stench of nicotine floated my way, causing my nose to itch. Annoyed, I waited for the smoker to pass me and noticed something familiar about him. He walked straight to Leighton's door, and I expected him to knock. But he didn't. The fucker stood outside of her window, peering into her house while smoking his cigarette. Son of a bitch! She was mine to stalk. I clenched my fists and moved closer, still sticking to the shadows.

A few feet away, something hit the window from the inside. Leighton. Her stalker bolted. I paused a beat, wanting to check on her and wanting to kill the fucker at the same time. As long as she stayed in, she would be fine. I took off after him. The asshole was quick, but I stayed on his tail for a few blocks and continued my pursuit, staying in the shadows as he turned down an alleyway and went downstairs to a basement-level apartment. Lights flicked on, and I pressed my ear to the door, listening for a sign that he had company. Aside from his heavy footfalls, all was quiet. I knocked on the door and stepped to the side, the darkness concealing my presence.

He opened the door and took a few steps outside, looking around. I stepped behind him, slipped into his apartment, and waited. He re-entered his place, closed and locked the door. Only then did I get a good look at his face. Well, hello, Number Three. I hit him over the head and watched his body crumple to the floor.

"I knew you had the hots for my girl." I kicked his foot and explored his abode.

The studio flat was less than pristine and smelled of rotten food. I held my breath while going through his things without touching anything.

Henry had an impressive gaming console for a college student and part-time barista. I paused at his cluttered computer station, pulled a pencil off the desk, and then used the eraser side to move the mouse. The computer flicked on, and there was a picture of Leighton on his screen saver. The photo had been taken from afar and at an angle. There was a blonde female—presumably Hallie—seated across from her. Leighton wore a sweet smile and held a cup of coffee between her palms. Fucker had been taking pics of her without her knowing. There was a file on his desktop with her name on it. A feral growl rumbled from my chest. Pulling down my sleeve to cover my hand, I clicked on the file and found more pictures of Leighton, her school and work schedule, her mother's address, and her home address, which was written on a notepad.

Number Three had a major hard-on for Leighton. Yeah, I was fully aware, so did I, but this guy was a textbook stalker.

He had separated his living area from his bed by stapling a sheet to the ceiling. I wasn't sure why he bothered until I saw it. There was a shrine beside his bed. Pictures of Leigh were everywhere, all of which were either random shots of her from afar or pics downloaded from a social media account. Leighton wasn't on social media much, but that obnoxious blonde had been.

Nestled on the altar he'd created were clothing items that made my palm reach for the knife hidden in my boot. And I had thought Number Three was the least threatening out of the three men on my list. The sick fuck had also collected used coffee cups with Leighton's name on them and lipstick prints.

I stomped over to where Henry's prone body lay on the carpet and kicked him in the ribs. "Wakey, wakey," I said in a sing-song voice. "Time for you to wake up and die."

It had taken hours for me to deal with Henry. He divulged a lot of information, proving he had been the threat. I was pleased to take him off my list. My girl was safe. Still, after returning home to clean up, I had to be sure she was okay. I returned to her place and let myself in.

Leighton was sound asleep. She looked impossibly angelic, snuggled up in her blankets. It took all of my willpower not to snuggle next to her. I watched her sleep, while leaning on the door frame. The rise and fall of her chest began to lull me into unconsciousness. It was time to go.

I walked over to her, kissed her forehead, and then went home, knowing that I may have taken out the threat, but I would be forever her shadow.

CHAPTER 10
LAZARUS

FOR THE FIRST couple of nights since I'd found Leighton, the nightmares had stopped, and I'd finally gotten some decent sleep until last night.

I'd thought dealing with Number Three had done the trick since he'd been stalking her and seemed to be the immediate threat. I'd learned that Henry had stalked Leighton over a year ago. He placed notes and red roses on her windshield, broke into her car several times, and stole her gym bag and other personal items. She'd stopped driving to school and started dating Keith.

Henry was heartbroken but moved on to his next victim, another student. Supposedly, he wasn't obsessed with the other girl like he had been with Leighton. The girl was an easy chase, he'd told me, and when he caught her, it wasn't intriguing anymore. The woman in the photos on his computer had been reported missing six months ago. When I asked him what he did with her body, Henry changed. As he told me about what he did with her body before and after he killed the poor girl, Henry became . . . aroused. I was so fucking glad I'd been stalking Leighton before this fucking psycho had gotten a hold of her.

After the kill, Henry began working at Buzzy's, where he ran into

Leighton again. The high he had gotten from ending Monique had worn off by then, and this time, Henry had decided to get a little more aggressive with his tactics. From what I could piece together, the time frame matched when my nightmares began.

I made Henry write out his confession in detail and give his statement on camera. There was plenty of evidence of his wrongdoings, and I'd made it look like a suicide. He was a sick man, and killing him had been the most rewarding kill of my twelve-year career. I'd thought for sure he was the man I was looking for.

But I was wrong. The nightmare returned, and it felt even more realistic than before. I didn't understand why. I was doing all I could to keep her safe.

I'd been keeping tabs on her through the home security system Leighton had added to her house after the Henry incident. If someone other than me were in her house, I'd get a notification on my phone. I even hacked into her phone and had been tracking her whereabouts. She walked to and from campus and work. And nothing out of the ordinary was happening in her life. If she wasn't in class, she was in the library working or studying.

Although she wasn't the social butterfly her friend had been, Leighton seemed to be withdrawing deeper into her private little bubble. She seemed to be withdrawing from social contact entirely, and her typical sunshine persona had been replaced with a down-turned smile. Being stalked by Henry had shaken her. And that meant I had to tread carefully with my brand of stalking. I didn't want to scare her, not even a little. But in my defense, it was necessary. And I wasn't ashamed of using every tool I had at my disposal.

If my nightmare was any indication, my form of stalking wasn't enough. I had to get more involved in her life.

I checked the surveillance footage from her house through my phone for the millionth time. Leighton and her friend had been chatting away while going through her closet. The rudimentary system she'd chosen was shit in terms of sound quality. I couldn't hear what they were saying, which sucked, but I knew where Leighton would be in a few hours, so I fired off a text.

Laz: Tonight 6 Compass

Zeke: U were serious about that?

Laz: U in or not?

Zeke: Shit, this is a first.

Zeke: Yeah. C U there.

Since this wouldn't be my usual stalk-my-nightmare-girl kind of mission, Zeke's presence would help make me look less . . . creepy. I wasn't a serial stalker like Henry. Leighton was my only obsession. Her opinion of me mattered, which meant I had to get creative with my seduction. I needed to work for it. Game on.

Leighton was supposed to meet her date at the restaurant at five-thirty. I'd told my brother six because my goal was to introduce myself to her by intercepting her in the hotel lobby. Hopefully, I could steal her away from the asshat she was going to meet. I had a feeling she had too much integrity just to leave the guy high and dry, and so I'd keep an eye on her throughout the night.

Still, I wanted time alone with her, which took careful planning and timing. I watched her get ready while I had gotten ready myself and then headed to the Thornefield Hotel to meet with the man in charge of security.

Everything had worked out even better than I had planned. I arrived at Thornefield before Leighton and paid the head of security a wad of cash to bring him into the fold. All I needed was a few minutes alone with her.

My nightmare girl strolled through the lobby, looking more beautiful than ever. My original plan to approach her with kid gloves went up in smoke. She was ten minutes late, and she was about to be even later. I casually walked behind Leighton and steered her into the elevator reserved especially for us.

CHAPTER 11
LEIGHTON

IT'D BEEN three nights since the stalker had made an appearance. The police had zero leads, which didn't surprise me. I got one of those surveillance cameras that synced with my phone and blackout curtains for the living room and bedroom. It felt like I was living in a cave, but made me feel more at ease.

It was date night with Nick, and I wanted to cancel, but Hallie insisted.

"You need a night out. Take your mind off of this week," she said. "And it's just dinner. You'll have a delicious meal and drink expensive wine with a hot guy. Hell, you may even get lucky." She wiggled her eyebrows.

"The last thing on my mind right now is sex," I told her.

"Leighton Parker! Get your head right! Don't let that psycho take away your feminine power by sealing your lady cave. It was a fucked up experience, I know that, but if you hide yourself away, you're letting that fucker win." Her tone was serious, and for the first time, I agreed with her philosophy. I was sitting at home playing the victim. And that mindset needed to stop.

"You're right. I'll get ready."

"Of course I am. Come on, I'll help you get ready." She tugged on my hand, and I sat dutifully on my vanity stool.

We spent another thirty minutes gossiping about her love life, making me twenty minutes late for my date.

I had to forgo the contouring and the smokey eyeshadow and wasn't sad about it. Nick was taking me to dinner tonight and not meeting me at the altar. If a man liked me because of all the makeup hacks, he wasn't for me. Better to know now.

The dress Hallie had picked out for me was a deep eggplant, making my porcelain skin look even more pale. The tight-fitting bodice pushed the girls up, putting them on display while the satin material flowed softly to mid-thigh, accentuating my curves. I'd only worn it once on a dinner date with Keith, but I didn't have many options in the dress department. I slipped on black heels and layered the ensemble with a trench coat to ward off the autumn night chill.

I breezed through the lobby of the Thornefield Hotel and went to Compass, the city's newest restaurant on the top floor. Hallie had chosen the restaurant when she'd arranged the date with Nick, but I insisted we meet at the venue rather than have him pick me up at my place. After the window stalker, I was being extra careful. Yeah, he seemed nice, rich, and handsome, but any man could have those qualities and still be a perv. I didn't want him to know where I lived. At least not yet.

The waiting area for the elevator was crowded, with people heading to the same restaurant. Apparently, there was only one elevator that went straight to the top. I sent a quick text to Nick, telling him I was on my way when another elevator opened behind me.

"This one goes to Compass if that's where you're headed." A deep male voice slid over my skin, setting off sparks deep in my belly.

"Oh. Sweet." I walked into the elevator, no longer paying attention to my phone.

"Who's the lucky guy?" That whiskey-coated voice asked.

I turned to see who he was talking to, only to find us alone.

"Umm . . . he's not lucky. He's just an acquaintance. And why did you assume it was a he? I could be having dinner with a girl-friend." I craned my neck to meet his seductive gaze. The man was big. Tall, broad-shouldered, and breathtakingly stunning. Dark hair framed his angular, clean-shaven face. His stormy eyes drew my attention.

The air between us sizzled, enticing me closer to him. It bespoke of possibilities. Promise. My palms itched with the desire for skin-to-skin contact. Without thinking, I stepped closer.

"Nah, you seem like the type of girl who appreciates a good D. Something I'd be happy to help you with."

I paused mid-step. He flashed me a devilish grin. Cheeky fucker.

"Is that what you're selling? You give good dick?" I narrowed my eyes at him. "Your parents must be so proud."

He tipped his head back and laughed.

"I guarantee it'll be the ride of your life." He casually leaned against the elevator panel, crossing his left foot over his right. Everything about him oozed confidence and something more . . . something dangerous yet alluring. He wore a well-tailored charcoal gray suit with a black button-down dress shirt. This guy was going to be a lot of work. But by the size of those big hands and the not-so-subtle bulge in his crotch, so worth the effort.

"Your shoulders must be killing you from carrying around that oversized ego."

He snorts and then the elevator lurched, making me wobble. Muscular arms caught me before I stumbled to the ground.

"You good?" he asked. His breath brushed my cheek, causing me to shiver.

I nodded and angled my face into his chest. His spicy male scent stirred my blood. Something about this stranger woke a part of me I hadn't realized existed. His hand remained on my waist, keeping our bodies pressed together, and I had no interest in separating myself from him. I cocked my head to the side, waiting for the warning bells to go off in my head, but nothing came.

This is building maintenance. Are you two okay in there?

The voice cut through my mental hiatus. Above the elevator buttons, a screen displayed an older gentleman in a security guard uniform.

"We're good," my handsome stranger replied.

Sorry for the inconvenience. We're looking into the issue with your elevator. Please be patient. We'll have you out of there in a flash.

"Take your time. We're not in a rush." The handsome stranger grinned down at me, his hand still on my waist.

I returned his smile. Stuck in an elevator with a hot stranger. The endless possibilities ran rampant in my head. "Not in a rush, huh?"

"He's only an acquaintance. He'll understand." He shrugged. "This will give us time to get to know one another."

"Don't you have a date? Or are you trolling for chicks in the elevator?"

He chuckled.

"No date. Just my brother." He stepped closer, and I stepped away until my back hit the opposite wall. He placed his arms on either side of me, caging me between them.

"Do you not know what personal space means?" I pushed against his hard, muscular chest.

He smiled. "I like the way you smell."

I could say the same about you.

"Ease up, stranger," I said in a breathy voice. What the hell was happening to me?

"Lazarus." His eyes roamed down the length of my body. "My name is Lazarus. And you are?"

"Leigh," I said meekly. Dammit, he was so intense.

"Lei, as in the string of flowers Hawaiians drape over your neck at luaus. I like it," he said in a deep, husky voice.

I laughed. "Not flowers. Leighton."

"Nice to meet you, Leighton," he said. "See, now we're not strangers."

"Seriously, can you back up?" I fiddled with the buttons of my coat.

"Am I making you hot?" He licked his lips.

"You wish. Do you always come on this strong?"

"Only when I see something I want." He reached out to pull open my coat. "Can I see your dress?"

I smacked his hands away. "Do you not have any boundaries?"

"You have have no idea." His gaze fixed on my cleavage.

"Hey!" I slapped his forehead. "Eyes up here." I pointed to my face.

He released a low laugh. "You're stunning." He traced the pad of his thumb over my collarbone.

My skin felt feverish and tingled all over. What was it about this man? I moved away from him, needing distance, which was impossible in the small space.

Lazarus shadowed me and tugged my coat down my shoulders. I didn't stop him.

He pressed his body into mine.

"We should have sex. Right now," he whispered into my ear.

"Oh, I see what this is about. You think this is the prehistoric era. Poor little caveman is lost." I patted his cheek. "This is the twenty-first century. It is no longer acceptable to hit a woman over the head with a club and take her back to your cave."

He released a low chuckle, then returned his heated gaze to me. "I'm going to ruin your sweet pussy. And you're going to love it."

Arousal throbbed between my legs. "Not going to happen, Caveman."

"Maybe not right this second, Flower, but it will happen." He ran his finger across my lips. "I know you want me. Your nipples are hard, your pulse is thumping. I bet your cunt is drenched right now."

"You know nothing." I angled into his touch. What was I doing? This man was a complete stranger. And I had a date to get to.

"I have a date tonight," I blurted.

"Fuck him. Come home with me." His hand snaked around my back and landed on my ass.

Yes. "Umm . . . no."

"Why not?" He dipped his head to the crook of my neck and ran his lips on my jaw.

As though my mind took the night off, my heeled foot slithered up and down his leg.

He caught my thigh and hooked it around his hip. Oh, fuck. I was doing this.

Ahem. Sorry sir, ma'am. We were able to fix the issue before the fire department arrived. We'll have the elevator moving.

Lazarus let out a groan and I pushed him away while smoothing down my dress. A moment later the elevator whirled to life.

"We can still get out of here." He bent to pick up my coat that had fallen to the floor and handed it to me.

"Dinner date remember?" I said. "I, umm . . . this is not me. I never do things like this."

He crushed me to his chest and nipped my neck. "I like that about you."

The elevator chimed and the doors slid open.

CHAPTER 12
LEIGHTON

I SMELLED Nick before I saw him. That man sure loved his cologne. I spied him waiting for me at the hostess stand. My stomach sank. Nick and I didn't have any type of relationship, but almost having a quickie with a stranger on my way to meet another man for dinner was wrong on so many levels.

I glanced over my shoulder at Lazarus, who gave me a wink, and I caught sight of my reflection. Shit. I panicked.

I waved at Nick and gave him a one-moment gesture, then went in the opposite direction to the restrooms. Shame washed over me as I stared at the mauve lipstick smeared all over my mouth.

The door opened, knocking into me.

"Sorry!" Lazarus said.

"What are you doing in the ladies room?"

"This isn't the ladies room. It's a non-binary something or other," he replied with a grin. "And you didn't lock the door. Some might call that an invitation."

"In your dreams. You smeared my lipstick, you pain in the ass. Now get out and wait your turn." I dampened a paper towel and removed the streak of color.

"I didn't come here to use the bathroom." He moved my hair to one side, and his hot lips pressed against my bare shoulder. "Honestly, after being stuck in the elevator with you for thirty minutes. I came in here to rub one out. But since you're here, I'm here. Maybe we can help each other out."

"How about I introduce my knee to your crotch?" I retorted.

"Do you really want me to stop, Flower?" His tongue flicked under my jaw, making me shiver.

"Caveman." I clenched the countertop and tilted my head, giving him greater access. "This is too much. Too fast. Not to mention horrible timing."

"Tell me you don't want me, and I'll stop." He ground his very large, very hard cock against my ass. "Tell me you don't want my hard cock."

Oh my God.

"Nope. No, it's . . . gigantic. And gross." The lie tasted sour in my mouth.

He released a husky chuckle. "You're a horrible liar." His fingertips found the hem of my dress. "Let me make you feel good. I'll keep my fingers above your panties. You are wearing panties, right?"

"Of course." I snapped.

His hands slid up my thigh as the door handle jiggled, bringing me back to my senses.

"Enough, Lazarus. Please." I pleaded and pushed him away.

"I hate that you're having dinner with someone else." He pressed his forehead against mine. "You have integrity, my flower. Rare. Very rare. He doesn't deserve you."

"I know, it's just dinner."

He adjusted himself and opened the door. Before I exited, he whispered into my ear. "Enjoy your *just* dinner, Leighton. But know this—I won't be far, and you will not leave his building without me. Understood."

Ooookay. That was creepy and possessive and hot as fuck. Like I'd lost my sense of self, I nodded.

"Words, Leighton. Say the words." His eyes bore into mine.

"I won't leave this building without you," I said, my voice breathy.

I walked into the hallway and looked back at the bathroom door as it closed.

"Leighton," Nick said as I approached. "Everything alright?"

"Yeah, sorry I'm so late. And then I had to pee," I said. "If you want to cancel, I understand."

"No, no. The night is still young, and you must be hungry." He took my coat and handed it to the hostess.

"Thirsty, actually. I could use a drink," I told him as the hostess handed him a claim ticket.

"I'm glad you said that because they gave our table away, so it might be awhile. But we can go to the bar."

He led the way to the bar and chose a section that allowed us to see the restaurant entrance.

"Hi, are you two having dinner or just drinks?" the bartender asked as we sat down.

I looked over at Nick. "I don't mind eating here," I told him. It made it feel less like a date and more like getting together with a friend kind of night.

"Okay, sure, if you don't mind." Nick shrugged. "Yes, dinner here, and may we see the wine list."

I watched Nick speak with the bartender, scrutinizing everything. In my four-inch heels, he wasn't much taller, putting him at five-foot-ten. He seemed fit but not muscular. Lazarus made him look like a teenage boy. Where was that wine?

"Do you like red?" he asked.

I nodded and picked up the glass of water the bartender had just poured for me.

Nick was a handsome man. Clean cut and well put together. He was polite and articulate. He had a confident posture and an easy smile. He swirled the wine in his glass and took a sip.

"Delicious," he said to the bartender, who proceeded to pour me a glass.

I couldn't reach for the glass fast enough.

"Cheers," Nick held his glass to me.

I clinked his glass and took a deep pull of the delicious red liquid.

"Good?" he asked.

"Just what I needed."

He chuckled. "I've been here before. Do you want me to order?"

I always liked it when men took control of ordering.

"Please, as long as it's beef."

"A meat lover, my kind of girl," Nick ordered for the both of us and casually brushed his hand over my arm. I cringed inside.

I shook off the sensation and went back to staring at him while he spoke with the bartender, searching for flaws and couldn't find any. There was nothing wrong with the man. He was handsome, and he had a good job. By most women's standards, he checked all the boxes. He truly seemed like the perfect package, and yet I wasn't feeling any fanny flutters. He wasn't Lazarus.

As though I'd summoned him, I felt his presence at my back. I glanced over my right shoulder, and there he was, lowering himself in the chair next to me. An almost identical version of him sat on the other side of him.

The heat of his body made my pulse race. As if his presence wasn't enough, a warm, large palm grazed my knee. My brain short-circuited, making it impossible to hear anything Nick was saying.

"Earth to Leighton," Nick said.

I blinked, focusing on my date. "Sorry, what?"

"I should tell the hostess that we're eating at the bar. Save me some wine." Nick flashed me a brilliant smile, then strolled toward the hostess stand.

I uncrossed my legs, spreading my thighs apart.

"Alone again," Lazarus drawled.

"What are you doing here?" I muttered under my breath.

"Getting a drink while they prep our table." His hand traveled to my thighs.

"Behave, Caveman," I told him.

"You spreading your legs me tells me to do the opposite."

My breath hitched. Damn it, he was right.

"Lazarus, we already talked about this."

"I can't help it," he said. "I have a raging boner that won't leave me alone."

I groaned and swallowed the rest of my wine.

"Are you wet?" His finger traced the sensitive spot between my pussy and my thigh.

I gripped his hand, stopping him before it went any further.

"Let me touch you," he growled.

"No," I glanced around, ensuring no one could see what he was doing to me. Nick was still at the hostess stand with his back facing the bar, and Lazarus's brother was talking to a couple on the other side of him.

"One touch and I'll leave you to your date. I'll keep my fingers above your panties." He wiggled his hand free, and I let him roam.

We'd just met. We didn't even have our first kiss, and yet the second his digit touched my sex, I fucking wanted more. I rolled my hips, and my legs inched further apart.

"That's a good girl, open up for me," he groaned.

His touch was gentle, his finger thick. More, my body begged.

"Under," I pleaded.

He snaked a finger under my panties and ran his digit up and down my slit.

"So fucking wet." His voice was deep and husky. "Damn, baby. I want to drive my cock so far up your tight cunt."

I placed a hand on his thigh and squeezed.

"I . . . I need," My chest heaved.

"Come for me, baby."

I wasn't sure if it was the taboo situation or if it was because it had been so long since I'd been touched like that, but I was teetering on the edge, ready to explode.

I tilted my hips, granting him easier access, and he sank his finger into my depths. My body clenched, and I let go, biting my lip to stifle my scream just as Nick turned to face me.

Nick wasn't my boyfriend, but I was sure there was a special place in hell for people like me.

CHAPTER 13
LEIGHTON

MY SKIN WAS FLUSHED, and my breathing came in pants. I pushed Laz's hand away and reached for my water as Nick sat down.

"Sorry about that," Nick eyed me suspiciously. "Are you okay? Your skin is flushed."

Lazarus, the cheeky fucker barked out a laugh.

"I umm . . . must be the wine."

"You need to eat. I'll ask about our dinner," Nick replied and flagged down the bartender.

"Now, I feel bad," Lazarus said.

I glanced over my shoulder and found him licking his fingers.

"Delicious! Dessert before dinner." He winked.

I was speechless.

He smiled. "Do you want our table? To have a proper date?"

"Fuck off," I snarled.

He laughed. "I guess that's a no. Enjoy your just dinner, Leighton. Remember what I said."

He picked up his drink and followed his brother into the restaurant's dining area.

His absence made me feel empty.

"Ah, here it is, appetizers," Nick said.

With Lazarus gone and a pent-up orgasm released, I focused solely on my date.

We had a casual conversation through dinner. He was easy to talk to and engaging. He'd glanced at his phone a few times, which was a massive error in my book, but after what I just did with Lazarus, he got a definite pass.

"A couple of friends are meeting at the bar on the rooftop. It's called Firefly. Wanna check it out?" Nick asked as he removed the credit card from the billfold and slipped it into his wallet.

"Firefly?" I'd heard about the new hotspot but hadn't thought it'd still be open in the fall.

"Yeah, they have several fire pits and a bunch of heaters so you won't be cold. It's a popular spot." His smile was sweet and almost boyish. "Come on, one drink, maybe two. I'll even forgive you for being late tonight."

Guilt over my under-the-bar counter orgasm and for being late had me following Nick up the glass staircase to the rooftop even though I didn't want to. I wanted to spend more time with Lazarus. I glanced over my shoulder and saw him and his brother leaving the restaurant and moving toward the glass staircase.

Firefly had several fire features providing warmth and a sultry orange glow. Three six-by-six-foot fireplaces ran down the middle of the lounge area, with plush white cushions surrounding them. The twenty-foot quartz counter bar had heated lamps overhead, making it almost toasty despite the fifty-degree weather. We saddled up to the bar where Nick's two friends were.

They'd been drinking, and I learned this was their usual night out, except Nick had canceled on his friends to be with me.

"Well, now I feel bad for ruining boys' night out," I said, sipping a glass of water. I'd ordered another glass of red but was doing my best to hydrate in between sips.

"Don't be sorry, gorgeous; we'd rather have you here with us," one of his friends said in a creepy tone that made me cringe. I looked for Lazarus and found him at the other end of the bar.

Nick noticed where I was looking and said, "Good find. Chad, go get that table for us."

I grabbed my glass of wine and followed Nick and his friends to a high-top table. Lazarus gave me a wink as we passed by, and I blew him a kiss. For some reason, having him shadow me made me feel safer. I needed to get my head checked.

Nick's friends were funny and enjoyable to be around. We continued our banter back and forth. And as the night wore on, the wine had worked its magic, and the subtle brushes on my skin became more apparent and uncomfortable. Nick had scooted closer to me and I kept moving away. Not only was I feeling the effects of the alcohol, but so was he. It was time to go.

Nick placed another glass of wine in front of me. "Oh no, I already had more than my share."

"No pressure. Let's at least toast to making new friends," Nick said, raising his glass. I did the same and toasted the other guys at the table.

The men watched me as I drank, and then someone bumped into me, spilling my wine down my dress.

"Sorry about that, Flower. Are you okay?" Lazarus stood in front of me.

I nodded.

"We need to go right now. I'll follow you out." His deep voice was stern, and he wasn't taking no for an answer. I wasn't sure what made him get bossier than usual, but I was covered in wine and didn't feel like arguing.

"Are you okay, Leighton?" Nick asked while trying to push Lazarus away from me.

"Yeah, I'm good; I need the restroom. Excuse me," I said.

"Dude, watch where the fuck you're going," Nick said to Lazarus.

I didn't wait around to hear them bicker. I made my way to the bathroom and felt the room sway.

CHAPTER 14
LAZARUS

I STROLLED AWAY FROM LEIGHTON, feeling like a big man. My fingers were still sticky with her cum. She'd let me touch her. My ego was inflated, which was a bit ridiculous because she was still having dinner with the cologne guy, number two on my kill list. Oddly, that didn't enrage me as much as it should have. She was mine. Still, I kept an eye on the back of her head as Zeke and I sat to have dinner. We ordered and chatted about mundane things for a bit.

"Ah, I see what this is about." A satisfied grin spread over Zeke's face.

"Um, what?" I replied, not paying attention to what he was saying.

"She's hot. I can see why you're obsessed." He placed a napkin on his lap as the food was brought to our table.

"What did you just say?" I snarled. Was he talking about my girl? I already hated the idea that she was on a date with that asshole. But my brother noticing her as well added an extra dose of anger to the fire.

The waiter placed our food in front of us and made a hasty retreat.

"Chill, dude. I was paying you a compliment." He raised his hands in mock surrender.

"How is that a compliment to me?" I frowned.

"I only meant you have good taste," he added. "Sheesh. Touchy, touchy."

I grunted something incoherent and began eating. I was ravenous and wondered if my Flower was too. I glanced at the back of her head, taking special note of her body language. Her back was straight, and she maintained a safe distance from her date. If he leaned close, she leaned away. I liked it. It made me less angry that she was eating with that asshat instead of me. Deep down, I knew I'd be tucking her in tonight. I'd make sure of it. She wasn't leaving this building without me.

Ezekiel and I finished our meal at the same time as Leighton did.

I tracked her as they ascended the stairs to the rooftop—Firefly's signature lounge.

"I guess we're going upstairs," Zeke said, paying the bill.

"Shit, I can get that." I reached for my wallet. I'd invited him to get that brotherly bonding time out of the way and to stalk my girl without seeming like I was stalking her. The least I could do was pay for dinner.

He shrugged. "Company expense."

"In that case, yes, we are going upstairs."

He laughed as we took the stairs.

The packed lounge was making me twitchy. Zeke ordered two glasses of cognac, and we stood off to the side, watching my girl. Nick and two other men surrounded her, and I'd already committed their faces to memory—two more to add to my kill list.

"You can't kill all of them, you know," he said.

"Why not?" I asked.

"Because killing is a crime." He snorted.

I sputtered, nearly choking to death on my drink. Considering I was our family's hired hitman, his comment was fucking hilarious.

"Seriously, Laz. What are you planning to do? You can't stalk her forever." His voice took on that same condescending tone our father always had.

"I'm not stalking her. I'm shadowing her. It's different," I retorted.

"Shadowing? Is that what the kids are calling stalking now?" He quirked his eyebrow at me.

"Fuck off, Zeke. Stop calling me out on my shit," I growled.

"What is she doing with guys like that anyway?" he asked.

"Her friend set up the date," I said absently, my gaze fixed on my dark-haired beauty. At least she was laughing. She hadn't smiled much in the last few days. When she was with me, I'd see her smile all the time.

"What? How do you know that?" His interrogation continued. I should've known this would happen.

"I watched it happen," I replied.

"How long have you been stalking the poor girl?" I felt his gaze on me harden.

"I told you, I'm not stalking. I'm shadowing. I am trying to get to know her without being overly aggressive," I said defensively.

Zeke laughed. "What happened? Crooking your finger stopped working on the ladies?"

I gave him a dry look.

"Ah, I see. You like this one." He grinned. "What makes her so special?"

I couldn't answer that. Wouldn't. I felt Zeke's eyes burning a whole into the side of my face. He was piecing it together.

"I didn't know you still had those." Concern laced his voice.

I shrugged, ignoring his comment. My brother sipped his drink, and my eyes locked with Leighton's. She gave me a small smile of . . . relief, which made me feel wanted. I might have been shadowing her, and she was definitely on a date with someone else, but that smile told me she was glad I was there.

Nick and his friends moved to a table nearby. Leigh strode past me, and I winked at her. She blew me a kiss.

Too Much Cologne Guy gave her another glass of wine even though the one she'd been drinking was half full. The asshole was trying to get her drunk. Or . . . I tipped my head to the side and eyed Nick and his friends.

Nick said something, and they all raised their glasses. Then, all three men fixed their gazes on Leighton as she pulled a deep drink.

I stood abruptly. A thread of alarm tugged at the back of my neck.

"I gotta run." I pulled out my wallet and threw some money on the counter.

"Go. I'll go over and stall those guys." Zeke patted my back.

"Thanks, Zeke." I patted his shoulder. He was the best wingman and an even better brother. I needed to make a better effort to return the favor.

I pushed past people and bumped into Leighton, spilling her wine on purpose.

"Sorry about that, Flower. Are you okay?" I gazed into her eyes, and her pupils were blown wide. Fuck.

She nodded.

"We need to go right now. I'll follow you out," I told her.

"Are you okay, Leighton?" Nick asked while trying to push me out of the way.

"Yeah, I'm good. I need the restroom. Excuse me," she said.

"Dude, watch where the fuck you're going," Nick said to me.

I leaned in close and growled in his ear. "If you slipped something in her drink, I will rip your entrails out and then shove them down your fucking throat."

Nick blanched, and I stomped off.

CHAPTER 15
LAZARUS

LEIGHTON DISAPPEARED down a corridor that led to the elevators and the bathrooms. The hallway was packed with people waiting for the elevators. My girl took neither. She maneuvered through the crowd, bypassing the elevators, and took the stairs that led back to the restaurant. I pushed my way through the people not so graciously as she had and hurried to catch up with her. By the time I reached the bottom of the stairwell, I found her pointing an accusing finger at the hostess.

"I won't forget this." She scowled and turned to get into an elevator car.

I took a few long strides and squeezed in beside her. Usually, I hated being close to so many strangers, but this time, the crowded elevator had me pressing close to my nightmare girl. There was a slight tremble in her hands, and she inhaled visibly. Her breasts rose with a deep breath and slowly relaxed.

The car stopped on the next floor, and another passenger got in. I angled my body behind her, so close I could smell the sweet scent of her skin, and her long dark hair brushed against my chest. My fingers twitched, eager to graze the bare skin on her elbow.

She hadn't noticed me yet, or anyone else for that matter. She focused solely on her phone, tapping away a text to . . . I leaned closer. Hallie. She was contacting her friend for support. Leighton switched the app to check on her ride-share pickup. Her car was three minutes away.

The elevator stopped at the parking level, and the crowd behind us exited. I remained close to her, not willing to allow anyone to touch her.

We remained alone in the elevator, as it continued its descent, and she hadn't moved away from me. Or rather, I didn't move from her. Our bodies were so close, and still, she hadn't made eye contact with me. Okay, my girl got a massive fail for situational awareness—no big deal. We could work on that together.

"Leaving without me?" I asked.

Leighton swung around and swatted me across the face. Her movement was so fast it startled me. My face stung, and I was . . . proud.

"Fuck, Caveman. Don't sneak up on a girl like that! You're lucky I didn't have a gun."

My lips twitched at the sound of the sweet little thing using profanity. "You would have shot me?"

"Yes, I would have shot you."

"Do you even own a gun?" I asked.

"No." All of the bravado she'd just displayed physically left her body and made her look vulnerable. She swayed on her feet.

My protective instincts took over. "Are you okay?"

"I'm . . . I don't know. I feel weird," she replied, still looking at her phone. "It hasn't been the best night."

"Not the worst if I remember correctly." Trying to lighten the mood.

Her lips curled up at the corners, and color stained her cheeks. The elevator reached the ground level, and she stepped out with me right on her heels.

"You're coming with me, Leighton," I told her.

"No. I'm not. I'm not in a good mood. Those men were weird,

and I shouldn't have been out with them in the first place. And that bitch of a hostess." She stomped through the lobby, her heels clacking on the marble flooring.

I opened the glass door for her before she could reach out.

"Can you believe the bitch wouldn't give me my coat because I didn't have a claim ticket?" she continued.

Ah, now her incident with the hostess made sense. I unbuttoned my suit jacket.

A gust of wind blew her dress. Her hands shot down her sides, holding the fabric down as she shivered.

I placed my jacket over her shoulders.

"Oh! This isn't necessary." She shook her head.

"You're cold. I'm warm. Wear the coat," I said gruffly, then signaled the valet guys.

She slid her arms through each sleeve. On instinct, I gathered her hair at her nape and pulled the silky strands free from under the collar.

"Thank you." She turned and craned her neck to look up at me. "I know I made a promise, but I just can't. I want to go home."

"You don't need to thank me. And technically, you did leave the building with me," I said. Her blue eyes had silver streaks, and I found myself at a loss for words for a second.

She pulled my jacket tighter around her body, tipped her nose to its collar, and inhaled deeply. She was taking in my scent, and that slight movement got my dick's attention.

A commotion from the building made the both of us turn.

"Oh fuck," she cursed.

Her date and one of his buddies were on their way out, and my brother was causing a scene trying to delay them.

My girl moved to stand behind me.

"I'm going to kill that fucker," I growled.

"It's fine. I need to leave," she said.

"Let me drive you home," I said, barely retaining my anger.

"Umm . . . no, my ride is here." She wobbled, and I placed a hand on her waist, holding her steady as she looked down at her app. A car pulled up to the curb a few feet away from us.

"Uber for Leighton," the female driver called out.

My nightmare girl walked to the car, and I followed. "Oh, I almost forgot." She stopped at the curb and began to take off my jacket.

"No," I stilled her arms. "You're coming with me, Leighton."

"But . . ." She began to protest.

"I insist." I cut her off, pulled a hundred-dollar bill from my wallet, and gave it to the driver.

"My car is right here." I steered her to the passenger side of my Maserati.

I held the door open, and she paused before getting in. Her gaze dropped to my lips, and her tongue darted out and licked her own. "Umm . . . okay. Thanks." Her breath fanned over my mouth; my fingertips grazed her jaw.

She smiled, and my whole world turned on its axis, making me forget the urgency of the situation.

My brother's voice reached my ears.

"Let's get you home, baby." She slid into the car, and I closed the door once she was seated.

I rushed to the driver's seat, tipped the valet guy, and sped off. Leighton's head lolled to the side, and she mumbled something incoherent.

Fucking fuckers were so going to die.

But Leighton first.

She mumbled again, her speech slurred. I imagined she was telling me her address, not that I needed it. Because of my "shadowing," I knew exactly where she lived. I sped through the streets, ignoring traffic laws. I wanted to take her to my place but knew she would feel more comfortable at home. She was going to be sick, and it wouldn't be pretty.

By the time we reached her place, Leighton was barely lucid. I dug her house keys out of her purse and went to the passenger side just as she exited the car. She stumbled, trying to walk the short distance to her front door, and I caught her before she hit the sidewalk, carrying her the rest of the way. I punched in her alarm code and kicked the door closed.

"Don't feel right," Leighton mumbled. Her words were slurred, and her voice weak.

"I know, babe. You need to get the poison out of your system." I told her while setting her on the bathroom floor.

I got on my knees and guided her to the toilet.

She tried pushing me away. "No. I don't want you to see me like this."

I also hated seeing her that way. Vomit didn't bother me. I'd seen plenty of brain matter, blood, and guts to be squeamish about anything. No, I hated seeing her vulnerable and scared.

She rested her head on the toilet seat. "Go, Lazarus, please."

"I'm not leaving, Flower. I'm going to stay until I know you're okay. And then I need to tear out Nick's innards." I pulled her hair back. "Let it out, Leighton. I'll be right here."

Her body heaved, but nothing came out. "Leighton, you will feel better once you purge."

Tears streamed down her face.

"I'm right here, babe. I'll take care of you." I used my free hand to massage her back, and she let go.

Leighton emptied the contents of her belly; she was a wreck, skin pale and make-up smeared all over her face. Still, my nightmare girl was the most beautiful woman I'd ever seen.

I turned on the faucet and let the bathtub fill while helping her brush her teeth. With that done, she leaned on me while I helped her undress. She still wore my coat, so I reached under it to unzip her strapless dress, letting the purple satin fall to the floor. Next, I unclasped her bra and slid her panties down her legs. She was exquisite, and I was so close to her bare sex. I breathed her in and remained the perfect gentleman.

Leighton braced her hand on my shoulder, keeping her weakened body steady. Her skin was clammy, and she leaned her head against the wall. Fucking Cologne Guy. I stifled a growl and slid my coat off her shoulders. She curled in on herself, trying to shield her body. I murmured assuring words, picked her up and placed her into the warm water.

I let her soak in the tub while I went to the kitchen. Aside from a tomato and several packages of ramen noodles, her refrigerator and pantry were bare. I launched a delivery app on my phone, ordered a few essentials, and returned to the bathroom.

It had been an hour or so since she took that last sip of wine, and Leigh was completely out. I imagined she wouldn't remember what had happened since we arrived at her place. I pulled her out of the tub, dried her naked body, and carried her to bed. She was like a rag doll. Her body was limp and listless. She was completely unaware of me and extremely defenseless. In Nick's hands, he could have done disgusting things to her. My body was tight with hot, fiery rage.

Why any man would find a woman in this state arousing was sickening to me. Those fuckers had nefarious plans, and I was salivating at the thought of killing every one of them.

I was a covert assassin. Clean. Efficient. No fanfare. Just dead bodies. Nick Hanford and his friends would suffer public humiliation and gruesome deaths.

My phone chimed, alerting me that my delivery was near. Three minutes later, I accepted the items I'd ordered and began putting them away in their respective places—bottles of Pedialyte for hydration. Aspirin and ibuprofen, in case she had a headache. And some canned soups and crackers. Leighton would need real food, but wouldn't have an appetite for a while.

I filled a glass of water and placed the headache remedies on the nightstand.

My nightmare girl was still out. I scrubbed my hand down my face and slipped into bed, fully dressed. The rise and fall of her chest gave me comfort. She would be okay. It had been close, but she was home and safe. I reached for her hand, linking our fingers together.

Everything about Leighton was beautiful. She had satiny, smooth skin and delicious womanly curves, and I wasn't even remotely aroused. The only thing I wanted was to hunt down Nick and his friends and paint the town blood red. I stared at the ceiling thinking about all the ways I'd make those assholes pay.

I must have dozed off and slept soundly. When I woke, sunlight filtered through the windows, and Leighton rested on my chest.

Gently, I rolled her over and slipped out of bed. I wasn't planning to leave, but I didn't want her to panic when she woke and found me on the bed beside her.

I knelt by her bed, watching her sleep. Her arm slid over the mattress like she was looking for me, so I extended my hand and grasped her fingers. She clung to my palm and brought my knuckles to her lips.

"Thank you," she murmured. Her lids were still closed.

I kissed her forehead. "You never have to thank me for taking care of you, Leighton. You are mine to care for and protect. Now and always."

CHAPTER 16
LEIGHTON

I WOKE FEELING groggy and confused. My head ached, and my mouth was dry. It felt like I had been run over by a bus or had a three-day bender in Vegas. I raised my aching head off the pillow, prying my crusty eyes open. What happened? I slowly sat upright. Pain lanced my brain, and I slumped back down to the mattress.

"Easy," a deep voice said.

My eyes snapped open, and I rubbed at them to clear my vision.

"Lazarus?" My throat felt raw. How? And then it all came crashing back to me. The wine. Nick. And Lazarus rubbing my back while I puked my guts out. Fuck.

"I'm here, Flower. Would you like some water? And maybe some aspirin?"

I nodded, then realized I hadn't restocked supplies and was out of Advil. Shit.

"Water," I croaked.

Lazarus was beside me in the next instant, helping me sit up. He held a glass of water to my lips, and I drank . . . all of it.

He set the glass down and brought another. I glanced at the cup, which was filled with a pinkish liquid, and frowned.

"It's just Pedialyte, Leighton. You need electrolytes," he said.

I took the glass from him and sipped. It was sweet, like straw-berries.

"Thanks." I drank more.

"Aspirin or Ibuprofen?"

I pointed to the Advil bottle. He cracked it open and handed me two green pills.

"You went shopping and came back?" I asked after taking the pills.

"Never left. I ordered delivery. There's more to drink and some soup and crackers when you're ready." He took the empty glass from me.

I collapsed onto the bed, my body still feeling the effects of the drugs. Fucking Nick. Fucking Hallie. Fuck me. Why'd I have to go on a date with that asshole?

Lazarus turned his attention to me; his gaze was soft, and there was a slight stubble covered his jaw. He was so handsome, and I prob-ably looked like a train wreck. I reached up to caress his face.

"Thank you, Caveman. For taking care of me. For staying." My eyelids felt heavy.

He kissed each eye and then my forehead. "Rest, babe."

I closed my eyes.

It was dark when I awakened again. I glanced at my phone in disbelief. I'd been out for nearly a whole day. It was early evening, and although I slept the entire time, I still felt lethargic.

On my nightstand was a glass carafe filled with water, a bottle of ibuprofen, and a note.

Leighton, Had a few things to take care of. If I'm not back by the time you awake, drink plenty of water and have something to eat. And rest. I'll be back soon. Xo, your Caveman.

I closed my eyes and went back to sleep with a smile.

————

Days later, the effects of whatever drug Nick had given me wore off, and Lazarus never returned. He texted twice to check in, and that was it. He probably didn't want anything to do with me after watching me make a complete ass of myself. He was so sweet, though. Not only did he get the essential items I needed to recover, but he also cleaned my house. There wasn't a trace of vomit anywhere, no clothes on the floor. Even my towels had been freshly laundered.

But he was gone, and I didn't know if he would return. For some stupid reason, I was hurt more by his disappearance than by Nick's actions.

Lazarus wasn't only kind and caring, he also had that sexual magnetism that took up space in my brain, body, and . . . my dreams. He had left his coat hanging on my bedroom doorknob, and I'd become obsessed with wearing the damn thing and went so far as to keep it on my bed. Pathetic, I know. But he smelled so good and damn those strong hands.

Sometime in the middle of the night, I woke, my skin heated, and moisture dripping between my thighs. I turned over on my belly. I smooshed my face in the coat, inhaling his scent. Thoughts of strong hands roaming all over my nakedness had my clit pulsing with want. I reached into my nightstand, looking for the one thing that could bring me my release. I pulled out a tube of lube. And found nothing. I sat up and peered into the drawer. My vibrator was gone.

He wouldn't have. Would he? Motherfucker.

I smashed my face into my pillow and growled. Great. Now, I was both sleep-deprived and sexually frustrated.

Hours later, my mood hadn't improved. I stomped through the library, aggravated with myself.

"What?" I snapped at the person who'd tapped on my shoulder.

"Whoa. Someone's in a mood," Keith said.

"Yes. Yes, I am." I shouldered past him with a stack of books in hand.

"Leighton, talk to me." He stood before me and placed his hands on my shoulders. "What's wrong?"

"Nothing. I've been on edge since I caught someone peering into my window and then my stupid date. And things have not been going my way." I didn't want to tell him about my missing vibrator. And I certainly wasn't going to tell him about my hot caveman who had vanished.

"Who the fuck has been stalking you?" he asked.

"No idea," I replied.

Keith pulled me in for a hug. "I know you don't trust me much, Leighton, but you should know I'll always be here for you. If you feel scared or need someone to talk to, you can count on me."

I sighed into his chest. I didn't want to rely on him; he'd broken my heart, and I didn't want to go through that again. But, the reality of it was . . . I didn't have anyone else to rely on.

When I'd called Hallie after my date, she hadn't been there. She didn't even call me until the following afternoon. And when she did, she went on and on about her night out and hadn't bothered to ask about my date even though I texted her 911 messages until Lazarus brought me home.

Thoughts of my deep-voiced savior had me pulling away from Keith. "Thanks, but I'm okay. Or I will be."

"The offer will always be there. I was heading to Buzzy's. You want to join me? My treat."

"Ummm . . ." I glanced at the clock on the wall behind the counter.

"Perfect timing. Your shift is officially over." He smirked.

I shrugged and gathered my things.

A crowd gathered around Buzzy's as we approached.

"I wonder what's happening," I said.

"Let's find out." Keith grabbed my hand and led me inside.

The staff at the coffee house were in tears, and people were whispering. Keith and I approached the counter.

We placed our orders, and then I waved at Claire, one of the managers. She came around the counter and hugged me. "Hi, what's wrong?"

"It's awful," she said softly. "One of our employees is gone."

"Who?" Keith asked.

"Henry Feldman. He called in sick last week. And then he stopped contact completely." She sniffled. "I called his emergency contact last night because no one had heard from him. And she just called and said his body was found at his apartment." She sniffled.

"Dead?" I gasped.

She nodded.

"Oh no! Not Henry."

Keith walked me home after we left Buzzy's. The news was unsettling, and I hadn't wanted to be alone, but I didn't want him to stay either. With everything that had happened a few nights ago at my date and the news about Henry, I felt vulnerable and needy. And with our history, it'd be too easy to fall back into old habits. The last thing I needed was to get naked with my ex and then deal with the ordeal of having to kick him out.

I tried studying, but my mind drifted to what had happened to Henry. Aside from Buzzy's and the occasional hello around campus, he and I had never spoken. He seemed like a nice enough guy, always smiling and cordial. People seemed to like him, and he had friends. Claire didn't have much information aside from confirmation that he was dead. The how was a mystery, which seemed to bother me more than anything.

A firm knock on my front door startled me. I peeked out the window to see a police officer standing at my door. My heart galloped. When was a visiting police officer ever good news?

"Hi, Leighton, I'm Officer Daniels, and this is Officer Chan. We were here about a week ago regarding the stalker situation. May we come in?" the man in blue said.

"Umm . . .I guess so. Did you catch the guy?" I stepped out of the way, let the officers in, and motioned for them to sit at the dining room table in my kitchen.

"Well, yes, we think so." Officer Daniels said. "Ms. Leighton, where were you this weekend?"

"Here. Except Saturday." I waved my hand, gesturing to the apartment. "I went out Saturday night. Aside from that, I was home in bed. Why?"

"Do you know a Henry Feldman?" he asked.

"Yes, he works . . . or worked at Buzzy's. I just heard the news," I answered, my head swiveled back and forth between the officers.

"What news?" Officer Chan asked gruffly.

I told them about my visit to the coffee shop.

"News travels fast," Officer Daniels muttered. He rested his elbows on the table and massaged the bridge of his nose. "Do you have anyone who can corroborate your whereabouts?"

"Yes, of course. What is this about?"

Officer Chan glared at me and said, "Henry was found dead in his apartment late last night. We have every reason to believe he was your stalker. We found several pictures of you along with personal items."

"Do any of these items look familiar?" Officer Daniels opened the envelope he'd brought and pulled out a few pictures.

I did a cursory glance at the pictures and nodded. My stomach dropped, and my mouth began to sweat. The familiar pink scarf, wooden hairbrush, and my favorite lipgloss stared back at me. Items that had gone missing over a year ago when a stalker had been leaving notes and red roses on the windshield of my car. My stomach swooped.

"Um, is there anything else I need to do?" I asked.

"No. We wanted to let you know and confirm these were yours in case they belonged to one of the others."

"Others?" I asked.

"Other females," Officer Chan answered curtly.

I clutched my stomach. "What's going on? Did you think I had something to do with his death? How did he . . . was he murdered?" My shrill voice was a clear indication of what I was feeling internally.

Neither officer said a word for a moment.

I slammed my hand on the table. "Listen, you can't come into my house and drop bombs about an acquaintance being my stalker and that I might need an alibi and then go all silent on me. What the actual fuck is going on?"

"Calm down, Leighton. No one is accusing you of murder." Officer Daniels lowered his tone, and his brown eyes softened with concern. "We're just conducting an investigation. We found photos of one other woman, one who had been reported missing. We won't know all the details until the autopsy is done. And yes, we suspect foul play. There were inconsistencies."

"Inconsistencies? What kind of inconsistencies?" I pressed.

Officer Chan huffed. "It appears that he shot himself. However, there were multiple contusions on his torso. Someone worked him over pretty good before killing him, or him killing himself."

I would have heaved if there was anything else left in my belly.

"Well," I swiped my wet cheeks. "It wasn't me. I didn't beat him up, and I'd never k-kill anyone."

"We're sorry to have upset you." Officer Chan stood. "I think we're good."

Officer Daniels stayed rooted in his seat, and his gaze hadn't left my face. "Is there someone you can call to be with you tonight? You shouldn't be alone when you're upset."

"I'm fine," I snapped. I opened the front door and motioned for them to leave.

Officer Daniels gathered the pictures and pulled a business card from his wallet. "My number, in case there's an emergency. Oh, um. One last thing: we have been getting reports about break-ins in this area. Be sure to lock up and keep your alarm on." He placed the card on the table and then followed his partner out.

CHAPTER 17
LAZARUS

"WHY THE HELL would you get Josiah involved in this? This is a personal matter; I can handle it myself," I snarled at Ezekiel.

"I did it to help you," Zeke argued.

"Did I fucking stutter?" I snarled. "I can take care of this myself. I don't need help!"

"Lazarus, you made a very public display at Firefly, leaving with your girl—who was on a date with someone else. If that someone else suddenly winds up dead, you can bet your stubborn ass they'll pick you as suspect number one. Hence, Josiah and I will be helping you with this hit." He propped his elbows on my desk. "Let us help you. I've done preliminary research, and trust me, you'll want more eyes on this. Those three men have influential ties and are into some sinister shit."

I glared at my brother. He wasn't wrong about me becoming suspect number one. I'd lost count years ago of how many lives I'd taken, but there was one certainty out of the triple digits, only four were personal. Two orderlies, one nurse, and the psychologist—all from Bright Haven. They'd never be able to find those bodies, let alone pin their deaths on me. It had taken years of careful planning to pull that off and right now, because Leighton was involved, I was pissed as all hell and not thinking clearly. Fuck. I hated to rely on anyone, but my brother had a point.

"What do you have?" I ground out.

"I did a background check, and you're not going to believe this." Josiah strolled into my office.

He was my father's brother from a different mother. Yes, there was a pattern with the men in my family, one I had no intention of repeating. Josiah was the youngest of my father's brothers and only five years older than me. I was more like him than the other men in my family, which was probably why we got along so well.

Josiah powered up his tablet and used the sixty-five-inch television in my office to display his findings.

I watched the images of Nick and his two friends flash on my screen and wanted to kill them all ten times over.

Nick Hanford wasn't only an investment banker; his father owned a chain of banks in the state. The Hanfords had wealth. Not Ford family wealth but they had it all the same. His wife and three children lived in Los Angeles and had been for the last two years. They were separated, but there was no record of a divorce filing.

Alex Yoo was a first-generation Korean-American. His parents immigrated to the United States and made their wealth via an import-export business. Alex hadn't worked for the family business as one might have guessed. He was a social media influencer and had a huge following online. From what we could tell, he offered dating and relationship advice. It didn't seem legit because although he was married, he and his wife had lived in separate residences for years. We contacted an associate in Malaysia to sign up for the membership and contact us with his findings.

Chad Johnson was the most concerning. He worked in the state prosecutor's office, and his father was also a senior partner in one of the state's largest law firms. From what we could tell, Chad was on the fast track to becoming the first black prosecuting attorney at twenty-six. He was well-liked and had a bright future.

So, why were these three men drugging my girl? Simply because they could. Although all three were married and had children, they never wore wedding rings. They were well-educated, reasonably good-looking, and charming. They presented the perfect package to unsuspecting women.

Our preliminary findings showed that they got together once a month on a Saturday night. They went to a different bar, found a pretty girl, plied her with alcohol, and she left with them. If I hadn't witnessed what had happened to Leighton, I'd think this was perfectly normal behavior. I had a hunch they'd done it before and was determined to find the evidence.

I spent the entire day and most of the night working alongside my uncle and brother. We dug up their financial, phone, and email records. All illegal, of course, and thus none would hold up in court. That was fine because I wouldn't give them the right to a jury.

It was after business hours when my father knocked on my door—a courier right behind him.

"What are you three up to?" he asked, then motioned the courier to place the to-go packages on the coffee table in my office. "It's late."

"Sentinel stuff," I replied, not bothering to look up from my screen.

Solomon cleared his throat. "In case you forgot, I own this place. Don't make me ask again."

I side-glanced at my father. He was right, sure. But I was a stubborn cunt, and I didn't like being pushed around. I rose to stand and faced him. He was shorter than me. And I had a good forty pounds of muscle on him. I didn't want to fight him. For the most part, I respected the man. But I was a man, too.

"Will you two stop," Josiah stated. "Solomon, why don't you pull up a chair, have some Chinese takeout with us, and we'll fill you in."

My father and I gave each other a curt, respectful nod and he joined us to brainstorm on the job. I'd told my father and uncle what had happened to Leighton. All four Ford men were in agreement for once in our lifetime. The three men were serial date rapists, and we needed to put an end to it. It was an interesting bonding experience, one I wouldn't have imagined in a million years.

An hour or so later, another knock on my door had all four of us turning to see the intruder.

Davis, the youngest of our father's sons, peered in. "What do you want?" I asked.

While Zeke asked, "What are you still doing here?"

My father and uncle also wanted to know the answer to that question.

"Oh, I was working on something and noticed a light on. I thought I'd check to make sure everything was okay."

"You're not needed here, Davis," I stated.

"Go home, son. We're good here," my father said.

"But . . ." Davis began.

"Get out," Zeke barked.

Davis left.

My father, uncle, and brother left an hour after Davis's intrusion, and I kept working, determined to find something. Finally, I uncovered the motherload. The trio communicated via a private web chat service, which revealed what we suspected. They were serial date rapists, getting a unique brand of fentanyl from Korea and using it on girls to test its effects with hopes of selling the stuff on the black market. They'd been doing this since the beginning of summer. If they'd been successful, Leighton would have been victim number five. Who the other four were, I didn't know . . . yet. How had they gotten away with this shit for the last few months? Easy. I glared at their photos. Nick had the financial means. Alex had access to the import and shipping industry. And Chad had connections in the police department. Yep, the bullshit ran deep, and it would take a while to unravel. I massaged the bridge of my nose, glad to have help from my family.

It was well past midnight when I'd decided to call it quits. I took what I could home to the penthouse and sent an apologetic text to

Leighton. I'd wanted to get back to her, but it was late, and I didn't want to disturb her.

Leighton hadn't responded to my text, which was understandable. I checked her security camera feed, and she was sleeping facedown in bed.

"Good night, Flower." I closed my eyes. "Don't worry, those fuckers will pay for what they'd done to you."

CHAPTER 18
LAZARUS

IT WAS MID-AFTERNOON, and you wouldn't know it. Dark gray clouds blocked out the sun, making it look and feel like the sun had already sunk below the horizon.

I parked in front of Leighton's place and got her coat out of my car. It had been a week since the incident at Firefly. I hadn't planned to stay away from her for so long, but dealing with Nick took longer than expected. I'd been working on it non-stop, gathering information, and for the first time in my hitman career, I felt like I was doing good work. As a hired assassin, I thought I was the big bad wolf, and fuck me, I'd been dead wrong. The date rape crew, as we'd begun to call them, made me look like a virginal Little Red Riding Hood.

We had uncovered a lot of incriminating info on the trio and were still working on plans to take them out. I'd wanted to kill them and stage it as an unfortunate accident, but my elders wanted more. They wanted to expose these trust fund brats for what they were—elitist assholes using their power and position to cover up illegal activities. Sure, they'd die, but not without public humiliation first. For the sake of the victims—one had been found dead, and the three were still on the missing persons list—I was okay with their plan.

A drizzle descended upon me as I strolled to her front door. I knocked and saw her open and shut the curtains.

"Just a minute," she called out.

I heard her shuffling around and chuckled. I'd checked the surveillance cameras earlier and knew her place was messy. She was trying to tidy up for me.

I knocked again. "Open up, Leighton. It's starting to rain out here."

She opened the door, drawing it back with a whoosh. Her hair was up in a messy bun, her cheeks flushed, and she wore my coat. The one I'd given her when we left Thornefield.

"Hi." I grinned. There was no way for me to hide the satisfied smile on my face.

She shut the door again, and I laughed.

"Leighton. Seriously, I'll catch pneumonia out here." The light rain became a steady rainfall in a matter of seconds.

She opened the door again and motioned for me to enter.

I stepped in, and she closed the door behind me. "I came to drop this off." I handed over her coat.

"Oh, thanks. How'd you manage to get it?" She took the coat and hung it in her closet.

"I went back to Compass and asked the manager for it." I glanced around her home and smiled.

"I should have thought of that. But I suppose I wasn't in my right mind at the time." She chewed on her lower lip, thinking. "I umm . . . thank you, Caveman, for everything. I'm unsure what would have happened to me if you hadn't been there."

"Flower, I told you, you never need to thank me for taking care of you." I pulled her lower lip free of her teeth.

"I only remember bits and pieces of that night. Things were fuzzy from . . . when we left Thornefield." She looked off to the side, thinking. "I don't even remember how we got here."

"I drove, Leigh. You gave me your address, and then your head started to list to the side. You were pretty out of it when we reached the front door," I told her.

"Ugh. I'm so embarrassed." She placed her face in her hands.

"Don't be. You're alive and well. That's all that matters, babe," I said.

"So umm . . . can I get you something to drink?" She moved into the kitchen and peered into the fridge. "Eat? Well, maybe not eat unless you want a tomato or ramen noodles. I ate the soup and crackers you had delivered."

"Good, I'm glad you ate something somewhat healthy. But uh, ramen noodles?" I arched my brow. "Haven't you had any real food since I was here last?"

She paused momentarily, tapping her finger on her chin. She hadn't left the house since. She cast her eyes down.

I'd been keeping an eye on her periodically. I had a feeling she'd received news about Henry somehow, and that had been bothering her. She didn't know about my involvement in the situation, which wouldn't change anytime soon. However, I wanted her to talk to me about it.

"What happened, Leighton?" I asked.

She wrung her hands together nervously.

"Come here." I steered her toward the couch. "Talk to me, babe." I flopped on the cushions beside her.

"A few days before we met, I had a stalker," she began.

Yes, I know. I was stalking you first, and then he showed up.

I feigned surprise.

"I called the police, and then a few days ago, they showed up and told me they caught the guy, and he'd been found dead."

"They made a house call for that?" I arched my brow. This time, my surprise was genuine. Possibly ill-timed, but surprised nonetheless.

Leighton wasn't phased.

"Well, that's the interesting part," she continued. "They said the cause of death was suicide, but . . . they suspect foul play and thought I had something to do with it."

"Oh, shit? Why you?"

"Apparently, he'd been stalking me for a while. And although his death was a suicide, there were bruises all over his torso."

"And they thought you beat him up?"

"I know, ridiculous, right? It's just unsettling. All of it. Finding out someone I barely knew had been stalking me, and then he's found dead, and the police come to question me as though I had something to do with it." She tipped her head back on the sofa, looking at the ceiling.

"The odd thing is . . ." She nibbled her lower lip again. "I'm not sorry he's dead. I'm kind of glad he is."

That's my girl.

"Does that make me a bad person?" She raised her chin and looked me in the eye.

"No. Not at all. It seems like the guy was a creep, and he got what he deserved," I said.

"Yeah, it's been hard navigating these emotions. I haven't been back to school or work since the police arrived. I'm not worried about school; my professors have been cool. Work is another issue, or rather non-issue, since I don't work there anymore, which is fine considering it was a shit job that paid minimum wage. My boss is just an ass."

"What kind of work?" I asked as though I didn't already know. *Yep, master manipulator at work here, folks. Lies upon lies upon lies, for now.*

"I worked at the library. My supervisor said she wouldn't hold my position for me because, and I quote, 'I need to evaluate what it is about me to attract these psychos.' And I had to admit she does have a point."

"Well, she sounds like a complete bitch," I fumed. Now I had to add the damn librarian to my kill list.

"To be fair, it's been a shit week, and I haven't been the model employee," she said.

"Don't be so hard on yourself. You've been through a lot. Is your life always this exciting?"

"No. Not even close." She chuckled and eyed me warily.

"And then there's you. With how my life has been going, you're probably the worst of them all," she said. Her gaze studied me.

Ooof ouch. And so true.

"Leighton, I would never harm you in any way. With me, you're always safe; however, if I make you uncomfortable, say the word, and I'm gone. But . . . I'd rather stay."

There was an awkward stretch of silence while she mulled my statement over, and I was glad she was thinking things through; still, I had to steer her in the right direction.

"Do I?" I asked in a low, seductive tone.

She tipped her head to the side.

"Do I make you feel uncomfortable, Flower?"

"No," she replied immediately. "I'm not sure why, but even from the first time we met in the elevator—you never gave me creepy vibes. And there's the fact that you watched me vomit my guts out and still took care of me. Maybe you're not such a caveman after all."

I flashed her a smile, which she returned.

"So, yeah, I guess you can stay for a while. Oh, sorry, did you want something to drink or eat? I was about to get you something before I got distracted unloading my problems on your lap."

"Well, you're not feeding me ramen noodles. And you can talk to me about anything anytime. I'm happy to listen or help with your problems however I can," I told her and meant every word. Despite my shadowing prior to our actual meeting, I wanted Leighton to trust me and willingly allow me into her life.

I pulled out my phone and began tapping away on it.

"I could use help figuring out my choice in men," she muttered.

She falsely blamed herself for those men and their actions, so I ignored her statement and asked, "Italian or Greek?"

"I'm sorry, what?" A line formed between her brows.

"Italian or Greek? Food? What do you feel like having?"

She laughed. "I thought you were asking me what kind of men I liked."

I already knew the answer to that question. "You like me. And I'm neither. Food?"

"You? Is that right?"

"Food, Flower. Stop changing the subject," I chided.

"Greek," she replied.

"Done."

She narrowed her gaze. "How do you know what I wanted to eat?"

"I got a little of everything." I winked.

CHAPTER 19
LEIGHTON

LAZ ORDERED ALL of my favorite dishes from my favorite Greek restaurant. It was as if the guy knew everything about me.

He ordered enough to keep me fed for a week. The sweet man was concerned I'd go hungry now that I didn't have a job. And he ordered a bottle of wine. I eyed the wine; apprehension flitted through my belly. It'd been a week since the night at Firefly, and I wasn't sure I was ready to drink again, now or ever.

Lazarus noticed my hesitation. He wrapped an arm around my waist and rested his chin on my shoulder, "Leighton, you don't have to drink the wine now or ever. And honestly, I didn't even ask for it. I order from them all the time, and they always include this bottle."

I pressed my cheek lightly against his and exhaled. There was no way I was letting what Nick did to me affect me for the rest of my life. And for fucks sake, I was at home, and Lazarus was with me. "I think I'd like to try it," I muttered.

"Okay." He pecked my cheek.

My dining room table was covered with books and papers, so we ate and drank in my living area, choosing to lay everything out on the coffee table, picnic style. After dinner, Lazarus helped me clean and put the leftovers away, all while making fun of the shit job I'd done trying to tidy up when he unexpectedly arrived.

I excused myself to the bathroom for a moment, and when I returned, he was standing like he was ready to leave. Disappointment shrouded over me, making the food in my tummy gurgle.

"Why don't you have a television in here?" he asked.

"I prefer reading in here, and watching television in there." I waved toward my bedroom.

Laz waltzed into my room, making himself at home. It warmed my insides to see him so comfortable in my personal space. For some reason, I wanted him to feel welcomed.

"Ah, here it is." He picked up the remote and then flopped on my bed.

"I don't have cable, and my Netflix subscription expired." I sat beside him, suddenly embarrassed. "I'm a student who just lost her job, remember."

His gaze fixed on me for a moment, his expression neutral.

"This," he twirled his finger in the air. "Doesn't give off the struggling student vibe. How do you pay for a duplex off campus? Let alone tuition. I'm pretty sure working at the library doesn't pay well."

My shoulders slumped. I hated talking about my family. "Well, I have a student loan. And this place belongs to my mother's husband. He . . . he bought it for me. And pays the utilities."

"So he pays for your household living expenses but not your personal expenses?" he asked.

"Well, no, he does. Or he would. I don't want to ask for anything more than the household stuff."

He waited for me to continue.

"He's the biggest creep of them all," I added, which was the god-awful truth. "My mother married him when I was fourteen. She's beautiful and ill-equipped to hold down a real job. And he's wealthy. Long story short. I don't like him. And I don't want to owe him anything. I tally what he pays and intend to pay him back someday. Somehow."

"Hmmm . . . interesting. So you work part-time to afford personal things like Netflix, and I'm guessing, books?"

He pulled a book from under his shoulder and glanced at it.

"Yes." I motioned to snag the book from his hands, but he moved out of reach. "Don't read that."

He held his arm out, holding me back while he read through the last page I'd bookmarked. Oh god. I scrambled atop him, fighting to tear the book out of his hands. He easily flipped me over and pinned me down to the mattress.

"Give that back!" I snarled.

He laughed while dodging my attempts to take the book from his hands.

"This is a dirty book." He smirked.

"No, it isn't," I said under my breath, my cheeks flaming hot.

"Uh yeah, it is. It's pornographic. The elemental princess has five mates. Five?!"

I bucked him off me and snagged the book from his hands.

"Do you know how utterly ridiculous that is? Five men would never share one woman, princess or not."

"It's called fiction, Lazarus. It's supposed to be far-fetched. It's part of the appeal."

"Oh, and I suppose having one mate isn't appealing." He quirked his eyebrow.

"Well, sure it is. But if you want 'real life' stories, watch the freaking news," I told him.

"I would, but you don't have cable. Having a television with no cable is practically useless." He paused, then sat up to face me.

"Did you? You know." He tipped his chin to the book in my hand.

"Did I what?" I asked, perplexed. *Have five mates? In my dreams. I'm not that cool, nor do I have the stamina.*

"Have you had sex with more than one man at the same time?" he asked.

Oh . . . well.

"That's a personal question," I replied.

"You did, or you would have said no. How many? Five? Fuck."
Lazarus rubbed his hand down his face.

I laughed.

"Who I slept with is none of your business," I said

"Who the fuck were they?" Laz growled.

"Again, none of your business, Caveman. Who I sleep with is
personal," I told him.

"Personal? Really? We're in your bed. You're half-naked. A
personal question about your past is completely within range here,"
he retorted.

"Umm . . . well kind of, sorta, but not really. Anyway, how about
you answer a personal question for once?" I replied.

"Ask me anything you want?" He threw up his hands as if saying
he was an open book.

I tapped my chin. During dinner, he'd told me he was a downsizing specialist, which sounded like complete bullshit.

"What does a downsizing specialist do? Exactly?" I asked.

"Kill people. I take out people who are no longer necessary," he
stated bluntly.

I gaped. It took me a minute to fully register his words.

"You're fucking with me. If you're going to bullshit, come up with
a better lie," I finally said.

"Hey, just because you don't like the answer doesn't mean it's a
lie." He placed a pillow under his head and crossed his ankles.

I rolled my eyes.

"Did you just roll your eyes at me?"

"Stop deflecting and answer the question." I raised my chin.

"You stop deflecting and answer my question first." He shrugged.

"Fine! Next question. What—"

He cut me off. "Nope, my turn."

He repositioned himself on my bed to face me while propping his
head up with his elbow.

"Why are you wearing my coat?" he asked, his tone serious.

I'd been wearing his coat on and off since he'd left it a week ago. I knew he noticed as soon as he walked in my door, but he had the decency not to bring it up until now.

"You've been dying to ask me that all night, haven't you?" I asked.

"Yes. I like seeing you in my clothes, so I didn't want to bring it up, afraid you might take it off," he replied.

"And now?"

"I'm curious about why and hoping you might take it off so I can see what you've got on underneath." He hooked his finger into the lapel and tugged gently. I slapped his hand away and pulled the coat tighter, trying in vain to hide my cleavage.

He smirked. "And that's three questions. Time for you to pay up."

"I . . . um . . ." I paused, trying to come up with a lie.

"No. No bullshit. And no half-assed answers either."

He drummed his fingertips on the mattress between us.

I took a deep breath. Ah, shit. Fine.

"I like it. It's comforting."

"In what way?" he asked, not missing a beat.

I swallowed hard, then turned over to look at the ceiling.

"Leighton." Lazarus hooked my chin with his fingers to meet my eyes. "Truth."

"It smells like you. Wearing it reminds me of the man who brought me home after my date and his friends tried to drug me. The man who stayed and took care of me while I puked my brains out. The man who had the opportunity to take advantage of me while I was drugged out of my mind but didn't, despite what transpired between us earlier that evening. The man who was a complete gentleman and a good friend when I needed one the most. It reminds me that despite my hellish week, good men do exist. It makes me feel safe."

I didn't know where those words had come from, but everything I'd said was one hundred percent true.

Lazarus stared at me—disbelief and shock written all over his face. I'd said too much. That was a girl thing, wasn't it? We were always confessing too much too soon, effectively scaring men off.

Before I could doubt myself any further, Lazarus crashed his lips against mine.

CHAPTER 20
LAZARUS

AT AGE ELEVEN, I became aware that I was a killer. After the incident with the psychologist at Bright Haven, my father agreed and had me training to become the assassin that I am today. My path in life was decided, and I began training after school, forgoing social activities or sports. I never complained; it was a good life, one I accepted and enjoyed. My father had warned me that the path as a killer would be one of solitude. Love and family weren't something I'd ever considered . . . until Leighton.

The words from her beautiful lips left me speechless—never had anyone thought of me as a protector. Never had anyone said I made them feel safe. I was the monster hiding in the shadows, the thing people ran from.

From the first night Leighton entered my dreams, she became my nightmare girl and mine to protect. And now, after her confession, she was mine to love.

I crashed my mouth to hers, taking her by surprise. Her pillowy lips parted for me, and my tongue delved into her mouth. She tasted minty and floral and utterly intoxicating. I breathed her in, stealing the very air from her lungs. I wanted to consume her—all of her. Make her completely mine. An undeniable hunger enveloped me.

Every kiss became more. More demanding. More possessive. More claiming. I wanted to eat her alive, body and soul. My crazy was out front and center. A part of me, my sensible side, knew I had to rein it in. But fuck . . . Leighton responded in kind. Her fingers threaded through my hair, keeping our faces pressed together. She uncrossed her legs and spread them for me, allowing my body to settle between hers.

Keep it together, Laz, I reminded myself, yet the thought evaporated the second it was formed. She was mine. And she was giving herself to me.

I'd ruin her and myself in the process. My brand of crazy would surely scare Leighton away, which was the last thing I wanted. With the strength of pure will, I hovered mere inches from her body, in full plank position, determined to slow things down. The heat of her sex soaked through my jeans. Fuck. A deep growl rumbled from my chest, and I drew away.

Leighton lifted her head off the mattress and gripped the back of my head, keeping our lips locked. She moaned into my mouth. A low, sultry purr. She slid her foot alongside my outer thigh and wrapped her leg around my back, pulling me down on top of her. Her responsiveness spoke directly to my crazy, and my attempts to resist the temptress snapped.

I pushed my coat off her shoulders while keeping our lips fused and palmed her full breasts, pinching her nipples through the thin fabric of the lacy bralette she wore. Leighton clawed at my t-shirt, tugging it off my back. Her hands roamed over my chest and down my arms. I nipped at her neck, sucking and licking a path down to her chest. She wriggled out of the lace, granting me access to her pert tits. I squeezed the heavy globes, kissing and sucking each nipple.

"Mmm . . . Lazarus," she moaned.

I bit the taut, rosy bud. She writhed under me, grinding her pussy on my length. I reached between her legs and found the thin fabric covering her cunt soaked. My hand wormed under the lace. My fingers slipped between her folds. So fucking wet. I ran my thumb over her swollen clit. Her body quivered. Leighton groaned and began pushing down her panties.

Her eagerness fueled my desire. I unbuttoned my jeans and rolled them down my hips. My cock sprang free, painfully hard. I lined up my tip and pressed at her slick entrance.

Leighton pushed on my chest. "Condom, Laz. Please."

I always wore a condom and never had a problem doing so. Leighton was different. For the first time in my sexually active life, I wanted to bareback. But I'd respect her wishes . . . for now.

"Where?" I growled.

"What? What do you mean where? Don't you have one?" Her skin flushed, and her chest heaved.

"No. Don't you?" I asked.

"No. I haven't had sex in months. Fuck." She palmed her face.

"Fuck is right. God damn it!" I snarled. I always had condoms on me but hadn't thought about it. Well, okay, I did. I just didn't want to wear one. But I wouldn't do anything against her will.

Leighton rolled away from me, closing her legs. Oh no. That wasn't going to happen.

I gripped her leg and forced on her back, then pinned her body with mine.

Her eyes were wide, questioning.

I kissed her gently, suckling her top lip and then the bottom. She relaxed and kissed me back, her eyes squeezed shut.

"Leighton," I said. "Look at me."

Those big blue eyes peered at me.

"I would never hurt you. I will never do anything to you against your will. Whenever you say no, I will stop."

I held her gaze.

"Do you trust me?"

She nodded.

"I need to hear you say it, Leighton baby."

"I trust you." Her voice was strong and sure, and she didn't blink.

Thank fuck. My crazy was already unleashed and had to be sated . . . with at least a taste.

I took my time trailing kisses down her body, paying special attention to her breasts. Her heart was hammering in her chest. I grinned.

My hands roamed over her narrow waist, and I kissed down her flat stomach, rolling her belly ring with my tongue. Leighton's body trembled beneath me. Her responsiveness made my ego soar. My lips grazed over her mound and hovered over her clit. I blew on the sensitive nub, and Leighton arched her back.

"Lazarus," she said with a breathy voice.

I peppered kisses all over her outer lips; the taste of her desire filled my mouth.

"Yes, baby," I cooed.

"Stop." Her body quivered. Her voice was shaky. "Teasing. Me."

I released a raspy chuckle. She jerked her hips. I flicked her clit with my tongue, then ran it down her slit to her tight entrance. Up and down, driving her mad. Her pink, smooth flesh fit perfectly into my mouth, and I sucked it whole. Her body vibrated under me. Her juices coated my tongue and dripped down my throat. She was so fucking sweet. I drank every drop, slaking my thirst, and ate her whole as though it was my last meal.

Leighton pumped her hips wildly. She was teetering on the edge of release. But I wasn't ready to let her fall yet. I wasn't nearly done feasting on her delicious cunt. I eased off on my assault when she gripped the back of my head and forced my face to her pussy.

"I need to come," she said.

"Beg me." I made a slow, lazy circle around her clit, then pulled away.

"Please, Lazarus. Please, please, please." She chased my mouth with her hips.

I caught her clit between my teeth while plunging a finger into her hole.

Leighton thrashed on the bed and screamed her release. Wave

after wave of cum poured from her spasming cunt. And I drank every fucking drop.

Her skin glistened with sweat, and tremors rolled through her body with the aftershocks of her orgasm.

"That was . . . wow," she panted.

I kissed and suckled pussy lips. Leighton jolted, her flesh ultra-sensitive. She'd had enough for now, and I crawled up her body with a smug smile of satisfaction, feeling like the king of the world.

Her honeyed taste lingered in my mouth, and her juices covered my face. I didn't bother cleaning up; I wanted to savor her taste and share it with her. Leighton initially welcomed my kisses delicately, and then her mouth became more urgent. Her body responded again.

I gently pushed her away. "Sleep, Leighton baby."

"But," she protested.

"There will be another time." I kissed her forehead, then rolled over, bringing her to rest on top of me.

She wiggled, molding her body against mine, and fell asleep in seconds.

CHAPTER 21
LEIGHTON

I ROLLED to tuck my head into my pillow that wasn't there. My face pressed into a hard chest, and a strong, steady heartbeat thumped under my cheek.

My caveman, my Lazarus.

I breathed him in, savoring his masculine scent of leather and spice. The events of the night before came flooding back to me. He'd shown up uninvited after being gone for a whole week, and yet I wasn't mad about it. There was an intensity to him which could be overwhelming, but he was also intelligent and thoughtful. We had an easy-going camaraderie as though we'd known each other for much longer than a few days. Having him in my home felt . . . natural. And that talented mouth of his was something. Arousal stirred in my belly, making my pussy clench. Slowly, I tipped my head to take in his handsome face. He smiled slightly in his sleep, softening his angular features. I wondered what he was dreaming about.

Needing to pee, I slipped out of bed, did my usual morning things, and returned to find him still sleeping peacefully. He'd said he was a downsizing specialist, aka hit man, which had to be bullshit. Even so, he didn't seem to be on a schedule because he'd been sleeping like he had nowhere to be. He hadn't said much about his past, and neither did I. We seemed content to get to know our present-day selves versus the past that may have shaped us. We didn't talk much about family; although, he did mention that he worked for a family-owned business. And I did mention my dislike for my mother's husband, but he hadn't pressed for more information, which I was grateful for; that was a sour subject. From what I'd heard and seen, I liked him just as he was—more than just liked him, if I was being honest.

He rolled over and pulled my pillow to his chest. His biceps flexed, and his back . . . my breath caught in my throat, and before I could think better of it, I strode to my bed, dropping my towel on the floor. The cool morning air nipped at my flesh. *Thank god I didn't wash my hair.*

I crawled onto my bed and up his body. I kissed his broad shoulders and down the puckered flesh of his back—the uneven, discolored flesh bespoke of pain and trauma. I didn't know his story or where the scars had come from. Still, my heart hurt. *Who did this to you, Caveman?* Another emotion overwhelmed the sorrow I'd felt, an emotion I wasn't familiar with . . . rage. I'd never been a violent person, but the sight of his scarred flesh made me angry. Whoever had done this had landed the top spot on my newly formed kill list.

Lazarus' body went rigid under my touch. I increased the pressure of my mouth, kissing and licking over each scar and the length of his spine to his neck, then whispered in his ear. "You're beautiful. Every inch of you is strong, masculine beauty." His body relaxed, and I caught his lips with mine, swiping my tongue through his mouth. He tried to pull away, but I cupped his face, then rolled him onto his back and straddled his waist.

"Good morning." I kissed each eye, then worked my way down his chest. His stiff cock, poked at my center.

Damn it, Leigh, why didn't you put panties on first?

I was dripping. My cunt perfectly poised over his crown. The cotton briefs he wore did nothing to inhibit my need to slide over him. I groaned and rocked over his cock.

"Leigh, baby," Lazarus said, his voice laced with sleep and sex.

Reluctantly, I moved and settled between his legs. I kissed his belly and slid my tongue down his happy trail, rolling his briefs down past his hips and thighs.

I stared. He was perfect. Even his balls were perfect. Hair trimmed short, skin smooth and velvety. He had the most beautiful cock I'd ever seen. And he was huge. Long and substantial girth. This was not a ride-all-night kind of cock. This was a make-you-walk bow-legged kind of cock that you'd feel for days. My pussy pulsed, juices coating my thighs. I caressed the smooth skin from tip to root. His cock bobbed, nearly smacking me in the face. I smiled and then gripped his length. He was thick and heavy.

Where was a condom when I needed one? And I desperately needed one.

I took him into my mouth. Laz hissed. I swirled my tongue over his crown, licking his precum. To my surprise, I didn't want to spit it out. It wasn't overly salty or bitter. It was delicious, and I wanted more. I wanted to swallow. I opened wide and worked him with my tongue and my lips. He was a big man; there was no way I'd fit the gigantic dick in my mouth. My eyes watered as I took him until he hit the back of my throat and still had almost three inches of length. I used my hand and my mouth. Sucking and stroking.

"Leighton, fuck." Lazarus sat up. His breathing ragged. "I want your pussy."

I released him with a wet pop. "My pussy wants you, too."

I swirled my tongue over his tip. He pulled my hair back and held it with one fist.

"Damn, baby. That mouth of yours feels so fucking good."

I kept my gaze locked with his and sucked him down deep.

"Fucckk." His balls tightened. His eyes rolled back in his head.

I sucked harder, stroked faster. Tears streamed down my cheeks.

Laz tugged on my hair, pulling me off his cock. "You're going to make me explode."

I inched up just a tad, catching his cock between my breasts, sliding him up and down. "I want you to."

He pumped his hips, fucking my breasts. His crown slapped the tip of my tongue. I reached between my legs and rubbed furiously over my clit.

Abruptly, Laz rose to his knees and pushed his cock into my mouth. "Swallow."

He kept his hand tangled into my hair and fucked my mouth. I gripped his thighs and held on for dear life, breathing through my nose. His crown entered my throat. He grunted his release. Hot ropes of cum filled my mouth. I swallowed and swallowed, and still, his seed dripped down my chin.

He pulled out, his grip on my hair loosened, and then he peered down at me. "Good morning, beautiful." He swiped his cum from my chin and put it back in my mouth. He smiled as I licked his finger. "Suck me clean."

I did as he asked while massaging my clit. He slapped my hand away. I glared at him.

"Clean?" he asked, looking down at his still-hard cock.

I ran my tongue over his shaft again, eager to please him. He groaned and then shoved me back on the bed.

"As much as I wish I could, I won't be able to come again." His tip nudged at my entrance. "But I will sink my dick so deep inside you and make you come before I soften."

With one harsh thrust, he plunged into my depths. I dug my nails into his arms and bit into his shoulder. *Owww.*

He shuddered. "Fuck. Sorry. Did I hurt you?"

I didn't say anything. Metallic-tasting liquid filled my mouth. Shit. Fucking Caveman was going to split me in half.

"Leighton, talk to me. I . . . I knew you were on the smaller side. I should have been more careful. Are you okay?"

I nodded.

"Look at me," he demanded.

My eyes fluttered open. His eyebrows were scrunched together.

"Words, babe."

"I'm okay."

He nodded and moved to get off me, but I locked my legs behind his back. I rocked my hips. I felt so complete. I needed him to move.

"I'm not finished." I brought his face to mine and latched onto his lips.

He pumped into me, taking me higher. Sucking him off and swallowing his hot cum was beyond arousing, it wouldn't take long. My body was primed for release, and his cock was hitting me in all the right places. Laz draped one of my legs around his bicep. He dug in his heels, each thrust searing me on the inside.

"You cunt feels so fucking good," Lazarus said through clenched teeth. "Come for me."

"Yes, Lazarus!" I arched my back and detonated. An explosion of pleasure rolled from the tips of my toes up to the crown of my head. Everything tightened. Goose flesh prickled over my sweat-covered skin.

"Leighton, fuck." Laz let out a pained growl. "Your pussy is milking my cock, babe. You're gonna make me come again. Relax. Don't move." He gripped my hips, keeping my body still.

His forehead was knotted in concentration. Lazarus was doing everything he could to hold off his release. It was cute. And I was the devil. I pressed my lips to his, and my cunt squeezed his shaft.

"Ahh fuck. I won't be able to hold off," he growled.

I smiled against his lips and moved my hips, rocking back and forth over his cock.

"Naughty girl." He moved with me, picking up the pace. A second wave of pleasure rose within me.

"Don't stop, Laz. I'm almost there."

He growled. Each thrust was wild, rough, and frantic. He clamped onto my nipple with his lips, and his teeth grazed over the sensitive flesh. My climax overwhelmed me. My walls closed in on his cock, and then Lazarus came with a primal grunt. He continued pumping into me as though he was pushing his seed deeper inside my tunnel.

Lazarus consumed every part of me right then. His deep, masculine moans of pleasure filled my ears. His thick cock stretched me beyond anything I'd ever imagined. The weight of his body felt like a protective shield. He'd claimed me, and I wanted him to do it over and over again.

He peppered kisses all over my face as we caught our breath. "Please tell me you don't hate me." His downcast eyes were hooded with guilt.

"Hey," I caressed his cheek. "I wanted this as much as you did. Maybe even more."

I smiled, and he smiled back.

"But we can't do this again."

Anger and annoyance flashed over his face. He eyed me. The intensity of his gaze bore into me, and suddenly, I felt like a small animal caught by the big bad wolf.

"Yes, we will," he told me.

"I didn't mean it like that," I chuckled. "I meant without protection."

"Again, yes, we will." He sealed his lips to mine, and I made a mental note to make an appointment at the clinic, or I would be in trouble.

CHAPTER 22
LAZARUS

MY PHONE VIBRATED in my pocket. Zeke was having a fit since I should have been in the office two hours ago. I sent him a text telling him I was on my way and placed my phone on silent. I didn't feel bad about ignoring him or missing a meeting. For the first time in months, I'd slept soundly two nights in a row. I winked at my flower as she ran around her place, gathering what she needed for school. She flashed me a brilliant smile.

I rinsed our coffee mugs and placed them on the drying rack. We had toast and coffee for breakfast and were heading to campus.

"Are you ready?" she asked me.

"I am. You?" I snagged her around the waist and kissed her neck.

She nodded. I took her book bag from her, and then we left her apartment.

"Leighton!" her friend slash neighbor screeched.

She was wearing a tight body-con dress that was too small. Her hair was a mess, and her make-up smeared. Ah, the walk of shame.

"Hey! Are you just getting home?" Leighton asked.

"Yeah. I missed my morning classes, but . . . oh well. I need sleep, girl."

Leighton laughed.

"Who's this?" her friend asked, eyeing me appraisingly.

"Oh, this is—" Leighton began.

"Her boyfriend." I finished for her, taking the apartment keys from her hand, and proceeding to lock up.

"Really?"

"Yes," Leighton said. "This is Lazarus. Laz, this is Hallie."

Hallie, whom I'd already done some research on, was a spoiled brat. She lived off her daddy's money, barely had a two-point-oh GPA, and wasn't interested in much except getting as many social media followers as possible, sleeping around, and partying.

She extended her hand, and I ignored it, grasping Leigh's instead.

"Nice to meet you." I tugged at Leigh's hand.

Yep, I didn't like Hallie much. Perhaps I should have been more cordial, but I disapproved of the friendship. I wasn't trying to tear down Leigh's support system, but Hallie didn't offer the type of support and friendship my woman deserved—case in point: Nick Hanford.

"Alright, girl. Get some rest." Leigh leaned into me. "I need to get to class."

Hallie released a dramatic yawn. "Boring! But someone needs to follow the rules." She laughed. "Nice to meet you, Lazarus." She jutted out her hip in what was supposed to be a seductive pose.

Gross. "Yep." I draped an arm around Leigh's shoulders.

"Boyfriend, huh?" Leighton asked me as I steered her to the car.

"For now," I replied.

"For now? Does that mean you already have a break-up date in mind?" She craned her neck to peer at me through her dark lashes.

I opened her door and waited until she got in. Before closing the door, I bent down and whispered in her ear. "Wedding date."

I closed the door before she could answer and placed her book bag in the trunk of my Bentley Coupe.

The wedding date remark wasn't a joke. It was a fact. My crazy was not only out, it was permanently attached to Leighton Parker. The only thing I could do was stay close to her or I'd fucking lose my shit and go on a killing spree. My mind whirled with all the things that needed to be changed.

Leighton was silent when I got behind the steering wheel. She didn't say anything until we pulled out of her driveway.

"Umm . . . I am going to pretend I didn't hear what you just said," Leighton muttered.

"Going to pretend? I think you've already been doing that." I reached for her hand and brought her knuckles to my lips. "Leighton, Flower, you can ask me anything."

"So, what does a downsizing specialist's daily schedule look like?"

I laughed. "Guess this means I am going to do all the planning."

"Not funny, Lazarus. And no more talking about weddings." She yanked her hand away from me and placed it on her lap.

"Okay, okay. Geez, touchy subject." I grabbed her hand again. "I have a meeting today and must go out of town. One day only. I'll be back tomorrow."

"Where?" she asked me. "Do you travel a lot?" She frowned and turned her face away from me.

"To the city. And yes, a few days a month. And no, Leighton, I'm not leaving you. I was serious about what I said."

She turned to face me.

"The 'w' word," I muttered.

She rolled her eyes.

"You need to stop doing that," I growled.

"And you're going the wrong way," she said as I pulled up to the gate designated for faculty parking.

She turned to face me, and I pointedly rolled my eyes.

I lowered my window at the guard gate, and the guard waved me in.

"Well, aren't you special?" Leigh eyed me.

"Me? No. My car, yes." I pulled into a random spot. "Don't move."

She looked at me with round eyes.

I exited the car, hurried to her side, and opened the door.

"What was that about?" she asked.

"Unless we're pulling into valet, I open your door."

"Oh my gawd, Caveman."

"Do not roll your eyes, Leighton."

She narrowed them instead.

I pulled her bag out of the trunk and motioned for her to lead. I knew her schedule, but it wasn't time to tell her about that yet.

"You don't have to walk me to class, Lazarus." She linked her fingers with mine.

"I don't, but I want to and will every chance I get," I told her.

We reached Clarkson Hall within minutes.

"Faculty parking is so much closer," she groaned.

"It's the car," I replied. "You're welcome to use any of my vehicles anytime."

She peered up at me.

"Don't . . ." I began.

"Roll your eyes," she cut me off. "Well, I wasn't so in your face with that."

I barked a laugh. "I will enjoy swatting your ass for being such a brat."

"Promises, promises," she said in a sing-song voice.

We stopped at a classroom where students were entering. A man about my age stopped before entering and addressed my girl.

"Oh hey, Leighton. Good to see you." He switched his book bag from his left to his right shoulder. "I was going to call you this weekend."

I snaked an arm around her waist. She leaned into me.

"Did you need help with something?" Leighton asked.

His eyes flicked up to me nervously. I glared.

"This is my boyfriend, Lazarus. Laz, this is Justin. He's the professor, and I'm his aide for this period," Leighton said.

Aww fuck. Professor Justin just landed a spot on my kill list. I did my best not to snarl.

"Uh . . . hi. Nice to meet you. And um. No. I mean, yeah, I

needed help grading some projects, but no worries. I'll see you in class." Justin made a hasty retreat into the classroom.

Leighton turned in my arms and caressed my cheek. "You can't snarl at everyone I know," she said.

You shouldn't have let me come inside you, I wanted to say, but didn't. That wasn't the cause of my crazy. But it didn't help either. "I'll only snarl at the bad people."

"What if I only know bad people?" she asked.

"Then I'll kill them all and be the only good person you need." I brought my lips to hers.

She kissed me back, telling me I hadn't scared her off yet.

"Tomorrow?" She licked her lips when we broke our kiss.

"Tomorrow," I promised. "Leighton, I have a serious request."

"If you say the 'w' word again, I'm running away."

"You run away, and I will hunt you down and then chain you to my bed," I told her.

She shook her head. Just barely refraining from rolling her eyes.

"Fine. What's the request?" She rested her hands on her hips.

"Don't go out without me. Just school and nowhere else," I said. She laughed. I didn't.

"Oh shit, Caveman, you're serious. Why are you serious?" Wariness replaced the laughter in her eyes.

Because I'm fucked up crazy.

"What's one day?" I asked.

She thought about it for a minute, then said. "Fine, one day."

I released her and draped her bag over her shoulder, then turned on my heel and returned to my car with a big smile.

A few strides away, she called out my name. I turned to see her drop her bag and run toward me. She jumped into my arms, a little breathless.

"I have a special request, too," she said. A big smile stretched over her beautiful face.

"Anything."

She wiggled out of my arms, and I set her down on her feet.

"This." She wormed her hand under my sweatshirt and tugged on my t-shirt.

"You want the shirt off my back?" I arched my brow and started stripping.

"Sounds weird when you say it like that, but . . . yes. Yes, I do." She nodded emphatically, hurrying me along.

I gave her my shirt and pulled on the hoodie. She brought the cotton to her nose and inhaled.

Leighton reached up, brought my face down to meet hers, and graced me with a gentle kiss. "Thank you," she said against my lips, then stepped away. "Now, go . . . downsize someone unnecessary."

I watched her until she disappeared into the classroom, completely speechless.

Oh, Leighton, my sweet nightmare girl. I am so fucking in love with you. You will never escape me.

CHAPTER 23
LAZARUS

"WHAT THE ACTUAL FUCK, Laz? Where the hell have you been?" Ezekiel asked.

I found my brother pacing in our office lobby, wringing his hands together. Geez, someone needed to get laid.

"I'm here. No need to get your knickers twisted in a knot," I replied.

"This is important, Lazarus. And when are you ever late?! I'll tell you when. Never." My elder brother followed me to my office. "Once this is done, we can focus our time and resources on the date rape crew project."

I'd spent the last forty-eight hours with Leighton and was in a grand mood until Zeke had to bring that shit up. And fuck, he was right. Our father and uncle insisted on us finalizing today's ticket and then we could focus on the DRC.

"I haven't forgotten about the job today or about the DRC. My flight leaves in two hours. I have forty minutes on the plane. My gear is packed and ready. Unless something has changed, all will go as planned. Chill the fuck out."

I stood behind my desk and logged onto my computer. "I do need food, though." I strode to the far corner of my office, where I kept a mini beverage cooler under the counter and pulled out a water bottle. Zeke stood in the middle of the room, staring at me. I threw a bottle of water at him, which he let drop to the floor. I shook my head and grabbed another bottle for myself, then popped it open and took a swig.

"What, Zeke? If you're going to stand in my office, make yourself useful. Like order lunch or something," I told him.

"Something's different about you. What happened?" Zeke stepped closer to me, leaned into my chest, and sniffed. I cocked my eyebrow. *What is the fucking weirdo doing now?*

"You smell like sex. Oh shit! You spent the night with Leighton. Damn, this is serious."

I should have showered. Leighton offered, but I'd made up an excuse about not having clothes. I did. My bags were packed for the mission. The truth of it was I didn't want to wash away her scent. Strange, yes. Borderline creepy, possibly. Unhygienic, some might agree. In my defense, I'd just had sex with the girl of my dreams without a condom. Hell, it was the first time I had sex without a condom, period. I was savoring the experience. At some point, I'd have to shower. But not yet.

"How does she feel about the . . . what did you call it? 'Shadowing'?" Zeke asked.

"Haven't told her about that." I scratched my jaw. "I did tell her about my line of work, though."

"Of all things, why that?"

"If she can accept me for what I do, then the rest of my sins won't seem as bad." I shrugged.

"Not sure she'll see it that way, but hey, I'm no expert. Aren't you concerned she might share that information?"

"Not in the slightest."

"That is so unlike you to be so trusting. You must really like her. Or are we talking about love here? Tell me more, little bro." He grinned.

I gave Ezekiel a dry look and ignored the question. The Ford men didn't talk about feelings, nor did we share secrets or anything else for that matter. I didn't know who my brother or uncle was dating. They didn't know about my life either. And I'd been okay to keep it that way . . . until Leighton and the fucking DRC. It was already out of character for me to have shared the shadowing part, and I wasn't quite ready to divulge more. The conversation thus far was already giving me gas.

Zeke wasn't bothered by my refusal to talk. He had lunch ordered and made himself comfortable in my office.

I worked on the tasks I needed to complete for the mission while Zeke fiddled on his phone, glaring up at me every five minutes. My mission was simple: there was one target who would be at a conference in the city. I checked his itinerary. His flight had already taken off and would arrive at the city's primary airport in three hours and eighteen minutes. He had two men with him as his personal security detail, and his suite at Wellington Hotel had already been prepped for his arrival.

My flight plans were already in place. The weather pattern held, and the flight was a mere forty minutes. We'd be taking one of our small jets; both myself and Zeke were licensed to pilot. But we'd hire pilots for this job. They'd deal with the plane while I got a rental car, which was already waiting for me. I'd arrive at the hotel before the target did, do my thing, and return shortly after.

Our well-trained and loyal staff had conducted thorough research on our marks. Zeke managed the employees, and they did good work. Still, I always followed up with research of my own. It was safer that way. Despite all the intel, the mark was just a mark to me. I had plenty of personal information on him, but the reason he was on my list was utterly unknown. Aside from the demons of my past, my kills were never personal. Those demons were long dead. Now it was pay to slay, except for my kill list pertaining to Leighton. Fuck I'd blow up the entire world if that meant it'd keep her safe.

My brother waited not so impatiently for me to divulge details about my nightmare girl. His tapping fingers did nothing to distract me from my tasks as they would have usually. I was focused and eager to get this done and be back in her arms by morning, if not sooner.

Tasks completed, I faced my brother. "Don't you have your own desk to tap your fingers on?"

"Took all of fifteen minutes for you to notice. I'm either losing my touch at being annoying, or you're pussy drunk." He snorted.

"Don't you have other things to work on? Like the DRC?" I glared at him.

"DRC? We're using acronyms now?" He shrugged. "I like it. Calling them date rape crew was too on the nose. And no, I don't have other things to do. The team is gathering the info on that mission, which we'll need to present to our elders. Because of the players, they want that job thoroughly vetted. But today's ticket is the priority. It's a high-paying job; we can't fuck up."

"Your lack of confidence in me is annoying as shit. When have I ever botched a job?" Impatience was evident in my voice.

"When have you ever been in love?" he snarked.

I was about to deliver a nasty retort when a knock interrupted. "What?!" I shouted.

"There he is, the grumpy sunshine we all know." Zeke got out of his chair and opened the door. "It's lunch, asshole."

He took the take-out bags from one of the staff members, some dude I wasn't familiar with. My stomach growled, and I wondered if Leighton had gotten lunch. I pulled out my phone and glanced at her schedule. Yep, I had programmed her class schedule into my phone. It wasn't that creepy. I'd told her I was doing it, and she just shook her head at me. I'd left her two hours ago, and she should have been done with one of her classes and heading to the library.

I sent her a text.

Me: Have you eaten anything?

Leighton: Not hungry.

Me: You need to eat, babe.

Leighton: Go back to downsizing, Caveman. I'm studying.

Me: If you don't take a break and eat something, I will send someone there to deliver food. And when I get back, I'll follow you around campus to ensure you take proper care of yourself.

Leighton: I'd laugh, but I know you're not joking.

Me: Eat, Leighton.

Leighton: Stop bossing me around, Caveman.

Me: I'm not being bossy. I care about your well-being.

Leighton: Aww. Heart eyes emoji.

She attached a pic of a granola bar.

Leighton: Happy?!

Me: If you didn't have leftovers, I'd be worried about dinner.

Leighton: I forgot about that. Now I am hungry. Thank you for overfeeding me.

Me: You're welcome. Lunch tomorrow.

Leighton: Promises. Promises

Me: I always keep my word, Leighton, baby.

Leighton: Kiss emoji.

Something hit me in the face, then thudded in my lap. A fucking egg roll.

"I'm glad to see you smiley and in love. But food, which you requested." Zeke waved his hand at the food laid out on the desk.

"Who's in love?" a nasally voice asked. "Can't be Lazarus. He's immune to feelings."

"Get the fuck out of my office, Davis," I growled.

My mood soured at the presence of my younger brother.

"What? Am I not invited to your precious brother bonding luncheon?" Davis asked.

"NO," Zeke and I said simultaneously.

"Didn't want to be here anyway." He backed away. "Good luck with your mission. Father said he expects excellence with this job; the client is very important. Don't fuck up."

I threw the water bottle at him, which he tried to duck. It caught his shoulder and spilled all over his suit.

Zeke burst into laughter, and Davis scampered out the door.

Less than two hours later, Zeke and I were deplaning and heading to the Wellington Hotel. Typically, I did these jobs alone and had preferred it that way. Zeke and I discussed it after Davis declared this job important to our father. We researched both the target and the client that had ordered the ticket further and found nothing new. However, it was a new client referred by one of our regulars. Yep, some people had a long list of enemies. The new client was paying thirty-percent higher, which was a red flag in my book. And that was Zeke's department. It was a money exchange, and since it was never personal, I never cared so long as I got paid. We discovered a few discrepancies that caused us to scratch our heads.

Potential setup? Highly unlikely, but possible. If anyone dared, I'd tear their entire operation down and their families. But I was a death dealer, and that meant dealing with unsavory characters. Anything was possible.

I checked in with Leighton, happy to see her at home and happier to have heard her voice. Eventually, I'd have to confess and stop peeking into her security cameras. Soon.

"Your girl okay?" Zeke asked.

"Yep," I replied, and he left it at that.

Over lunch, I'd told him about Leighton and the reasoning for my shadowing. He knew she was special to me. It was written all over my face, and I even heard it in my voice. Fuck, she'd changed me. Zeke patted me on the back, telling me how happy he was for me. He teased me about setting a wedding date and when we'd be having kids. I told him to stop being childish. There was no way I'd admit to already planning all of the above in my head.

I was coming on too strong as it was and needed to back off, lest she ran away from me. The thought made me grind my teeth. A longing stirred in my gut. I rechecked her cameras. She padded barefoot from her kitchen to her living room with a glass of wine in one hand and her smut book in the other. She was wearing my shirt. My heart soared. I sent her a text.

"I love you," I typed, then deleted it. Too much. And tacky. The first should be in person.

Me· See you tomorrow, beautiful.

Leighton: Heart emoji. Kissy face emoji.

She was mine, and even if she did try to leave, I'd follow her, even if that meant to the grave.

I breathed deeply and let my killer instincts wash over me like a second skin.

Get the job done and return to Leighton.

CHAPTER 24
LAZARUS

AS PLANNED, we arrived at the hotel earlier than the target. The hotel was crawling with unmarked security guards. Zeke and I didn't bother checking in. Instead, we grabbed a drink at the hotel bar and then hightailed it to the airport. We were able to catch up with the target and followed him and his two men. They didn't go to the Wellington Hotel. They drove straight toward Block 9. A city block that had been taken over by the homeless.

The men stopped in front of a two-story building resembling the rest of the block. Faded paint, broken windows, and discarded items littered the premises. People wrapped in worn clothing and blankets huddled against the building walls, shielding themselves from the constant drizzle and cool night air.

People scattered as soon as our target and his guards exited their car. Interesting. The main door of the building opened, and out stepped a bald man dressed in a suit. He said something in his earpiece and let them in.

I'd planned on following them alone, but Zeke got out of the car. I shook my head. "I work alone on this, brother. Keep the car running."

"Not going to happen. We don't know what or who we're dealing with," Zeke replied.

"Ezekiel, someone needs to watch the car. If one of us doesn't remain with the vehicle, it will be gone in ten minutes. You need to stay."

Zeke was about to argue. He scrubbed a hand through his hair and walked back to the car. "You have ten minutes, or I'm coming in there."

I broke into a jog and went up the side of the building using the fire escape stairs and crawled into a broken window on the second floor. The broken window opened to a three-by-five space with a black false wall. Fuckers were hiding something, and although not my mission, I was curious. Muffled voices from the other side had me pressing my ear against the false wall. I couldn't make out any words. Taking a chance, I pushed gently on the wall, which swung open with a squeak. I waited. No one came.

I slid out of the room and did a double take. The inside did not look anything like the outside. The room looked to be recently renovated. The tiled flooring was swept clean, and throw rugs with dizzying geometric patterns were placed under or around simple furnishings straight from an IKEA catalog. Overhead, the fluorescent lights flickered on and off. I stayed in the shadows and moved toward the voices coming from a doorway on the opposite side of the room.

As I approached the door, I noticed a small kitchenette in one corner and a smaller room with a sink, probably a bathroom. Someone was living here or hiding out.

I pulled out my Beretta, attached the suppressor and crept closer.

The doorway led to stairs that opened up to the first floor. My target was yelling at someone on the phone. His guards and baldy were standing idly by.

"I already told you. My contact said they arrived and left!"

"I don't know! You're the one with the faulty information!"

"Fuck you. You said all we needed to do was take out one. There were two. The boss is going to be pissed. This is your mess. Fix it!"

He tossed the phone.

Huh? I tapped my gun on my chin. It sounded like someone wanted to take me out. Better see who it was.

"Someone get me a drink!" my target yelled. Baldy moved toward the stairs. I hid in the shadows and waited.

He rounded the corner, and I pressed my gun to his temple.

"Don't even breathe." I urged him forward, closing the door behind us, and locking it for good measure. I led Baldy to one of the chairs in the middle of the second floor.

"Who do you work for?" I flicked off the safety.

"Fuck you."

I wrapped my hand around his mouth and shot him in the knee.

Blood poured from his wound.

"Who do you work for?"

"Black Sheep Enterprises."

"Who's your boss?"

"The man downstairs. Octavius."

"Who was he talking to?"

"I don't know. We don't have a name."

I pressed the gun to his wound.

"I don't know! I was told to wait here until Octavius arrived. All I know is Black Sheep wants The Sentinels."

Thump. Thump. Thump.

"Rick? Open the door," someone called from the opposite side of the door.

"You have two seconds to tell me something useful."

Rick screamed. I shot him in the head, then rolled to the side as the door burst open.

Shards of wood flew everywhere, and I fired my weapon, shooting someone in the foot and the second assailant in the shoulder.

Bullets came at me, and I rolled to the ground, using the sofa as a shield. Cotton filling floated in the air. Peering around the shot-to-shit sofa, I emptied my clip, killing the two guards, and then went downstairs to look for Octavius.

"Octavius, come out to play," I said in a sing-song voice, reloading my weapon.

A sharp whistle sang past my shoulder. Another caught my left bicep with a crack. Ah, shit, there went my phone.

I dropped to the ground and feigned a groan, then waited. Octavius snuck out of his hiding space and came toward me. I shot him in the arm. He dropped his gun. I shot him in the knee. He crumpled to the floor.

"Who were you talking to, Octavius?"

"Why should I tell you? You're going to kill me anyway."

"True. But, if you tell me, you'll die knowing I killed the man who put you in this position in the first place."

He thought about it. "I . . . I don't know his real name. They call him the Chosen. His number is on my phone."

"Show me."

He pulled out his phone with a shaky bloody hand. I glanced at the number, committing it to memory, and then shot him in the head. Then I took his phone just in case there was more exciting information.

"Laz! You've got company. Get out of there!" Zeke screeched into my earpiece.

Perfect timing.

I hurried into the car and told Zeke what I'd learned as we sped out of Block 9.

"Shit," Ezekiel said. "Someone has a case of the ass for you. And our company. But especially you."

I laughed. "Wouldn't be the first. Won't be the last."

"We need to switch cars. Hole up somewhere for the night and do some research," Zeke replied.

"Yeah, I got the number." I scratched my temple. "And his phone. There's probably a tracker on the thing, so let me see what I can do."

I wiped the bloody phone on the seat and began tapping away.

"Bet you're glad I'm here now, huh?" Zeke said.

"Just drive, asshole."

CHAPTER 25
LEIGHTON

"WHERE ARE YOU OFF TO? Going to see your hot boyfriend?" Hallie teased as we both locked our apartment doors.

"I'm going for a run," I replied. "Where are you going? New boyfriend. You look amazing!"

She wore thigh-high black leather boots, a black leather miniskirt, and a black cropped turtleneck. A tan trench coat hung off her shoulders, and gold hoop earrings framed her perfectly contoured face. It was noon on Friday, and Hallie looked like she was going to a swanky party in the city, which was her normal state. She was always stunning.

"Why, thank you." Gold bangles jingled as she moved her hand to place her keys in her Birkin. "Not boyfriend. But maybe. I like this one."

"Can't wait to meet him," I told her. This guy must be special. Hallie wasn't the type to use the term *boyfriend*.

"Where's your man? I haven't seen him around. Are you two done already?" she asked, giving me her best doe-eyed look. The hint of sarcasm did not escape me.

"He's out on business," I replied with a smile I certainly did not feel. "He won't be back until next week."

That was a lie. Why I said that, I didn't know. What I did know was absolutely nothing. I hadn't heard from Lazarus in days. Not a single word. No calls. No texts. I called and messaged, and no response. We had sex, and the fucker ghosted me. He acted so incredibly sweet for a couple of days and then vanished. That seemed to be his thing. Great for a day or two, then disappeared for seven. Hired assassin, my ass. He probably had a wife in the city. I was such a sucker.

"Well, well, well. Since he's away, we need to hang out. The football team is having its annual Halloween bash tomorrow night, and I have the perfect outfit for you. I'll come over at five. Let's have drinks and get ready together."

"Five?" Usually, frat parties didn't start until nine.

"Drinks, remember? We'll get a good buzz with good alcohol before we get there. And no, I'm not taking no for an answer. Love you. Bye!"

She sauntered away from me before I could respond.

I crossed the busy street onto university grounds, took a right onto a path that hooked around the campus to one of the many parks and started in a light run.

Dark, fluffy clouds blanketed the sky, making it seem like it was early evening rather than midday. Perfect weather, in my opinion. I was a rainy day and dark skies kind of girl. I wasn't an emo kid. I just loved how the silvery grays made it always seem like twilight. And rain was a blessing . . . if you're dressed for it, which I was not. The weather forecast had indicated a zero percent chance of rain, which I'd been banking on. It was unseasonably warm, and my skin glistened with sweat as I picked up the pace. My heart rate increased, and my muscles began to burn. The exertion felt good and kept my mind from spiraling.

I'd been running daily since Lazarus ghosted me. It kept me sane.

Lazarus. What a massive disappointment. I thought we'd had something. I certainly felt like we did. It seemed like he felt the same way. How could I have been so wrong?

Sure, there was a possibility that he had been unable to call me. Maybe his phone had been stolen. Or broken. Or there weren't any phones within a hundred-mile radius from where he was. Excuses. Poor, lame excuses.

Well, okay, he could be injured and in the hospital. Or maybe he was dead. I tripped over my feet and barely righted before face-planting on the trail.

Okay, the thought of him dead was not welcome, moving on. It was easier to be mad at him. Sort of. Fuck.

I felt utterly ridiculous. I was pining over a man that I had sex with . . . without protection, and he fucking vanished. Un-freaking-believable! Why did I attract these losers? Henry, Nick. Even Keith wasn't exactly a winner. What was it about me?

I shook my head and focused on my breathing. In through the nose, out through the mouth. In through the nose, out through the mouth. I tapped the volume on my watch and let Ms. Swift encourage me to *Shake it Off*.

An instinctual unease niggled my nape. I picked up the pace as I rounded the lake, heading down the path that led home, which was empty. Not a single soul in the vicinity. I reduced the volume until I could no longer hear Ms. Swift complain about her ex.

The sounds of my feet pounding on the pavement accompanied me, but that disquiet of being watched pressed on my back. I turned around. Nothing. I kept going. Fuck I had another two miles to go. And still not another soul. Where was everyone? It wasn't nighttime. It wasn't raining. It was as though the universe was purposely fucking with me.

Or maybe it was all in my head.

I focused on my breathing for a few minutes, then turned around. Nothing. I slowed. Walked backward, and still nothing. Jesus, Leighton. I faced forward and continued home.

A moment later, someone gripped my elbows. I screamed and turned with my arms swinging and fists connecting with a hard chest.

"God damn it!! Keith, you motherfucker!! Why would you sneak up on me like that?!"

My asshole ex rolled to the ground, laughing.

"You scared me!" I kicked his shin.

"Sorry! Sorry, Leighton." Keith held his hands up in supplication. "I'm sorry. Peace."

"You're an asshole." I walked away.

Keith came up beside me and draped an arm around my shoulders.

"I'm sorry, Leigh. Truly, I am. I wanted to surprise you. Stupid, I know. I'll never do that again."

"You're an awful human being, Keith Maynard." I shook off his arm.

"I'm sorry, okay, let me make it up to you. Coffee?" he asked, his voice holding a hopeful tone.

"No. I'm annoyed."

"Ah yes, I forgot. Grudge holder." He hooked his thumb in my direction.

I glared.

"Okay, okay, I'm batting zero for three at this point. What can I do?" He grinned.

"Nothing. I'll get over it. Just stop doing that, asshole! It wasn't funny the first time. It's not funny now! What if I'd had a gun and shot you?" I told him.

He scrunched up his face. "I hadn't thought about that."

Of course, you didn't. Idiot.

"So, umm . . . I wanted to remind you about the party we're having tomorrow night," Keith said.

"Yeah, Hallie told me," I replied.

"Are you two still friends?" he asked.

"Why wouldn't we be? We've been best friends for the last two almost three years." I narrowed my eyes at him.

He shrugged. "She's always out, and you're never out. I thought. I don't know what I thought. Anyway, it doesn't matter. I hope you come to the party tomorrow. Please."

"Keith . . . there isn't a you and I anymore. You know that, right?"

"Yeah, but I still like being around you. Maybe if we try to be friends like we used to be, we can find our way back to each other."

I gave him a sidelong glance.

"And if not, we can still be friends. Nothing wrong with being friends, right?"

I looked at the ground as we walked. Keith and I had met in a math study group. We both sucked at numbers. We used to joke about how we'd never make it as a couple or business partners because neither of us could barely count. Those were simpler days. Probably the most fun I'd had as a college student, and I was graduating soon. And Keith would go off and play professional football somewhere.

A pang in my chest filled me with...I wasn't sure what. I didn't love Keith anymore but appreciated having him as a friend. My life would be different soon. I'd be getting a real job and a different apartment, and shit, I would have to become a full-fledged adult.

"You're right." I finally said.

"Cool. See you tomorrow." He leaned in and pecked my cheek.

I swatted him on the ass as he turned away. He squealed.

"Stop scaring girls running alone in the park!" I called.

He jogged off with a big grin.

Lazarus was gone, and Keith was here offering friendship. A party was just what I needed.

CHAPTER 26
LAZARUS

I BOLTED UP IN BED, my body covered in sweat. My heart was hammering in my chest, and my eyes darted around the unfamiliar room.

"Laz? You good?"

I flinched. Startled by the sound of my brother's voice.

"Nightmare?" he asked. He swung his legs off the double-sized bed across from mine.

We were still dealing with the setup. After I'd taken out the primary target and his men, Zeke and I had done some research and decided to stay behind and follow up on leads. We checked into a ratty motel to keep out of sight and had been doing some undercover work. The person responsible for the setup was a sneaky fuck. He'd hidden his identity under layers and layers of bullshit. We'd wanted to find concrete evidence before bringing the situation to the elders—our father and uncle. It'd taken more than a week, and we'd just gotten the information that revealed the actual plot: take out the muscle—me, take out the brain—Ezekiel, take out the mentor—Uncle Jo, then take down the original—our father. Black Sheep Enterprises was a new player from the East Coast who wanted to take out The

Sentinels. From what we could tell, we'd taken out someone important to someone who called himself the Chosen. We'd just gotten the intel the night before and had decided to get some sleep before heading home. And I wish we hadn't waited. It was already mid-morning.

"Leighton," I croaked out, my throat parched. "I need to get home."

I pulled on my jeans and a sweater, then stuffed my feet into my shoes.

Zeke got dressed, and we had our gear packed up in minutes.

"I'll drive," I said.

He nodded and got on the phone with the pilots. They had stayed near the private concourse, and I trusted my brother to ensure they were ready to go by the time we reached the tarmac.

The nightmare was still fresh in my mind as I peeled out of the parking lot, leaving dust and pebbles in my wake. I had thought I was done with them. I reached into my pocket for my phone, which wasn't there. We'd been so preoccupied I hadn't had a chance to replace the phone that had taken a bullet for me. I tried calling from the motel's phone, but she never picked up, and I hadn't bothered to leave a message. She must be pissed. And possibly in danger. I punched the steering wheel.

"You want to talk about it?" Zeke asked.

I growled in response. It was unfair to take out my anxiety over my nightmare on my brother, who had been nothing but supportive of me all my life. But fuck! I couldn't find the words.

Ezekiel didn't pressure me for answers, so we drove silently for two hours to the private airstrip. The flight staff was ready to go when we arrived, and we hopped on the plane.

"Wheels up," I said to the pilots as soon as I boarded.

The pilot nodded at me, and Zeke and I strapped in.

Five minutes later, we hadn't moved. My knee bounced up and down, and I cracked my neck from side to side.

"Let's go!" I shouted. The cockpit was a few feet away from me, and I knew they'd hear me.

Five minutes later, I got up to storm into the cockpit.

The door opened. The pilot's eyes nearly popped out of his head. "Apologies, sir. We're unable to take off. Fog has impeded air visibility. The FAA is not allowing any planes to take off. It looks like we're grounded for at least another hour."

FUCK! I punched the wall.

"Keep us posted," Zeke said to the pilot, who nodded and skulked to the cockpit.

"Laz, call her," Zeke handed me his phone and moved toward the cockpit, giving me some privacy.

I dialed Leighton's number and, this time, left a message. She was screening her calls, which was typical for her. I tapped the phone on my forehead and decided to send a lengthy text, giving her a synopsis of why I hadn't called, that I was on my way, and, most importantly, telling her to stay home. I waited for her to respond.

Two minutes passed, and it felt like two months. I clenched my fist around the phone and drew back my arm, ready to toss the fucking thing, when Zeke said, "I wouldn't break that if I were you. That's the only means of communication we have."

"How much longer?" I asked. I could have said thank you for the phone and support, but my nightmare girl was in mortal danger.

"Flying . . . will be a while. The fog is thick, and with all the other private and commercial flights grounded, it'll be a few hours. Driving time is about the same."

I paced the aisle and tugged at my hair. Drive or wait. Drive or wait. Fuck! I dialed Leighton's number, and it went straight to voicemail. I texted. She didn't respond. She was probably pissed. I said I'd be home, but that had been days ago. Fuck my fucking hitman life. If I didn't care what happened to my brother or my uncle or my father or this fucking company, I would be with Leighton keeping her safe. I continued pacing. Flying time was forty-eight minutes in the air.

Driving four, maybe five hours. Fog in this city was always unpredictable. Drive or wait, Laz. Drive or wait.

"Fuck this. I can't sit here and wait." I grabbed my bag, and Zeke followed me out of the plane.

CHAPTER 27
LEIGHTON

MY PHONE RANG. "Can you check who that is?" I called out to Hallie. She'd come over hours earlier than expected with boxes of clothes for us to try on for the Halloween event.

"It's says unknown. Probably a telemarketer," she replied.

"Eeww, turn it off!" I told her as I signed for the box that had just been delivered. I glanced at the discreet box with an unknown sender and tried recalling what I had recently ordered. And then I remembered it wasn't a purchase. It was a replacement. I slid the box out of the way, trying to hide it from Hallie as she strolled out of my room wearing a shimmery white floor-length Grecian goddess number.

"Beautiful!" I exclaimed.

She spun in a circle.

"Your turn, come on!" She dragged me into my room.

Hallie was into cosplay, so she had countless of outfits to choose from. I'd never been into Halloween until I'd met her. This was our third Halloween party together, and every year, her costume collection grew. As per our ritual, we started out trying on outfits, ordering takeout, and then graduating to drinking good liquor. Her father had zero problems with her spending money on expensive wine, champagne, or whatever spirit desired. Last year, we'd gotten recipes for making specialty cocktails. They were sweet, and we both had gotten puke-faced. This year, we'd decided to keep it classy, and Hallie had splurged on two pricey bottles of champagne.

After the Nick incident, I'd been hesitant to consume alcohol, but Laz had eased me back into it. The night he ordered Greek food, we had some wine. At first, I didn't think I'd be able to handle it, but by the end of the night, I'd finished an entire glass.

"So . . . Hallie, you haven't mentioned your new guy. How was your hot date?" I asked, wanting to distract my brain from the man who had ghosted me.

Her shoulders slumped, and the little frown on her face told me it wasn't going well. Looked like I wasn't the only one with boy problems. "It's . . . I don't know. Sex is good. Not the best. But I like him. A lot."

"But . . ." I prodded.

Her eyes flicked to mine, and then she looked down at her hands. "I think he's still in love with his ex."

"Oh! Well, fuck him. Tell him to stop wasting your time and move on," I told her. The guy sounded like an asshole.

Hallie shrugged. "Yeah, maybe. Anyway, what about your new guy?"

Shit. My turn to fess up.

"I lied." I blurted. "He . . . he's disappeared. I haven't heard from him since you saw us leaving."

Hallie blinked rapidly. "Well, fuck him, too. What is wrong with these guys?! Don't they know how lucky they are? Fuck them."

We clinked our glasses together and took a long swig.

After trying on a dozen or more costumes, we were thoroughly sauced. In our drunken state, we decided to go full-stop slutty. A hot cheerleading uniform for her and a scandalous schoolgirl outfit for me.

We poured the last champagne into two plastic cups and made our way to the party, leaving our boy problems behind us.

The dormitories were located a short distance from our apartments. Whether they lived on campus or not, all students converged on Dormitory Row, where every chapter house would host a Halloween party. Revelers decked out in Halloween regalia often party-hopped.

Ashmore University was privately owned and funded. The athletics department was small in comparison to other schools, but the small community were huge supporters of the team. Alpha Phi members were primarily athletes and had the largest dormitory on campus. The Tigers football team has been number one in their division for the last two years. Every student knew if you were invited to an Alpha Phi party, you were part of the cool kids' club. I'd never be asked to hang out with them if it weren't for Hallie and Keith.

Hallie and I bypassed the long line of people waiting to enter House of Madness, Alpha Phi's chapter. We approached the pledges guarding the door with an extra sway to our hips. "Leighton, right?" one of the pledges asked me.

"Yep." I popped the p. I needed water or wouldn't make it till midnight.

"Ummm . . . can you wait here while we get Keith? He asked us to notify him when you arrived."

"Aww, you're so good at this." I caressed the guy's cheek. "Tell him I'm here, and I'm sure he'll find me."

I brushed past him, with Hallie right behind me. We navigated our way through the crowds of people and went straight to the dance floor. Bass thumped in my chest as Hallie and I swayed to the beat, our bodies pressed together.

One guy pressed into my back while another pressed into Hallie's.

"You two fine ladies shouldn't be dancing alone," one guy slurred.

"We're not alone," I called out over the music.

Hallie looked at each of them. "Yeah, we're together. And we're not nearly drunk enough."

"We'll go get drinks."

"We're good!" Hallie and I raised our cups and kept dancing.

They moved away, and another two brave souls took their place.

Both tall and muscular. Younger, probably sophomores. And both wore black slacks and a bowtie, but no shirt. Hallie and I looked at them and then at each other.

"Approved!" we said simultaneously.

We clinked our cups and took a drink. I turned to face the guy behind me while Hallie rubbed her body against my back.

"And you are?" I asked.

"Leaving." Keith shoved the guy away.

"Oh. Fuck. Sorry, Keith. I didn't know she was with you." Bowtie guys trudged off.

"Fucking pledges. Every. Fucking. Year." He shook his head. "Hi. You look fucking amazing."

"You didn't need to do that," I said, shouting over the music.

"Yeah, I did . . ." A string of muffled words came out of his mouth, but I couldn't hear a thing.

I shrugged.

He placed a hand on my waist and leaned in. "Let's go somewhere a little quieter."

I shook my head. "I'm not leaving Hallie."

"She's already occupied," he told me.

I turned around to see Hallie locking lips with some random dude dressed like a pirate. I smacked her ass. "I'll be back. You good?"

She released the guy's mouth and faced me. "Where are you going?" She glanced over my shoulder. "Oh, it's you." She gave Keith the middle finger and then continued kissing the pirate.

I followed Keith to the kitchen, which was marginally quieter. "Drink?" Keith asked.

"Water," I replied.

He handed me a bottle of water and grabbed a beer for himself.

"Thanks, Spartacus." I tipped my chin to his outfit, or rather lack thereof. He wore a black pleated leather kilt with a matching harness that crossed over his bare muscular chest. I had to admit, my ex looked damned good. Of course, he knew it. Just calling him Spartacus had him puffing his chest and flexing his biceps. I gulped my water.

"I'm glad you're here, Leigh. I have um . . . something important to tell you." He averted his eyes.

"Are you okay?" I asked.

"Yeah, yeah, I'm good, it's . . ."

An amorous couple entered the kitchen, interrupting him. Aladdin hoisted Ariel on his hip and perched her on the counter right next to me.

"I am sure Princess Jasmine would not approve, Aladdin," I muttered.

They continued making out as though I weren't even there. Aladdin lifted Ariel's shimmery skirt fin, and Keith and I burst into laughter.

"I guess we should go somewhere else," Keith guided me out of the kitchen.

"Bathroom first." I broke off from him and headed to the bathroom.

Fortunately for me, there was no line to get into the bathroom, but as I exited, the crowd seemed to double, and it took forever for me to cross the room to the stairwell, where Keith waited for me.

"This is insane," I said in a raised voice.

"I know. I can't hear myself think," he shouted.

He pointed upstairs. I nodded and followed him to his room, dodging the partiers and the many couples getting handsy in the hallway.

Keith took out a key hidden in his leather wristband and unlocked his door.

I entered his room just as one of his frat brothers approached. Keith talked to his friend while I perused his dorm. He'd lived in the same house when we'd dated. The room was different now. Being a senior and his position on the football team had given him a larger space that, aside from square footage, wasn't that much different than before. He had the same bed with the same tan comforter set. The furniture, a light oak three-drawer dresser with a matching night-stand, was dorm-issued.

The typical everyday items cluttered the top of his dresser: athletic tape, receipts, air pods, chargers, and a picture of us taken last winter. *Uh oh.* I moved past it to the nightstand, pretending I didn't see that, and my breath caught in my throat. Familiar gold bangles sat atop a neatly folded black turtleneck.

I wasn't angry or jealous about him seeing other women. I had been with Lazarus just days ago, so there was no room for me to harbor those types of emotions. It was the who that bothered me.

I turned to face him just as he closed the door.

"Sorry about that," he said. "The new batch of pledges are learning the ropes."

I stared at him, unable to find the words.

"What's wrong?" His face scrunched.

"You tell me, Keith. What did you want to talk about?" I asked.

His eyes went wide, and then the door swung open.

A tall, broad form wearing a long, black, hooded cloak and a reaper mask pushed his way into the room, slamming the door behind him.

"What the fuck?" Keith shouted.

In a seamless, lightning-fast movement, the reaper man put Keith in a sleeper hold and dropped his body to the floor.

I swallowed past the lump in my throat, trying to find my voice, and froze.

CHAPTER 28
LAZARUS

THE DRIVE HOME took twice as long as it should have. Fucking traffic. It was like the universe was literally trying to keep me from Leighton. She hadn't picked up the phone. She hadn't called back. I was ready to have a fucking heart attack, and I had just turned thirty.

Zeke dropped me off at my house, and I went to my penthouse, grabbed my keys, and drove like a bat out of hell to Leighton's place. She wasn't there. I let myself in, keying in the alarm code; I'd seen her enter the code when we left days ago.

Her house was a mess. Costumes of every color were laid out all over the place. Two bottles of champagne empty. She had gone to a Halloween party, and she was drunk. The nightmare flashed to the forefront of my mind. Damn it, Leighton.

I kicked a box that had been lying on the floor. I picked it up and saw the familiar toy. Fuck. She bought a replacement. Grinding my teeth, I tucked the box under my arm, activated the alarm, and drove to campus.

It was Halloween, and I suspected where she'd be. I should have thought of it earlier. Hell, I should have told her about my dreams. The only reason I hadn't was . . . pride. I didn't want her to know how crazy I truly was. I wanted her to fall in love with me and keep my crazy in a bottle, releasing it a little at a time. If I'd said the truth, there was no way she'd want to see me again. But then again, if I'd had, it may have kept her alive. Stupid. I ground my teeth.

Out of fucks to give, I drove on the campus grass, taking a shortcut to Dormitory Row.

I got out of my truck and slammed the door.

"Bruh, you can't park here." A kid about my height and weight, said to me.

I snarled at him. Then, I pulled out my wallet. "Hundred bucks for that." I whirled my finger at him.

"Two hundred," the snarky fuck said.

I scowled. "Fine. Two, and you sit here and watch my ride."

I moved past the revelers, doing my best to avoid the bodies bumping and grinding on the dance floor or the couples getting frisky on the sofas pushed to the side to make room for the overcrowded space. The bass thumped in my chest, and the smell of stale beer permeated the air. I walked through the party, moved through the living area, and froze. The world around me faded into the background as she breezed through the room, seemingly in slow motion. Her hips swayed with each graceful step. She tossed a stray strand of silky dark hair over her shoulder, and a playful smile spread across her plump pink lips.

She followed her ex upstairs, and I nearly threw my knife at the fucker's back. There were too many witnesses, and I didn't have a clean shot. I stalked them, shoving people out of my way.

At the end of the hallway, Keith closed the door. His frat mate passed me in the hall, and I stomped to his room, closing the distance in two straightforward strides. I shouldered the locked door, pushing it open.

"What the fuck?" Keith shouted.

I had the asshole in a sleeper hold in two seconds flat. His body dropped to the floor. He'd be out for a few minutes, but one could never be too careful. I picked up a jump rope lying on the floor and tied his hands and arms together. Then, I stuffed his mouth with a sock sitting on top of a pile of dirty laundry. I was ready to drag my blade across his throat when I heard a stifled gasp.

Leighton was backing up toward the bed, and then she scrambled onto the mattress and moved to the farthest corner, putting as much distance between us as possible. Her eyes were wide with fear. My gaze trailed down her body. Her torso was exposed. Her short skirt revealed a hint of white panties. I growled; my dick hardened. She was beautiful. And mine.

I stalked to her retreating form.

"Leighton." I tore off my mask and chucked it to the side.

"Lazarus." Her shoulders sagged with relief so palpable I felt it in my bones.

I crawled on the bed, closing the distance.

Thwack!

My head whipped to the side.

"That's for scaring me, you asshole. I thought you were going to kill me," she snarled.

Thwack!

My head whipped to the other side.

"And what did you just do?! Is he dead?"

"I wouldn't have bothered tying and gagging him if he was dead. I'll let him live. For now."

She struck out with her fist, but I gripped her wrist.

I smiled at my future wife and gently raised my fingers to caress her cheek. "I missed you too." I glanced down between her legs, getting a full view of her white lace panties. "Nice costume."

She slapped my hand away and placed her foot on my chest, trying to keep me from getting too close. "Can't say the same about yours. Now, fuck off."

I stood and shrugged off the reaper robe I'd borrowed. Well, no, paid for, fucking kid. Leighton lunged off the bed, trying to escape, but I was faster and stronger.

"You will listen to me, Leighton." I shoved her back onto the mattress and pinned her body down with mine.

She struggled to get free. Her core rubbed against my torso.

"All that's doing is making me hard. And making you wet," I told her.

She stopped squirming, and I smirked.

"Fuck off, Caveman. You disappeared. For a whole fucking week. Not one call or text the entire time." She struck out with her fist, catching me on the chin this time. I had to hand it to the little one; she could throw a punch.

"Are you done?" I raised an eyebrow.

"No! I don't want to hear your lame excuses." She bucked wildly, which only made me chuckle.

"This isn't a joke, Laz," she snarled.

"Calm down, Leigh baby. Let me explain."

Her body relaxed a tad, and I released my hold. Leighton, my naughty girl, kneed me in the stomach, just barely missing my groin. I gripped her thighs, spread them apart, and settled my full weight between her legs.

"That wasn't nice," I said.

"Get the fuck off me, Lazarus. I don't want to hear how you lost your phone and how you could not find a single working phone in this entire fucking city!"

"I did call, but you never answered. I should have left a message. That's on me."

She rolled her eyes, then tilted her head away, avoiding my gaze.

"Look at me." I hooked her chin, forcing her to face me. "I wanted to come home to you as planned, but I was set up. Someone was trying to kill me. It's a long ass story. The important part is that I came as soon as possible, and yes, I could have handled the situation better. I apologize, Flower. I'll never do that again."

"Someone was trying to kill you?" she asked in a small voice.

I nodded. The tension left her body. But her brow furrowed. She didn't believe me.

"Here's proof." I sat back on my knees, took off my sweater, and showed her my bandaged shoulder.

She sat up and inspected the bandage, which was seeping blood. It was a low-caliber bullet that had gone straight through, causing a minor injury. I wasn't worried about it, but I did like her worrying about me. She gently brushed her finger around the bandage. Her ire melted into concern, and then something fiery flashed in her eyes. "Who did this?"

"Some scumbag. He's dead now."

"Good," she said under her breath.

Crisis avoided, I smiled. I knew we had things to work on and discuss, but I was in her good graces for now, and she was still breathing. Win-win.

I kissed her chin. She didn't slap me again. I kissed the corner of her mouth. She let out a soft sigh. I kissed her lips slowly and delicately, savoring her taste. She deepened our kiss. Her lips were hot and welcoming.

She straddled me as I undid the knot that held her short top together. Leighton shrugged off her top and unclasped her bra. Her full tits bounced free of the lacy fabric and I pinched her hard nipples.

My hands moved down to grip her ass. I snaked my fingers between her legs. She was so fucking wet. "Lazarus," she moaned, tossing her head and arching her back.

I pushed her back onto the mattress and removed her panties, then tucked the small wet material into my pocket. Leighton crashed our mouths together. Our lips and tongues collided in a heated mess of urgency. I unbuttoned my jeans, not bothering to take them completely off.

My raging hard cock bobbed, and I mounted my girl. Leighton placed her foot on my chest, stopping me. "Condom, Laz. Please."

"No," I growled.

"Yes. You must. I couldn't get an appointment at the clinic; they were too busy. I did what I could even though you didn't call me back for days. I did my part. You do yours," Leigh said with a defiant glint in her eyes.

"Fuck." I couldn't argue with her logic. I leaned over her and pulled on the drawer of the nightstand. Bingo. Number one on my list had a large variety. I randomly chose one, tore the packet, and slipped on the prophylactic. I never had an issue with condoms; I'd worn them all my life, every single time, except once, with Leighton.

Her legs were spread wide, her fingers strumming her clit. I slapped her hands away. "Mine."

"Have at it then, Caveman," she teased, her wet pussy on display.

I flipped her onto her stomach and propped her up on her knees. My palm struck her meaty flesh. "That's for leaving your house when I told you not to."

She gasped, then glanced over her shoulder at me, her eyes narrowed. I smirked and spanked her other cheek. "That's for coming to your ex's room."

Leighton's lips parted, her eyes hooded with lust. I rubbed her round ass, massaging the handprint. Her pussy dripped. "You like this," I said.

"More," she moaned.

I struck her ass again. And again. Her fists clenched the sheets. She screamed with pleasure. Her juices trickled down her inner thighs. I rubbed her flesh again, then drew back and smacked her pussy. Her body quivered, her release so close.

My cock was painfully hard, and the fucking condom was suffocating me. I flipped her over, positioned myself at her wet entrance, and nudged myself inside. Slowly. Fuck she was tight. I covered my body with hers and pressed our lips together.

I sank in a little further.

"More, Lazarus," she moaned and tilted her hips, granting me further access. I pushed in deeper. "Yes! Just like that." Her voice was breathless.

I slid all the way in, driving my body deep into hers. She moaned wildly. My thrusts were rough. I wasn't angry. I was starved. We'd been together, really together, for two days, and being apart felt like an eternity. My body wanted to brand her as mine. I fucked and fucked Leighton as though my life depended on it. And honestly, it did. I was nothing without her.

She came, screaming my name. Her nails dug into my back. Her walls clenched around me, and I let go. Ropes of cum exploded out of me. The fucking condom made it feel like my spend was being shoved back into my body. I growled, breathing heavily.

Leighton was a heap of beautiful, sweat-covered flesh. I kissed her pouty lips, and she gave me a sweet, lazy smile. I released her and sat back.

"Don't go." She reached for me. Her skin prickled.

I would have covered her with a blanket, but we were on her ex's bed. The thought of the asshole lying on the floor stirred my anger. I slipped off the condom, detesting the damn thing.

"Come here." I pulled Leighton to a seated position, gripped a fist full of her hair, and tipped her head back.

She let out a breathy moan and reached between her legs.

"Open your mouth and stick out your tongue."

Her gaze caught mine, and she hesitated for a second. Then, her lips parted slowly, and she ran her tongue over her lower lip.

"This is the last time I'll ever wear these fucking things again." With the condom in my other hand, I raised it over her mouth and poured my cum all over her tongue. "Swallow, Leighton."

She did as I commanded. Milky white liquid dripped into her mouth, and she lapped it up. Swirling it with her tongue. "Fuck baby," I groaned. My cock was rock hard all over again.

CHAPTER 29
LAZARUS

SOMETHING ABOUT LEIGHTON kept me perpetually hard. I'd fucked her twice and came hard both times and still, I couldn't get enough of her.

"Done," she said, clinging to my chest. "I'm done. I need a shower."

"You're not taking one here." I kissed her cheek. "Let's get dressed and go home."

She nodded and unwound herself from my arms.

"Stop staring perv," I said over my shoulder.

Keith had gotten up during round two. Tied and gagged, he hadn't been able to say a word or move, and I didn't mind him watching the show. But I did mind him watching my nightmare girl getting dressed.

Leighton, startled. "Is he awake?"

We both looked at Keith's prone form. His eyes were closed, and his head lolled to the side. Faker.

I shrugged and helped Leighton into her barely-there costume. "I'd make you wear this reaper robe if it didn't smell like smoke," I told her.

"What?" She placed her hand on her waist and cocked her hip to the side. "You don't like my costume?"

I snagged her by the waist and kissed her belly. "I love it. I don't like other men loving it, too."

"It's Halloween, Caveman." She cupped my face and kissed me. "And this is just a costume."

"Wait outside," I said.

"Why?" She glared. "You can't kill him."

"Why not?" I asked. If she told me she still had feelings for this asshole, I was going to plunge my knife into his heart.

She side-glanced at his nightstand, where some gold jewelry was sitting on top of a black top. "He doesn't deserve to die, Lazarus. Maybe an STD or something that will make his penis fall off but not die."

I smirked, then tipped her chin to face me. "You're vicious." I pecked her nose. "And I like it."

"Do not leave this house without me. And for the love of all that's holy, do not drink anything being passed around in this house." I shoved Keith's body away from the door.

She stepped over Keith and pulled open the door.

"Leighton?" I gripped her elbow.

"I heard you, Caveman. I'm going to pee and will meet you at the bottom of the stairway. Hurry."

I watched her walk down the hall, then closed the door and faced Keith.

"You can stop pretending to be asleep now," I told Keith.

His eyes snapped open, and he stared daggers at me. I laughed.

"I'm not supposed to kill you even though I really want to." I tugged the sock out of his mouth.

He gulped a lung full of air and spat obscenities at me.

"Now, now, that's no way to treat someone who had given you a front row seat to the best show."

His face went red.

"Yeah, I know you were watching. You missed round one, though.

That was a hell of a show. There will definitely be a repeat performance, but you're not invited. Of course."

"Fuck you, you fucking pervert. As soon as I get free of these ropes, I'm going to kill you with my bare hands!" Keith shouted, spittle dripping from his mouth.

"Please do. I am looking for an excuse to kill you, after all. Self-defense and all that. Leighton won't hold it against me."

I pulled a knife from my boot and cut the ropes.

I sat back on his bed and spread my arms wide. "Come on. Let's get to it."

"Fuck you! What do you want?"

"From you? Simple. Stay the fuck away from my woman. Come near her or talk to her ever again, and I will kill you."

Keith let out a nervous laugh. "You can't control her, you know. She's going to do whatever she wants. And if you try to keep us apart, she will return to me. Just you wait."

I stood to put the stupid reaper costume back on. I didn't want to stand out in this party full of underage drinkers. Keith flinched and made himself small against the wall.

"Follow my orders, Number One. Or come at me anytime. I'll be waiting."

I stepped over his legs and walked out of his room.

A witch was fucking a zombie at the bottom of the stairs. Leighton was nowhere in sight. And, of course, she didn't have her phone on her. At six foot two inches, I was taller than most and had been able to see the crowd. It had thinned out a bit since I arrived. From what I could see, people had migrated outside where the DJ had moved. Idiots should have done that in the first place. The house was trashed. Oh, the idiocy of college years. For some. I had never been that stupid.

Leighton was not amongst the crowd. I scanned the room, and my palms began to sweat. The scene looked familiar. I stomped through the house, pushing people out of my way until I found the kitchen. My vision tunneled as I caught sight of my nightmare girl sitting on a bar stool, reaching for a bottle of water. I rushed toward her, knocking people over. She saw me coming and smiled. She reached for me. I lunged and pulled her in for a crushing hug.

"Leighton, baby."

"Caveman?" She gazed at my eyes through the mask. "Everything okay?"

I hoisted her into my arms and dashed to the door.

A few feet from the entrance, chaos broke out behind me. Screams rent the air as bullets flew in every direction. The crowd went into a manic frenzy. People stampeded toward the back door. The music cut off. I was being pushed and dragged in every direction. I held onto Leighton with a death grip. One hand wrapped around her waist, the other covering her head. I plowed through the crowd. Bullets kept coming. *Who the fuck has an automatic rifle at a frat party?*

I spared a glance over my shoulder and caught a clown aiming his weapon at the crowd.

"Everybody down! And shut up!" He walked over to two girls cowering on the floor and compared their looks to something on his phone.

Ahh fuck. He was looking for someone specific.

All I wanted was to keep my girl safe. I wasn't a hero. Never wanted to be. But I found myself stepping into a crowded hallway and crouched to pull my knife out.

"Leighton, wait here." I unwrapped her arms from my neck and stepped out of the hallway just as clown face popped in another magazine. I threw my knife. My aim hit the fucker in his chest, and he went down. I crossed the room to the clown's prone form to retrieve my knife, snagged the phone out of his hand, and then rushed back to Leigh.

Pop! Pop! Pop!

Another gun went off. My leg stung. I spun as the crowd in the hallway went into a frenzy again. Leighton was knocked to the side. Her head hit the edge of a credenza she had hidden behind. I picked

her up and ran out the backdoor. Sirens blared in the background. I
didn't stop until I reached my truck.

I opened the passenger door and placed Leighton on the seat.
Her head lolled to the side.

"Baby, are you okay?" I checked her over. "Did you get hit?"

She didn't respond. My hands slid all over her body and came up
clean. I checked her pulse; it was strong and a little fast.

"You're okay, baby. You're okay." I crushed her to my chest and
kissed the top of her head. My leg ached.

As I rounded my truck to the driver's side, my babysitter popped
his head out from the truck bed.

"What's going on, man?" the kid asked.

"Shooter. You have somewhere safe you can lay low? I need to get
my girl home."

"Just drive off campus, man. I'll hop out at the first stop light."

I got in and drove, leaving the chaos of a mass shooting
behind me.

CHAPTER 30
LAZARUS

GRIMACING, I pulled my brother's phone out of my pocket and dialed. There were a few numbers I committed to memory, and Dr. Hernandez was one of them.

"I need you," I said.

"Ezekiel? Is your brother okay?" Dr. Hernandez asked.

"Uh yeah. This is Lazarus, I'm using Zeke's phone. My place, five minutes."

I sped to my building and carried Leighton upstairs, leaving a trail of blood behind me. Doc was already waiting at my door. He took my keys out of my hand and opened the door.

"Fuck, Laz you're bleeding out," he said.

"Her first." I laid Leighton on the white leather sofa, not giving a fuck about the bloody mess I was leaving behind.

"What happened?" the doctor asked.

I gave him a rundown of what had happened while he checked on Leighton.

"She's fine, minor concussion. Let me see your leg."

While he tended to me, I called Paul, my connection to the police department. I told him what happened, and he said he'd keep my involvement off the books. The other shooter had been apprehended.

The guy was blindly following his friend in hopes of being paid for his efforts. The clown guy was the mastermind behind it all and I had his phone. Stupid kid was going to spend the rest of his life in prison for being a sheep.

"This is going to hurt. The bullet is lodged into your hamstring."

"Just pull the fucker out," I shouted.

Leighton stirred. Fuck.

Doc made quick work of removing the bullet and stitched me up. He even looked at the other wound Zeke patched up a few days ago. Fuck me, I was getting shot left and right these days.

After Dr. Hernandez left, I pulled out the phone I'd taken from the clown and almost threw the fucking thing against the wall. If Leighton hadn't been sleeping on the couch, I would have razed the town to ashes. There were two pics on Clown's phone, one of me and one of Leighton. Fuckers were looking for us.

I scrolled through the text messages and came across the unknown number that had attached the texts along with a promise to pay. I immediately called Zeke at home and gave him the info. He'd be able to track the phone log.

Leighton woke after I hung up the phone. "Lazarus?"

"I'm here, baby. We're at my place. How are you feeling? You, uh, have a minor concussion." I pulled her into my chest.

"What happened?" she asked.

I retold the tale. She cried.

Most people weren't accustomed to killing or seeing dead bodies. I'd been desensitized to it since I was a teenager. Seeing Leighton fall apart made me realize how very different I was from normal society. I let her cry herself out on my shoulder, all while wondering if she'd think differently of me from here on out.

We hadn't known each other long, and although I'd done my digging into her life, she didn't know me at all. Fear squeezed my heart and almost made me laugh. I hadn't felt an ounce of fear for myself when dealing with the Clown gunman but losing Leighton scared the shit out of me. I'd have to tell her the truth about everything: the stalking, the killing, my family, my past. The latter was a topic best left in the grave, but I'd known from the minute I'd fallen for her that the past would have to be dug out of the ground and laid at her feet. That was the only way to move forward.

"Whose blood is this?" Leighton pulled away from me, her mouth agape at all the bloody towels I hadn't had a chance to clean up.

"Mine, Flower. All mine," I said in my best assuring voice.

"What happened!?" She looked me over. Her shrill voice thick with panic. "You didn't say one word about you getting hurt. Did you get shot?"

She was worried about me. I gave her a lopsided grin.

"Lazarus! This isn't funny," she scolded.

"Sorry. I like that you're worried about me."

"Damn it, Caveman! Let me see!"

"The doc patched me up." I stood. "The bullet didn't go as deep as he thought. He stitched it. He even checked my shoulder. I'm good as new."

Leigh looked me over, then wrapped her arms around my middle. "Thank you, Lazarus. You saved everyone."

"I don't give a shit about everyone, babe. Just you." I kissed the top of her head.

She kissed my chest and peered up at me. "What can I do for you?" she asked.

Her question took me by surprise. I couldn't remember when someone offered to do something for me. Quite possibly, it had never happened before.

"Uh . . . nothing. It helps that you're here," I told her.

"How about I help you with a shower then?" She flashed me a coy smile.

Although I had to keep the fresh stitches dry, I wasn't an invalid, but I wouldnn't say no to her attention.

Leighton perused the penthouse, becoming familiar with it. I was pleased to see her making herself comfortable in my home. It was hers now. I didn't want her to leave. I wouldn't allow it.

She covered my wounds with a trash bag and sealed them with duct tape. I smiled as I watched her work. She found a plastic folding chair I'd had in one of the storage closets and placed it in the shower.

I leaned on the doorway to the bathroom, not saying a word as she turned on the shower, testing the temperature. It was a massive shower that could easily fit four people. Removable shower heads were on both ends, and a rainfall shower head came down from the ceiling. She figured out the buttons and reached up to remove one of the shower heads from its cradle.

Everything in my home had been designed to my size. I hadn't thought about sharing my space with anyone. Marriage hadn't been part of my plan. But here she was, the woman that had changed all that. Leighton was five-feet-five inches, not short, but certain things in my home would be beyond reach. I moved to help her, but she waved me off, stood on the chair, and then turned toward me.

"Well, you can't shower with your clothes on, can you?" She shut off the shower and sauntered toward me.

She undressed me and then took off her costume. My cock stood at attention. We'd had sex a few hours ago; I'd gotten shot, and she had a concussion, but my dick was vigilant.

Leigh placed a soft, quick kiss on my crown and then made me suffer through a thorough shower. She was even kind enough—or wicked—to cover her body with suds while I watched helplessly.

It was only until we landed in bed that she took my cock in her mouth.

"Let me come in your cunt," I pleaded.

Her mouth was amazing, but my seed belonged in her channel.

"No," she said with a defiant tone. "Twice already, Lazarus. We've pushed the limit twice now."

"Did you hate it?" I tugged her hair back, pulling her off of my cock.

"No. I loved it," Leigh admitted. Her cheeks flushed.

"Me too, and I don't give a fuck about the consequences." I flipped her over and slid in, making her scream.

I fucked her good and hard until we were both spent and exhausted.

My leg throbbed—the pain muted by the bliss of sated lust. I'd surely busted a stitch and fallen asleep the happiest man alive.

A few hours later, Zeke called with info. "Wait, Lazarus," he said.

"No," I told him. "The fucker paid two gunmen to shoot up a college dorm party. There will be casualties. He went through all that trouble to find me and Leighton. He doesn't get to live to see another day. We have enough evidence to incriminate him. Just cover my tracks."

I left Leigh sleeping soundly as I went to take care of number two on my list.

CHAPTER 31
LEIGHTON

"LEIGHTON, BABY, TIME TO WAKE UP," Laz's deep voice purred into my ear.

My body responded. Liquid heat seeped between my legs. *No, no, no,* I scolded my body. After all the fucking the night before and at sunrise, my pussy needed a break.

"It's almost two in the afternoon. Your friend called twice and sent texts."

Hallie. I called her from his phone and left a message.

"Is she okay?" I sat up, rubbing my eyes.

"I didn't talk to her. I sent a message back saying you were fine and asleep. That was three hours ago. She just called again."

"Thanks."

He left me a phone and exited. I called Hallie, grateful for memorizing her phone number.

"Hallie? Are you okay?" I said as soon as she answered.

"I'm fine. You disappeared with Keith, and I left early with that guy in the pirate costume. He was fun. I didn't hear about what happened until I woke up this morning," she told me.

"I'm glad you weren't there. It was fucked up," I replied and told her what had happened and why I was with Lazarus. I didn't mention that I'd seen her things in Keith's room, though. That was a topic I hadn't wanted to address. Nor did I say that Laz had knocked him out and tied him up. Or the sex part. I didn't feel the need to overshare.

"From what I've heard on the news, it was a random shooting. The two shooters were drunk, had gotten hold of weapons from somewhere, and started shooting for no apparent reason. Six people were killed and fifteen were taken to the hospital for various injuries. The clown guy took a knife to the heart. There are dozens of conspiracy theories about that. And the other guy dressed as a panda bear is in custody."

"Unbelievable! I'm shocked. How's Keith?" What I said to Lazarus about Keith was the truth. He didn't deserve to die.

"I talked to him, and he asked about you. I told him you were with your new beau," she replied. There was nothing unusual in her tone. I wondered if she'd ever tell me about her and my ex. Weird.

"Good. Are you at home?" I changed the subject.

"Yeah, I'm leaving, though. We'll catch up soon, okay?"

I hit the end button and felt a twang of pain in my heart. In the blink of an eye, my relationship with Hallie had changed, and I had no idea how to fix it.

I pulled on one of Laz's hoodies, forgoing undies because I didn't have a clean pair, and searched for him.

He was sitting at the kitchen counter with a tablet in his hands. The television in the other room flashed scenes of Dormitory Row. Laz saw me approach and hit the mute button on the remote beside him. He wrapped his arm around my waist and drew me into his body.

"Hi." I rested my chin gently on his shoulder, avoiding the bandage. "How are you feeling today?"

"Fine. Busted a stitch somehow, but Doc has already fixed it up. He's umm . . ." Lazarus peered at my face and paused. A million thoughts flickered across his features. "Did you want to watch the news?"

I shook my head. Hallie and Keith were the only two people I was close to on campus. They were fine, which was a relief. The entire situation was horrifying to live through, and I wasn't ready to relive it again. Lazarus made me feel safe. Hell, he kept me safe. And I'd wanted to remain in this safety bubble as long as possible.

"You must be hungry. I was gone longer than I'd thought and didn't have much here, but food will be delivered shortly. Do you want some coffee or something else?" Laz asked me.

There was a hint of hesitation in his tone. He was keeping something from me.

"Spit it out, Lazarus. What aren't you telling me?"

"Come." He stood and led me by the hand to a part of his penthouse I hadn't explored. We passed an entertainment room with a pool table, bar, leather sectional, and big-screen television. I counted four yesterday, and this made it five. I slowed as we passed an alcove showcasing at least a hundred bottles of different types of whiskey.

Lazarus paused as I gaped, then continued as we passed a gym fully equipped with weights, a spin bike, a rowing machine, heavy bag, and a treadmill. I glanced around me wondering if there was something else . . .

"Pool is on the other side," Lazarus told me as though he'd read my mind.

Before I could comment about it, he knocked on a door, the only solid one I'd seen thus far, and waltzed in.

In it was a massage bed and counter with a glass sink. A spa room. Really? *I would die if he tells me he's been getting facials.*

"Leighton, this is Dr. Hernandez. He's the man that patched me up last night," Lazarus said and stepped to the side, revealing a short man with a deep tan and thick glasses.

"Nice to meet you, Leighton." Dr. Hernandez extended his hand. A huge smile splayed over his face.

"Likewise," I shook his hand and noticed the medical instruments on a tray beside him. I eyed the tools suspiciously.

"Oh umm . . . Lazarus asked me to do this. I assure you, I am a professional. This is perfectly legal and safe. Also, my wife is a nurse. She'll be here in mere moments. You have nothing to fear. I've implanted IUDs countless times. And this copper is the best. You won't feel a thing, and you'll have nothing to worry about," the doctor told me.

Son of a bitch! I glared daggers at Lazarus.

"Doc, give us a minute. Natalie should be here soon. You can let her in," Lazarus told him.

"Of course!" The doctor hurried out of the room.

"What the actual fuck, Caveman?" I shouted before the door closed.

"Don't overreact. You said you couldn't get an appointment at the school clinic, so I'm taking care of it," he said evenly.

The fucking nerve of this man. "You can't just make me get an IUD without speaking to me first!" I shouted.

"I'm not forcing you to do anything," he replied calmly.

"This is my body, Lazarus." I waved my hand down my front. "I make the decisions, now and always."

"Of course, but . . ."

"But nothing, you insufferable caveman! Don't you think we should have discussed this before having a doctor meet me in your treatment room?" My voice shook with anger.

"Baby . . ."

"Don't baby me! I'm leaving!" I stepped toward the door, fuming.

Lazarus blocked my path and picked me up. He sat on the bed and kept me on his lap with his arms wrapped around me, keeping mine fused to my sides.

"I'm sorry. I wasn't trying to assert my dominance," he said.

"Yes, you were," I spat.

"Okay. Fine. I was," he replied.

His chest rose with a deep inhalation, and then he released it slowly. He shifted my body so that I was straddling him.

"Leighton. We just met, but I know how I feel about you. I know what I want." He hooked a strand of hair behind my ear. "I don't expect you to feel the same, at least not yet. What I do want is the absolute truth."

I huffed, then nodded.

"Do you want to have my babies?" He snaked his hand under the hoodie I wore and rubbed my belly.

That one question snuffed out my anger, and I spat out the first answer that formed in my mind.

"Yes." I blurted without hesitation. Oh shit. *Where did that come from, Leighton?* "But maybe not yet."

A bright smile spread across his lips and reached his eyes. He placed his large hands on my face and kissed me deeply.

I kissed him back and clung to him. He hardened beneath me, and I wanted nothing more than to feel him inside of me.

He broke our kiss. "I don't need to wait, Leigh. I'm ready to impregnate you right now. I can tell the doc to fuck off. But only if that's what you want."

His cock pressed my panty-less center. And I wanted it. I wanted to say yes. *Too soon, Leighton.*

"We don't know each other, Lazarus," I replied.

"I know enough," he replied without missing a beat.

I gazed into his eyes and caressed his jaw with the tips of my fingers. We were practically strangers, and yet . . . *He loves me.* I felt the emotion in his touch, his gaze, his voice. His love for me oozed out of his pores when we were together. *When we were together.* Those four words brought me back down to earth.

"Not yet, Lazarus. Someday. But not today."

"I understand." Not a hint of disappointment in his voice. "Someday. Soon."

I pressed a chaste kiss to his lips.

"I can wait, Flower. What I will not do is wear a condom ever again. You are the only woman for me, and I won't wear that shit. So . . . what would you like to do until someday soon comes?" he asked.

And there it was, the hope he had latched onto. We both did.

"Call the doctor."

Dr. Hernandez and his wife, Natalie, came back to the treatment room. Lazarus tried to escape, but I forbade it.

"Oh no, you don't. You get to stick around and be supportive."

He tried to fight me over it but lost the battle.

The procedure was over quickly and with minimal discomfort. I laughed when Doc told both Laz and me no sex for twenty-four hours.

"Leighton." Natalie handed me a box before leaving. "Morning after pill, just in case . . ."

"Thanks."

I walked into the kitchen, grabbed a bottle of water, and then sat with the pill in front of me. Lazarus watched me as I stared at the pill.

Sure, I'd wanted children. But that was a dream for later. Much later. And yet, I found myself overwhelmed with a longing I'd never experienced before. Maybe it was the trauma. Or perhaps I was falling for a man I hardly knew. I popped the pill in my mouth and swallowed.

CHAPTER 32
LEIGHTON

"THANKS, LEIGHTON," a student said as she hugged me on her way out of the classroom.

"Thank you," another said, and another.

We'd just finished a support group meeting, one of many held at the library since the shooting. As a psychology major, I'd been asked to assist with the grieving process. I wasn't a psychologist or counselor yet, but the student body needed help, and there were less than a handful of professionals on campus.

I'd been hosting two support groups a day, three days a week, for the past two and a half weeks. It counted as credit for my last psych class and looked good on my resume. In many ways, the work was gratifying; in others, it was also draining. My work seemed to be helping those who sought it. And that reinforced my decision to pursue my path. On other days, it drained me. I slumped behind the desk and gathered my things.

"Knock, knock."

I raised my chin and beamed at the gorgeous man entering the classroom. Lazarus strolled toward me, wearing jeans and a sweat-shirt that read BOSS across the chest. Everything about him oozed confidence and swagger. He was definitely the boss and so devastatingly handsome.

"Hi," I stood.

Lazarus leaned over the desk and greeted me with a wet kiss.

"Ready?" he asked.

I nodded and rounded the desk. He picked up my book bag and linked our fingers as we exited the classroom and headed toward his vehicle.

We'd spent every day together for the last several days. Some nights we stayed at his place, some nights at mine. He took time off due to the GSW he'd received at the party. He was healing quickly, and I imagined he'd be back to doing his missions soon.

While I was studying, he worked on his laptop or made business calls, and I began to learn more about his work—most of what he did while at home was research. I didn't get details on who he was researching; I just knew that each ticket, as he called it, had a target, and the person who paid for the ticket was called the client. The target and client needed to be researched thoroughly for him to do his job. The man wasn't lying when he said he killed people for a living. The Sentinels, his family's business, was a software firm specializing in creating programs for various types of data analysis. That was the public persona. Although it wasn't the company's primary source of revenue, Laz had said that was one hundred percent legit. The money making part of the business however, was gun for hire, and Lazarus was the weapon.

Oddly, his occupation didn't bother me. If anything, it only endeared me to him further. After seeing what he'd done to take out one of the shooters at the party, I quickly realized that people with his skill set were needed in the world. He was good at what he did. In my eyes, he was a hero, a true protector.

But no one would see it that way because no one would know. He had worn a costume and mask at the costume party. No one knew his identity. And he wanted to keep it that way. He had contacts within the police department who had helped to conceal his involvement. And the one guy he'd gotten the costume from had been found and his silence bought off. My Lazarus didn't want the fame and accolades he deserved. And that made me love him more.

Yep, I had fallen hard for my caveman. He was intense, possessive, and demanding. All red flags, which I conveniently ignored. It wasn't that hard to do. He was hot. And oh my god, the sex. I couldn't get enough of the man.

"How was the support group, babe?" he asked.

"Good." I leaned into his body, and he draped an arm over my shoulders. "A lot of people are still having nightmares over what had happened. I hope they'll heal from the trauma someday. But I'm not sure."

"You really enjoy this psychology stuff, don't you? Think you'll take it further?"

"Yes, I do. I wasn't sure if I wanted to pursue the doctoral program, but after doing these support groups, I decided to continue."

"Hmmm . . ." Laz said. "Well, I'm sure they appreciate you." He removed his arm from my shoulder, opened the passenger door, and held it open for me.

"Thanks." I tiptoed to plant a kiss on his bottom lip.

"How was your day?" I asked when he slipped into the driver's seat beside me.

"Still going, babe. You okay with hanging out at my place? I need to finish some work, and then I'm all yours." He wiggled his eyebrows at me.

I giggled. "Sorry to repeat myself but . . . you don't have to drop me off and pick me up from school every day."

He gave me a rueful glare.

"Don't give me that look."

"I'm not trying to smother you, love. However, I can meet you halfway," he said.

"Oh, this oughta be good," I muttered.

"You're itching for a spanking, aren't you?" He leaned over and nuzzled my neck.

"Eyes on the road!" I scolded him.

He pulled into his parking garage minutes later and said, "We're out of coffee. Buzzy's?"

"Yes, please."

We'd been to Buzzy's a few times in the last couple of weeks. Laz's building was around the corner from the coffee house. After Henry had passed, I hadn't been back. It felt awkward. But with Lazarus beside me, I didn't feel uncomfortable at all.

As we approached the coffee house, I noticed the homeless woman who called herself Elaine. I hadn't seen her for a while, so I disentangled myself from Laz's arms and approached her.

Lazarus stopped me before I got to her and said, "I'll place our orders." He kissed my temple and went into the cafe.

"Hi, Elaine!" I greeted the woman who looked the same as the last time I'd seen her. I'd met her when I first came to Buzzy's three years ago. I had just moved into my apartment, which was a twenty-minute walk. That seemed so far in comparison to walking from the penthouse.

"Leigh!" She gave me a toothless smile. *Oh! That was different.* Her front teeth were missing. They'd been yellowish before, which was why I remembered.

"Oh my." She placed a hand over her heart and watched Lazarus enter Buzzy's. "Your forever is easy on the eyes. Good on you!"

Right. Elaine was different. I wasn't an expert in psychology, but I did study a little about psychosis and mental illness. Elaine, however, didn't quite fit into those clinical boxes. Over the years, she'd often say uncanny things to me. The first time she met Keith, she'd said, "Fun, but you don't love him." I remembered being grateful Keith hadn't heard her. Last year, before I went on the road to visit my father for Thanksgiving, I stopped in to get a cup. Just as I left Buzzy's, Elaine hobbled to me and said, "Today is a bad travel day. Wait. The day after tomorrow is better." The urgency in her tone that day made me change my plans. And I was so grateful I'd listened. An insane storm had blown through the city, causing multiple accidents and stranding people on the freeway for hours.

"It's good to see you," I said, ignoring her comment. "How've you been?"

"Happy looks good on you, Leigh. Beware. The jealous one will harm you." She sat on a bench and made herself comfortable. "Oooh wee. I need to rest my dogs. I had a dog once. It was white with black spots. No, black with white spots. She was cute but mean! She'd bite your hand clean off." She slapped her leg and hooted.

Uh oh. The businesses in the area got pissy if people sat at their tables and didn't order anything. I needed to get her something to eat.

Lazarus appeared with three cups of coffee and a paper bag. "I wasn't sure what your friend liked, so I hope coffee is good. And I got a variety of pastries." He placed the items on the table in front of Elaine.

"Oooooh!" Elaine rubbed her hands together, then dug into the bag.

I cupped Laz's face and gave him a big smooch. "You're the best."

"So good!" Elaine exclaimed, her mouth full of raspberry filling.

Lazarus and I laughed.

"You did good!" Elaine nodded, her gaze fixed on Lazarus. "So good! Your mama is so proud."

My eyebrows shot up to my hairline. I side-glanced Lazarus, who cleared his throat and then said, "Uh, my mother's been dead for fifteen years."

Elaine shook her head and began rocking. "The dead see all, Lazzy boy."

Lazarus turned sheet-white. I grasped his hand, and he squeezed. Hard.

"Who. Are. You?" Lazarus asked through clenched teeth.

"Just a person who sees." Elaine pulled a butter croissant from the bag and continued eating.

Lazarus was crushing the bones in my hand.

"Laz," I said. His narrowed gaze remained fixed on the homeless woman. I tilted his chin to face me. "I'm here. Always. No matter what. Even if you break my hand."

"Oh shit." He released his grip and brought my reddened fingers to his mouth. "Sorry, baby."

"It's okay." My phone rang. "You good?"

He gave me a stiff nod and pressed his forehead to mine.

"Oh, I know he should give her the ring," Elaine said to thin air.

Laz and I both turned to face Elaine. My phone rang again. I pulled it out of my pocket. Hallie. I hit decline. A second later, I received a 911 text.

"Hallie is sending me 911 texts," I said to Lazarus.

"The blonde with the first-world problems. Always so dramatic about something." Elaine sipped her coffee. Lazarus smiled. Neither of them thought very highly of Hallie. I sighed as another text came in.

I brushed a hand down Laz's arm and stepped away to call Hallie while Elaine babbled about something I couldn't hear.

CHAPTER 33
LAZARUS

I WAITED for Leighton to step away, then gave her unusual friend a stern gaze. "Tell me what I need to know, Elaine," I said.

The homeless woman leaned back and laughed. "Oh Lazzy, you know how these gifts work. It comes, it goes." She waved her arm in a dramatic back-and-forth motion. "You did good saving her. She is important to you. And one day she'll help a lot of people."

She began packing her things as Leighton returned to my side, a grave look on her face.

"Don't forget what I said, Leigh. The jealous one is not to be trusted." She turned toward me and gave a flourishing bow. "Thank you for the tea and crumpets, good sir." She said in a horrible British accent. "Toodles."

Leighton and I stared after the her, completely speechless.

"Umm . . . yeah, that's Elaine. She's different," Leighton said.

"I gathered." I handed her a cup of coffee, which was probably lukewarm. "What did your friend want?" I asked at the same time she asked me who was Lazzy.

"We need to get home." She had a faraway look in her eyes. "Umm . . . Hallie said there's some breaking news on the local station I needed to see."

"What's going on?" I asked, grateful we weren't talking about the nickname my mother had given me as a boy.

"Something about Nick. The guy who spiked my wine."

Ah, I knew where this was going, but I still had a role to play. I wasn't quite ready to confess my sins yet. Soon, but not quite.

"I won't forget that asshole anytime soon. Come on. Let's go home," I replied, steering Leighton toward our penthouse. It hadn't escaped me that she'd referred to my place as ours. Every time she'd said it, it sent a thrill of elation through me.

"He was found dead. And it sounds disturbing," Leighton said.

"Hmmm," I grunted. It took them long enough.

As I had already known, the news reported the death of Nick Hanford. It was a gruesome scene and must've stunk like all hell. I'd paid him a visit in his rental home, which was a place he'd go to meet his mistresses. As I promised, I gutted the fool and shoved his intestines down his throat. It was a fucked up way to die and a fucked up way to kill. And more than that, it was justified. After Zeke had confirmed that Nick had paid the clowns to come looking for us at the Halloween party, I went a little rabid.

Before killing him, I'd learned that someone had fed his friend Chad info about me, specifically hunting them down. How that got out to them was a puzzle we hadn't pieced together. It had to be someone in the office, so we were doing a massive overhaul of the staff and our computer systems. It didn't matter much since we had already obtained incriminating evidence through pictures, videos, and messages. Our illegal way of acquiring said details of their misdeeds was inadmissible, but we didn't care. I'd gathered the evidence proving Nick's shady character, leaving copies splayed across the floor around his dead body. His family had been humili-ated, and their business had taken a severe hit. The Hanford family name was forever tarnished. I couldn't care less. If they'd cared so much about their family's reputation, then they shouldn't do bad shit. Simple. Nick had done a lot of bad shit. He lured women, drugged them, raped them, and filmed it. The clown bullshit was the tipping point. His friends would meet the same fate.

The evidence we'd found was enough to put the DRC away for a long time. That wasn't good enough for me. We were digging into their lives, searching for every shadow. We wanted the details of how the drug was coming into the States. Also on the list were locating the victims. We knew they'd been planning to sell the drugs, but the elders thought there was something bigger at play. Thus, the research continued.

I couldn't tell Leighton the extent of what we'd found. She knew my job title, and that was it. I would spare her the details as much as I could. The media skirted around the truth, as they do. They reported that he'd been murdered, and evidence of his date rape schemes was found at the crime scene. But that was the extent of it. They hadn't mentioned his partners. I had kept those details from them on purpose. I was going to deliver justice for the victims, not the law. Jail time was not enough punishment for those assholes.

There was a lot of work to do, but my flower had all my focus. Leighton hadn't taken the news so well. Understandable after Henry, the shooting, and now this. After watching the news, she went to our home gym without saying a word. I wasn't a great communicator myself, so the best I could offer her at the moment was space. I scrubbed a hand down my face. Could I be the common denominator in all the upsetting events swirling through her life? I propped my feet on the desk and contemplated the question. Perhaps I was, but Leighton was alive, and that was all that mattered. The chaos would die down, and we would have a normal life, or so I hoped.

Elaine's comments niggled in the corner of my mind. She was an unusual bird. A lot like Aunt Pol and my mother before she'd passed. Elaine had called me Lazzy, a nickname my mother had used when I was a boy. And the jealous one she mentioned to Leigh had to have been Hallie. Dealing with Henry, Nick, and Keith had kept my hands full. I hadn't done much research on her friend and knew I had to keep a closer eye on her. Elaine had been talking to thin air about the ring, which was also unnerving.

I wasn't joking when I told Leighton about a wedding date. I hadn't proposed, but that was a *when* not an *if*. I'd been thinking about the ring that had been a family heirloom on my mother's side. The ring I'd give to Leighton. It was a four-carat diamond with a platinum filigree setting. It was beautiful and delicate. It wasn't expensive considering my level of wealth, but it was priceless to me. It had been my mother's and had been passed down through the generations to the eldest female. My mother had only one child, me. And aside from Aunt Pol, I didn't have any relatives on that side of the family. The ring was mine, and I hadn't a clue what to do with it until Leighton—the woman who had become my world.

Deciding to put my brooding on pause, I strode down the hall to find Leighton, still in the gym. Solid thumps floated down the hallway, taking me by surprise. I paused in the doorway and watched as she punched the heavy bag. Her form was on point. Fists up, chin down, thumbs tucked in, elbows at her sides protecting her body. She was light on her feet as she moved around the bag and landed each hit with a thud. After drooling over her fine physique clad in a sports bra and tiny shorts, all of which revealed firm tits, a slim waist, and a tight ass, I noticed she'd wrapped her hands like a trained boxer would. She'd done this before and had been trained by someone. Who was the lucky motherfucker? Whoever had taught her had taught her well. The thought of her hot and sweaty with some dude salivating over her didn't piss me off as much as it should have. Nope. Instead, my cock swelled. My ego never needed to be a girl's first. Virginity was a stupid kink. Seriously, people, taking someone's virginity took all of two seconds, and then it was over.

What mattered to me was being the one and only in Leighton's present and future. She was a fucking smoke show. I hadn't had so many orgasms in such a short time since I'd first discovered how fun my penis was at the ripe age of twelve. Sweat coated her body; firm muscles flexed as she pounded the bag. I wanted to throw her down on the mat and impale her with my cock. She was clearly working through her emotions, which I could respect. My cock twitched. Greedy fucker. *Stay or go, Laz. Stay or go.* I stepped back when she noticed me.

"Hey, Caveman." Her voice was breathless.

"Hi. I didn't mean to interrupt." I stood in place. If I stepped toward her, we were getting naked.

"Your form is impressive. Where'd you learn how to box?"

"You really want to discuss my past right now?" She jutted out a hip, her chest heaving with exertion. "Or do you wanna help me stretch?"

Oooh yeah. That was an open invitation. Stretch meant fuck in this context.

I approached slowly, removing my shirt as I neared. Leighton stared at my chest. I flexed. She licked her lips and began tugging down her shorts.

"No." I shook my head. "That's mine."

My hands roamed over her slippery, sweaty skin. "Your skills surprise me, Flower. It makes me wonder what else you might be good at."

I gripped the meaty part of her ass cheek. With speed and strength I didn't know my little one possessed, Leighton executed the perfect hip throw, slamming me onto the mat. I landed with a thud, and a whoosh of air escaped my lungs. Leigh straddled my waist; a sly grin graced her lips. Sneaky little minx. She had skills, and I was impressed. And painfully hard. Rough play was kind of my love language. I flipped us over, pinning her under me, and wrapped my hand around her throat—the primal caveman dial in me turned up full blast. I was starved for her. I crashed my lips to hers, my tongue dipping into her mouth, claiming her very breath. With one hand, I released her throat and locked her wrists together above her head while my other hand pushed up her sports bra, giving me access to her breasts. I licked and nipped down her skin, savoring her taste. She was the perfect combination of sweet and salty. I kissed a path down to her hard nipples and latched onto the taut bud with my teeth.

Leighton moaned, "Lazarus, I need you."

She writhed beneath me, her hot core rubbed against my cock.

I bit her other nipple. She hissed and arched her back, pushing her tit into my face.

I slid down her body, my face covered in her sweat, then peeled down her shorts, tossing them across the room. Leighton was splayed before me, slick with her juices. I watched in fascination as she reached between her legs and slid her fingers over her core. She parted her pussy lips showing off her perfect round hole.

Fuuucckk. I almost came in pants. I wanted to take my time and savor my woman. This wasn't that kind of love-making session. This was going to be a hard and rough fuck. I pushed my sweats down past my hips and lined up with her entrance. The size of my crown dwarfed the size of her opening. It was hot. And it would hurt her. The first thrust always did. But I didn't care. I needed to be in her cunt. I shoved my cock into her. Leighton cried out, her back bowed. I gripped her narrow waist and worked my way in, deeper and deeper. She took it. Every time she took all of me, every fucking inch. Her tunnel squeezed around me. I drove into her, using my body weight, marveling at her beautiful pink cunt as it swallowed me whole. Leigh gripped my wrists, her nails digging into my flesh. Her breathing came in short pants. She was close. Thank fuck, because so was I.

"Lazarus . . ." She let out a breathy moan. "I need to . . ."

"That's it, baby girl, let it out."

She sucked in a sharp breath and shuddered under me. Her walls caved in on my cock, ripping my release from my body. I jerked my hips as my seed shot into her until there was no more to give.

I covered her body with mine, my full weight on top of her. She didn't complain; she didn't groan. Leighton wrapped her arms around me and squeezed me tight.

"Thank you, Caveman. For taking care of me," she whispered.

She was talking about the Nick situation again. I propped my body up with my elbows, keeping my softening cock where it should be, nestled in her pussy, and gazed into her big blue eyes. Before I could speak, she said, "I'm grateful to whomever it was that killed him. I'm glad he's dead."

That's my girl. I smiled down at her and then gave her a wet smooch.

CHAPTER 34
LEIGHTON

WEEKENDS WITH LAZARUS had always been too short. We hadn't spent a night apart since the Halloween party. He'd healed completely and had left early for a mission out of town. I didn't ask many questions, and he didn't offer answers either. Just as well, relationships were built on trust after all.

I hadn't let the news about Nick bother me. He'd had it coming. Drugging women and taking advantage of them in their inebriated state was appalling.

The Monday before Thanksgiving, I arrived at the library where I had been holding support group meetings to find it empty. Odd. Since we began these sessions, we typically had a packed room of ten to fifteen people. At the top of the hour, two women and one man came in.

"Hi," I greeted them. "Let's give it a few more minutes for stragglers to arrive."

"Uh . . . Leighton, I don't think anyone else is coming," one of the girls told me. Her name was . . . Erica . . . no, Erin. She had been one of the regulars I'd recognized at the meetings. She had flaming red hair and a vibrant personality, which made up for her petite four-foot-six stature.

"For the record, I don't believe the gossip." The male student sulked in his chair, his long legs stretched in front of him. Carl had also been a regular. He hadn't been at the party but had attended every meeting I'd held. He seemed to be a loner and the type of person who withheld his emotions. The party hadn't been the original cause of his pent-up trauma, but there was something else in his life that had been. If being in this support group gave him comfort, I wouldn't kick him out.

"What are the latest rumors?" I asked.

"You haven't heard?" Andrea, a fellow senior, spoke up. She was one of the popular girls. Perfect face, perfect body, and the perfect boyfriend. She dated the captain of the basketball team. Andrea had taken some coaxing to join the group. She'd stand outside the class for the first couple of sessions, chewing on her nails. The other attendees had coaxed her in somehow, and ever since, she'd been an active participant. Her unrestrained tears helped others open up, and I was glad for her presence within the group.

I shook my head in response. When I dated Keith, the football quarterback, it certainly had it's drawbacks. The rumor mill topped the list. I did my best to ignore the whispers and side glances that followed me everywhere during our relationship and after.

"Uh . . . the buzz is about you having something to do with the latest murder," Andrea added.

"What murder?" I blanched.

"The guy on the news. The one that drugged girls at bars and then took them home," Erin said.

"Oh . . . why would I have anything to do with that?" I asked.

"Someone started a rumor about you having known him and the guy from the coffee shop," Carl answered.

What in the world was going on!?

"Well, that's weird." I shrugged. "And for the record, I had nothing to do with either situation."

"But, we can continue if the three of you want to," I added.

The small group was eager to talk, and it ended up being my most rewarding session. With fewer people, each person had an opportunity to speak, and they were more open about their feelings.

I continued with my day, and sure enough, the rumor mill was in full swing. People snickered behind my back. Students gave me a wide berth in the hallways, and in all of my classes, no one wanted to sit near me, leaving me with an entire row of to myself.

My last class for the day was another group support session, which was also empty. The gossip wasn't going to be so easy to ignore. I closed the classroom halfway through the designated time and decided to visit Dr. Arkesh, head of the psychology department.

"Leighton? Don't you have a group session?" She glanced at the clock overhead.

Guess the rumors hadn't reached the faculty yet.

I told her what had happened and told her of my connection to two of the deceased, Henry and Nick.

Dr. Arkesh, being the consummate professional that she was, listened intently with a passive face.

"Well, rumors have a way of fizzling on their own. However, if you feel uncomfortable continuing your classes on campus, I am sure your professors will be willing to work with you. You're nearly done, correct?"

I nodded.

She jotted notes on a piece of paper. "That settles that then. It will be easy to complete your courses online. Email me your schedule, and I will contact each directly."

"On a personal note," she folded her hands on her desk. "Besides me, who knows of your connection with those men?"

I gaped. It was a fair question I hadn't contemplated, although I should have.

"Hallie," I breathed.

"Hmm . . . I don't know who Hallie is, but if she is the only person on campus who knows about these things, it is obvious that she is the source. Now, don't let this upset you, Leighton. Your friend may have told one person for a good reason. And maybe it got blown out of proportion. And you can't take responsibility for Nick or Henry's actions. Their actions were horrible and nothing you did had caused them to act the way they did."

I nodded.

"On another note," she continued. "Let's talk about your future in psychology. Doctorate program, or are you moving into the work sector after graduation?"

I'd spent an entire hour with Dr. Arkesh going over my options after graduation. Although she'd given me sound advice, none had sunken in. I left her office with thoughts about the rumors buzzing through my mind.

The realization that Hallie had told someone about my connection with Henry and Nick was disconcerting. Why would she do that?

I hadn't confronted her about Keith. She'd been sleeping with him. There was no denying that. It had been her jewelry and clothes in his dorm room. Sure, there could have been another explanation, but I wasn't counting on that. And honestly, I didn't care that they were together; I did, however, care that she didn't say anything to me. And now there was the issue with the rumor.

A harsh tug on my elbow pulled me out of my musings.

"Leighton? Are you okay?" Deep lines formed on Keith's forehead. "I've been calling you for the past five minutes."

"Oh. Sorry, I didn't hear anything. Lost in thought, I guess," I stammered.

"Do you mind if I walk with you a bit?" he asked.

"Sure. I'm just heading home. How are you holding up? I should have called you. I'm sorry."

"I'm fine. The situation is fucked up, though. The guys are shaken up. Some are pissed. We didn't lose anyone in our house, but yeah, I think that was the last Halloween party for Dormitory Row as a whole." There was a sadness in his eyes that I'd never seen before. Keith was Mr. Happy. He'd make a great motivational speaker if he didn't make it as a football player.

"Sorry to hear that," I replied.

"I heard you're doing a support group," he said.

"Not anymore. I think." I told him about the rumors and my meeting with Dr. Arkesh. She agreed with my plan to continue with the small group that I did have if they wanted to.

"I hope you continue with that group. I was going to bring some of my teammates to one of those. You're good at that kind of stuff. That sucks about the rumors, though," Keith said.

"Um, thanks." I glanced at him. "I think it was Hallie. She was the only one who knew about my connection to those guys."

He didn't say anything as we walked. His face was scrunched, and then he pulled me to a stop.

"Leighton." He ran his hand through his hair and looked up to the sky as though searching for answers from the heavens. "I don't know where to begin. I . . . Fuck."

"Hey." I grasped his hand and squeezed. "You don't have to tell me anything, or you can tell me everything. I will always be your friend."

"God damnit, Leighton." He pulled me in for a hug. "This would be so much easier if you were a bitch, you know."

I chuckled against his chest.

He released me from his arms but ran his finger along my jaw. "I love you, Leighton. I don't want to, especially after Halloween. But I do and always will."

After Halloween? What did I do? I thought about it, then remembered. Shit. *Please don't tell me you saw me and Lazarus together. Please.*

"I saw you and your boyfriend together." He dropped his hand.

That was a bitch move, Leighton. And at the time, I knew there was a possibility he'd wake up while Lazarus and I had sex on his bed. Who was he kidding? I was a bitch. The petty side of me wanted him to see. I had wanted to get back at him for sleeping with my best friend. It was a total bitch move. It was one thing to move on from a relationship. But to have sex with another guy on my ex's bed while he was in the same room. That was just cruel.

"I uh . . . I think you're wrong, Keith. I am a bitch. I'm sorry. That was awful of me." My voice wavered.

"It's okay." He pulled me in close again. "I'm not mad. I'm envious. And I deserve worse. Hallie . . . is manipulative. She's been sneaking into my room, and one thing leads to another. Every time I tell her to go away, she keeps coming back. I . . . didn't want to say anything because it's embarrassing. She . . . whatever. Let's just say there should have been a public beheading for that guy, Nick, for what he did. It doesn't feel good to be drugged and taken advantage of."

I didn't understand the correlation between his relationship with Hallie and Nick's actions, but Keith didn't say more. And I didn't pry.

"I hope he gives you everything you deserve, everything I couldn't." He cupped my face and kissed my forehead.

"I hope the same for you, Keith." My eyes watered.

"Hey, be careful around Hallie, okay? She has a mean streak and is hella jealous of you."

"Thanks, Keith. For everything."

He walked away, then turned. "Hey, Leigh. I hope you continue that support group. Maybe I'll bring the guys to the next session. I think it'll help."

I watched Keith Maynard stroll away, and for the first time, I felt like we were past the awkward post-break-up stage and had reached a place where we could be friends.

CHAPTER 35
LAZARUS

BEING AWAY from Leighton was more challenging than I'd thought it would be. Even without the nightmares, I felt a strong need to keep her close. We'd been together every day since Halloween. I'd been recovering from the gunshot wounds while working on research from home. Leighton studied in my home office beside me. It was a comfortable existence, one I'd planned on maintaining for as long as we could.

Graduation was right around the corner, and she was adamant about not doing the cap and gown thing. She didn't say why exactly, but I knew she wasn't one for seeking attention, and she didn't want her parents in the same vicinity. Family drama, I got, so I didn't push. I liked having her to myself anyway.

We hadn't found the mole involved in setting me up. I'd completed the job, the ticket was paid, and the trail went cold. The culprit had to be in our office. Our staff came out clean. Still, we'd been monitoring their whereabouts and everything they did online inside and outside the office. We didn't have a large staff working for The Sentinels, but we did have enough to keep Ezekiel, Josiah, and myself busy.

On top of that, the most rewarding aspect of my work was being able to hunt the rest of the DRC crew. Once Nick's illicit activities hit the news, his partners split town. The mere thought that they could escape their fate was hilarious. For the first time in Sentinel history, we had plenty of resources that were being used to deliver justice. It wasn't a paid gig, yet the entire staff had given two hundred percent to this project.

And that was what took me away from my girl and had me freezing my ass off on the other side of the border. Snowfall covered the towering mountains; the frigid air was cold enough to chill my bones.

I'd been watching Alex Yoo for a few hours. He had been hiding in his winter home since Nick had been found. Alex went about his day without a care in the world. He thought he was safe. Good. I thought. Let him believe that.

After following him most of the day, I'd decided to wait for him in his not-so-humble abode. I'd turned off his alarm system with a few taps on my phone and let myself in. His sprawling mountainside home was decked out in sleek lines and modern finishes. Views of the verdant forest could be seen from every window, making it feel like nature was a part of the home.

I liked it. A lot. It was secluded, and with a few modifications, it could be quite secure. Maybe Mr. Yoo could give it to me and Leighton as an early wedding present. I smirked as I set myself up in his home and waited him out.

It didn't take long. He had been at a local restaurant having dinner with associates, returned home before nine P.M., and dismissed his security detail. Alex was feeling mighty comfortable for a man who was about to meet his maker.

According to my research, Alex was a cigar smoker and would partake nightly before bed. He didn't disappoint. I watched him go to the humidifier and withdraw the only one left. He frowned at the case, which had been full before he left.

I patted my chest, where four cigars sat comfortably in my

pocket. Zeke loved cigars, too. My brother could never say I didn't get him anything.

Alex shook his head absently and proceeded to his study. In his study, he flipped on his computer and logged in. Then he pulled tools out of his desk, strolled to the French doors leading to the balcony, and cracked it open. He casually leaned on the door frame, clipped one end of the cigar, and lit it, taking a deep inhalation of the tobacco. Alex blew out a puff of smoke and returned to sit behind his desk. The computer screen flickered, and he moved the mouse around, making a couple of clicks, and a female moan filled the space.

Porn. Of course. I wasn't one to judge when it came to pleasures of the flesh, but there were things a person couldn't unsee. Alex unbuttoned his shirt, exposing his scrawny torso, and unzipped his trousers—time to end this before it got gross.

I stepped out of the shadows as the moans from his computer grew louder.

Alex sucked on his cigar, pulling the smoke deep into his lungs. His other hand disappeared under the desk. He hadn't even noticed me, an intruder, less than five feet away.

I cleared my throat.

Alex jumped out of his seat. His cigar dropped to his desk; his pants hung past his no-ass frame. Thankfully the desk was high enough to conceal his pecker. His gaze finally landed on me.

"Who the hell are you?" He grasped his cigar tremblingly, and the other reached beneath the desk, presumably depressing the alarm button I'd already disabled. "How the fuck did you get in here? My guards will be here any minute!"

A ski mask concealed my identity, not that it mattered if he recognized me from Firefly. It was cold out, and I didn't want to handle the hassle of scrubbing every surveillance camera in the little town.

"Let's not waste time with questions I won't answer and get to the questions *you* will answer.

"You and your friends have been bad, bad boys. Do you know what happens to bad boys that prey on innocent women?"

"It was just . . . just a test," he stammered. "We've stopped."

"Bullshit, Nick told me differently. He said it was all your idea. The drugs from your home country. The girls you prey on online. All of it was part of a larger scheme." Now, I was the one bullshitting, but Alex didn't know that.

"It was not my idea. I mean, yeah, there are the girls online." He wrung his hands nervously.

Through our contact in Malaysia, Alex lured underage girls through his online membership under the guise of offering dating advice. It was all friendship and camaraderie until the end of the hour when he'd whip out his little pecker and give his followers a show. And society thought the hired assassin was an evil man.

"Everything I do is consensual. And the drugs, well, that was an opportunity we wanted to try. Then Chad got carried away. And one test run turned into . . . seven."

Seven? Shit, we'd found four, and Leighton was supposed to be number five. And this was why we were still researching the fucks.

"If you want to live, you'll have to give up all the intel. We found a lot, but . . . the answers all point to you."

"Not true! I have the evidence. Recorded conversations between the three of us."

Excellent. We'd found call logs on a burner phone, but the conversations were golden.

"I suggest you start downloading those right now." I pointed at his computer with my gun.

Alex didn't hesitate. He pulled out a thumb drive and pressed a few buttons. I strolled over to his desk and propped my ass on the edge and watched him work. Took him all of two minutes. His skills would have been valuable to our operation. Too bad he was a scum bag.

I took the thumb drive from him and pocketed it. "Who told you about me?"

It was a long shot. Not even Nick could tell me how he'd found out about me and Leighton being at the Halloween party. Someone had been following me, but who?

He cackled. Saliva caught in his throat, and he let out a ragged, wet cough. "Someone is out to get the Ford family . . . hard."

I pointed my gun at his face. "Tell me who it is."

His body shook, and he began stammering again. "He called himself the Chosen One, and he approached us. He said someone was gunning for us, so Nick went after the guy and his girl."

"You're not telling me anything helpful, Alex." I flipped the safety off my gun.

"I don't know," he sobbed.

The moans from his computer got louder. I shot it.

The fucker rushed to the open door and tried to throw himself over the balcony.

His suicide attempt was pathetic. With his pants around his ass and his micro penis flopping out like a wilted peanut shell, his hurried movements made him look like a malnourished, drunk penguin.

I grabbed him by the scruff and threw him down to the wooden planks.

"I'll give you one more chance," I said.

"He contacted me once," he cried. "There's a phone in my brief-case. Mostly, he talks to Chad. I think they were friends."

"Why didn't you say that in the first place? Get up. And for fucks sake, put your micro dick away."

Alex did as I asked, and I followed him to the foyer, where he'd left his briefcase.

Sure enough, someone had been watching. In the last two minutes, he had sent a message threatening death to his family. Alex broke down in sobs.

I dialed the only number on the phone and placed the call on speaker. A modified voice answered. "You'll never find me. And thanks to you, Alex's wife and young children will die."

I laughed.

"You call yourself the Chosen One?" I laughed, clutching my belly. "If you have to hide behind a voice modifier, you ain't chosen for anything but cowardice. Now stop fucking around."

Silence.

"Seriously, dude, if it's me you want, I'm right here."

I spread my arms wide and spun in a slow circle. My gaze swept the room. I'd already dismantled the alarm and security surveillance in the house. There was something else here—something I missed.

"Fuck you, Lazarus," the voice said.

A flash of red caught my eye. "Run!"

I bolted out the door, hauling Alex with me. We made it two feet from the front door, and the beautiful mountain house exploded into pieces. The concussive force sent me flying thirty yards. By the time I came to, sirens were approaching. I caught sight of Alex's lifeless form, sprawled awkwardly over a boulder. A puddle of dark liquid bloomed over the rock under his body. *Yep, he was gone.* So much for getting more info from the bloke.

The contact phone had been lying in a demolished heap on the sidewalk. I picked it up and strolled out of Alex's neighborhood, replaying the voice in my head. There was something eerily familiar about that voice.

———

A few hours later, I was back at my penthouse, which was empty. Fuck.

I exited my place and drove to her apartment. Her door was locked but not bolted. Damn it, Leighton.

She was asleep and hadn't even heard me enter. I growled. She startled awake.

"Hi! You're home early." She gave me a sleepy smile.

The irritation over her lack of security and vigilance vanished. "Leigh, baby." I pulled her into my arms, knowing I was covered in dirt and smoke.

Leighton didn't seem to mind. She melted against me, all heat and lust.

I removed my t-shirt from her body with a smile. She loved wearing my clothes, and I loved seeing her in them.

My mouth latched onto her nipples. Leighton groaned under my touch. I shoved my hands under her panties. Her core was slick and ready for me. I teased her clit. Leighton humped my hand.

"Lazarus," she moaned my name and tugged off my sweater.

Her hands roamed over my chest and down the scarred flesh of my back. I didn't even flinch. I'd never allowed anyone to touch my back. Not since the day I'd received the scars. With Leighton, it was different. I was different. Her hands roamed the puckered skin, warm and wanting.

"I missed you," she whispered.

"Missed you too, babe." I pushed her onto the mattress. She spread her legs wide, and I dove into her wet center. Her pussy glistened. I captured her swollen clit between my lips. Leighton cried out, her body quaking beneath my touch. I loved how responsive she was. I licked up and down her folds, suckled her clit, tongued her entrance. Her breaths came in short gasps. She was close, so close.

I backed off to unbutton my jeans, then pulled them down with my briefs. I didn't bother to undress completely. I wanted to be inside her. Needed to be inside her.

Leighton's need was just as great. She collided her petite frame with mine and rolled us over. She straddled over me and threaded my tip into her hot, wet cunt.

"Fuck, yeah, baby." I pushed up with my hips.

She hissed. Her nails scored my chest. I bucked while she sank. She paused with me halfway in. I smacked her ass, and she dropped down, sheathing me entirely into her tight hole.

I gripped her thighs and rocked her over my cock.

"Oh! Lazarus, you feel so good," she said. Her voice was low and breathy.

Leighton rolled her hips slowly at first. Then she picked up the pace.

Fuck. Shit. Damn. My toes clenched. My release rose to the surface, desperate to be freed.

She arched her back; her hair flowed wildly over her shoulders. Her tits bounced with her movements.

"Make yourself come, baby." I slapped her ass again, and she let go. Her cunt tightened around my cock. A rush of liquid pooled between us.

I flipped us over and hooked her leg around my arm. She felt so fucking good. I plowed into her pussy with deep, punishing thrusts. Leighton took it. Took all of me. I wanted to give her more. Give her everything. Give her at least one more orgasm before my release. But her sweet, tight pussy had me in a vice-grip and wrung my orgasm from me.

Her lips found mine, and she stole my breath while breathing into me simultaneously. I was consumed entirely. My heart, body, and soul belonged to her.

I growled as my seed coated her walls.

We came down from our climax with quivering muscles and ragged breaths. I kissed her tenderly, then released her and went to the bathroom. I turned on the shower to let the water warm, then returned to collect her.

She snuggled into my chest as I carried her in the shower, letting the warm water glide over us.

It wasn't until I had set her down on her feet that she opened her eyes to peer at me.

"Hi. Did you have a good day at the office?" She smiled.

I laughed. "More or less." I kissed her forehead and proceeded to wash her hair. She rested her cheek on my chest as I lathered her tresses, rinsed them, and ran conditioner from her scalp to the ends of her hair.

"That feels so good." She released a contented sigh.

I chuckled. "Yes, you do like this."

After rinsing her hair and scrubbing her body, she took the loofah from me and said, "My turn, although I won't be able to wash your hair, Caveman. You're too tall for me to reach."

I took care of the parts too high and let her wash my body. As she'd done before, her touch was gentle and loving. Unlike the last and only time we'd been in the shower together, she took her time washing my back. Her tenderness soothed the phantom aches I'd thought were long gone. Each kiss chased away the past and paved a path to a brighter future.

"Thank you," I said into the dark room. We were back in bed, and Leighton had snuggled against my side.

"For?" she asked.

"For not asking." In my experience, whether it was a lover, friend, or stranger, the questions were instantaneous the minute they glimpsed my scars.

Leighton wiggled away from me and brought her face close to mine. The moon's light shone through the window and bathed her skin in an angelic glow.

"I don't ask because I already know how the story goes," she said.

I chuckled. "Is that right?"

"Well, not everything, obviously. But the parts that matter. I know that you are no longer a victim. I know that you are brave, resilient, and a survivor. Whoever did that to you didn't break you. Didn't even come close. You are a strong, powerful man—the story of who, when, or why is yours to tell when you're ready. I'll be right here when you're ready to talk about it. And if it hasn't been done already, I'll stand by your side when it's time to make the fucker pay."

My heart threatened to leap from my chest and wrap her in it. "I love you, Leighton."

I sealed my lips to hers, and for the first time in my thirty-one years of living, I made love to the only woman I'd ever truly loved.

CHAPTER 36
LAZARUS

I WAITED outside the classroom for Leighton's support group to finish. A couple of people I'd recognized from previous meetings exited the room, and a broody kid with long dark hair had propped the door open on his way out. He wished Leighton a happy Thanksgiving, and I heard her call out, "Same to you."

Moments later, a familiar blond athlete strolled out of the room with another jock, Leighton, between them. Fucking Keith. I thought we had an understanding, chump.

I ground my teeth, my arms crossed over my chest as Leighton moved to shut the door. The two athletes waited for her to discuss something that didn't interest me. They backed up, giving her some space, while she fiddled with a wad of keys, looking for the correct one to lock the door. They hadn't noticed me yet, and if I'd take my ego out of the equation, nothing untoward was happening between them. I just didn't like my girl's ex.

Leighton found the right key, locked the door, and glanced over her shoulder. Our gazes locked, and she smiled brightly. That smile stopped the world, and all the jealousy slowly ebbed out of my consciousness.

"Hi," she greeted me with a heated kiss. I deepened the kiss further, staking my claim in front of the two men, and glanced in their direction with narrowed eyes.

Keith glowered at me, and his friend let out a cat-call whistle and said, "Dammmnn." I liked his friend much better.

"How was the support group?" I asked.

"Good," she replied. I then turned toward Keith and his friend. "I'm unsure if you have met Lazarus, Keith, and Toby. Guys, this is my boyfriend."

Keith clenched his jaw but extended his hand. I flashed a shit-eating grin. His friend, Toby, was much more amiable.

"Nice to meet you, dude. Your girl is going to make a helluva psychologist one day. One group meeting, and I feel better than I have in weeks," Toby said.

"Glad to hear it," I replied.

"We gotta run," Keith added. "Thanks again, Leighton. Enjoy your holiday weekend. Lazarus." He tipped his head and turned away.

Toby pulled Leighton in for a hug. "Thank you, Leighton. That helped. See you after the break." He released her, shook my hand, and then trotted to catch up with Keith.

"Guess support group is working out," I told her as we dropped off the classroom keys at the library's info desk. "You like this psychology thing, don't you?"

"I like helping people." She shrugged. "The support group is neat. I've never used what I've learned in a group setting. I enjoy it. I'm not sure how much longer we'll be doing this, though. Or, at the very least, me. Graduation is right before Christmas." She pulled out her phone and glanced at the screen with a frown.

"Everything okay?" I asked.

"Yeah, I need to call my Dad." I opened the car door for her, closed it when she was settled, and went to the driver's side.

We were supposed to spend Thanksgiving at her father's place. Well, she was supposed to, and I invited myself. Holidays weren't a thing in my books. My father, his wife—Zeke's mom—and the other half-brother got together for the holidays, but I made it a point to be busy, even though most times I wasn't. Aside from Josiah and Zeke, I avoided the rest of them at all costs.

"I need to stop in the office real quick. Do you mind?" I reversed out of the parking spot and proceeded to drive off campus.

"Oooh, I get to see your office. How exciting." She beamed.

I chuckled. "It's a building with office furniture and people working there. No big deal. What'd your father say?" I changed the subject. I was curious about meeting her father. Leighton didn't talk much about her past or her family. Hell, neither did I, which may have been why we got along so well. I was okay with that. As far as I was concerned, she was everything I needed. And I was everything she needed; although, she may disagree with me. She had a fierce streak of independence.

"Umm . . . I don't know, let's find out." Leighton put her phone on speaker, and a phone rang.

"Leigh!" a gentlemanly voice said. "Thanks for calling me back. How's my favorite daughter?"

"I'm your only daughter, Dad. And I'm fine."

"That's why you're my favorite." He laughed. "I'm going into a meeting, but I had to tell you there's been a change of plans. Molly wants to head back east for Thanksgiving. I'm sorry, kid. I hope you're not disappointed."

"Nope, not at all." Leighton's voice sounded upbeat. I caught her reflection in the window, and the slight furrow in her brow told me differently.

"Well, I am. I wanted to meet your new fella. He better treat you right," her father said.

Leighton rolled her eyes. I rested my palm on her thigh. She moved her phone into her other hand and linked our fingers together.

I brought her fingers to my lips and kissed each digit.

"Next time, Dad. Let's talk when you return from your trip," she said.

"Okay, Leigh. Happy Thanksgiving; I love you."

Leighton hung up and said to me, "Sorry to disappoint you, but you won't be meeting my father on Thursday."

"I don't care. I don't need his blessing or anyone else's. And now, I get to keep you all to myself."

She laughed.

"Thanksgiving to me is all about takeout and football. But we can do something special if you want. Go to a fancy restaurant or something," I told her.

"I like takeout and football," she replied.

"You're the perfect woman." I leaned over and smooched her cheek.

We arrived at The Sentinels' headquarters and headed into the elevators when Leighton suggested, "Since this is our first Thanksgiving together, maybe we should do something different."

"Like?" I arched my brow.

"Football and cook a nice meal at home," she suggested.

I pressed the elevator button for the twentieth floor and sideglanced her. "I'm not picky when it comes to food, babe, but ramen noodles aren't my idea of a nice meal."

She swatted my arm. "I can cook more than just ramen noodles."

"Sure you can," I teased. "But fine, we can do whatever you want. I'll be prepared to order takeout just in case."

"Challenge accepted, Caveman." She hopped into my arms and wrapped her legs around my torso. "I'm cooking, and you will eat every disgusting morsel."

I tipped my head back and laughed. Our lips clashed just as the elevator chimed and the doors opened.

Leighton tried to wriggle out of my arms, but I gripped her body and carried her into the lobby.

"Put me down, Caveman! Everyone is staring."

I answered with a laugh and didn't release her from my clutches until we reached my office.

"You're a pain in the ass." She smoothed down her sweater dress, then removed her coat. I placed her coat and mine on the hooks behind the door.

"This is fancy. And unused." Her fingertips brushed the empty bookshelves. While Leighton looked around, I strolled to my desk.

"You are correct. I come in for meetings and to do work that requires me to be on our servers. Other than that, I am in the field or working from home."

I logged onto my desktop and began typing. Zeke had our think tank tear apart the ruined contact phone I'd gotten from Alex. The analysis was done, and I needed to peruse the reports.

"Is there anything I can help with?" Leighton asked as she came to stand beside me.

I pulled her onto my lap and fondled her tits through the soft, fuzzy fabric. She moved her hair to one side, giving me access to her neck. I sucked and nipped the sensitive skin below her earlobe, making Leighton roll her hips over my hard cock.

"When I said help, I didn't mean to distract you. You have work to do," she murmured.

"Fuck work. Spread your legs for me," I growled.

She did as I asked, and I tore a hole through the crotch of her stockings. Her panties were nice and wet, eliciting a deep growl from my chest.

"Good girl," I praised. "Strip for me, baby."

"Ummm . . . should we maybe make sure the door is locked?"

"I don't give a fuck who sees. Get. Naked."

She stood to face me, then removed her boots and stockings. Her hands inched up her dress, slowly revealing her black and pink boy shorts. She raised the fabric of her dress, tugging it past her hips, then up her torso. Higher and higher her dress went until she stood before me, wearing a bra and panties. I spun her around and placed her back down on my lap.

"Boots. On."

"Yes, sir." She pulled on each boot.

I made her stand before me again. My gaze traveled the length of her body. "You're so fucking beautiful." I unzipped my trousers and pulled out my swollen cock. Leighton slid her tongue over her bottom lip. I wanted that mouth.

"On your knees, baby."

She knelt between my legs and peered up at me through her long lashes, waiting for my instructions.

I ran the pad of my thumb across her lips. "While I'm working, I want you to suck. Do a good job, and I'll reward you later." I slapped my heavy cock across her cheek.

Defiance gleamed through her narrowed gaze.

"Open. Your. Mouth."

She opened wide, and I bucked my hips, forcing myself deep into her mouth.

"Take it," I said as she worked me over with her lips and tongue. "All of it."

I gripped the back of her head and pressed her down over my cock. "God damn. You suck a good dick," I hissed.

My climax rose within me, and I clenched my fists, forcing it back. I wanted this to last. I focused on my computer screen while Leighton sucked me off. The information blurred together as my girl did extraordinary things with those beautiful dick-sucking lips.

"Ffffuck," I groaned. My need to come was fierce. I tried to slow it down but those fucking lips. So soft. So wet. And those beautiful eyes. Every time I looked down, Leighton's gaze locked with mine. She sucked and stroked. Little moans escaped her while she slurped on my cock.

I managed to air-drop the report to my phone. My balls tightened. I gripped the back of her head and slammed my cock down her throat, and released with a deep groan. Hot ropes of cum jetted through my cock and filled her mouth.

She released my dick with my cum dribbling down her chin. Her tongue darted across her lips, licking every drop. A wicked self-satisfied smile spread across my face.

I was spent, but I wasn't going to leave my girl wanting.

"On the desk," I ordered.

———

We were in my office for three hours, and ninety percent of that time had been spent between Leighton's legs or her between mine. Totally worth every second.

Leighton excused herself to the restroom when Ezekiel popped into my office.

"Took you guys long enough," he muttered.

"Fuck off."

Zeke chuckled. We talked shop for a while until I heard Leighton's voice drift in from the hallway. A nasally voice responded. She was talking to Davis, and my protective instincts kicked in.

I stormed out of my office to find Leighton right outside my door, with Davis smiling at her.

"I can see why my brother keeps you all to himself," Davis said. "You are stunning."

Fucker was begging for an ass whopping. I extended my hand toward Leigh, and she gripped it.

"Thanks. And uh, nice to meet you, Davis."

"You too, Leighton. Don't be a stranger." He gave my future wife a sleazy smile. I glared at him over her head as I ushered her into my office and closed the door.

Ezekiel chuckled as we entered my office. "Met the other one, have you?" He grinned. "I'm Zeke. The favorite brother."

Leighton chuckled. "Nice to meet you," Leighton shook my brother's hand. "I remember you from the restaurant."

She was radiant. Her skin was flushed, her hair mussed a little.

"Ah, you remember. Yeah, um, good to formally meet you." He glanced at me and asked. "So, what are you guys doing?"

"Nothing you need to concern yourself with," I told him.

"We're going to get groceries. For tomorrow's dinner," Leighton answered. "If you're not busy, you can come over."

"For Thanksgiving dinner? At Laz's?" Zeke asked, sounding like he was the lead in the soprano section of the boy's choir.

Leighton smiled at me, and although I wanted her to myself, I nodded at my brother.

"Fuck yeah, I'll be there." Zeke clapped me on the shoulder.

"Is there anyone else we should invite?" Leighton asked. I knew she had been referring to Davis, who would never be invited to my home. Ever. I could feel his presence lingering outside my door.

"No!" Zeke and I said simultaneously.

"Okay. Well, as the favorite brother, you're welcome to bring a date, Zeke," Leighton offered.

"Oh no, just me. I'm going to enjoy every minute of this, Leighton, my lovely." He took her hand and kissed it. "You are a good influence on my brother." He turned toward me and gave me a sly grin. "I'm digging this new you, bro."

I rolled my eyes and gathered our coats. "I'll text you."

"Bye, Leighton, nice to meet you!" He waved.

Despite his antics, I had to agree. Leighton was a good influence, and I liked the new me too.

CHAPTER 37
LAZARUS

THE BED beside me was cold and empty. "Leighton," I called out and got no response. Worry flitted through my thoughts as I stumbled out of bed and prowled through my apartment. Voices from the front entrance had me racing in that direction.

"Thanks, Mike!" Leighton said. "I'll take it from here."

"I don't mind, miss. This is a lot for one person to carry."

I glared at my woman, and Mike, the head of security for my building, with my arms crossed over my chest.

"Good morning," Leighton drawled. She glanced down, and that was when I realized I was standing in the middle of the hallway, butt-naked, sporting an impressive case of morning wood.

Mike had the decency to avert his eyes. "Sorry, sir, I'll leave the rest of these bags here for you. He tapped on the elevator button several times until a door opened. He hurried in without glancing back.

Leighton hopped into my arms. "Are you happy to see me?" She giggled.

"I'm glad you're amused, Flower. Why didn't you wake me?"

"You were sleeping like a baby, so I thought I'd get an early start."

She hopped out of my arms and began taking grocery bags to the kitchen.

She shooed me out of the kitchen to organize her things, and I was happy to give her space. She was making herself at home, and I couldn't have been happier.

I worked out, showered, and returned to find Leighton in the kitchen. "Breakfast?" she asked.

"Sure. You've been busy." I sat at the kitchen counter while she brought me a cup of coffee.

"Uhh, yeah. It started with a grocery list for tomorrow, and then I wanted avocado toast. And then I remembered you saying you loved peanut butter sandwiches, but you didn't have any, and the next thing I knew, I had a grocery cart full of stuff."

She removed the frying pan from the stove and slid two sunny-side-up eggs onto open slices of toast topped with an avocado spread.

My stomach growled, and I took a bite. "This is good," I said with my mouth full.

"Don't sound so surprised. Avocado toast is not hard."

"Well, I am, honestly. Why do you eat ramen noodles when you can cook?"

She laughed. "I happen to like ramen. And the only reason I don't cook much is because cooking for one person is depressing. And truth be told, I've only cooked Thanksgiving dinner twice."

"I'm sure it will be fine, babe," I told her between mouthfuls.

"If it isn't, blame Google. I downloaded recipes."

I laughed. After eating, I asked, "How did you pay for all of this?"

"I have money, Lazarus."

"I have more. Next time, take my wallet with you."

She snorted. "I don't need your money, Caveman."

"You don't need it, but you will take it," I told her.

"I won't take a dime from you. End of discussion." She walked out of the kitchen.

Of course, I followed her.

She sat on a plush white leather sofa in the living room with her legs folded beneath her.

"What's this about, Leighton." I parked my ass on the stone coffee table in front of her.

"Nothing." She fiddled with her phone.

I snatched it away and threw it on the chair opposite us.

"Leighton? Don't make me go caveman on you."

"You already have," she crossed her arms over her torso.

I gave her my mean glare.

"Fine."

She let out a breath of air. "My mother never worked a day in her life and depended on my father for everything. He left her for a younger woman, and she panicked. She didn't have the means to care for herself or me. My father provided for us, but a year after the divorce, he made a large amount of money, which she wasn't entitled to. His new wife reaped the benefits of it, and that sent my mother into a tizzy. She lost weight and began taking care of herself. I thought she was going to get a new job or career. She didn't. Instead, she found herself a new man. One that was much wealthier. They married when I was fourteen, and we moved into his house. He's not a good man, but my mother would be lost without his money. For a while, I thought I'd go to school, get a good job, and take care of her. But I realized she didn't want that. She was content to be with a man who provided for her every need. He treats her like shit, and she allows it because, in truth, what are her options? She doesn't have an education. She doesn't have a skillset. She doesn't have the desire to fend for herself. I vowed to never, ever put myself in that position. I will pay my way, Lazarus. I appreciate your generosity. But, no."

Well, fuck. I brushed a hand down my face.

"You are nothing like your mother, Leighton. I appreciate your independence and would never take that from you in a million years. But . . ."

I paused to find my words.

"Everything I am, everything I have is yours. All of it. The shirt off my back. Every penny to my name. The blood in my veins. My heart. My soul. All of it belongs to you. I love you, Leighton. You will never be rid of me. Whether I live or die, you will never be without."

Her eyes watered. I took a deep breath and pressed onward.

"Your father and stepfather sound like complete assholes." I placed my hands on each side of her face. "Never, ever compare me to either of them again. I am nothing like them."

"That's fair," she replied in a quiet voice.

She studied me for a long moment. Quiet. Her fingers traced the planes of my face, then she climbed into my lap. "I love you, too, Lazarus."

———

Thanksgiving was delicious and, hands down, the best holiday I'd ever had. Leighton downplayed her skills in the kitchen. She refused my help, and we ate early in front of the television with Zeke. After the game, my brother and I kicked her out of the kitchen and took care of clean up. She'd used every pot, pan, and dish in my kitchen. There were things in there I hadn't realized I owned.

"Did you get a chance to look at those reports?" Ezekiel asked.

"I glanced at them." Sort of. I was busy getting my dick sucked.

"Sure you did," Zeke said. "We have a problem."

"I noticed the coding. It looks familiar," I said. There was an IT coding that we were able to trace with our technology. As a tech firm, we had access to software no one else had. It left a signature, like an IP address, allowing us to see who was communicating with whom and from where. The code was brand new. We'd been using it for our purposes but hadn't launched anything yet.

"That's because it is," he added.

I dropped a pan in the sink. The loud clang reverberated through the kitchen.

"You need help in there?" Leighton called from the kitchen.

"We got it, babe," I answered, rinsing the pan.

"Someone on the inside is plotting against us," I muttered. Only one person came to mind. Fucking Davis.

"I thought it was Davis at first, too. But I have someone tailing him. And I've bugged his office and his computer and his phone. He's coming up clean."

"Since when?" I asked.

"Since our mission."

"Good thinking," I placed the cleaned pan on the drying rack. "That voice I'd heard did sound familiar."

"The one before the explosion?" Zeke put another pot in front of me. He washed, and I rinsed. "I'll keep an eye on him."

"It has to be him," I muttered. "Who else would have the nerve to pull something like this off? Have you told our father?"

"Fuck no. He babies that asshole. Feels sorry for him," Zeke replied.

I scoffed. Yeah, because he's the son who got thrown in a mental institution where they burned him alive as treatment.

There were a million things I could have said that would have highlighted the misplacement of my father's concern. But fuck them. All of them.

"He's excited to meet her. Leighton," Zeke said.

I glared at Zeke. "You told him you were here?"

"Yep. Bragging rights. Besides, the entire office is buzzing about the woman in your life. If you wanted to keep her a secret, you shouldn't have brought her there and had loud, crazy sex in your office for hours."

"We weren't that loud," I retorted.

He laughed. We finished cleaning the kitchen and found Leighton napping on the sofa. I draped a blanket over her and kissed her cheek. Zeke and I moved into my office to discuss business things.

"Almost forgot." I pulled the cigars I'd taken from Alex out of my desk and handed them to him.

"No way! Where'd you get these?" He sniffed the Cohiba.

"The target. Alex," I told him.

"Sweet. Thanks." He patted his pocket and then pulled out a lighter.

I shook my head. "Take it outside."

"Seriously?" He sulked.

"My house, my rules."

"Alright, alright. Your girl made me a lovely meal and packed leftovers for me, so I'll abide. While I drink some of this expensive scotch you have sitting here collecting dust."

Zeke helped himself to a bottle of Macallan and poured two fingers into a glass for each of us.

"Davis is behind this. We need to prove it," I said.

"Well, let's come up with a plan." He guzzled the scotch and poured himself another glass.

"I'll need a day to think this through," I told him.

"I'll do the same." He tapped his glass. "You gonna marry her?"

"Yep." I leaned back in my office chair and propped my feet on my desk.

"Wow. Zero hesitation. How long has it been? A month?" His eyebrows shot to his forehead.

"I knew from the first time I laid eyes on her."

"Does she know . . . everything?" he asked, his voice cautious. My past was a sore subject. I never talked about it to anyone, which would have to change. Leighton would have to learn about all of it.

A sinking feeling in the pit of my gut churned. "Not yet," I said, then gulped the rest of my scotch.

"She loves you, Lazarus. She'll understand." My brother told me.

I hoped to hell he was right.

Later that night, I lay in bed, my mind churning over the long list of things I needed to tell Leighton while my nightmare girl slept soundly on my chest. There was so much. If I had been in her position, I'd run screaming. And yet I knew if I didn't say anything, she'd never forgive me and leave anyway.

Relationships are fucking hard. No wonder I'd remained single for so long. Leighton was worth it, though. It'd be worse to lose her all because I lost my nerve.

"Leighton, baby, wake up." I shook her tiny body. "Wake up, babe."

"What's wrong?" she asked sleepily.

"I have to tell you something," I said

"Right now?" Her eyes were still closed.

"Yes, it's important." I shook her arm until her eyes flicked open.

"Mmmkay." Her eyes drifted closed again.

"I did something I can't take back. And just so you know, I wouldn't have if I'd known how you felt about financial independence . . . So, I, uh, I paid off your student loans."

"What?"

"I paid off your student loans," I repeated.

"Why? And how? You can't be serious, Caveman?!" She pushed me with her feet.

"I'm sorry! I didn't know how strongly you felt about your financial independence. I meant it to be a grand gesture of love. And yeah, no refunds. So there."

"So there?! That's all you have to say? I can't even with you. I'm so freaking furious, but I'm too tired to kick you out of bed and yell at you for real."

"Is that what you're trying to do? Kick me. Feels good. Like a massage." I snorted.

"Fuck off." She slammed a pillow on my face. " Let me sleep! I'll fight with you about this in the morning."

Leigh rolled over, giving me her back. I chuckled and snuggled into her body. She tried pushing me away, but that only made me hold her tighter.

Well, that could've gone worse. I smiled, happy with the results. Maybe I'd confess my sins every time she was asleep. That was pushing it. But so worth it. One down and a million more to go. At least I was making progress. Mind at ease, I drifted off to sleep.

CHAPTER 38
LEIGHTON

THANKSGIVING WEEKEND CAME AND WENT, and it had been probably the most pleasant holiday I'd ever had in my entire life. Lazarus and I had family dramas we never discussed, which was fine with me. I knew I'd have to be more open about my situation, especially with Christmas right around the corner and Laz's insistence that he accompany me to my mother's. I was happy he wanted to go. I hated the idea of having to deal with my family on my own.

Laz and I were approaching the front door of my apartment when Hallie was exiting hers.

"Hi," I said.

She jumped, then placed a hand on her chest. "Shit, Leigh. You scared me."

"Sorry," I chuckled.

She pulled me in for a hug. My body stiffened, and then I patted her on the back. I hadn't seen her since the Halloween party. Nearly a month now.

"I have your stuff. Your costumes. I was going to drop it off, but I haven't been home much."

"Oh. Right, I forgot." She left her door wide open while Laz opened mine.

"I'll get them," Laz offered.

"So, um, it's been a while," I said.

"Yeah, a lot has happened," she replied.

The tension between us was awkward as fuck. It bothered me that she hadn't told me about her feelings for Keith and that she'd told everyone else about my connection with Nick and Henry, but . . . shit, she was my closest girlfriend.

"Listen, Keith told me about you two, and I wanted to let you know that I'm not mad about that. Okay?"

Hers eyes widened with surprise.

"You're not mad at me?"

"No, Hallie, he and I have been over for a long time, but we're still friends. I want him to be happy. And you, too."

She pulled me in for a hug again. "Thanks, Leighton. But he and I will never be. He still loves you, you know."

I shrugged. "I'm with Laz now. Keith knows that. He'll move on if he hasn't already."

Laz came out of my apartment with two heavy boxes and placed them just inside Hallie's door.

"Thank you, Muscles." Hallie brushed his arm with her fingertips.

Lazarus recoiled from her touch and snarled at her. "Never. Touch. Me."

Hallie flinched like she'd been slapped, and Lazarus turned on his heel and walked back into my apartment.

I gaped at both of them.

"Sheesh. No touchy. I get it," Hallie muttered.

I didn't even know what to say.

"So, I better get going. Good to see you, Leigh. Maybe we can do a get-together soon." Hallie stormed past me.

In my apartment, I found Laz casually lying on my bed.

"What was that about?" I asked him.

"Don't like her. Any woman that would sleep with her best friend's boyfriend is not a good friend, Leighton."

"I don't disagree, but Keith and I haven't been together for months."

"And what about the rumors she started?"

"Okay, you have a point," I replied. As much as I hated to admit it, he was right. Still, were those two things enough to end a three-year friendship? I shrugged off the thought and proceeded to the closet to pick a few items.

————

A week later, I was finishing my support group. The last one I'd held, since graduation was upon us, and I was officially done with school.

"How does it feel being done with college and all?" Keith asked.

"Odd, to be honest, but I may start graduate school next fall. Got into the doctoral program and am qualified for financing," I told him as I locked up the classroom.

"Good for you! You'll make a great psychologist, Leigh," he said, then stopped in the hallway to look around him. "No boyfriend to pick you up?"

I chuckled. "No, he's out of town."

Keith walked me halfway to my house.

"How are things with you and Hallie?" I asked.

"There's no me and Hallie. There will never be a Hallie and me ever. We had to change the locks at the dorm so she couldn't get in, and I talked to the Dean about her sneaking in. They talked to her, and she still tried to get in. Be careful of her, Leighton. She's jealous of you."

"Sounds like you should be the one to be careful," I replied.

He laughed. "No, I'm good. I did have to threaten her with a restraining order, though."

"Wow, that's . . . weird. I can't imagine why she's so unhinged." I shook my head.

"She's always been that way, Leighton. She puts on a different front when it suits her." He shrugged.

Elaine's warning floated into my mind. Weeks ago, she said to be wary of the jealous one, and I'd already realized I needed to be wary of her. But I thought the rumors were the extent of the harm she'd cause.

Keith and I parted ways, and I continued to my apartment, deep in thought, when my phone rang.

"Hello, Mother," I answered while unlocking my door.

"Leighton, I wanted to remind you about next week."

"I haven't forgotten Christmas, Mother."

"Well, I'm just making sure there are no excuses. Your father is hosting an important dinner with esteemed guests. It is imperative that you're here. You haven't gained any weight, have you? I've bought you a few dresses you must look . . ."

I placed the phone on my kitchen counter, went to the bathroom, and returned. She was still droning on about how I must watch my weight now that I was getting older. For fuck's sake, I was twenty-three, I wanted to say, but there was no point in arguing with the woman.

Someone rang my doorbell.

"Okay, yep, got it. I am swamped right now, and someone's at the door. See you soon," I said into the phone and hung up. I shouldn't be rude to my mother, but sometimes it was hard to tolerate the woman.

I peered out of the peephole and then opened the door.

"Hi. Am I disturbing you? I brought some wine." Hallie held up a bottle of red. "I thought we could catch up."

"Sure," I motioned for her to come in and went to get glasses while she went into the drawer and pulled out a bottle opener.

She and I used to do drinks all the time. She'd come over, or I'd go to her place. It sucked that things had suddenly changed.

"No classes today?" I asked, trying to shrug off the warning I'd received from Keith and act natural.

"Not for the rest of the afternoon, and I have a late start tomorrow. No boyfriend?"

"He's out of town. He'll be back later."

"You really like him, huh?" She opened the bottle of wine.

"I do. He's good to me." I took the bottle and poured wine for both of us.

"I'm glad you're happy, Leighton," she said.

I handed her a glass of wine and moved our conversation to the living room.

"Cheers." I held up my glass to hers.

She clinked her glass with mine, and we both took a sip. The tension between us was god-awful.

"I'm sorry, Leighton. I should have told you about how I felt about Keith from the start. I . . . I've had a crush on him since freshman year. I did all sorts of things to get his attention, and he ignored me. Ignored. It became a challenge in ways, and then I thought maybe he was into guys. Then you showed up, and he was besotted. By then, you and I were already friends, and I had plenty of other guys, so I pretended not to care. Then, when you broke up with him, I thought maybe it was my turn, and now here we are. It's weird between us now, and I . . . I hate it. I wish I never slept with him."

"Hallie, it's not that you slept with him that bothered me. It's that you didn't mention it before. I would've been okay with it because I knew Keith wasn't my forever. But, whatever. Bygones, right?" I waved my hand dismissively. "I don't want our friendship to end because of a boy. Your friendship means more to me than that."

"Thanks, Leighton. Let's start all over." She gave me a big smile. "Tell me about your new beau. Who hates me."

Hallie and I spent the next few hours drinking wine, ordering takeout, and chatting about everything. It was like old times. For a moment there, I felt lighter. Relieved. Good friends were hard to find, and I truly wanted to move past the whole Keith situation. But . . . there was something amiss. She'd skirted around the Nick and Henry topic when I'd asked and said everyone knew about Henry's obsession with me, which had been news to me. She was adamant that she'd told only one other person about Nick, some random girl I'd never met. The way her eyes shifted, and the change in her tone had told me she was bullshitting me.

My heart bottomed out, and the wine in my stomach turned to acid. I clutched my middle.

"Are you okay?" she asked.

"I umm . . . no. My tummy has gone sour," I replied.

"Oh no! Too much wine? Here, let me get you some water."

Hallie went to the kitchen and returned with a glass of water.

"Do you want to lie down?" she asked as I downed the water.

"Yeah, I think I better." I stood and went to the kitchen to place my wine glass in the sink.

"Okay, I better go anyway. Look how late it is?! We need to do this more often." She brought her empty glass and food containers to the kitchen counter. "I'm just going to use your bathroom, then help you clean."

I rinsed our glasses and tossed the empties. When Hallie returned, the kitchen was nearly cleaned, so I ushered her out with promises to call her soon.

After she left, I leaned against the door, filled with disappointment. *Why Hallie?*

Later that night, I heard my doorknob wiggle. I'd fallen asleep in my living room, reading a book. I peered out of the peephole and saw a male figure walking away from my door. He was much shorter than Lazarus and stocky. Aside from the fact that he wore a baseball cap, jeans, and a dark, long-sleeve shirt, I couldn't tell much else from his retreating form.

I grabbed my phone and went to my room. I lay in bed for a minute, then heard rustling sounds in my backyard. Fuck.

I dialed 911—more rustling noises. My entire body shook with fear.

911, Please state your emergency.

"Someone tried to get into my front door," I whispered. "And now I think he's in my backyard."

More rustling noises came from the back door, which I had

double-checked before Hallie arrived and was bolted. Whoever he was must be desperate to get in.

My heart thundered in my chest. I didn't have a weapon and didn't have anywhere to go . . . except the closet. I hid under a pile of clothes.

The operator asked me for my address, a description, and a bunch of other questions I answered robotically, all while the noises from outside got louder.

Officers are on their way. Just stay on the line with me until they arrive. Where are you now?

Click.

The intruder had opened my front door.

"He's inside." My voice was shaky, my cheeks wet.

I've let the officers know. They're racing toward you. Just hold on. Stay quiet. Help is on the way.

Loud footsteps reverberated through my house. It was a small house; he would find me in seconds. I clamped a hand over my mouth to stifle my whimpers.

Rustling noises from the living room. More footsteps.

My bedroom door creaked open. The footsteps were louder. He was in my room. My chest heaved with every breath.

He was in front of the closet. I could see his jeans through the seam of my closet door. He had a gun in a gloved hand.

A bone-chilling feeling raced up and down my spine. The sound of my heart racing thumped in my ears.

He raised his hand slowly. Every sensation felt razor sharp, and time seemed to stand still. Death hovered over my head, and I was paralyzed. Fear had me in its grip, with death as its only vow of release.

His hand stopped mid-air. He paused for a moment. Something caught his attention.

Suddenly, he turned away and stomped through the house.

I didn't move. I didn't dare make a sound.

A heavy thud snapped me to attention.

Leighton? Leighton, are you still with me? Talk to me. The officers have arrived.

"I'm here. I'm going to stay right here, okay?"

"APD. Leighton Parker?" a male voice called out.

It's okay, Leighton. The officer entered your premises through the back door. I'll wait right here until you talk to them, alright?

"K," I peeked out of the closet and slowly stood.

"I'm Officer Wilson. Are you Leighton?"

I nodded.

"There's no one else here. My partner is rechecking the area, and we have another patrol car in the neighborhood. Why don't you come outside so we can talk?"

"K," I said. "I think I'm okay now," I said into the phone.

I'm glad. The officers will take it from here.

I disconnected the call and sat with the two officers, reviewing the details. I numbly went through the motions as they had me going through the house to see if anything was missing. The perpetrator had taken my purse, with sixty dollars, IDs, and credit cards. He'd also taken my tablet. There was no sign of forced entry. According to the police, the intruder busted the door lock, and it looked like the deadbolt wasn't engaged.

Damn it, Leigh.

"Is there someplace you can go? Or someone you can call to stay with you?" Officer Smith asked before he left.

I said yes, even though the only two people I could rely on were Lazarus and Keith. I gathered my blanket and returned to the closet. It was three in the morning, and I had no idea where he was or how long it'd take him to reach me, but I dialed his number anyway.

"Hey, baby. What are you doing up so late?"

"Can you come home?" I asked. Tears streamed down my face.

"What happened?" he growled into the phone. Then I heard him shout. "Get this fucking plane in the fucking air right fucking now!"

"I'm on my way, babe. Talk to me. Tell me what happened."

CHAPTER 39
LAZARUS

THE SOUND of her terrified voice nearly broke me. Leighton had another fucking stalker. Or was it a random burglary? She didn't have much in her place to steal, which wasn't a deterrent. A desperate person looking for money would take the next best thing, and that very well could have been her. He had a gun, she'd said. He could have shot through that flimsy closet door and riddled bullets through her precious body.

I clenched the steering wheel, ignoring all stop signs and red lights from the private airstrip to her house. The flight was forty long-ass minutes, and the drive was nearly twenty. I cut the driving time in half, the only thing I could control, and raced toward her.

I'd looked into Leighton's life before we met, and everything had seemed so . . . vanilla. Nothing was exciting about her life, and now she had a stalker, a date rapist, and an intruder. Was it me? I mean, yeah, I was an issue with my brand of shadowing, but I'd never hurt her. Henry had stalked her prior, which could have been disastrous. Nick was a random meet-up at a coffee shop. I was convinced she wouldn't have gone out with him if Hallie hadn't arranged the date. The intruder was a puzzle I was determined to solve, i.e., kill.

When I arrived, all of the lights in her apartment were on. I used my keys to let myself in and was about to punch in the alarm code, then stopped myself. The police had told her the alarm had been cut from the outside. Stupid, cheap-ass alarm system. I almost punched through the fucking thing.

Leighton wasn't in the living room, and she wasn't in bed. She wasn't in the bathroom either.

"Leighton?" I called out in a tightly controlled voice.

She didn't respond.

I tore open the closet door, and my heart sank. She was huddled in the corner of her closet, shaking like a leaf. Fuck. I scrubbed a hand down my face, gently scooped her up, and sat on the bed with her on my lap.

"It's okay. I got you." I rocked her in my arms, and she flung hers around my neck and squeezed.

Her body heaved with sobs. Somebody was going to die for this.

And this was what stalkers did to innocent women. They violate personal space and instill fear. They make a woman feel helpless and vulnerable. It wasn't about the money, IDs, or a stupid fucking tablet. It was about robbing a woman of her right to feel safe in her own home.

I'd been her stalker. I was still stalking her in a way. I'd told myself everything I'd done was out of love and for her safety. But was it? In some ways, yes. But if I were to be honest with myself, it still violated her privacy. And I fucking hated myself for it. Worst of all, if and when she found out, she'd hate me, too.

I pushed those thoughts aside and held her close, whispering loving, reassuring words.

"Take me home," she whimpered.

"Of course." I stood with her in my arms and carried her to the car.

As soon as she got to the penthouse, she took a shower, returned to bed, and fell fast asleep. I held her until her breathing evened out and then slipped out of bed.

I turned on the feed in my home office that held her surveillance videos. The live feed was dead, as expected. Whoever it was had dismantled it a few minutes before she'd called the police. I tapped on my keyboard until I was in the cloud, looking for anything out of the ordinary that would have happened that day. I waited patiently, forwarding now and then until Leighton came home. She talked on the phone and went to the bathroom. After that, Leigh walked down the hallway and checked the deadbolt. She returned to the kitchen and continued talking to someone. Then, her neighbor showed up. I disliked the blonde, but Leighton had to make decisions regarding her friends. She and Hallie spent hours in the living room chatting and drinking wine. Then Leighton placed her hand over her belly. Hmm . . . she hadn't mentioned she wasn't feeling well, but with everything that had happened, that was probably not important.

Hallie got up to use the bathroom while Leighton cleaned the kitchen. I watched my girl work, and a line formed between her brows. She was upset, not sick. Interesting. Hallie returned moments later and left in a rush. Leighton locked the door behind her and turned on her alarm.

She showered, got comfy on the sofa with a book, and dozed off. Hours later, the feed went offline. I rewound the video.

During the second run-through, I followed Hallie after she placed her empty wine glass and the food containers on the counter beside Leighton. She went to the bathroom, then came out slowly minutes later. I sat up and paid closer attention. She crept along the hallway to the back door and reached for the deadbolt. Motherfucker. I was going to kill the bitch.

"Lazarus?" Leighton's voice cut through my murderous thoughts.

I flipped off the computer hastily before she approached my desk.

"I was looking for you," she said. Her eyes were red and puffy, and her hair was mussed. In my eyes, she would always be breathtaking.

I rounded my desk and pulled her into my arms. "Sorry, I had things to do. Let's go to bed."

Leighton was asleep within moments while I stared at the ceiling, wondering how I was going to kill her friend. I had to question the bitch first, and that would take a certain finesse. She was working with someone, and I needed to know who and why.

Leighton snuggled closer, her body molded to mine. I pulled her on top of me, her soft skin and weight making for the perfect blanket.

"I'm sorry I wasn't there to protect you, baby. It won't happen again," I murmured into her hair and fell asleep.

CHAPTER 40
LEIGHTON

IT HAD TAKEN me a few days to recover after the intruder incident. I felt violated and fearful. Lazarus was attentive and being with him made me feel secure. And as much as I appreciated him, I hated it as well. I hated feeling defenseless and dependent on a man for protection. I never told him that because I didn't have an alternative solution.

Luckily, finals and the upcoming holidays had kept me busy. I finalized my schedule for the doctoral program and was able to squeeze in one class starting at the end of January. I also had gone on a couple of interviews as a peer counselor.

Laz stayed by my side for the most part. He even went with me to the DMV to replace my driver's license, which took hours. He worked from home, and when he had to do things at the office, he was only gone for a few short hours. But he couldn't be my shadow forever. I had a life to live, and so did he.

"You don't have to do this," Lazarus argued. We were at my apartment, where he would leave me until he returned from an out-of-town job. "You are welcome to stay at the penthouse. Our house."

Moving in with Laz was not an option for now. He loved me, and

I loved him. But moving in because I was scared to be alone wasn't right. I didn't want to start a life with him based on fear.

"I have to confront my fear, Caveman," I told him, even though my stomach clenched with the thought of being alone.

I'd called Hallie the morning after the incident, just in case the prick was a serial burglar. She sounded freaked out, which was all the excuse she needed to begin her holidays in Mexico. She left that night. I couldn't blame her. It had taken me days for me to have the courage to return to my apartment, and Laz was at my side. I hadn't been alone in the place or alone, period, since the incident. That needed to change. I couldn't play the victim card for the rest of my life. I wouldn't. I steeled my resolve.

"I can do this, Lazarus. It's just a few days, and then you and I will be on our way to my mother's. Spending days with my mother and her husband is actually worse than me staying here alone." I smirked.

He wasn't keen on the idea and had only left after I promised to check in often.

Two days later, I was still alive, and I fell apart only once. My mother was having a fit about needing me to visit sooner than expected, so I drove home with plans to meet Laz there after he finished his job, which was closer.

My mother's house was a five-hour drive. Since I didn't want to go at all, I took my time and arrived several hours later.

The house was massive, an eight thousand square foot monstrosity. My stepfather was a stockbroker. He was often on the East Coast, leaving my mother alone. She never complained. She kept busy with lunches, shopping, and frequent trips to the dermatologist's office, getting every known beauty treatment under the sun. She'd told me it was a requisite for keeping a man. "A woman must do everything in her power to look her best, or your man will leave you for a younger version." She was speaking from experience. And that just made me sad. Especially since her current husband was a bald, fat, creepy fuck.

I drove through the gates and down the long driveway until I pulled to the front door, where staff members greeted me. One man removed my suitcase from the trunk, and another drove off with my car. Both men were strangers I hadn't met before.

"Leighton!" My mother greeted me, placing an air kiss on each cheek. "What are you wearing?"

"What I always wear, Mother." I waved a hand down my body, clad in an oversized hoodie and baggy jeans. Unlike my casual garb, my mother was wearing a deep burgundy Versace gown that fanned on the steps behind her. She was dripping diamonds. Her earlobes, her neck, and each finger sparkled. Her skin was pulled tight around her face, and her lips were bee-stung, swollen, and coated in a glossy red that matched her dress.

She took in my attire with an odd look, which I imagined was meant to be a disapproving frown—if her forehead could move. In comparison to her, I was severely underdressed, and I couldn't care less.

My mother and I had moved in with Ron—my mother's husband—and his son, Andre, shortly before I turned fifteen. At that time, my mother and I had lived alone for almost two years. During that time, I went from a flat-chested little girl to a curvy 36C. It was just the two of us, and I never thought twice about wearing crop tops sans bra around the house. Moving into Ron's house had been a wake-up call. My mother's husband leered openly, and the sexual innuendo was over the top and downright creepy. And that was just the beginning.

"There she is. My gorgeous daughter." Ron spread his arms open. "Come give Daddy a hug."

I wanted to vomit. I kept my overnight bag in front of me, keeping him away from my body.

"You must be hungry," my mother said, tugging me away from her husband.

"Umm . . . yeah, sure." I followed my mother.

Her heels clicked on the shiny marble flooring as she chatted away. I tuned her out and counted the Christmas trees. It was the only time of the year her husband gave her free reign to decorate as she saw fit. I'd counted twenty from one end of the house to the other. She went way overboard this year.

"Are you listening to me?" She pursed her lips.

"I umm . . . sorry. No. I was admiring the beautiful Christmas decor."

She preened. "Oh! I'm glad you like it. They did everything exactly as I wished. Down to the very last detail. Champagne?"

"No, thanks. I'll have a quick bite and get to bed if you don't mind. It was a long drive."

"Of course, darling."

The chef fixed me a quick but delicious sandwich, and then I retreated to my room before nine P.M.

The following day, I woke with the feeling of being watched. I scanned the room and found nothing suspicious, so I went about my routine and found my mother in the sunroom—my favorite room in the house. The gardens were covered in white, fluffy snow, making everything look soft. Muted sunlight streamed through the glass-paned windows, and the roaring fireplace made the room feel nice and toasty.

My mother sat at a table covered with breakfast goodies, her back to the fireplace. She wore a plush robe, and her hair was pulled into an artful bun. She'd skipped the warpaint but not the diamonds. Aside from the bee-stung lips, this was the mother I remembered.

"Good morning, Mother," I kissed her cheek.

"I take it you slept well." She smiled.

"You made changes to my room," I said. The decor had been a frilly pink when I moved in at fourteen. I returned for Christmas every year, and it had always remained the same. It didn't matter to me since I had never considered this house home and hadn't cared what my room looked like.

"Your father said it would please you if we made some updates," she replied.

"He's not my father," I retorted.

"Leighton." She smacked her hand on the table. "Stop that hate talk! After all that he's done for you. For me. You shouldn't be so disrespectful!"

It took all of two point five minutes for this pleasant morning visit with my mother to turn ugly. And I had nearly a week of this shit. *Fuucckk.*

"Right. So why am I here before Christmas?" I asked.

"For me, of course." Ron strolled into the room, leading with his paunch. He kissed my mother on the forehead and leaned over to kiss my cheek. I raised my glass of orange juice and turned, blocking his attempt.

He frowned. "Leighton," he began. "Come to my office when you're done with breakfast. I will apprise you of what's expected of you this evening."

"Sure."

"Oh, Leighton, you will love the dresses I picked for you! I will have them brought out to you after your meeting." My mother beamed.

She'd changed so much since I was a kid; she was an alien to me.

I forced down my breakfast and trudged my way to my room, needing a moment to myself before meeting with Ron.

In my room, I dug out another sweater from my suitcase.

"I told you to meet me in my office," Ron leaned on the doorframe.

I nearly jumped out of my skin. Vulnerability was getting old. I was so tired of being afraid.

"I needed another sweater," I said through clenched teeth.

"No matter, we can chat here on your bed." He parked his fat ass on my bed and patted the mattress.

Hell no. I sat at the desk instead.

"You're a willful one, aren't you." He leered. "I like that about you."

"You had something to tell me about this special dinner?" I asked.

"I want you on your best behavior for my guests. These are important men, Leighton. And I invited them here for you."

"For me?"

"To show you off, of course."

"Yeah, no. I won't parade around like a piece of meat in front of your vultures." I raised my chin.

"Yes, you will. If you don't, I'll cut you off completely," he told me.

I rolled my eyes.

He strolled closer to me and stroked my jaw with a stubby finger. I cringed.

"From now on, I want you to call me Daddy."

I gagged. Breakfast threatened to spew out of my mouth. Ron stepped away.

"You're going to do as I say, Leighton." He stopped at the doorway. "If you defy me, I will cut off your mother as well."

And there it was, my Achilles heel. Fuck my life.

"One more thing, you should lose those baggy pants. Those leggings you have on under them are so much more appealing." He walked out.

Fucker was watching me. I fucking knew it. I stood abruptly. My eyes darted to each corner of the room, searching for hidden cameras but coming up empty. Fuck these men. I grabbed my purse and my coat and went out the front door.

"Miss, your father said not to let you drive. Snowy conditions and all," the man who had taken my luggage to my room said.

"Oh, I'm not driving. I'm just going for a stroll before it starts snowing again." I shuffled away from him and kept going until I got to the gate, where I had to convince the gate guard to let me pass.

I walked for a half mile, fuming. Fury sang through my blood. There was no way in hell I'd go back there. Could I do that to my mother, though? I couldn't be responsible for her life. I pulled up a ride-share app and frowned. Shit. My phone was nearly dead. I shifted from foot to foot to stave off the cold until my ride arrived.

CHAPTER 41
LAZARUS

> Leigh baby: Left my mother's. Phone battery is dead. Checking into a hotel. Will text soon.

I READ Leighton's text a million times and called her twice as many. Something had happened to her at her mother's, and I hadn't a clue what. I floored the gas pedal, pushing the rental car as fast as possible.

The job I'd been on was closer to her mother's house than our home in Ashmore. As soon as I'd received her text, I finished the job and sped off.

My phone chimed. I glanced at the incoming text and frowned. Not Leighton. Credit card alert. Mission Bay Inn. I smiled. At least I had an address, and she used the credit card I'd given her. Probably out of necessity since her cards hadn't been replaced yet. Still, it felt like a step in the right direction.

Chad Johnson, the last person on the DRC list, was still on the run. As a public figure, he had a lot to lose. It was just a matter of time before his indiscretions became public knowledge.

After Alex had been found dead, we leaked his videos and pictures. Most of what we shared was information on how the drugs were imported into the country. His family's business was toast. We'd also leaked the info on his social media following. The web chat service he'd used was now under heavy scrutiny. Too many predators like Alex were on the site, preying on underage teens.

The media had a field day with all the info, and my contacts at the police department had told me they were looking into other suspects. I could have handed Chad's information to the authorities, but this was personal. Not only did they drug my girl, but they'd come after us. And I was chomping at the bit to find who'd leaked info from my office. My money was on Davis, but he was squeaky clean so far. We had a team tailing him and had bugged his place and his phone.

I hoped Chad would fess up since he had been purported to be the "Chosen One's" primary contact. Publicly, Chad's office had stated that he was on an extended leave of absence due to health reasons. Total bullshit, but he couldn't hide forever, and it didn't matter how far he ran, I'd find him.

The latest lead had him staying at a five-star hotel in the city. Unlike Nick or Alex, Chad had a team of security guards surrounding him. I'd spotted one team loitering outside the hotel entrance and several guys guarding the commercial entrance. The lobby was crawling with security, although none of that mattered. I was in disguise as a hotel employee when something spooked him. I walked toward his room when his team ushered him into the elevator. I ducked into the stairwell, then jogged to the next floor and watched from a room window as they sped off.

My phone rang. "What's going on, Zeke?"

"Somebody tipped him off!" He shouted into the phone. I held the phone away from my ear as he spat out a string of curse words.

"Yeah, I figured that out, Zeke. The question is who."

"No idea. There are only four of us that knew about your mission. You, me, Dad, and Uncle Jo," Zeke huffed. "None of us on that list would leak that information."

"That means our communication has been compromised," I said. That was a scary thought, but it was the only plausible solution.

My brother was silent for a minute.

"You're right. Fuck. New phones, email accounts, and passwords for everyone. I'll have our offices swept. Maybe even homes. Fucking Davis. I'm sure it's him, but Sol refuses to believe it." I heard him tapping on his keyboard. "Where the hell are you anyway?"

"On my way to Mission Bay Inn."

"Leighton? I thought you two were going to her mother's or something like that," he asked.

"We are or were. I'm not sure." I told Zeke the rest of the story as I sped down the highway.

"Well, shit. Hope she's good. I'll send a new phone to your hotel," Zeke said. "And Merry Fucking Christmas, asshole. Thanks for leaving me with the family."

He hung up.

Two hours later, I valeted the rental and waltzed into Mission Bay Inn.

Mission Bay Inn's lobby was festive. There were decorated trees everywhere, ten-foot-tall toy soldiers, reindeer pulling Santa's overflowing sleigh, and bright lights sparkled like it was the Las Vegas strip. In the middle of the seasonal craziness was a twenty-foot tree with chairs that resembled wrapped presents surrounding it.

I spotted my nightmare girl talking to an older couple, a mug with a mountain of white foam in her hands.

She hadn't seen me yet, and I almost hung back to watch her and caught myself; I needed to stop my stalker-ish behavior.

From several feet away, our gazes locked. A bright smile spread over her beautiful face. She set the mug down, ran toward me, and hopped into my arms. Our lips clashed.

"Ahem." A male voice broke our sweet reunion. "Take it upstairs, kids."

I released Leighton with a chuckle.

"How'd you find me?" she asked.

"Credit card alert."

"Yeah, about that . . ."

I cut her off with a kiss and bit her lower lip to prove a point. "I don't care how much money you spend or where you spend it. You never owe me an explanation, Leighton. Understood?"

She nodded.

"Words, babe."

"Yes. I understand. Thank you," Leigh replied.

I pecked her forehead, then waved at the decor. "This is . . . a lot."

"This is nothing. My mother's house looks like Christmas arrived and vomited all over the place."

I laughed, then placed a wet smooch on her lips. "You had me worried there, Flower. But you seem to be in good spirits."

She gave me a lazy smile. "I've been drinking."

"Ah, I see. Everything okay? Where's your phone?"

"Better, now that you're here. And upstairs charging." She tugged my hand toward the elevator, then did a U-turn back to where she'd left her drink.

She introduced me to the couple who had wanted to get to know me as though they were her grandparents. I wasn't a chatty person, but Leighton was in a good mood, so I indulged the couple while my flower sat on my lap and sipped her cup of spiked hot chocolate.

Thirty minutes later, we were finally heading to the room. There was something about being in an elevator with Leigh that made my cock swell. Or maybe it was having her perched on my crotch for the last thirty minutes, or perhaps it was the way she licked whipped cream off her lips. It was all of the above, and it was just Leighton. Everything she did stirred a primal need in me. I pressed the emergency stop button on the elevator and had her bottoms off in minutes.

CHAPTER 42
LEIGHTON

I'D CHECKED into Mission Inn, a day spa and resort on the coast. It was beautiful and fuck-all expensive. If Lazarus hadn't left his credit card in my purse, I wouldn't have been able to afford the suite, the only room left. Due to the influx of holiday travelers, the hotel was fresh out of standard rooms. Reluctantly, I handed the credit card over. Lazarus was well off and very generous, but financial independence was never something I'd let go of. I wasn't sure what that meant for our future, but presently, going back to my mother's was not even an option. And yes, I could have found a cheap motel, but I was rattled by Ron's threat and pulled up the nearest hotel a couple of blocks from a swanky outdoor mall I'd been familiar with. Plus, I needed a stiff drink. I checked in, went to the room, and realized I had no clothes or toiletries, and I didn't even have a charger for my phone.

The hotel didn't have a spare charger, so I walked a few blocks to the mall, crowded with last-minute shoppers. It wasn't my scene; I was an online shopper, but I needed that damn charger. At least I was getting in my steps. I had to use Laz's card again and again. I kept all the receipts and only purchased what I could pay back. With any luck, one of the job interviews I'd gone on would hire me, and I'd have work beginning in January.

After my little shopping spree, I dumped the bags in the posh suite, plugged my phone into the charger, and went downstairs for that drink.

An hour later, the most stunning man prowled through Mission Inn's lobby with a deep furrow marring his features. How did he find me? It didn't matter. What mattered was that he was here, and I wasn't alone. I ran to him and hopped into his arms.

We chatted with Ruth and Bill, an older couple I'd met while having my second adult hot chocolate, and then my caveman ravaged me in the elevator and again in the suite.

"Do you want to tell me what happened?" Laz asked.

I buried my face in the crook of his neck while he traced small circles with the pad of his thumb over my thigh.

"I . . . left my mother's," I said.

"I can see that." He chuckled. "What did she do to make you leave? Or was it your stepfather?"

"Don't call him that! He's my mother's husband, and that's it. He's not my anything!" I snapped and moved away from Lazarus.

He regarded me with wide eyes. Yeah, that was uncalled for.

"Sorry, I shouldn't have taken my disgust for that man out on you."

"Don't apologize, babe. Tell me what happened." He rolled to his side, facing me.

"That man is creepy. He came into my room and insisted I behave for his guests tonight. And he made an odd reference to what I was wearing, which tells me the room has cameras. Seriously, what kind of pervert sets up cameras in a woman's bedroom? Gross." I cringed.

Laz's body stiffened. I tilted my head to peer at his face. The deep furrow in his brow was back, and his jaw clenched.

"He threatened to cut me off and my mother if I didn't behave tonight. Fuck him. I'm not going back. And I'll have to figure things out for my mom," I continued.

Lazarus remained silent for a beat and then rolled us over so that I was pinned beneath him.

"Leighton, I hope you can trust me and umm . . . I hate to be insensitive about the situation, but I need to know. Did he touch you?" His voice was deep and growly.

"No. Umm . . . not really." My eyes shifted to the ceiling because I hated talking about this.

"Look at me, Leighton."

I did.

"There's something you're not telling me."

Damn it, I had to tell him everything. Or did I? Talking about my past was my least favorite thing.

Laz's silvery, intense gaze made me squirm. As though he could sense my discomfort, he pressed our foreheads. "Baby, there's more to this story. Your disgust for that man is palpable, and I . . . I want you to feel comfortable talking to me. I won't judge you, no matter what happened. Let me help you."

Despite my caveman's assurance, I knew the dredging up the past was going to suck, but I had to open up. I had to trust someone. I pushed him off me, sat up, and placed my face in my hands as the unwanted memories flooded my brain.

Nine years ago

The mattress dipped, and something brushed my feet. I bolted upright in my bed and found my mother's new husband sitting on my mattress.

"What are you doing here?" I asked.

"Ssshh, you don't want to disturb your mother's sleep. I was checking on you." He touched my foot. I snagged it away and scrambled up the mattress, putting distance between us.

He licked his lips, leering at me.

"Are you still a virgin?" my mother's husband asked me.

"That's . . . that's private," I stammered.

"You are, aren't you? Good little girl. Stay that way. We men like virgins."

The door swung open, "Dad?"

"Go back to sleep, Andre," Ron hissed.

"What are you doing here?" Andre asked.

"Checking on my daughter," he said nervously.

The light flicked on, and I felt relieved.

Ron hastily got off my bed, his face beet red, his eyes wide. "Good night, Leighton."

He stomped out of my room, tugging on Dre's elbow.

The next day . . .

Thanks to the weirdo my mother married, I couldn't sleep well. I felt sluggish and didn't want to leave my room, but I was hungry, and my room didn't feel safe anymore.

Mother was polishing her nails in the living room, and Dre was somewhere in the massive house. I grabbed a donut from the kitchen and passed Ron's office. The bald man was creepy. Why my beautiful mother married him was beyond me. Oh wait, he had lots of money, that was why.

I lingered outside his door and listened to his conversation. What could I say? I was a curious teen.

"Fully developed and so naive. The way she flaunts herself." He groaned. The sound he'd made was disgusting.

"Virgin. I'm sure of it." Ron laughed. "No, not yet. But you can bet I'll be sampling that soon."

He laughed again. "How about you sweeten that contract with an extra percentage or two, and maybe I'll share. Call it a virgin tax."

I backed away from the door. The donut in my belly souring. Was he talking about me? Whether he was or wasn't, the entire conversation I'd overheard made me feel icky.

"Hey!" Andre said as I bumped into him. "You okay? You look like you've seen a ghost."

I looked down at my tank top and immediately crossed my arms over my chest.

Andre tilted his head to the side.

"Umm, can you give me a ride to the mall?" I asked hastily.

"Sure, I need to stop at Jenny's house first."

Later that day, at the food court in the mall, I asked Dre, "Why do men like virgins?"

The French fry he had been holding paused before entering his mouth. He dropped the fry.

"I'm sorry, what? Where did you hear that? And why are you wearing a coat? It's summer?" His eyes squinted.

"I'm cold," I lied. I'd wanted to conceal my body. "Why do men like virgins? Do you like virgins? Is Jenny a virgin?"

"Stop saying virgin!" Dre shifted in his seat uncomfortably and looked around. "I'm not sure where this is coming from. Well, I can guess. The answer is no. Real men don't like virgins. Insecure men like virgins. They prefer being with a girl who is inexperienced because it makes them feel superior. She doesn't have anything to compare to."

"Oh. Maybe I should have sex so that I'm not a virgin anymore. Then insecure men won't be interested in me."

"That's not a good reason to . . ." He ran his hand through his hair and tugged on the short strands. "Ahhh shit. Okay, you need to have this conversation with a woman. Come on."

Later that night, I wedged the chair under my doorknob just like Dre showed me and slept like a baby.

Dre and his mother, Rosa, took me to breakfast the following day. Rosa was a lovely woman, kind and motherly. She was soft around the middle and huggable. So unlike Rachel, my mother, even her round figure couldn't soften her sharp edges.

After breakfast, we knocked on my father's door. It was Sunday, and his new wife was out to brunch. Dre and I sat in the living room watching television. I wasn't paying attention to the program; I was eavesdropping on the adults.

"Are you sure?" my father asked.

"My son is not a liar. Neither is your daughter. Either you take her out of that house, or I will take her myself!" Rosa answered.

"Fine. Fine, I'll talk to my ex and make it happen."

I was moving in with my father. Yet I'd rather have lived with Rosa instead.

There was a heavy silence in the hotel suite after I'd told Lazarus about the awkward event between myself and my mother's husband.

"Fuck." Lazarus muttered and rested his head on my chest. After another long pause, he raised his head. "So, this Dre, will he be there tonight?"

"No. After I moved into my dad's, it became a nightmare for him. Like I said, once my dad found out, he told my mother. She confronted her husband, who blamed his son. My mother refused to believe me. I felt horrible for Dre, but he'd said he wasn't sorry, and he'd rather take the blame than have me in the house with his father lurking in the hallways. At the time, Dre was already a senior in college. He had been living at home and commuting. After the incident, he moved out also, and our parents decided to keep us apart at all costs. He visits on Thanksgiving; I go there for Christmas. We text on birthdays, but that's it."

"Well, if his father is such a shit, why does he even bother? Why not turn him in to the authorities?"

"Money. Dre has recently done well for himself. But his mother is dependent on Ron's money."

"Fuck, and I thought my family was bad. And they are but fuck." Laz stared into space for a beat and then returned his gaze to mine. "What time is this party thing?"

"Dinner is promptly at eight," I told him. "My mother sent a million texts."

Laz glanced at the digital clock on the nightstand. "Plenty of time, let's go shopping, babe. We've got a party to get to."

"You can't be serious?" I asked as he got off the bed and pulled me up.

"Absolutely. After tonight, that blowhard won't threaten you or your mother ever again. Come on." He swatted my ass and strolled into the bathroom.

CHAPTER 43
LAZARUS

THE ONLY THING remarkable about Christmas was the mall stayed open late, and we were able to get outfitted for Leighton's mother's soiree. I didn't want to go, but I added her mother's husband to my kill list. The perv would have taken advantage of her at fourteen if his son and ex-wife hadn't intervened. And the way her shoulders curled in defensively while she told me what had happened indicated she was still uncomfortable around him. He made her feel vulnerable and scared, which pissed me right the fuck off.

Yeah, I admit my shadowing didn't make me much better. I'd have to come clean. The camera I'd installed in her bedroom needed to be dismantled. Soon. She was going to hate me when she found out. Fear, an emotion I was not familiar with, bubbled in my gut. *She was going to leave you.* The thought of losing her because of my stalker-ish behavior flooded my brain. I shoved the thought away with a swig of the wine we'd gotten during our shopping excursion. *Soon, Leighton. I'll tell you everything soon. But not today.*

Leigh exited the bedroom wearing the deep red gown I'd picked out. The strapless gown showed off her sculpted shoulders and porcelain skin. The sweetheart bodice pushed up her huge boobs, showing off plenty of cleavage. The satiny fabric cinched at her waist and then fell softly around her hips and then down to the floor in a magnificent train that trailed behind her.

I drank her in with my gaze. Blood rushed to my cock.

"You're breathtaking." I crossed the room in two easy strides and brushed my lips across her collarbone. Her breath hitched, and I felt her pulse quicken.

I reached under the slit of her dress and sought out her core. "Mmmm baby, so nice and wet." I snaked my finger under her panties and strummed her clit.

She let out a low moan; her eyes fluttered closed.

I slid a finger into her pussy.

"Oh my god, Lazarus."

Her phone beeped. Her mother had been texting non-stop.

"As much as I want to continue this, we have to go." I released her cunt and slid my wet finger into her mouth. "Later." I captured her lips with mine and led her out into the hallway.

Twenty-five minutes later, we drove through the gate of her mother's mansion.

"Keep it up front. We won't be staying long," I said to the valet attendant and placed a hundred dollar bill in his palm. He nodded, and I rounded the car and laced my fingers with Leighton's.

We entered the overly decorated mansion—every inch covered in something to celebrate the holiday.

"You weren't kidding about Christmas vomit," I chuckled. Leigh gave me a small smile; anxiety radiated from her in hot waves.

"Don't worry, babe. You have nothing to fear from this man ever again," I assured her.

She squeezed my fingers and gave me a grateful smile.

"Remember the plan," I told her.

She nodded and then directed me to her room while she went to find our host and hostess.

A few minutes later, I found everyone in the study. I stood just outside the door and watched the crowd, which was predominately male. While I was perusing the upstairs, I'd passed photos of her mother and Ron and picked out the creepy bastard in the crowd. As I anticipated, Ron was seated next to Leighton.

"I love your dress." He leered at her. His friends agreed.

"Thanks," Leighton said in a tight voice. "My boyfriend picked it out."

"Boyfriend? Ron, you didn't say anything about her having a boyfriend," a man old enough to be her grandfather said.

"Boyfriends, husbands, they come and go. I'm sure we have a more suitable replacement for this boyfriend of yours," Ron replied. He scooted closer to Leighton. She moved farther away from him until she finally ran out of cushion and stood. Ron also stood and reached for her elbow, and that's when I walked in.

"Sorry, it took me so long, babe. This place is like a maze." Leighton's gaze locked with mine.

She beamed at me with a grateful smile. I pulled her into my arms and laid a lingering kiss on her lips.

Someone let out a low whistle, and we broke our kiss.

"Pardon us," I said and then turned my attention to Ron. "You must be the host."

"I . . . I . . . yes. I am," Ron stuttered. He extended his hand to me, and I looked at it, then lifted my gaze to meet his.

"You and I need to have a conversation," I said, disregarding his attempt to shake my hand.

Rachel, Leighton's mother, breezed into the study like a prima donna. She was weighted down with enough jewelry to make Tiffany envious and wore a long, sequined, gold gown. Rachel and Leighton shared the same dark hair and that was it. I imagined Rachel had been attractive once, but it was hard to tell with the warpaint and the plastic expression on her face.

"Darling!" she exclaimed, and then air-kissed Leighton on each cheek. I rolled my eyes.

Leighton made the introductions, and then her mother announced that we should move into the formal dining room.

"Since I just arrived, I'd like some male bonding time. Just one drink." I smiled at the men in the room and then addressed Leighton's mother. "If that is okay with our hostess, of course."

"Of course! Come on, ladies," Rachel exclaimed, and she directed the other women out of the room.

Leighton hesitated a minute and then pulled my head down to whisper in my ear. "You can't kill him."

I growled.

"Seriously, Caveman. If anyone takes his life, it's me."

That made me smile. My killer instincts were rubbing off on my little flower. "As you wish." I gave her a reassuring kiss on her cheek.

After the women had left, I helped myself to the bar and poured myself a healthy dose of scotch.

"So, what were you all talking about before I arrived?" I asked the men.

"Oh, nothing . . . the men were just complimenting my daughter's dress."

"She is beautiful, isn't she?" I sipped the liquor.

The men in the room murmured their agreement.

"If I ever see any of you looking at my woman again. I'll rip your fucking throats out." I withdrew the pistol from the holster on my hip and leaned casually on the bar.

The men blanched.

"Now, now, Lazarus, no need to get territorial," Ron said. "She is mine, after all. Virgin or not, I still hold sway over her life. And you aren't her husband."

I crossed the room in two easy strides and pistol-whipped the fucker, while still holding my drink in the other hand.

Ron fell face-first into the couch. The other men froze in place, their faces a mask of panic and distress.

I closed the double doors and strolled back to the bar and refilled my scotch, then dumped the alcohol over Ron's face.

He startled awake, sputtering.

"What . . . what's going on? Lazarus?" Ron looked around the room wildly.

I gripped his face, squeezing his swelling cheeks. "Disrespect my woman again, and I won't hesitate to pull the trigger. And from now on, you will address me as Daddy. Understand?"

He nodded.

"Say. It."

"Yes . . . Daddy," he muttered.

"I can't hear you?"

"Yes, Daddy."

I turned toward the other men. "The rest of you can stay for the ass-kicking, or you can get the fuck out," I told them.

The five men stepped over each other to get out of the room. Ron tried to leave.

"I didn't say you could leave." I yanked him by his tie and forced him back to the sofa. Then I smacked him across the face for good measure.

"Stop hitting me! I'll sue!!" he stammered.

"Ah, ah, ah. What are you supposed to call me?"

"Daddy." He dropped his gaze.

"Not great. But we'll work on it. And yes, you could sue. If you live long enough." I sat across from him. "I heard what you said to Leighton. Boyfriends come and go . . ."

"Is that what this is about?" His face turned beet red. "Fuck her. She's just a wh—"

I pointed my pistol at his face. "You may want to think real hard before you finish that sentence."

"I . . . I . . . I'm just saying you can have her, Daddy."

"Oh, I already have her. I want *you* to stay the fuck away from her." I pressed the pistol between his eyes. "And your bullshit threats to her and her mother stop now. You break my rules, and I will shove my foot so far up your ass you won't be able to shit right for the rest of your life."

"You . . . you . . . can't make me—"

I pistol-whipped him again, cutting him off.

"I can and will do whatever the fuck I want."

"Fine! Fine. I won't bother her ever again."

I glared at him. "Say again?"

"Yes . . . Daddy. I won't bother Leighton or her mother again."

"On that note, here are a few more conditions."

I whistled on my way to the dining room, happy with my meeting with Ron, who was trailing behind me.

At the dining room, I stopped at the entrance and said, "Ron has something to say." I moved to the side, allowing Ron and his swollen face to take center stage.

"I . . . um, I'm not feeling well. Thank you all for coming." He turned to leave.

I cleared my throat.

Ron stopped, then turned back to face me.

"Thank you, Daddy, for stopping by," he said in a small voice.

"And?" I asked him.

Ron turned toward Leighton. "I . . . I'm sorry for my inappropriate behavior, Leighton."

Leigh narrowed her eyes at him.

"Ron? What did we discuss?" I scolded.

"Sorry, Daddy," he said and then cleared his throat. "Leighton, I apologize and promise not to threaten you or your mother again."

Leighton gave him a curt nod. It wasn't enough to erase the memories, but it was a start.

"Daddy, may I leave?" Ron asked in a defeated tone.

I laughed.

"Before you run off. I have a surprise." I dug into my pocket, pulled out a bundle of wires connected to a tiny camera, and placed them on Rachel's dinner plate. "Guess where I found these? I'll give you a hint. Leighton's room needs to be remodeled again because there's much more where that came from."

Ron's swollen face turned a spectacular shade of red and purple.

"Shall we?" I helped Leighton stand.

She gave me a big smile and took my hand.

In the car, Leighton burst out laughing. "I can't believe you made him call you daddy!"

She held up her palm for a high five. I slapped her hand with mine and drove back to the hotel with a big smile.

My future wife was laughing beside me, and I'd gotten to pistol-whip a pervert.

Best fucking Christmas ever.

CHAPTER 44
LEIGHTON

I WAS WALKING on a cloud with a huge smile plastered to my face as I made my way to Buzzy's. Christmas with Lazarus had been the best holiday of my life. We didn't exchange presents and didn't attend any parties. It had been just us. After leaving my mother's place, we returned to the hotel and spent nearly thirty-six hours in our room.

I'd texted my mother on Christmas Day, and she had yet to respond. She was probably embarrassed with how Laz handled things, and for the first time, I couldn't care less. He'd found the proof of the cameras in my room and had told me he left wires hanging all over the place in case she needed more evidence. I'd hoped she'd found them and was working on an exit plan for herself. Via voicemail, I'd asked if she was okay and told her how much I loved her. If she didn't respond in twenty-four hours, I'd leave another message about calling the police to check on her. Maybe that would spark a callback.

Two days after Christmas, we were back at the penthouse. He had work, and I was done with school. I hadn't heard from the potential employers I'd interviewed with. Originally, I planned on escaping to Europe for a couple of months, but now that I had Lazarus, I didn't want to go anywhere without him. What was happening to me? I shook my head. It was sappy and so out of character for me. But . . . fuck me. I was in love. And he was so worth it. He was passionate and broody sometimes, okay, all the time. But his protective nature made me feel safe. I hadn't felt safe since Mother and Ron had gotten married. And now . . . Lazarus had me wrapped in a warm cocoon of protection.

I stumbled and caught myself before falling to the icy ground. Was I following in my mother's footsteps? The thought made my stomach queasy. Oh, no, that would not happen. I needed a plan. My one class wouldn't begin until the end of the month, and I hadn't considered taking a summer course. I'd been on two interviews and hadn't heard back. Perhaps I needed to call them and follow up. That couldn't hurt.

There was a short line at Buzzy's, and all the tables were occupied, which was unusual considering it was past breakfast rush hour. I glanced at the patrons and didn't notice anyone familiar. I placed my order at the register with the cashier, who was in training. She fumbled with the payment terminal and my credit card, and I moved to the side.

"Hey, Leighton, are you okay?" Claire, the manager, came around the counter and pulled me in for a hug. "I just heard. How awful!"

"Hi. I'm great. I just returned from a short but wonderful vacation," I replied.

"Oh shit. You haven't heard." She covered her mouth with her hands.

"No, I haven't heard a thing."

"Well, okay. Umm . . . here's your latte. On the house," she said hastily.

"What happened?" I pressed.

"I . . ." Her shoulders slumped. "Shit. I hate to be the one to tell you. So, umm . . . you dated Keith, right?"

I nodded. Dread crept up my spine.

"It was on the news day before Christmas Eve. He died. Horrible car crash."

My latte dropped from my hand and splattered on the floor at my feet. The room swam, and gravity didn't work for me anymore. Arms wrapped around my torso, and I was seated in a chair.

"Leighton?!" Someone patted my face. "Leighton?"

I blinked. My mouth felt dry, and I couldn't get enough air.

"Give her some room!" someone said.

"Here, Leighton, drink some water," another voice said.

It took me a moment to formulate a single coherent thought. I took the offered cup of water and gulped it down greedily.

Keith gone? It couldn't be.

"Here, Leighton." Claire handed me a wad of napkins.

I stared at the napkins in my hand and didn't know what to do with them.

"Dab your eyes, hun," she told me.

I dabbed my eyes and was surprised the napkins had come back wet.

"I umm . . . sorry for making a scene and the mess." I sniffled. "I should go. I need to make some calls."

"Do you want some help?"

"No, it's okay." I robotically walked out of Buzzy's.

As soon as I left the cafe, I called Keith's mother. Mrs. Maynard wasn't taking calls, so I left a message with his aunt, offering my condolences. I called Hallie next and got her voicemail as well.

On autopilot, I began walking. My thoughts were going in a million different directions. Fifteen minutes later, I realized I had been going to my apartment and continued until I reached my complex.

There was a business card jammed between the seam of the door. I unlocked the door and glanced at the card. Detective . . . Why did he stop by? I turned off my alarm and threw the card on the kitchen table when my phone rang.

"Hi baby," Laz said as soon as I picked up.

"Hi," I replied.

"What's wrong?! You sound upset."

"I um . . . yeah, I'm not in a good place. I just learned that Keith is dead. Car accident."

"Whoa. No shit. Sorry, Leighton. He wasn't my favorite person, but I know he was your friend. Do you need anything? I can come home right now if you want," he told me.

"No, it's okay. I'm at my apartment right now. I'll check my mail, pick up a few things, and go home."

"Take your time, babe. I need to take the truck to an auto body repair shop. Somebody side-swiped it in the parking garage while we were gone. Fuckers."

"What? That's unbelievable. Did you get to look at the surveillance in the building?" I asked.

"Not yet. That is next on my list. I'll be home in a couple of hours; you good?"

"Yes," I said.

"K. I love you. And sorry about your friend." He hung up.

A loud thump on my door startled me.

I paused in my kitchen with my hand on my chest, then answered the door.

"Officer Daniels. You're back. Again. What can I do for you?"

"You've been a frequent guest on our follow-up list. How strange! Do you mind if we come in?" he asked. "We have some questions about Keith Maynard."

Aww fuck.

The officers left fifteen minutes and a million questions later. It was the longest fifteen minutes of my life. Keith's parents had told the police that I was his favorite girl and that I had recently called their house, which led them to stop by my place and question me about Keith's potential enemies. According to the scene of the accident, there was another set of tires and skid marks before Keith's car careened off the road. They presumed he had been forced off the road. Keith's car had tumbled down a ravine and caught fire. The driver's side of the vehicle had been damaged, and they were still in the process of determining the make and model of the vehicle that had side-swiped Keith's car and forced him off the road.

I wrung my clammy hands together as I listened and answered their questions. It seemed to have taken hours. Once it was over, I was grateful to show them the door.

"One more thing, Leighton," Officer Daniels paused outside my door. "Have you heard from your neighbor, Hallie Garner? You two were close, correct?"

"Umm, yeah, and no. Yes, we were close. No, I haven't heard from her for almost a week. I tried calling after I found out about Keith but got her voicemail. Why?"

"His frat buddies said the two were arguing the day of the crash."

Fuuuckkk. This kept getting better and better. I swallowed hard and did my best to keep a neutral expression on my face.

"Okay, then, if you think of anything useful, please use my card."

I closed the door and then slumped to the floor.

What were the odds? My ex is pushed off the road to his death, and my current boyfriend's truck had been side-swiped and needed repair.

CHAPTER 45
LEIGHTON

"I'M SORRY, I can't go with you to the service today, babe," Lazarus said.

He'd left town last night, leaving me alone again.

"It's okay. It's probably best that I don't show up to my ex's funeral with my new boyfriend." I told him.

"I'm a phone call away if you need me. And I'll be back tomorrow night no later. I love you." He hung up.

Mixed emotions swirled through me as I drove through the cemetery parking lot, looking for an open spot. When Lazarus and I were together, any doubts I had about him and our relationship went out the window. The minute he left my presence, my mind bubbled over with questions. Had he killed Keith? We were both out of town when the accident happened. I was driving to my mother's, and he was presumably working.

We had yet to discuss what he did at work. He never offered details, and I never asked. Not talking about it made it less real. Although I wasn't bothered by the concept that he was a paid assassin, the less I knew, the better.

As far as the situation with Keith, I couldn't decide if I should ask Lazarus directly or snoop around. He'd be brutally honest if I asked, and I feared he'd say yes. What would I do with an answer like that? Lazarus knew what Keith meant to me, and I'd specifically asked him not to kill him. At the time, I didn't think it was a remote possibility. But now? Like his line of work, generally speaking, ignorance was bliss.

I thought about snooping around his office. I never asked for his login credentials for his home computer and didn't need to. He'd created a login for me specifically, and I wasn't tech-savvy enough to figure out a way to search his files. His desk was clean, not a single paper out of place. And there wasn't much in there anyway.

A few minutes later, I parked the Maserati a block away from the graveside where the funeral would be held. Keith was a popular guy, and I was sure his teammates, friends, and family had come to pay their respects. I wished Hallie was with me, but she hadn't answered my calls or texts.

The graveside was packed, as I expected. I stood in the back, content to go unnoticed, when his friend Toby, the one who had come to my group sessions, waved at me. I waved back, and he motioned for me to sit amongst him and his teammates. I shook my head. His friends noticed, and they all turned. A couple of them waved me over, and the crowd had begun to notice. I quickly made my way to their row and squeezed in beside Toby and Mark. Both men gave me a somber nod, and we sat silently through the service. By the time the service and burial had commenced, I was emotionally wrung out.

"Are you coming to the reception?" Toby asked me.

"I don't think so." I lifted my sunglasses and dabbed my wet face.

"Leighton?" A woman's voice caught my attention.

I approached Keith's mother and enveloped her in a warm embrace. "I'm sorry for your loss."

"Yours too. I'm glad you're here. Stop by the house when you have some time, please. It's good to see you." She squeezed me again and walked away with her husband, who'd given me a sad smile.

This sucked.

Toby and Mark walked me to my car. "So, um, any news from Hallie?"

"She hasn't returned my calls," I replied.

"Good, I hope that bitch stays gone," Mark muttered.

"Why? What happened?" Keith had told me about her coming over uninvited and all that mess. I didn't think his friends were that upset about it.

"You know that she was trying to date him, right?" Toby asked.

"Yeah, I spoke with both of them about it," I acknowledged.

"I'm not sure what she said, but that chick is bad news. Be careful around her," Mark said.

"She was not the person you thought she was, Leighton. We all thought it was weird that you were friends with her, but after I went to your support group, I realized you didn't know. You're different. Hallie is wild. And she wanted Keith badly. She'd sneak into his room when he was asleep. A couple of times, he was with another girl, and Hallie went ballistic. When he told her he'd never sleep with her again and to leave him alone, she got a wild hair up her ass and decided to have sex with all the pledges right there in the middle of our house."

"What?" I stopped in my tracks. Hallie was a free spirit. I knew that, but was she that wild and manipulative? I guess I didn't know her at all.

"Yeah. We changed the locks and told the guys not to let her in. Keith talked to the dean and the coach. Finally, Keith got a restraining order on her a couple of days before the accident. The day of the accident, she was outside the dorm shouting about how she'd have him killed."

"That's insane! But wait, wasn't she out of town?" I tried to recollect what she'd told me about her plans to leave town. She'd told me about her plans to go to Mexico after the intruder broke into my apartment.

"That's what she told everybody, but she didn't. Supposedly, she was staying with some rich guy. I asked her straight up, if you have a

boyfriend who is so rich, why the fuck are you bothering Keith?"
Toby shook his head.

"What did she say?" I asked.

"Told me to fuck off and stomped away," Toby replied.

"Jesus, this is all so crazy. It's like I didn't even know her." I
leaned against my car door.

"Well, be careful. And umm . . . I know you're with that other
guy, but Keith did love you. He only cheated because he was insecure. You . . . you were always the one. You were always his girl."

I said goodbye to the guys, got in my car, and sobbed.

It was early afternoon by the time I returned home. Instead of
going to the penthouse, I decided to go to Buzzy's. It felt like a good
day for some hot chocolate to soothe my soul.

Chocolate goodness in hand, I sat on a bench a dozen or so feet
away from the cafe when someone called my name.

"Hi, Elaine," I gave the woman a weak smile. Elaine was bundled
up in layers of sweaters and a ratty coat. She had gloves on and
approached me with a hitch in her step. In her arms was a large paper
bag. "How are you?"

"Good. Good. I'm just making my way to church."

"That's nice. Do you need anything?" I asked.

She stopped beside me, placed the bag on the ground, then
twisted her torso, stretching her back. "I wouldn't mind the company."

"Sure," I said. "Do you need a hand with that?" I pointed at
the bag.

"Oh, you're too good, me girl. These old bones aren't what they
used to be."

I hefted the bag, which, from what I could tell, was filled with
blankets or maybe coats. It wasn't all that heavy, but who knew how
long the woman had been carrying it.

We walked silently for a while, moving along at a slow but steady
pace. The weather had been warm-ish for the end of December, and
the snow had melted off the sidewalks.

"I can feel your sorrow, Leigh," Elaine said. "Who did you lose?"

"Keith. Ex-boyfriend with the blond hair," I told her.

"I remember. The not forever one." She nodded. "Sad indeed. Not easy to lose people. The only guarantee in life is death, Leigh. It comes for us all. Some much too soon, like your friend."

Although her words were facts, they didn't provide me any solace. I was a loner, and it seemed like my already small circle was getting smaller and smaller. My relationship with Hallie was strained at best, and now Keith was gone. Sure, there were a few acquaintances in school and from working at the library. But I started dating Keith a few months after I started school at Ashmore. He didn't interfere with my studies, but he encompassed my social life. When we broke up, I focused on finishing my studies to graduate a semester earlier, and I had Hallie for the occasional outing. And now . . . Lazarus was my world. Was I doing it again? Living my life for man. What was wrong with me?

"What else is bothering you?" Elaine asked.

"Oh . . . uh . . . just life, I guess. I wasn't in love with Keith, but he was one of my few friends. And now . . . now I have Lazarus. You met him a few weeks ago. I love him, but he's intense. Maybe that's a good thing. I don't want to lose myself in the process of being swept off my feet."

"Good men are hard to find, Leighton. He has a darkness about him. But that darkness can sometimes be exactly what you need. And you provide him with a steady foundation to keep him from drowning in all that dark. It is a good match; you two balance each other out. Life doesn't provide easy answers. What would be the point? Trust your gut to make the right choice. Let his darkness consume you. Or run and live the life you know you can provide for yourself. Both are good options," Elaine said in an articulate-sounding tone.

I side-glanced her. Since the day we'd met, Elaine had always been odd. There were times when her eyes darted to and from, her hands fidgety. Sometimes, she went off on tangents and spoke about strange things. Occasionally, we'd have everyday conversations. Most of the time, she looked tired and hungry. While we walked and discussed my love life, Elaine looked like a wise older woman concerned about my welfare, and I appreciated her sage advice. She wasn't wrong. Laz's darkness was full of power, passion, and possessiveness. And I agreed with her one hundred percent about one thing . . . his darkness would swallow me whole. He loved me. I knew that without a doubt, but was his love a healthy kind of love?

CHAPTER 46
LAZARUS

"CAN HE BE ANY WEIRDER?" Ezekiel said as he followed the ride-share Davis had gotten into. "Odd trips to Mexico, and the team can't get a read on his private residence. He seems to be hopping between places."

"That in and of itself is suspicious," I said.

After the Christmas holiday, our team at the office tracked Chad Johnson while Zeke and I followed Davis. The crew we had following our other brother hadn't found anything interesting, which was suspicious, so we'd decided to follow him ourselves.

Davis had taken a commercial flight to San Diego, got a rental car, and drove across the border to Tijuana. Once there, he'd gone to a motel, stayed for nearly an hour, then went to a bar and talked to the locals.

"Why'd he go all the way to Mexico, fuck a prostitute, and then kill her?" Zeke raised the question that had us scratching our heads.

"Maybe she wasn't a prostitute. Maybe she was someone he knew." I scratched the stubble which had grown out over the last few days. "I'll reach out to my contacts and see if they have a positive ID on the body. That doesn't give us the info we need to present to our father."

Zeke had followed Davis into the motel and had checked out the room after he left. What Zeke had found in the apartment had been disturbing. He'd taken a picture of what he'd seen, which was a naked woman lying in the tub with her face bashed in. She was unrecognizable. I'd done my fair share of killing, but women and children were a hard pass for me. Why Davis had gone after the brunette was anyone's guess.

While all this was happening, I stayed outside and monitored the exits. An hour or so after Davis entered the motel, he went to a bar where he spoke with the locals. Money exchanged hands, and he returned to his car and drove across the border.

We'd taken a jet to San Diego, getting us home quicker than his commercial flight. We'd waited for his flight to land and followed him from the terminal to wherever the Uber driver was taking him.

"Honestly, I didn't think he had it in him," Zeke said. "He didn't seem like the type of guy who could pull the trigger."

"The sneaky fuck is capable of anything. What I can't figure out is his motivation. He's always hated me, but what is his end goal? What does getting rid of me do for him?"

"Both of us. He hates both of us." Zeke continued following Davis's car, which was heading back to Ashmore. "I'd asked Solomon that, and he didn't have an answer."

"Did he have anything to add that might be helpful?" I asked.

"Not really," Zeke replied. Then, he changed the tone of his voice, mimicking our father. "He's had a rough upbringing. His mother was cruel to him and still is. We need to stop ignoring him and leaving him out. He is just as much my son as you and your brother."

"Same shit then," I replied.

"Yeah, same shit. Davis had been given the same trust fund as you and I got. He will inherit his share after Solomon passes. But seriously, aside from how you and I treat him, he's had it pretty good."

"I should have killed him for what he did to me when we were kids," I said.

Zeke didn't say anything.

"Do you think you'll ever forgive him? No offense. I don't know what had happened at Bright Haven, but we were kids, and you turned out okay."

I gave Zeke a dry look.

"Do you think you'll ever forgive him?" I retorted.

Zeke and I had never discussed what had happened when we were kids. And it wasn't something I cared to discuss. I reclined in my seat and closed my eyes, which did nothing to shut out the memories of Bright Haven.

Nineteen Years ago—

"I'm not lying!" I shouted at Dr. Nunes.

"Lazarus, come sit." He patted the cushion beside him.

Dr. Nunes, the psychologist and head honcho of the behavioral institute, sat casually on his sofa. He'd have private sessions with patients—some more than others. I'd watched the kids go into his office trembling, and they returned to the common areas looking like zombies.

I eyed the doctor warily and moved slowly to the couch.

"The staff here are heavy-handed, aren't they?" Dr. Nunes asked. Fucker knew they were. They'd been whipping me repeatedly since day one. My back was a mass of scarred flesh.

"You know how this works, Lazarus. Those prophetic dreams are nothing but your imagination working in hyperdrive. Nothing wrong with that. But when you start spouting prophecies, then that is the work of pure evil. And we don't want to be evil. Only bad people are evil. If you keep making up stories, we have to hurt you. We don't want to hurt you," he continued.

I clenched my fists, my focus fixated on the stupid ballpoint pen on the coffee table in front of me.

"You want to be a good boy, don't you? Here, I have something that will make it better." Dr. Nunes grabbed my hand and placed it on his crotch.

I snatched my hand away, grabbed the pen with the other, and stabbed his pecker.

His cries were music to my ears.

Later that day—

I gazed at Solomon Ford from the passenger seat with a new perspective as he drove his Rolls Royce away from the behavioral institute. My father's face was still red from all the screaming he'd done. "Mark my words, I will shut this whole fucking place down!" He bellowed. His knuckles were still bleeding from him knocking out the male orderlies who had tried to subdue him. They feared my father. I didn't. No, I wanted to be just like him. Mean. Ferocious. I was going to beat people up so they'd never mess with me ever again.

We drove in silence.

"Wake up, Lazarus. We're home," he said.

I followed him into Ford Estate and the kitchen.

"Feed him whatever he wants. Not too much sugar, though," he said to the chef.

"I'll be right back, Laz." He patted my head, then turned on his heel just as Margaret, Ezekiel's mother, stepped into the kitchen.

"Solomon? What are you doing at home so early? I thought you were in Europe for another month. And what's he doing here?" She pointed at me.

"Outside." My father exited the kitchen. "Now!"

Margaret followed, and I sat there quietly and listened.

"Never, ever make any decisions regarding my sons without me!" my father shouted.

"But, he was . . ." Margaret stammered.

"Don't fucking argue with me! Never again, Margaret, or I will throw you out on your ass so fucking fast and leave you with fucking nothing. My sons are off limits to you!" he roared.

My father stormed back into the kitchen and sat beside me. His body was tight with pent-up rage. He was scary, and I liked this side of him.

"Whiskey!" he said in a stern voice.

The chef placed a glass full of amber liquid in front of him. He swallowed it in one gulp.

"Bring me the bottle," my father said, his tone going back to normal.

The chef did as he asked and slid me a plate with a grilled cheese sandwich.

"Leave us," My father said to the chef. "Eat, Lazarus."

I ate. My father sat beside me, drinking his whiskey, and said nothing until I finished.

"Did he hurt you?" he asked.

"No, sir. I mean, well, the doctor didn't touch me. The orderlies punished me, is all."

"How?" The muscles in his jaw ticked.

"My back. It's okay, Dad, you hurt them way worse," I said.

The fury in his eyes faded a bit.

He turned to face me. "How did it make you feel when you stabbed the doctor with the pen?"

"Great! Like a superhero!" I grinned.

My father smiled. "My boy." He patted my arm. "I'm sorry you were sent away. I'm sorry you had to go through what you went through. But . . . a path has been placed at your feet. It will be a hard path. A path I didn't wish for any of my boys. It will be difficult; it will be painful; it will be lonely. The path that is meant for you is one of solitude. But as much as I don't want this, you will be perfect at it. Today, you rest. Tomorrow, your training begins."

"Get up," Zeke roused me awake.

I scrubbed a hand down my face and noticed we'd come to the office where Davis was getting out of the ride-share. I glanced at the clock on the dashboard.

"Why is he going to the office at this hour?" I asked. It was five-thirty P.M. the night before New Year's Eve.

"Don't know. Should we go up?" Zeke asked.

"Drive around first. I have a feeling he's not going up," I replied.

Zeke drove into the parking garage just as his phone rang, and he answered on speaker phone.

"Sir, Davis just returned, and it looks like he is going to the garage. Should we follow?"

I nodded.

"Yep. And stay on him," Zeke replied, and then he turned toward me. "You were right."

"Let your guys take over. I want to get home," I told him.

Zeke nodded. "I'll drop you off, then return this beast."

I stared out the window for a minute, thinking about what had happened at Bright Haven and what Zeke said earlier. Was it time for forgiveness? It had been nineteen years ago, and thanks to having Leighton in my life, everything turned out pretty good for me. Even after all these years, though, something wasn't right with my youngest brother.

"I don't think I can," I said.

"What?" Zeke eyed me suspiciously.

"Let me rephrase that; yes, I could probably forgive him for what he'd done to get me thrown in Bright Haven. But I don't think I could ever have a relationship with him. I'll never consider him a friend, colleague, or brother. And it's not because of the past. It's because he's not the kind of guy I want to be around," I explained.

"I understand completely," Zeke nodded. "I feel the same way. He's like the DRC dudes. Just wrong. I can't put my finger on it, but something about him is off."

"Exactly."

"Let's see if we can get answers from him at dinner tomorrow night. You're coming, right?" Zeke asked me.

"Yeah. I guess," I replied. I didn't want to subject Leighton to my family, but the elder Fords were being pests about meeting her.

Plus, Zeke was right. Forgiveness aside, Davis was odd, and it'd give us an opportunity to corner him.

"You better. Elsa is coming too," Zeke added.

"Why'd you invite Elsa?" I glanced at my brother as we pulled in front of my building.

"Paid, not invited. I figure it'd be good to have someone there to run interference so that we could talk to Davis. And I figure another woman would make Leighton feel more at ease since you know how my mother is."

"Smart move," I said. It was genius. Elsa was a paid actress slash sex worker. She'd be good to keep Leighton company while we talked to Davis and be able to flirt her way into Davis' head if need be.

Zeke dropped me off in front of my building and I trudged upstairs to deliver the news about having dinner with my family on New Year's Eve.

CHAPTER 47
LAZARUS

WE'D ARRIVED at Ford Estate on time because I was nothing if not punctual. Strolling into my father's home with Leighton on my arm lessened the angst usually overwhelming me when I returned home. It helped that my love was stunning in a black velvet halter gown that molded over her curves and accentuated her assets. Like the red dress she'd worn to her mother's, it distracted me to no end. I couldn't keep my hands to myself.

"Did you grow up here?" she asked me.

"Uh, yeah. I lived with my mother until I was six and a half. As soon as my father found out I existed, he fought my mother for custody and won." My hand trailed down her back and brushed her ass.

"Oh, wow. I bet your mother wasn't happy about that," she muttered.

"No, she wasn't, but I spent most weekends with her and my aunt. Do you want to see my room?" I asked.

"Yes, I do." She flashed me a huge smile.

I led her to the grand staircase.

"This place is magnificent." She eyed the cathedral ceilings overhead. "You could bungee jump from the top floor."

I chuckled.

The Ford Estate was at least three times the size of Ron's eight thousand square foot home. The house was more like a hotel resort. It was unnecessary to have a home so large. The upkeep took round-the-clock staffing, and the cost to maintain it was exorbitant. I was glad I'd never have to live here ever again.

"My father came from old money," I explained.

"Did you like living here?" she asked.

"No. It's cold and uninviting." I swooped her into my arms and carried her down the long hallway bridal style.

"I can walk, you know." She frowned.

"I know you can, but trust me. You'll thank me for this. We have a long way to go."

She glanced down the hallway. "You've got to be kidding me."

I chuckled. "No, babe. The children stayed in this wing with twenty-four-seven servants and security keeping watch."

"That's no fun for a kid. But I could remove my heels, Caveman."

"I like holding you close, Leighton. And you weigh practically nothing."

I kicked in the door to the room that used to be mine and then set Leighton on her feet. The room hadn't changed at all. The furniture was the same dark wood. The flannel bedspread was the same. I had been into hunting back then, so I had a few weapons lying around. Aside from those weapons, there was no emotional connection to the room. It meant nothing to me. Material things didn't hold much value to me. I had money. I had nice things. But none of it held sentimental value.

Leighton perused my belongings, taking note of the automatic crossbow.

"How old were you when you started to hunt?" she asked.

"I was seven when I shot a gun for the first time. My weapons training started early, mostly because I tagged along when Uncle Jo and Zeke were taught how to hunt. They're not much older than me.

I was a natural at it and started to take hunting seriously at around eleven."

"Well, this all explains your current profession." She gave me a sly smile. "What'd your girlfriends think about your hobbies?"

"I never brought girls home."

"Why not?" She perched on the double bed.

"I didn't want girls in my personal space. Still don't." Girls were for fucking. And that was it. I didn't say the last part, but that was how I viewed things until I met Leighton. I stood before her and caressed her jaw.

"Aww, you make me feel so special." She peered up at me through her long lashes. I ran my thumb over her bottom lip, and she separated her lips, allowing me to slide my thumb in her mouth. My cock had been hard since we left the penthouse, and now it was painful.

"You are more than just special, Leighton. You are my one and only," I told her. "Now, take off the dress."

I shrugged off my tuxedo jacket and unbuckled my belt, keeping my gaze fixed on Leighton as she let her dress pool to the floor. She bent over to pick up the black fabric, draped it over the bedpost and slowly climbed onto the mattress. She knelt on the bed, her ass resting on her calves. Her knees separated just enough, allowing me to see her pretty pink pussy.

Of course, she wasn't wearing underwear. I groaned.

"You're so fucking beautiful," I told her and pulled out my cock. "I want that red lipstick all over my dick."

She got on all fours and took my crown in her mouth, sucking and licking like it was her favorite lollipop. She worked me over with smooth, long strokes. Her tongue trailed along my shaft as she guided my length down her throat. She kept one hand at the base, and the other massaged my balls.

Up and down, she bobbed over my cock. I gripped the back of her head, pulling at her hair. I was so fucking close. "Fuck, babe," I growled through clenched teeth, doing my best to lock down my orgasm. "I want your pussy. Turn around."

I pulled her off my cock and had her turn, showing me her ass. I gave her meaty flesh a hard smack, then massaged the firm muscle. Leighton moaned my name. I separated her pussy lips, admiring the slick pink skin, and slapped her ass again, leaving another handprint. Juices dripped from her cunt.

"Lazarus, please," she begged.

Her pleas heightened my arousal, but I wasn't done toying with her yet. I slapped her cunt. Her body pitched forward, smashing her face into the mattress.

"This beautiful pussy is mine," I told her and slipped a finger into her hole.

She didn't respond, so I slapped her ass again.

Her cunt contracted over my finger.

"Yes," she whimpered. "Yours."

I removed my finger and replaced it with my cock. It wasn't an even trade, and I should have given her time to adjust, but my cock was dripping with precum. If I didn't get in her cunt soon, this would be a one-sided affair.

Leighton gripped the sheets as I pounded into her sweet pussy. Her cries got louder, and I didn't care. She came hard, clamping down on my cock. Her back arched off the bed. I didn't stop, each thrust driving her body deeper into the mattress. I chased my release until stars exploded behind my eyes. I slumped over her petite frame, my breathing ragged. Her sweet skin was sticky with sweat. I moved her hair away from her face, placing soft kisses from her ear to her mouth.

"Lazarus!" My father's voice boomed from the hallway. "Finish up, son. The rest of the family is waiting."

"Oh shit," Leighton cursed and tried to push me off her.

I laughed.

"Quit laughing, Lazarus! You heard your father."

I rolled over laughing while Leighton went to the ensuite bathroom.

CHAPTER 48

LAZARUS

WE FOUND everyone in one of the eight ballrooms on the estate having a before-dinner cocktail. Zeke gave Leigh a brief hug and introduced her to Elsa. The two seemed to get along just fine, but I'd pulled her away from the actress to introduce her to the others.

Margaret sat primly on a divan, bottle-blonde hair pulled into an artful bun. She had been a lovely woman once, but now the bitterness of being married to my father was apparent in her scorn-filled gaze and thin lips, which never smiled. I made the introduction quickly and moved on to the next family member.

Seated near Margaret was my grandfather, Jeremiah Ford, and his fifth wife, whom Zeke and I had referred to as Number Five since neither of us could remember her name. Leighton, being the lady she was, shook Number Five's hand and had gotten a name that I didn't care to remember. Not that it mattered; she was forty-plus years younger than Jeremiah. Their marriage wouldn't last, and soon there would be a Number Six. My grandfather was pushing ninety but still spry and horny as a dog. He beamed at Leighton, and I maneuvered my body, shielding her from him, and moved on.

"Leighton, this is my father, Solomon, and my uncle, Josiah," I said.

They both kissed the back of her hand. My spine went rigid. I didn't like anyone touching my girl. She smiled demurely, and I pulled her away from them, too.

Davis was sitting off in the corner; he gave us a weak smile, and waved. Leighton smiled back at him, and I could tell she'd wanted to say hello, but I guided her into the dining hall.

Dinner was mediocre. If Leighton hadn't been beside me, I would have never lasted through the entire meal.

My love was the perfect lady in every way. Elegant. Polite. She was intelligent and a great conversationalist. My stepmother had peppered her with a million invasive questions, which pissed me right the fuck off. I'd almost told her to get fucked with her asinine questions, but Leighton placed a firm hand on my thigh, telling me she didn't need my help. She took it all in stride with grace and poise but wasn't a pushover either. Margaret, the dragon lady, had tried to rattle my woman with off-handed questions. She'd pointedly asked, "How long have you been having sex with my stepson?" I glared at Margaret, who had no right to ask the question. She was not my mother and what I did was none of her business.

I clenched my fork and was ready to lunge across the table and stab the bitch in the eye. Leighton laughed and replied, "That's an awfully personal and inappropriate question for the dinner table. How about we save that one for when we're better acquainted? No need to make the rest of the family blush with S-E-X talk. Am I right?" I tipped my head back and laughed. My father's eyes widened with disbelief. Zeke choked on his food. Uncle Jo nodded his approval, and Davis muttered, "Damn." Margaret's face turned beet red with fury. She wasn't pleased with the response she'd gotten, but it did shut her up.

After dinner, we moved into a sitting room so the elders could smoke cigars and the women . . . I wasn't sure what the women of the family did. I'd always steered clear of the dragon lady and Number Five.

Zeke gave me a stiff nod, which I returned, and then he said to the room, "I think I, as the eldest, should take our lovely guests for a tour of the east wing." He made a flourishing bow and offered his arm to Elsa and Leighton.

"See you in a few." I kissed Leighton's temple and watched her stroll out of the ballroom.

"You love her," my father said. "I'm happy for you, son. She's a good match."

My jaw dropped. I made a show of glancing over both shoulders in case I'd been mistaken and he had meant the compliment for someone else.

"Don't," he growled. "I can dole out positive sentiments when the need arises."

"Well, knock me over with a feather," I said in my best Scarlet O'Hara impersonation.

"Why do I fucking bother?" He scowled. "You're childish."

"And he's back," I said. My father walked away, shaking his head.

Jo came up beside me and clapped me on the shoulder. "My brother's wrong. That girl is too good for you." He grinned.

Out of all the men in my family, I was closest to Josiah. He was only five years older, and we both had a penchant for weaponry and killing shit.

"Kiss my ass," I told him.

He laughed. "Brave of you to bring her here, but she handled herself well. I'm happy for you. We all are. Don't fuck up. And if you know what's good for you, marry the girl." Josiah raised his glass and then strolled away to speak with his father.

I walked toward the bar where Davis had been perusing the liquor shelves. He had always skirted on the outside of the family, never really in or out. It wasn't that unusual, considering we'd all inherited the anti-social trait from our father. Unlike Jeremiah, Solomon was never one to have lavish parties or a lot of friends over.

I stood behind Davis for almost a full minute before he noticed me at the bar. He jumped when he finally realized I was there.

"Shit. You scared me."

I smirked. "Didn't mean to. What are you looking for?"

"Not sure. It seems all we have here is scotch."

"If you're looking for something sweeter, there should be some cordials in the bottom cabinet." I tapped the counter to my left.

Davis looked under the counter and pulled out a bottle of amaretto. The dude was so freaking weird. No wonder I didn't like him.

"Your girl is stunning."

"Do not look at her," I snarled.

"Whoa! I was just complimenting the young lady." He poured himself a full glass of amaretto. "Does she know?"

"What she knows and doesn't know is none of your concern." Fuck this would be so much easier if I could just snap his neck.

He raised his hands in surrender and said, "Fine."

"What have you been working on? I haven't seen you in the office. Usually, you're always there," I asked.

"Umm . . . yeah, I've been moving," he stammered.

"Moving? Where to and why?" I prodded.

"Uh . . . I wasn't happy where I was. And I've been looking at an apartment in your building. Haven't fully moved in yet," he replied.

Fuck. The last thing I wanted was him as a neighbor.

"Where are you now?" I fired off the question.

"Huh?"

"You said you haven't fully moved in yet. You must be staying somewhere." I was a shit conversationalist but excellent at interrogation.

"Oh, um . . ." Davis thought about his next lie. Asshole.

"My old place near the edge of town. It's a duplex," he answered.

"Interesting. North Forty is a great location. When do you think you'll be moving in?"

"I'm already renting a spot on the fifteenth floor. 1507. I'll be moving after the new year."

"So tomorrow then."

"Uh yeah, I guess tomorrow."

Zeke and the ladies returned. Thank fuck. I'd gotten enough info for Zeke and me to follow up on. My part was done. It was time to go.

Leighton came to stand beside me. "Are you ready, baby?" I asked.

"Yes." She pressed a light kiss on the corner of my mouth

We said our goodbyes to everyone and got our coats from the staff waiting by the front door.

As soon as we drove away from the estate, I grasped Leighton's hand and pressed her knuckles to my lips. "Let's never do that again," I said.

She giggled. "It wasn't that bad," she replied. "But yeah. I'd rather enjoy the holidays with just us. Ezekiel and Elsa are fun to be around, though."

"Ummm, so they're not a couple. She's a pay-for-hire kinda gal," I told her.

"Really?" She wore a pensive expression as she gazed out of the window. "Why would a guy like him need to pay for a service like that?"

I laughed. "We are complicated men, us Fords."

"Complicated is a nice way to put it." She gave me a devilish grin.

I nipped at her knuckles.

She squealed and tried to pry her hand free from mine.

"Davis is . . . strange. He kept staring at me but didn't say a word. The first time I met him, he was all smiles and talkative. I got the feeling he was desperate to belong. Like he wanted to hangout with the cool kids or something. I almost felt sorry for him." She shook her head. "Tonight, he was weird—like there was something scheming behind his shifty eyes."

"I noticed him staring at you." I squeezed her hand. "Stay away from him, Leighton. He might be moving into our building. Never let him into our house unless I'm there."

"Umm, okay, sure. Lazarus?"

I glanced at her.

"You're hurting my hand."

I relaxed my grip and kissed her palm. "Sorry."

She let the topic drop, and I let my mind wander. Why the fuck was he moving into my building? Something was not right, and I needed to find out what his plans were. If it were just me, I wouldn't fret over the situation. But I had Leighton now, and I would not hesitate to murder my brother if he ever hurt her. And he was the type of sick fuck who would.

"Will you tell me about it? What happened between you and Davis? It doesn't have to be today or tomorrow, but maybe someday?" Leigh asked.

"Yes," I vowed. And I would keep my word, just not on New Year's Eve or New Year's Day. I wanted to forget our families, enjoy what was left of the year, and welcome the new one with my woman in my arms.

"You handled Margaret very well," I said, changing the subject.

"She's just a bully. I feel bad for her."

"Why? She's always been nasty. We used to call her the dragon lady."

Leigh chuckled. "Well, from what I can tell, she's just a bitter woman. She had to raise two children that were the result of her husband's affairs. That had to be a tough pill to swallow."

"True, but she could have left. Solomon would have cared for her financially."

"Maybe she loves him."

"A man like that, after what he'd put her through." I raised my eyebrow at her.

"Love sometimes means we focus on the good and turn the other cheek to the bad," Leigh replied.

"Ahh, I see. So that's why my hitman job doesn't bother you?" I teased.

"I keep hoping there's a metaphorical meaning to that title, like how the death card in tarot readings doesn't mean death. And maybe you're not an assassin but a vigilante superhero."

I laughed. "Paint it whatever color you want baby, I am what I say

I am. I do, however, like the superhero bit. Sounds way cooler than a downsizing specialist. I'm gonna start using that one."

"Sure, change the narrative to fit your agenda. Politicians do it all the time. Maybe that'll be a new career path for you."

I laughed again. "I wouldn't make it as a politician. I don't like people to begin with." I paused and thought about her tarot comment. "I didn't take you for a mystical arts believer. Especially because of the psychology thing."

"Caveman. My interest in psychology is not a thing. I plan on becoming a doctor someday. If I didn't know better, I'd say you had issues with psychologists." She looked at me, and I suddenly felt uncomfortable. I clenched the steering wheel; it wasn't a discussion I was ready for, and thankfully, she didn't press for more.

"I'm not a believer, but I am not a disbeliever either. It's part of my interest in psychology, I guess. It goes against mainstream teachings, but I believe psychology practitioners have a duty to their patients to remain neutral on those topics because some people have strong belief systems in the arcane, whether reading palms, cards, or deciphering dreams. As a professional, I want to be sensitive to a person's beliefs and consider those beliefs when addressing their issues. It's not a bad thing for a person to be intuitive. It's only bad if those beliefs harm the person or others," she said.

"Interesting. My family . . ." I cleared my throat. The way she was studying me made my skin feel hot. I released her hand and ran a finger around my collar. Damn bowtie was strangling me. I unraveled the darn thing. "My mother and my aunt were into those things. Prophetic dreams especially."

"Really?!" she said. "Is it a family thing? Have you had any?"

I nodded—a lump caught in my throat. It was the perfect opportunity to tell her everything, but I choked.

"That's so cool." She smiled and reached for my hand. "I hope to hear about them someday."

Leighton wasn't making fun of me. No, she was generally interested in the subject. Damn, this woman was perfect.

"Someday." I returned her smile and placed her knuckles to my lips.

Her gaze returned to the window as we passed our favorite fried chicken joint, which was still open two hours before the new year. I made a sharp turn.

"Are we getting fried chicken?" she asked.

"Yep. Dinner was total shit."

She giggled. "You're my superhero, Lazarus." She threw her arms around my neck and pecked my cheek.

CHAPTER 49
LEIGHTON

FIVE DAYS after the new year, everything was falling into place. I'd received a paid position at the local Catholic Charities center as a guidance counselor for abuse victims. Doctor Arkesh had recommended me for the position, and the nun who ran the center guaranteed me a flexible work schedule that would help when I returned to school.

"Congratulations, babe!" Lazarus said. "We'll celebrate when I get home."

"Okay, thanks. I love you." I hung up the phone and unlocked my apartment. I wasn't sure why I kept the place, considering I spent every night with Laz and had no reason to return. I checked my mail and had been gathering more clothing items when my doorbell rang.

I groaned inwardly. Every time the doorbell rang, it wasn't good news. I peeked out of the peephole, expecting to see the same police officers, but it was much worse.

"Hi, Leighton," Mrs. Garner, Hallie's mother, greeted me.

"Hi, Mrs. G." I pulled her in for a hug. "Is Hallie okay? I haven't been able to reach her for weeks."

Mrs. G shook her head back and forth, and tears began to fall down her cheeks.

Shit!

"She's gone, Leighton. Her body was found at a resort in Puerto Vallarta."

Mrs. G fell into my arms. I guided the weeping woman to the sofa.

Hallie had stayed in touch with her mother via texts, which Mrs. G allowed me to read on her phone. Hallie had gone on vacation to Puerta Vallarta with a new boyfriend. They got into an argument, and he left her there. Hallie wasn't phased by his departure because the stay was prepaid, and she met someone new and had a great time. The last text she'd sent was the day after Christmas, over ten days ago. Something wasn't right. Either Toby and Matt had been mistaken about Keith and Hallie having an argument two days before Christmas, or Hallie hadn't been in Mexico when she said she was. I was about to ask Mrs. G if Hallie had talked to her about Keith, but the woman was grieving. It didn't seem right to bombard her with questions I was unsure about.

Mr. Garner came to collect his wife, and I left my apartment with promises to help Hallie's parents in any way I could. Once again, my heart felt the heaviness of loss.

Two people who had played an integral part in my life for the last three years, had passed within a week of each other, and I had a niggling sensation in my mind telling me that the two were related.

I parked the Maserati beside Laz's truck and stepped around to the passenger side to look at the recent repairs. Not a trace of damage remained. The niggling at the back of my head returned with a consuming fierceness that was difficult to ignore.

"Miss?" Mike, the head of security, called me as I entered the lobby of North Forty. "A courier dropped off this for you."

He held out a padded manila envelope, and I took it. "Thanks, Mike."

My name had been scrawled over the envelope, and that was it. No sender, no nothing. Interesting.

In the penthouse, I set down the envelope and my other belongings and decided to pour myself a glass of wine. "To Hallie," I said to no one, letting the tears fall.

Cried out, I decided to open the envelope, dumping its contents on Laz's desk. In it was a single USB. I opened my laptop, popped in the USB, and opened the Lazarus Ford file.

After scanning the USB contents, I slammed my laptop shut, ran to the bathroom, and vomited.

It was him. My Lazarus. My stalker. He had been watching me. Stalking me. He snuck into my apartment while I slept and when I wasn't home. To add fuel to the fire, he'd killed them all. Henry. Nick and his friends. Keith and Hallie. It was his truck that ran Keith off the road. It was him in Mexico where Hallie's body was found. It was all him. The pictures were proof. There was no denying it—no sweeping it under the rug. My world began to close in on me, and I blacked out.

Hours later, Lazarus held me in his arms, rocking me back and forth.

"Leighton? Baby? What's wrong?" he cooed.

I jerked away from him, disoriented.

"Do you need a doctor?" he asked.

I took in my surroundings, realizing we were in the bathroom, sitting on the floor.

"I . . . um . . . no, I'm good. I must've passed out."

"And vomited. What happened?" Deep lines appeared on his forehead.

Oh, Lazarus, where do I begin? Where do we go from here? My heart was breaking. I couldn't find the words.

"Hallie's dead," I sputtered.

His eyes widened with shock.

"What? How?" he asked.

I told him what Mrs. G had told me, and his face was a mask of concern with not a trace of guilt or shock. How was I going to do this?

I sobbed. *This is the end.* I'd have to turn in the love of my life for murdering my ex and my best friend. Lazarus gathered me in his arms, and I cried myself to sleep.

———

Lazarus held me close through the night and had stayed by my side all morning. I hadn't said a word. I lay in bed with my grief and broken heart. Why Lazarus? How was I supposed to forgive him for this? How long had he been stalking me before we met? I'd been amazed that he somehow knew my likes and dislikes. I'd thought we had a special connection, and he got me on a level no one else ever did. Was any of it real?

Of course, the only truth he'd told me was about his occupation—the least likable trait he possessed. He'd told me about it from the beginning, so why was I so surprised? Appalled? Henry had tormented me for months. Nick and his friends were a menace. But Keith and Hallie had done nothing to him . . . or me. Sure, my ex and my best friend had been sleeping together, but they didn't deserve death over that. What either of them did with each other or other people was none of my concern. And I didn't care at all because I had Lazarus.

It was cowardly of me to avoid discussing this with him, but I knew he'd smoothly talk his way into my heart, and I'd forget about everything and easily forgive him. In his presence, I wasn't able to think straight. And I needed time. I needed space.

The proof was irrefutable, though, and I couldn't sit idly by with this weight on my shoulders. I'd have to turn Laz in. He was my stalker and a murderer. My love was a murderer.

The hard truth clawed at my insides with a thousand sharp spikes of flame. Why Lazarus?

By lunchtime, I'd made my decision. I left his penthouse and walked to Buzzy's.

"Hi Leighton, how are you?" Claire asked.

"Hanging in there." I plastered a fake smile on my face. "But I need a favor. I need to make a call but left my phone at home. Can I use your landline?"

"Of course." She showed me to the tiny closet, which had been converted into an office.

I dialed one of the few numbers I'd memorized.

"Hello," the male voice said.

"Peanut butter and jelly," I stated the password in a shaky voice.

The man on the other end of the line released a whoosh of air. "What's the address?"

I rattled off Buzzy's address and heard the familiar clickety-clack sounds of him typing on his keyboard.

"Got it. A black GMC Yukon, license plate FMC0742, will be there in three minutes. See you soon."

I disconnected the call, straightened my spine, and forced a smile.

"Thanks," I waved at the manager, left a twenty dollar bill in the tip jar, and then exited Buzzy's for the last time.

"ZEKE, CALL ME!" I ran down the stairwell, leaving Chad floating in a bathtub full of blood.

Before slicing his neck, he gave me everything I needed, proving Davis had been behind it all. Davis and Chad had gone to the same university and had been in a couple classes together. They weren't friends but they'd run into one another at alumni events.

As soon as Davis learned about The Sentinels tracking Chad down, he'd struck a bargain. He wanted them to take out me and Zeke and he'd make sure the info we'd found about their seedy dealings wouldn't go public.

I slid behind the wheel of my rental and emailed the video to my brother, then called Leighton. She didn't answer. I sent a text and then got on the road.

Thirty-two minutes later, I boarded the jet, and my phone rang.

"Where is he, Zeke?" I asked.

"Don't know. The slippery little shit has disappeared again. Are you heading back?"

"Yep, on my flight. I'll be in the office soon."

My phone rang as soon as I disconnected the call with Zeke.

I listened to the caller, clenching and unclenching my fists while he spoke. Fucking Davis.

"Thanks for the heads up, man. I owe you one." I hung up the phone. My legs bounced the entire flight.

"Zeke!" I stormed into his office.

"I have to go." My brother hung up his phone.

"We have another problem," I barked.

"You're freaking me out. What now, Lazarus?" Zeke raised one eyebrow.

"He's pinning this on you and me," I snarled. "Davis. He's pinning the murder of Hallie Garner, the woman in the Tijuana hotel room, on you. He's got pictures of you going into the apartment after her death. And he's got pictures of me waiting for you outside."

"Are you fucking serious? How did he pull that off?" Zeke asked.

I shook my head. "My contact in Mexico is doing what he can to destroy the evidence. We need to find him, like yesterday. The dead woman in the bathtub was Hallie Garner. She was a friend of Leighton's. She was blonde, so I didn't recognize her in the pic. Leighton found out about her death yesterday. The girl's parents were told she'd been found in Puerto Vallarta, which was bullshit. I did some digging, and that's when I got this." I handed him my phone. "Check the email. My contact received the pics anonymously. Luckily, he's the head of the department and corrupt as fuck. I need to wire some cash to keep him happy. We need to trace the IP address."

Zeke's cell rang.

"What?" Zeke answered on speakerphone.

"Sir, we're at the duplex that belongs to Davis. You may want to get over here," one of our employees said.

Zeke and I drove to the other side of town to a duplex that had been registered to his mother.

"Well, shit. He's smarter than we gave him credit for." I scratched my chin, gazing at the underground tunnel he'd dug under his home that went five miles to a lot closed off by a chain-linked fence. Within the fenced premises were several vehicles, a thirty-foot RV, and a truck that looked just like mine. Fuuucckk.

"He's planning to pin Keith's death on me," I growled.

"Who?" Zeke asked.

I told him the story about Leighton's ex while our team set up a blockade around Davis's property.

"We have the evidence against him now. I'll contact APD," Zeke said.

"Nah, man, you need to stay away from the police. I'll deal with APD. You head to the office and get that IP address traced," I told him.

After dealing with the police, I went to the office to check in with Zeke.

"Anything?" I asked my brother as I entered his office.

He gave me a rueful glare. "The fucker sent it from here."

"No fucking way. Clever little punk."

"How'd it go with APD?"

"Easy. They took the truck as evidence. Our team packed the contents from the RV. There's a lot of shit that'll keep us busy for a few days. You need to lay low. We don't know what his next move is." I checked my phone. No response from Leighton. "And I need to get home."

"I was thinking the same thing. There's an AirBNB open in your building. I'll give you a ride," Zeke said.

I redialed Leighton's phone and got her voicemail. "Fuck," I muttered.

"Still nothing?" Zeke asked.

"Something's wrong," I told him. I didn't have a prophetic dream about her, so I assumed she was fine. Although, that wasn't something I could rely on.

By the time we reached the penthouse, I was a bundle of frayed nerves. I stalked through each room.

"She's not here." I called her phone and heard it ring.

I found her phone lying amongst her things in the office.

Why would she leave this behind? I scratched my head.

"Go, Zeke. You don't have to wait around," I said.

"I'll be downstairs if you need me." Zeke shook my hand and took off.

I sat behind my desk with my head in my hands. *Where are you, Leighton?*

She wouldn't leave me, would she? Why would she?

And then I saw it. Amongst her things, on top of her books, sat a manila envelope with her name on it, the penmanship eerily familiar.

I picked the envelope up by the corners and tried to empty it. Nothing fell out. I set the envelope aside to dust it for prints, then looked at her things. Her phone, laptop, and tablet were all there. I'd monitored her through the surveillance cameras before she moved in with me and had done some digging into her background, but I hadn't gone through her computers . . . yet. I backed away from her things and decided to give it a few hours for her to turn up.

Leighton didn't return that night. The shit thing was her best friend was dead, and so was her ex. The only two people I knew of that would have had potential info on her whereabouts. Would she have gone to her mother's? Doubtful. Her father's? Possible but highly unlikely. I unlocked her phone and scrolled through the call list. Nothing unusual. I scrolled through the text messages. Nothing there either. I scanned her emails and deleted files and came up with nothing. *Fuck, Leighton.*

I glanced at her laptop and tablet and said fuck it. She can be mad later. Nothing. In all honesty, Leighton's life wasn't very exciting. She didn't even have nudes.

At midnight, I called my contacts within the police department, frantic to search for her. It hadn't been twenty-four hours, so that they wouldn't put out an APB. But my contact promised he'd have someone checking the traffic camera footage.

Early the next morning, I questioned the security guards at my building, and no one had seen her the day before. My aggravation levels were off the charts, not to mention my worry. She hadn't vanished into thin air. Mike sensed my ire and allowed me to review the building's surveillance. I spent hours watching videos and didn't see her get in or out of the elevators once. I moved on to the access points, including the back entrance used for deliveries and drop-offs. Sure enough, around noon the day before, Leighton exited the doors. She had walked down twenty-three flights of stairs. She meant to leave. Why would she do that?

I tracked her whereabouts out of the building and lost sight of her once she moved onto the side street.

The only thing between that area and the building was the strip mall. My first guess was Buzzy's. I went to the coffee shop and ordered a double espresso. The barista was familiar, but I wasn't the social type. I never smiled or had spoken a word to her or anyone else, for that matter. The likelihood of any of these strangers helping me was dismal, but I had to shoot my shot. People liked her, and maybe they'd help.

"Hey, has Leighton come by yet?" I did my best rendition of a friendly tone.

"Nope. Not today. I haven't seen her for a while, but then again, I've been off," the barista answered.

Thanks for nothing. I smiled and took my coffee to go.

My phone rang. "Zeke. Everything good?"

"Yeah, I was going into the office," he said. "How's Leighton?"

I told him the news.

"Shit, Laz. I'm sorry. Have you hacked into the cameras in your area?"

"I was going to do that next," I told him. "I need to take the envelope with her name on it and have it analyzed."

"I'll swing by and pick up the envelope. You check the cameras, then get some sleep. You sound rough. I'll call you as soon as I have something."

He hung up before I could say thank you.

CHAPTER 51

LAZARUS

SLEEPING while my body was still jacked up on espresso was an odd feeling. I closed my eyes with my heart thumping in my chest and reopened them hours later, still exhausted. The police department hadn't found anything, and neither had I. The only saving grace was the evidence in Mexico had been destroyed via Zeke. He'd sent a virus to my contact's email address. It effectively wiped out his hard drive emails and every file. Yeah, other pertinent info had probably gotten deleted as well, but I had zero fucks to give.

Leighton had been missing for more than twenty-four hours, and I had no leads. What would make my love leave me? She knew I was a killer. That hadn't bothered her before unless . . . did she think I had something to do with Keith or Hallie's death? Admittedly, I wanted to kill them both but had promised to leave Keith alone, and Hallie fucking deserved it. She had let someone into Leighton's home —a fact I hadn't shared with her and maybe should have. At the time, she'd been dealing with the shock of having an intruder in her home, and then the holidays rolled around, and Keith's death had happened. There wasn't an appropriate time to broach the topic. Was there ever an opportune time to tell someone their friend unlocked the deadbolt to your home, allowing a potential murderer in to kill you? No, there wasn't. I should have told her. I should have told her a lot of things.

My phone rang. "What," I answered.

"Uh, sir, this is Martin from the office. I have the print analysis you ordered. There are a few. Michael Sorenson, Leighton Parker, Amy McLaren . . ."

"Who's Amy? Did you find any information on her?" I cut him off. Sorenson was the security guard of the building. Amy was an unknown.

"Yes. She works for a local courier company."

"Send me the info for the courier company."

I was about to hang up.

"Um. Sir," Martin shouted.

"What."

"There's two more. Well, one. Your prints, of course, and your brother's. Davis."

I snapped a three thousand dollar Mikimoto pen in half. I disconnected the line.

"Has anyone found him?" I growled into the phone.

"Not yet, we are still sorting through his things from the RV."

"Call me as soon as you find something."

"Yes, sir."

Davis had said he was moving into 1507. I knocked on the door and then broke in. Aside from a couple of empty pizza boxes, the place was empty.

I returned to my penthouse and gathered a few things, determined to track Davis down. He'd done something to my Leighton. Scared her. Threatened her. Whatever it had been was enough to make her leave me. Damnit Leighton. Why couldn't she have talked to me first?

My phone rang. "I'm on my way back," Zeke said. "And umm . . . there's something you should see. I'm sending it to your email. Laz, don't do anything rash. Let me help you with this."

He hung up, and I waited for the email to arrive.

The email was a video file of Leighton. She left Buzzy's nearly forty-eight hours ago with nothing but a cup of coffee, and that was the end of the video.

Another email showed a different camera angle of Leighton getting into the back of an SUV with no license plates.

She'd left me.

The world tilted on its axis. My knees buckled, and I dropped to the ground.

Hours later, Zeke found me on the floor of my living room. How he let himself in was beyond me. But I was too broken to care.

"She left," I rasped. My throat was raw from weeping.

"She had a reason. She loved you. Something must have scared her off." Ezekiel helped me stand. "Are you going to wallow? Or are you going to find your girl?"

"I don't know where to begin."

I slumped on the arm of the sofa. A solid thud struck me across the face, whipping my head to the side. My jaw was on fire; coppery liquid flooded my mouth. *Fucking hell.*

"Don't be a pussy, Lazarus! You're better than this. Think!" He jabbed his finger into my forehead.

I blinked at him and rubbed my aching face. It took a minute for the pretty stars in my head to subside.

"Yep. I needed that," I said to him.

"What you need is a shower and a shave. And probably some food. Get. I'll order something to eat."

I slowly rose and stepped toward the hallway, then paused. "Thank you, Ezekiel. You're a good friend and the best brother a man could ever ask for."

My brother patted my back. "You'd do the same for me."

I took a shower and skipped the shave, saving my aching jaw from further discomfort.

Zeke had ordered Greek food, which almost had me choking up again.

We discussed the situation, created a timeline, and went through her electronics.

"She must have someone she's close to. Someone in her family," Zeke stated.

"She's an only child. Her parents are divorced. Her father has a kid from his second wife who is not even ten. Her mother married a scum bag. They didn't have any kids." I leaned back in my office chair with a frozen bag of peas pressed to my jaw. Fucker was lucky it didn't break. If anyone else had decked me the way my brother had, I'd have put two bullets in his skull.

"Fuck!" I sat up. "I just remembered something. Her mother's husband had a son. They were friends. Maybe. Just maybe."

I began researching Ron. He had a son—his only heir. There had to be information about him somewhere.

"What the hell is this?" Zeke held up a USB. "Leighton's?"

I shrugged. "Fire it up. I'm going to find this stepbrother."

CHAPTER 52
LAZARUS

THE WIND WHIPPED *around me as rain pelted my skin. Leighton ran along the shore. Away from me. I chased her. She stumbled. I struggled against the storm, desperate to reach her. She was under me, her body cold, her face pale and covered with thick red liquid. Blood. I wiped her cheeks and her forehead. The red liquid poured down in thick rivulets, and her eyes became vacant.*

I jolted upright in bed, panting. Fuck. Not again. The nightmares had plagued me for the past few nights.

Nine days after Leighton went missing, I still hadn't found her or her stepbrother. And we hadn't been able to locate Davis, either. His secretary couldn't reach him; it was as though he had also disappeared. Or was purposely hiding. I suspected the latter.

The USB had pictures of Zeke and me in Mexico. And a video of my truck running Keith's car off the road. Both made it look like I had committed both crimes. I had the proof to prove otherwise, but the evidence appeared damning. It was the pics and videos of me stalking Leighton that was of greater concern. She was going to be pissed. Fucking Davis, had been stalking me that entire time, and I hadn't known it.

To make matters worse, another picture of Zeke in the motel

standing over Hallie's body resurfaced. The asshole was taunting us. I was going insane.

Ezekiel and I had been working non-stop. Zeke tried to find the other brother. And I was trying to find my love. Amid everything we were juggling, Solomon called us into his office demanding an update. My strained relationship with my father had began after my first assignment. He came into my room to check on me and saw that I was unaffected by what I'd done. I remember holding his gaze and thinking, *I'm a man now. I killed for you. We are equals.* My father nodded as though he'd read my mind and walked away. And here we were more than a decade later still staring each other down.

Solomon Ford clasped his hands together and rubbed his thumb knuckles against his forehead. While he was deep in thought, I was losing time. Time that should have been spent tracking Leighton or, at the very least, her stepbrother.

"You have proof of his betrayal. When I find him, I will rip his throat out. End of meeting. I gotta go." I stood.

"Lazarus!" My father slammed his fist on his desk. "Sit." He steadied his breath and in a soft voice said, "Please."

I hit him with a stern glare. "Leighton is still missing. And I have my team working non-stop on finding her stepbrother. I'm hoping she went to him and hasn't been taken by your youngest son. Who we all know is a sick fuck. She could be in danger."

He returned my glare with one of his own.

"Two fucking minutes." I slumped into my chair.

"Damn it! You are headstrong." He shook his head. "I understand you need to do what you need to do. But . . . let me try to reach out to him."

He pressed several numbers on his phone and let the line ring. Davis's voicemail greeting came through the speakerphone and ended with a beep. "Davis, this is your father. I have some great news about your position in the company. Call me back, let's plan a dinner to celebrate."

My father hung up the phone. He then dialed his secretary. "I'm expecting a call from Davis. Stop everything when he calls and make sure the line is traced."

He disconnected the line with his secretary and faced me.

"That's the best I can do. If he calls me first, let me talk him down. If you find him before I do." Solomon took a deep breath. "You have my blessing. Both of you."

Zeke and I left his office. I didn't say it to my brother, but I was determined to find the fucker first.

"Sir." Martin rounded the corner. "We've got a hit on Ron Michaels' son."

———

Andre Guevarra, formerly Andre Michaels, wasn't easy to find. After Andre received his trust fund, he changed his name. He was an architect and married with two children, twin girls who were six months old. I wondered if Leighton knew about them.

"I'm heading out. Need anything?" I said to Zeke on my way out of the office.

"Um . . . nope. Good luck. I'll keep you posted on Davis."

A few hours later, I was knocking on a door in the middle of suburbia. It looked like any neighborhood in middle-class America. The homes had the same cookie-cutter design with a patch of grass, deadened by winter.

I knocked again and jiggled the door handle.

"Took you long enough," a male voice said from an overhead speaker.

"Let me in, Dre. I don't have time for this."

"You're in the wrong place. Go to 5925 Century Blvd. Number 306. It's not far."

His voice disappeared, and I kicked a dent in the door out of spite.

Ten minutes later, I was pounding on apartment number 306.

Andre opened the door to his loft. "You didn't have to kick in my door."

"You didn't have to keep Leighton from me." I pushed my way past him into his loft. The open plan was sparse and appeared to be un-lived in. There were two recliners in front of a fifty-inch television. One wall was lined with books, and the other had an extensive workstation with several monitors and more books. According to my research, Andre was an architect who had worked for himself. This wasn't a work-from-home situation, which meant I must've kicked in the door to his home where his kids were. I'm such an asshole. "Send me the bill," I added.

"I don't need your money," he scowled. *I've heard that before.*

"Where is she?" I asked, crossing my arms over my chest.

"Running from you," he retorted.

"Stop fucking around, Andre. I'm not in the mood."

"Right, because you might kill me." The smug shit turned his back on me and moved toward his desk on the opposite side of his apartment.

Andre was short for a man, about five foot four. His hair was a ruddy brown, shaved on the sides and tousled on the top. He had naturally tanned skin and deep brown eyes. He resembled his mother, a Mexican woman whom I'd been able to find online.

He tried my patience, and I didn't want to hurt him. I counted to ten in my head. Andre began speaking when I got to number six.

"She needed space, Lazarus."

"She's in danger!" I shouted.

Andre tapped away on his keyboard, ignoring me.

"If you care for her," I began.

"I have been caring for her since she was a child!" He cut me off. "I don't know you, but she loves you."

"And I love her. Tell me where she is!"

He huffed. "Perhaps you do love her. The million-dollar question is are you the best man for her, Lazarus? She didn't tell me the entire story, but it sounds like you live a dangerous life. Can you keep her safe? Can you give her a good life and all the things she deserves? Can you make her happy?"

His words were a mule kick to the gut. My line of work wasn't the type of work for a family man. But fuck him, for Leighton, I would die trying.

"I will prove myself worthy of her daily for the rest of my life," I said in a gentler tone.

Andre studied me for a second, then said, "Good answer. Give me a second. I'm booking you a flight. Here, she left this for you." He pulled out an envelope from his desk and handed it to me.

"Not necessary, I have my plane. I need an address," I told him.

"Fine." He waved me off and rummaged through his desk, looking for a pen.

Lazarus,

If you're reading this, you've tracked down the one person in my life who has been my friend and only family. Please don't hurt Dre. He's all I have left.

You probably found the USB among my things. I probably should have confronted you, but every time I'm in your presence, my heart swoons and rational thinking leaves me. I needed space to clear my head. I hope you can respect that and give me time. No matter what happens, know I love you and will forever.

Leighton

Water welled in my eyes, and my heart felt like it was breaking again. *I will make this right, Leighton.*

I glared at Andre. "I hate you for hiding her from me. But . . . thank you for what you did for her when she was fourteen. That was . . ."

"The right thing to do." Dre finished my sentence. "Despite how our paths crossed, Leighton will always be my little sister. I hope you bring her back."

Thirty minutes later, I was boarding my flight. My eyelids were heavy with exhaustion. *Why Leigh? Why didn't you confront me instead of running away?*

CHAPTER 53
LEIGHTON

NINE DAYS AGO—

The only good thing in my life that had come from my mother's marriage to Ron was the stepbrother that came with the package. With Hallie and Keith gone and my relationship with Lazarus blown to pieces, Dre was the only person I could trust, so I called him and gave him the password, which meant, "I'm in trouble and need to get out of town." I had been a child when we came up with our code language, and this was the first time I'd had to use it. At least it wasn't a peanut butter and strawberry jam call. That one meant I had been physically harmed. Small miracles.

The drive to my stepbrother's apartment hadn't taken as long as I'd thought it would. I moved to Ashmore because Dre and his mother lived nearby. I didn't realize how close because I never visited. I sighed.

Every ten minutes for the first hour, I'd wanted to ask the driver to turn around, but the farther we drove, the more sure I became of my decision.

I thought about the evidence. Where did it come from? Whoever sent it wanted to remain anonymous, which was a red flag. Why be sneaky about information that could surely put Lazarus behind bars? Maybe, like me, they didn't want that. But what did that person want? It was mind-numbing trying to figure out where the info had come from when it didn't matter. The evidence was damning and the root of the problem. How the information found its way to me wasn't the issue. The real issue was, how were we supposed to move on? How could I trust a man who had purposely killed two people I'd cared about? How could I ever find forgiveness for those deaths and for stalking me? He made me feel like we connected and understood me when he'd been studying me before and during our relationship. Was our time together a complete lie?

"We're here," the driver announced.

I thanked him and strode to Andre's apartment. After college, Andre moved into the apartment and had lived in it since. Unlike his father, Dre didn't care about flashing his wealth. He'd received his trust fund when he'd turned twenty-one, and the only thing he'd done with his money was take care of his mother.

The door to apartment 306 swung open before I knocked. Dre pulled me in for a fierce hug.

"Dammit, Leighton, you had me worried." He patted my back. "Come in, tell me everything."

Dre and I had bonded after our parents married. Ron and my mother had married the spring before I turned fifteen, and they had left us home alone while they were on their honeymoon. Dre was several years older and treated me like the kid sister he saw me as. And he became the sibling I'd always wanted. He saved me from getting molested by his father. I would have had a very different childhood if it hadn't been for his warnings. Thanks to Andre and his mother's help, I was able to move in with my Dad. It wasn't pleasant for him, though. Our parents blamed him, but Andre and I knew the truth. And ours were the only opinions that counted.

Even after all these years, his father forbade him from contacting me. In true Ron fashion, the man liked to threaten his son and Rosa, the mother of his only child. Dre and his mother had become my surrogate family over the years. They would always hold a special place in my heart, and one day, I would repay their kindness and generosity.

As it were, I was the one in need . . . again. Andre was my go-to when shit hit the fan. Thankfully, I didn't make it a habit of needing his help.

"How's Jenny?" I asked.

"Good, we, um . . . just had twins. Six-months ago." His chin tipped to a photo on his desk.

I glanced at the picture of him holding two bundles, wrapped in pink and white polka dot blankets.

"Dre, they're precious! I'm sorry I didn't know." I hugged him, tears leaking out of my eyes. "Where are they?"

"We moved a year ago. Ten minutes from here. I'd love for you to meet them. Another time of course. Sit, Leigh, tell me what's happened." He motioned for me to sit beside him at his computer station.

I told Dre a version of the truth. I was in love with a man and had recently received evidence that he'd been stalking me and had harmed people I cared about. I left out the hitman detail, stating that he had a dangerous job that often took him out of town. And although I wasn't afraid for my life personally, I needed to put as much space between Laz and me immediately.

"Are you coming back?" Dre asked.

"In time, yes."

"Do you want to disappear? Become untraceable?" he asked.

It took me a moment to decide. Lazarus loved me. It was the crazy, sick kind of love, but love nonetheless. He would hunt me down and hurt anyone who stood in his way. My asking Dre for help had already placed him in danger.

"Lazarus will try to find me. If possible, I need to travel under the radar for as long as possible. But if he shows up, tell him everything."

"If that's what you want, that's what I'll do for you. And you'll love me because I know just the place."

While Dre worked, I penned a note to Lazarus and left it with him. Not even thirty minutes after I'd arrived, there was a knock on the door. I sprang out of my seat.

"Relax, Leigh, it's just Mom. I told her you were visiting." Dre went to let her in.

I remembered to breathe and went to hug Rosa. She convinced me to take a ride with her to get some food.

"Tell me everything, *mija*." Rosa patted my hand when we got into the car.

After I'd moved in with my father, Rosa had become my surrogate mother. We spent a lot of time together for over a year. She was my friend and confidante. My mother had found out we had developed a friendship, and she was furious. My mother raged and forbade me to see her, which wasn't going to work. I didn't live in her house. When her anger didn't work, she played the victim card and would piss and moan about how I'd replaced her with her husband's ex. I felt horrible, so I all but cut ties to Rosa, who understood.

Something about Dre's mom made me want to spill my guts. Unlike my conversation with Dre, I was more forthcoming with particular details about my relationship with Lazarus, but I didn't tell her anything that could potentially make her a target. Rosa patiently listened while I talked, and when I was done, I slumped in the passenger seat of her van, feeling exhausted.

"What is it about me that attracts these predators?" I asked, feeling raw.

"Forgive me, but I think you're giving yourself too much credit in that department." Rosa regarded me with kind eyes and a soft smile. "Those predators weren't looking for you specifically. You caught their attention, but, honey, you're hardly invisible. I think you need to think about the situation objectively. First, I was married to Ron, and I'd suspected he had . . . dark tendencies way before he met your mother. That is not on you. Secondly, it sounds like the stalker and the men who drugged you were repeat offenders. You hadn't been the first, but you sure were their last. The intruder . . . yes, that must've been a harrowing experience. He may have gotten away, but his due will come. And you, my dear, are still alive."

I sat silent for a moment, letting her words sink in.

"I'm sorry about your friends, Leigh. It's frightening when the people you've come to care about are suddenly taken from you. But you're never alone. You have me and Andre always. I know it's an uncomfortable situation for you since your mother is married to my ex-husband, but I'm not trying to replace your mother. I do care about you as though you were my very own. You never have to isolate yourself from me or Dre. I hope you believe that."

Tears stung my eyes.

"As far as this new man in your life . . . he sounds like a very passionate man who is madly in love with you. I'm not saying you should run back to him. But I will say whether this incriminating information you anonymously received is true or not, trust your instincts. If your gut is telling you to distance yourself from him, then do it. Take a breath and give yourself time to process the information. If your relationship is meant to be, then it will. That might mean forgiveness. That might mean understanding. And it might mean saying goodbye to him forever."

Her last sentence felt like a bullet to the heart. *Say goodbye to Lazarus forever?* I couldn't.

"What is your gut telling you right now?" she asked.

Dre and Rosa had saved me from Ron. Both Henry, Nick, and his friends were dead and unable to harm anyone else, thanks to . . . Lazarus. But Keith and Hallie. Why would my caveman hurt them? His only motivation would have been to control me. To tear down my support system so that I was dependent on him and only him. And the stalking. Cameras set up in my room?! That was too much. *Damn it, Caveman.* I shook my head.

"I need time alone to sort this out," I told her.

"Okay, let's get some tacos and get you out of here." Rosa started her van and drove to a nearby Mexican restaurant.

A few hours later, I was wearing a disguise and on a private jet. My heart was heavy, and I was exhausted physically and emotionally, but overall, I was sure I'd made the right choice.

CHAPTER 54
LEIGHTON

IT HAD BEEN MORE than a week since I'd left home, and Dre was right. I wanted to hug him for choosing the island of Kauai in Hawaii as my hideout spot. He'd rented a guest house near the ocean, and I had spent most of my days swimming or walking the beach.

Kauai was a tropical paradise. Day and night for the past several days, I allowed the island's beauty to envelope me. Every morning, gentle rain stirred the earth, painting landscapes of vibrant green. The midday sun kissed my skin, its warmth a comforting embrace. Mesmerizing sunsets cast an awe-inspiring display of orange and pink against the enchanting indigo sky. As the moon rose, its radiant silver illuminated the tranquil waves crashing on the sandy shore. No doubt, it was all breathtaking. Yet, my heart and soul remained broken, unable to heal.

Drowning myself in the turquoise waves, I let my tears mix with the salty ocean. Despite all that had happened, my heart still yearned for Lazarus. *Would this ache never fade away?*

As the natural current brought me back to the shore, despair lingered in my heart, but clarity filled my mind. A profound realization settled within me—I could never turn in Lazarus for the unspeakable acts against my friends. This meant I could never face

Keith or Hallie's parents again. Ultimately, it meant I could not return home.

Without Lazarus, I wouldn't want to return home anyway. It wouldn't feel like home without him. Nowhere would. And then there was the stalking. How long had he been watching me? That was something I couldn't wrap my mind around. Tears welled in my eyes, and the ache in my heart smarted, once again reminding me it had never left.

"Leigh!" Nani waved at me from the house. I waved back and trudged through the sand toward her.

Nani and her husband owned the main house adjacent to the cottage I'd been staying at. They were lovely people and welcomed me into their lives with the warm Aloha spirit the *kamaainas* were known for. They made me feel like family. The Hawaiian couple owned a small restaurant and bar nearby, and I had spent time there helping if they needed an extra hand. I enjoyed the work. It kept me busy, and I loved the locals.

"Hi, Aunty Nani!" I learned quickly that everyone called their elders, related or not, aunty or uncle, out of respect. The couple insisted, and I wasn't going to argue. When in Hawaii, do as the Hawaiians do.

"Howzit! Me and Uncle going *mauka*. Storm's coming. You going be safe at the house, but you can come with us if you like."

"No, Aunty, it's okay. Thank you, though," I told her.

"K. You mind helping Bruddah Kai at the bar later on? We going leave this afternoon."

"Sure. I don't mind at all." I smiled.

"You look good, girl. Da island's healing you. Heart's still broken. But betta." She hugged me and then rubbed my arms. "Too skinny still. Go eat."

I chuckled and watched her walk away. Although Lazarus was always on my mind, being on the islands was soothing for my soul. I was getting fresh air, exercise, and was surrounded by warm-hearted people.

It was a temporary situation, though. At some point, I would need to make some serious decisions. I could stay, which wasn't a bad option considering my surroundings. Or face Lazarus in Ashmore. Or go somewhere else, someplace different. I wanted to continue my education, which meant Kauai was off the list. I couldn't stay in Ashmore either, which sucked because I was looking forward to the new job and school. I could go to Rosa's, which would hurt my mother but dammit, I was tired of being away from the good people in my life. One thing I'd learned from my stay on the islands was that family meant everything. And Rosa and Dre were family.

Later that day, I was at Pauhana's, bussing tables. Bruddah Kai was grateful for my help. The restaurant had enough tables to seat eighteen people. It was near the beach, and most people would order to-go and sit on the sand. The stormy weather deterred people from sitting on the beach, but there was a steady crowd coming to check out the waves throughout the night, making the restaurant busier than expected.

The winds had picked up, and the turbulent ocean crashed along the shoreline, reminding everyone that Mother Nature had arrived, and she had something to say. Tropical storms were common, and the impending storm wasn't a big deal, but Iz decided to close the restaurant an hour earlier.

A few patrons helped Kai and I lock up the restaurant at night's end. We tied down benches, tables, and umbrellas, anything the winds could toss around and use as a weapon.

After closing, Kai handed me a wad of cash before I got on my bike. "Sistah you going be okay or what? Not too safe in this kine storm. I can give you one ride."

"It's fine. I don't have far to go. And thanks for this." I held up the cash. Dre had set me up with money and credit cards, so I didn't need the cash, but Aunty and Uncle vehemently insisted, to the point that it seemed rude to deny their generosity.

"No worries. Aunty and Uncle betta give you one job. For reals."

I laughed. "Thanks, Kai! I can come back tomorrow if you need me." I pedaled my borrowed bike to the Kawaihae residence and wished I had taken Kai up on that offer for a ride.

In a matter of seconds, the typically pleasant, moonlit ride down a two-mile road turned into the ride from hell. Palm trees swayed angrily in the wind. The fragrant plumeria trees cowered under Mother Nature's might. The street was empty, and heavy clouds shielded the moonlight, casting ominous shadows on the otherwise peaceful road.

Halfway home, the heavens opened the floodgates, and rain poured on me. I was going against the direction of the wind, making every pedal stroke forward feel like I'd taken four steps back. I soldiered through the storm, constantly swiping water from my eyes like a damned windshield wiper.

It felt like Mother Nature was trying to tell me something. Or give me a warning. I shrugged the thought aside and kept moving.

By the time I made it to the guest house, I was a drowned rat. My sundress was plastered to my body. My mud-splattered sneakers squished with every step. And the wind tousled my wet hair into a massive bird's nest. I shivered as I parked the bike and hurried to the door . . . which was open.

I paused mid-step and glanced at the key in my hand. I locked the door. I know I did. I took a step back. Lazarus? My heart leaped, and I stepped forward, then stopped again. The house was dark, and my stomach clenched. *This didn't feel right.* I couldn't move. Thunder roared through the skies, prompting me to step backward. Slowly, I rounded the corner of the main house and found myself running down the main street.

CHAPTER 55
LAZARUS

THE FLIGHT to Hawaii did nothing to quell my nerves. My racing thoughts made it difficult for me to fall asleep, and when I did, the nightmare returned with a vengeance. Deep in my bones, I knew Leighton was in danger.

As soon as I landed, my phone chimed with a message from Montpellier. Aunt Pol's message was a garbled mess. Her voice was frantic, and all I got was one word 'left.' Whatever the fuck that meant. Despite the time difference, I called anyway.

"This is Lazarus Ford, calling for Polly Frasier. Is she still awake?" I barked into the phone.

"Oh, yes, there was an incident . . ." the receptionist trailed off. "Let me transfer you to someone that can help." She put me on hold before I could say another word.

"Mr. Ford, this is Lawrence, the night nurse," a male voice said. "Your aunt is asleep and fine. She had a nightmare and woke with a fright. We had to give her something to calm her down."

"Alright. When she wakes, make sure to tell her I called and did as she asked," I said, and then hung up. I'd call her again first thing in the morning.

Aunt Pol had a prophetic dream. Only one word from her

message was clear—*left*. What the hell did that mean? Leighton 'left' me. Watch my 'left' flank. Turn 'left'. Her words didn't make sense, but the message was clear: I or someone dear to me was in danger. I wasn't going to abort the mission. My sole purpose in life was to keep Leighton safe. Her needs and her safety would always take precedence before mine. Aunt Pol's dreams would have to take a backseat. Ideally, Leighton and I would both live and die at a very old age . . . together.

I drove to the address Dre had given me. Leigh wasn't there. Her floral scent lingered in the room, settling my frayed nerves to a manageable level. She was here, and by the looks of things, she'd be returning. I perused the studio and my stomach let out a ferocious roar, a reminder I hadn't had anything since breakfast. Aside from a brown spotted banana and a few packages of ramen noodles, there was nothing in the guest house to eat. Maybe Leighton had gone out for food. I left the guesthouse, locked the door behind me, and returned to my rental car. I drove through town, stopped at a few places she might like, and came up empty. I got some food to go and sat in my car while my phone charged. I called Dre.

He answered on the first ring.

"Did you find her?"

"No. That's why I'm calling. Have you talked to her?"

"Dude, you know our situation. We don't talk. She checked in when she landed, and that was our last communication. I should have warned her that you were on your way, but I didn't. You're welcome."

"Can you tell me anything about the place she's staying? The owners." I wanted to reach through the phone and snap the cheeky fucker's neck.

"Oh, yeah. Aunty Nani and Uncle Kimo. They have a small restaurant near the house," he said casually, like it was common knowledge.

I clenched the steering wheel. "The name of the restaurant would be helpful, Andre."

"I don't remember. It's a Hawaiian name. You can't miss it."

"I've been driving around town and checked out several places already." My voice was tight with anger.

"Are you in town? The little town just outside the airport?"

"Yeah."

"Wrong way. Drive back toward the house and go past it a couple of miles. It looks like a hole in the wall on the beach. Usually crowded because they have the best food."

I hung up the phone and got back on the road.

Just as Dre said, Pauhana was a little shack that was crowded. And there she was, my nightmare girl.

I stalked her with my gaze for a few minutes. The sight of her stole the breath from my lungs. She wore a blue sundress with yellow daisies and tennis shoes. Her skin was a sun-kissed bronze, and she wore a pretty yellow flower behind her left ear. And she was busy . . . working? I watched her from afar for some time as she wrote down orders, brought out the food, and cleaned tables. She was the only waitress, and the place was busy. She'd been there for all of ten days or so, and she'd already gotten a job. A part of me was fuck-all pissed that she was already living a new life so far away from me. And another part of me broke because she was already living a new life so far away from me.

Did she not love me at all? The sight of her moving on with her life was like she'd just stabbed me in the heart with a hot poker. Fuck, Leigh. Should I stay or should I go? Maybe she was better off without me. What kind of future did we have?

She moved through the crowd with the elegance and grace I'd always admired. She was efficient and amiable. And then I glimpsed the one thing that had given me a spark of hope. She greeted everyone with her beautiful smile, but the happiness she portrayed didn't reach her eyes. Leighton was going through the motions, keeping herself busy and faking it.

That bolstered my courage. Whether she wanted to stay in paradise or come home, Leighton was mine, and she would be coming home with me.

My phone rang before I slipped out of my hiding spot.

"Zeke?" I answered.

"Davis is there," he told me.

"Where?"

"There in Hawaii. On the island of Kauai."

"What the fuck? How?"

"He landed twenty minutes ago. He called Solomon, and they talked long enough for us to track his number. From what we can tell, he's been tracking our flights and followed yours to Hawaii."

"So, what does that mean? Where the hell is he?" I nearly shouted.

"The tracker we placed on his number has him near the airport. A motel or something. You may want to get over there."

"Fuck."

I glanced at Leighton. She was surrounded by people, and she'd be safe here.

"Send me the coordinates," I told my brother and returned to my car.

The beautiful evening had morphed into a menacing storm by the time I reached the motel.

Fucking Davis. He was the cause of all this, and now he was here. Murderous thoughts crowded my mind, and I pounded on the door that was registered to him. He didn't answer, of course. Oh, fuck this. I broke in. The room was empty, and his phone was charging on the nightstand.

I called Zeke. "His phone is here, but he's not. There's a storm brewing, and I need to get back to Leighton."

"Ah fuck. We need to microchip the fucker. Go find your girl. Let me know if he turns up."

By the time I returned to Pauhana, it was closed, and the storm raged overhead. I made a hasty U-turn and headed back to the guest house.

The rain came down in sheets. I flicked on the high beams; the windshield wipers were swishing away full blast, and I could barely see. Anxiousness gnawed at the back of my neck, yet I reduced my speed to a slow crawl.

Please be okay, please be okay, I chanted.

Out of nowhere, a lone figure suddenly appeared on the street. Familiar blue eyes locked with mine, and I yanked the steering wheel, making a hard left and slamming my vehicle into a coconut tree.

The airbags inflated and effectively punched me in the face. I sat in place, dazed and confused for a moment. *Leighton.*

The very thought of her made me move. I tumbled out of the rental. Blood streamed down my face. Rain pelted me from all angles while the wind whirled around me. I had no sense of direction.

Lightning flashed in the sky, illuminating the small figure lying on the asphalt a few yards away from me. *Did I hit her?* Bile roiled in my gut like bubbling acid. *No!* I rushed to her side and dropped to the ground.

CHAPTER 56
LEIGHTON

THE SOFT MUD felt comforting against my achy body.

"Leighton!" he shouted. His hands roamed over my neck. "Leighton!" He patted my cheeks.

My eyes fluttered open, and my heart soared. He came for me. He nearly ran me over, but he came for me.

"Thank fuck. Baby? Are you hurt? Anything broken?" He patted my body. His touch was jerky with tension and worry yet gentle at the same time.

"I fell," I said in a meek voice and rose to a seated position. "What are you doing here, Lazarus? You scared the shit out of me."

"We need to get off the road!" he shouted above the roar of the storm and picked me up.

"I can walk!" I insisted.

He didn't hear me, or he didn't care. He probably didn't care. Lazarus carried me to the side of the road.

"Down, Caveman." I wiggled free from his hold, and he set me on my feet and then squeezed my body to his.

"Don't ever leave me, ever again," he whisper shouted.

"Let me go, Lazarus." I shoved him away. As happy as I was to see him, I was still pissed. The things he'd done could never be undone. We had no future.

"Why did you leave without talking to me first?" he yelled.

"You know why." I pushed his chest. "How could you do it, Lazarus?!"

"Do what, Leighton? Tell me what you think I did."

"Oh fuck off. Don't act like you don't know. If you're here, you've seen the pictures and videos. All of it!" I stomped away from him, shivering from the rain.

"Get back here!"

I ran. I needed space just as much as I needed to warm up. It was dark, and the storm hovered above us. The downpour was unrelenting. I took a familiar bike path leading to the beach. Lazarus followed behind me. My foot sank into the sand, causing me to stumble.

Lazarus pounced, pinning me with his much larger frame.

"Ask me, damn it. Ask your fucking questions instead of jumping to conclusions," he snarled. Water and blood streamed down his face. "There's always two sides to a story, Leighton. You taught me that."

"You're hurt. We need to get inside." I reached up to his temple and noticed a gash on his head.

"No! We deal with this right now, Leighton. You owe me that much!"

"Stop being a stubborn pain in the ass! You need stitches. You're bleeding!" I pushed on his chest. He didn't budge.

"I don't give a shit." He crashed our lips together. His mouth and his tongue seared me with possession. My body melted against his, and my knees spread apart, welcoming his heat. My inner thighs rubbed against the gun he'd carried at his waist. His hands cupped my breasts, and his rigid length pressed against my core.

Lightning flashed overhead.

"Lazarus. No. Stop. We need to talk."

"I love you," he told me.

"I know . . . but we need to talk. Please."

He peppered kisses along my jaw and slowly sat up, bringing me with him.

"Oh fuck, you're bleeding." He patted my head gingerly. "Your face is covered with blood." Then picked me up and started walking.

"Lazarus, stop. That's not my blood. It's yours. Put me down."

"Are you sure?" He asked, genuine concern etched on his features.

"Yes."

He set me on my feet and gazed into my eyes. "Ask me your questions, babe," he said in an unsure voice, which made me pause.

Lazarus was never unsure. Did he have a concussion? He needed medical attention.

I stepped toward the house, hoping he followed me.

"No, Leighton. Right here. Right now. Let's deal with this."

I took a shuddering breath. "Fine. Did you kill Keith?"

"No, I told you I wouldn't. That was Davis. He rented a truck that looked like mine. He drove Keith off the road, returned to North Forty, and side-swiped my truck. Ezekiel and I found the truck he'd used."

"That makes no sense, Laz. Someone at North Forty would have heard an accident like that. Don't you think?"

"I'm not lying, Leighton. The police confirmed it," he growled.

I considered his answer for a moment, then asked, "Hallie?"

"No. Zeke and I tracked him to Mexico. He killed her in a seedy motel. Zeke checked out the room after he left and found her body. Her hair had been dyed dark, and well, she was unrecognizable. It was him, not me or Zeke."

"How about the others?" I pressed.

He paused.

"Damn it, Lazarus!" I stomped away.

"Get back here." He snagged me by the elbow.

"Why'd you do it?" I shouted.

"I had to! Henry was stalking you. I saw him outside your window. Nick drugged and would have raped you. He and his friends had been doing it for some time. I did the world a huge favor with all of those kills."

"Do you have any idea what those deaths cost me? The rumors in school. The students who refused to attend my support group. Do you know what a reputation like that could do to my career?" I smacked his arm.

"I didn't mean for that to happen. I never wanted you to get caught in the crossfire. Everything I did to those people was done to keep you safe."

"How long were you stalking me?" I shouted over the storm.

"Only a few days before we met. And I like to call it shadowing, not stalking."

"How could you?! You placed cameras in my room like my mother's creepy as fuck husband!" I caught his chin with a right hook and followed it with a jab to his nose. I kept hitting, unleashing all of the pent-up anguish, regret, and sadness. Lazarus took each hit like he wanted to be punished. I punched and punched until my arms hung at my sides like dead weight.

"Stalking is not cute or sexy, Lazarus. It's fucking creepy as all hell. You saw what it did to me when that intruder came into my house. It frightened me. It made me feel helpless and vulnerable," I said. "How could you do that to me? And then lie to me after you'd seen what I went through."

"I didn't realize how wrong I'd been until I found you hiding in your closet. But I didn't have a choice, Leighton. I had these fucked up prophetic dreams. You died in my dreams every fucking night. What else was I supposed to do? I needed to find you and learn about you and those around you. I needed to identify the threat. All of those men I killed were a threat to your life. I did all of it for you."

His shoulders slumped. "I know you hate me right now. But I'd stalk you, kill them and anyone else if it meant you get to live."

I broke down sobbing. Fury bled out of me like the rain that fell around us. My chest heaved with every intake of breath. Lazarus loved me more fiercely than any other person on the planet—more than my parents, who had given me life.

But his love was raw. Unfiltered. And it came with sharp, jagged edges. I wasn't sure I could survive.

The wind and rain came to a slow but sure stop, allowing us the quiet we needed to have an undisturbed conversation.

"And yes, I should have told you about the dreams. Fuck I should have told you a lot of things. The timing was never right. I messed up. Despite my many mistakes, Leighton. I'm yours. Whether you accept me or not. I will shadow you till the end of my days."

My heart caught in my throat. Prophetic dreams? He mentioned it on New Year's Eve. Was he telling the truth? How would I even know? He'd lied to me for months. I was at a crossroads, my future shrouded with a veil of doubt.

Lazarus took his gun out of the holster at his hip and extended it to me, butt first. "Take it," he said softly. I gaped at him. "Take it!" he shouted. His urgent tone made me flinch, and I took the gun, my hands shaking.

He knelt before me. "If you hate me or worse, if you fear me, kill me now. I'd rather be dead at your feet than see fear in your eyes when you look at me."

"Are you crazy? I'm not going to shoot you!" I tossed the gun in the sand. "Lazarus, I don't hate you, nor do I fear you. I just . . . I don't know what kind of future we have together. How can I trust anything . . ."

"You've got to be kidding me." A nasally voice cut me off.

Lazarus stood and brought me up with him.

"After all the evidence I gave you, are you seriously considering taking him back? Do you know the lengths I'd gone through to prove what a psychopath he is? You have no idea what I had to endure to incriminate him. And here I thought you were more than just a pretty face. You're fucking pathetic." Davis spat in the sand.

It had been Davis all along, which meant Lazarus was telling the truth. My gut lurched, and despite the cold, I felt hot. This was the fucker that had killed Keith and tried to tear me and Lazarus apart. And he nearly succeeded.

"Fuck you, Davis." Laz pushed me behind his large frame. "Why the fuck are you here? Haven't you done enough?"

"No. As a matter of fact, I haven't. You're still whining about your brief stay in Bright Haven like that was all my fault," Davis shouted.

I wasn't privy to their relationship, and so I remained silent, letting the brotherly drama unfold while inching toward the gun I'd thrown on the sand.

"It was your fault!" Lazarus circled his brother.

"It was a mistake made by a child. Solomon never forgave me for that incident. You never forgave me for that. I've been paying for a mistake I made when I was nine!"

"Really? That's your excuse. Why'd you hurt Zeke, then? Why'd you try to frame Keith's murder on me and Hallie's murder on Zeke? Why the fuck have you been setting me up on jobs? You're not a kid anymore, Davis. What's your excuse now?"

"Because with you and Zeke out of the way, Solomon will have zero options, and he'll have to recognize me as his only son and heir." Davis raised his chin.

"You fucking moron. Do you honestly think you can take me down? I'll snap your neck so fast you won't know what hit you," Lazarus spat.

Davis laughed. "Wrong, big brother. I've been tracking you for weeks—every flight. Everywhere you went. How do you think I knew where you were? Where Leighton was? Your assistant is an incompetent man whore, spilling all your secrets to the countless whores I paid to bed him. I was stalking you! I will succeed."

"And you," Davis sneered at me. "I would have killed you weeks ago if the police hadn't shown up."

"That was you?" I gasped. "You're the asshole who broke into my house?"

"Yes, sweetheart, that was me. All it took was for me to dangle a million dollars in front of your neighbor's nose to get her to unlatch that deadbolt, and I was in. The stupid bitch thought she could double-cross me, so I got rid of her, and now it's your turn." He aimed his weapon.

I dove for the fallen gun. Lazarus charged him.

Bang! Bang!

CHAPTER 57

LAZARUS

Time slowed and sped up at the same time. From the corner of my eye, I saw Leighton lunge for the gun she'd tossed to the side just as Davis fired his weapon. She screamed. I couldn't spare a glance to check on her. Rage propelled me forward.

"*Left!*" Aunt Pol's warning flashed in my mind. I stepped to my left. Another shot rang through the air. A battering ram hit me in my chest. Fuck me. I tackled Davis and drove my fist into his face. His jaw cracked under my fist. His body lay still. I tore the gun from his hand, then hurried to Leighton's side.

She lay completely still, her face covered with blood. Her pulse was weak but steady. The dark night made it difficult for me to see where she may have been shot, and I didn't want to jostle her body.

"Baby, talk to me." I wiped the blood from her face and pressed my forehead to hers. "Leighton? Please. Don't go," I pleaded.

Her eyelids fluttered open, and her eyeballs shook in their sockets. "No," she said with a hoarse voice. She raised her hand, the one holding the gun, and pulled the trigger. A loud boom reverberated over the beach.

"*Left!*" Aunt Pol's voice said as though she was sitting on my shoulder. I rolled to my left just as Davis struck the back of my head with a sharp piece of coral. I shook off the hit, raised the gun I'd taken from him, and fired. The clip was empty. Davis rushed me. I rushed back, using my heavier body to overpower his smaller one. Adrenaline surged through my veins. I heaved him overhead, then dropped to one knee and slammed his body down on my other. There was a sickening yet satisfying crunch. He spasmed, frothing at the mouth.

Slowly, I crawled back to Leighton. Her pulse was faint, her face was painted in red. My chest hurt like a motherfucker and a migraine stabbed the back of my skull. I slumped over her frail form, my cheek against her chest.

"Tell me you love me, Leighton. One last time, I need to hear you say it." Her heartbeat thrummed weakly.

In my head, I imagined her speaking the words I longed to hear, and then the world faded to black.

———

LEIGHTON

There was a loud buzzing in my ear, yet it seemed like the world around me was mute. Lazarus was speaking, but I couldn't hear him. The soft sand below me told me we were still at the beach, but I couldn't hear the waves.

Lazarus was lying on top of me. He had come for me. Even after I ran away from him, he still came for me. He'd been trying to protect me the entire time, and he had protected me from not one, but two predators. Three, counting Davis. Four, counting Ron. Those men would no longer hurt another soul. Lazarus, my caveman. Despite his many indiscretions, he truly loved me. And I had turned my back on him. If only I had communicated with him instead of jumping to conclusions. If only I could go back in time.

The weight of him nearly crushed me. Or maybe my body was

weakening from blood loss. I was dying. He was dying. We would die together on this beautiful, romantic beach. "I love you, Lazarus." My voice drifted out into the ocean.

I succumbed to the darkness and hung onto visions of Lazarus—my savior, protector, and only love.

CHAPTER 58
LEIGHTON

FOUR WEEKS later

I parted my hair to the side, ensuring my dark strands covered the left side of my head. The bullet had grazed my temple and taken off a chunk of my ear, tearing off cartilage on my helix. My hearing was fine, and I was alive, but still, it was a reminder of that night on the beach. And yes, I was vain.

It could have been a million times worse.

Although Lazarus and I had made it back in one piece, we did sustain injuries from the night we confronted Davis. The residents in the area had called 911 after hearing gunshots. Police and para-medics arrived, saving our lives. Neither Lazarus nor I had received fatal gunshot wounds, but we nearly bled out, me from the shot that grazed my temple, and Lazarus had taken a shot to his chest.

We spent a couple of days in the hospital, and then we got on a private flight home, where Dr. Hernandez and other specialists had told us to take it easy—a minor concession unlike what Davis had to deal with.

Davis would live the rest of his days with quadriplegia in prison. It was a horrendous state but one he had deserved. There was solid evidence of what he had done to Keith and Hallie. And unbeknownst to the Fords, he had killed his mother and biological father. His mother had shown him DNA evidence proving he wasn't Solomon Ford's son. From what Lazarus and Zeke had said, she wasn't a kind woman. Based on their recollection of the woman, along with evidence of what they'd found at his residence, there had been a lot more psychological abuse he had endured that no one had known about. Davis had gotten his revenge by smothering her with a pillow. His biological father had recently made contact with him, and Davis had shot him in the face. He'd buried both of his parents in the lot he used to hide his cars and RV. He had planned to eliminate Lazarus and Ezekiel to become the only heir to the Ford fortune before the DNA results were revealed. His schemes were elaborate and had impacted so many. I didn't have one ounce of pity for the man.

Aside from missing a chunk of my ear, less than two weeks later, the doctors declared me fully healed and okay for regular activity. I hadn't started my new job yet. I wasn't in the proper mental state to help anyone else with their issues when I hadn't fully dealt with my own. The nun at Catholic Charities understood and postponed my start date.

Lazarus, on the other hand, had to have surgery to remove the bullet and fragments. He needed more time to recover, but rest and recuperate were not in his vocabulary. My hot-blooded man was virile. The minute he had a hard-on, the man would not sit still. He argued with everyone and had become a total asshole. After one week of his assholeness, I ignored the doctor's orders and fucked his brains out. That calmed him down, sort of. We may have busted his stitches a few times because of our extracurricular activities.

He'd gotten shot in the chest at close range. My caveman had been lucky times two. Davis had used a low-caliber weapon, and the bullet lodged into dense muscle, missing vital organs, arteries, and bones entirely. It was still a wound that needed stitches and time to heal.

Laz's voice floated through the penthouse. It was easy to do since he was shouting at someone . . . again. He abhorred doctor visits. And he wasn't shy about letting the world know how he felt.

In the living area, Doctor Hernandez sat opposite Lazarus. The doctor looked pinched as he angrily stuffed his stethoscope and other doctorly gadgets into his medical bag. Lazarus crossed his arms over his chest, his chin raised in defiance.

I hung back for a moment while the two bickered. My caveman, for all his faults, had a big heart when it came to me. He'd proven time and time again that he would always put my life before his.

Laz and I had a long discussion about everything that had happened, starting with his first dream. It was a lot to unravel. The prophetic dreams were unusual and intriguing at the same time. The psychologist in me wanted to delve into his brain and study this phenomenon until he told me about his stay in Bright Haven. He had pent-up trauma from his childhood. That time in his life explained a lot about the man with whom I was in love. I only wished he'd told me all of it sooner.

And Lazarus wished I hadn't left without talking to him first. He was right. My actions were passive-aggressive. I ran at the first sign of trouble. Something I had learned from having to deal with Ron at fourteen. The minute Ron's creepy behavior was revealed, the adults removed me from the situation, which was the right thing to do. However, my teenage brain thought the best way to deal with challenging issues was to run away instead of solve my problems. It would seem this young, budding psychologist could use a little therapy of her own.

Both Laz and I were dealing with the traumas of our past. So, how do a man and woman who both have traumatic pasts make it in this world? Fuck, if I knew. I was still a student of psychology and learning this shit as I went.

I couldn't say I forgave Lazarus for stalking me, but I understood. And the hard truth was: because of his methods, I was still alive, and those men wouldn't hurt anyone ever again.

"Everything okay?" I asked Laz and Dr. Hernandez.

"Yep, doc was just leaving," Lazarus answered with a finality to his tone.

I glanced at the doctor and trailed my fingertips over Laz's shoulders as I passed his chair. Lazarus gripped my elbow, halting me before I could move away. He pulled me close, angling to place me on his lap. I perched on the arm of the chair instead, earning me a glare.

"No, Leighton, it's not. I told Mr. Ford here that he needs to stop his extracurricular activities, or his wound will never heal. But." He threw his hands in the air. "What do I know? I'm just a lowly licensed physician with over eighteen years of experience in the medical industry."

"Make sure to keep the area clean and dry," Dr. Hernandez added. "And please keep the activities to a minimum."

"We will do all of the above," I replied.

Lazarus scoffed. Dr. Hernandez shook his head, waved goodbye, and let himself out.

"You need to be nicer to him." I turned to Lazarus and checked his wound. It was red and irritated. The stubborn man wouldn't let the doctor redress his wound.

"I am nice," he said.

I rose from my seat to gather the supplies.

"Where are you going?" He snagged me by the waist.

"I'm going to clean your wound. It looks irritated," I told him.

"No. It's fine." He straightened in his seat and worked my leggings down over my hips.

"Lazarus, knock it off." I pushed him away. "You heard the doctor. We can't."

"I don't care. I need you in my mouth." He tugged my leggings down and pressed his lips to my pussy.

My body quaked. I rested my hand on his shoulder while Lazarus ran his tongue through my slit in slow, languid motions. He suckled my clit, gently taking the swollen nub between his lips.

"Fuck," I groaned.

His tongue slid back and forth through my folds. I gripped the back of his head. He moaned against my pussy. The vibration sent tiny pleasurable shockwaves up and down my body. I wanted more. More of him. My leggings trapped my legs together, and his firm hold on my ass kept me in place.

My climax rose; I tipped my head back, my moans louder. "Lazarus, sit back." My voice was low and breathy. "Let me ride you."

He peered up at me. My juices coated his sly grin. "Come on my face first." His mouth worked my cunt. His tongue, so soft and so wet, swirled around my clit with a gentle yet firm pressure that was perfect. So perfect. My release surged through me and left me panting and wanting more.

Lazarus leaned back into the chair. A smug look on his face as he whipped out his engorged cock. I removed my leggings and got on my knees. I grabbed the root of his length, opened wide, and took him deep in one smooth swallow. I'd been sucking his big dick to relieve the tension in his body and had been getting better and better, taking his massive size into my mouth.

He let out a deep groan. "That's it. Fuck, baby. You're so fucking good at that," he praised.

His half-hooded gaze locked with mine as I sucked and stroked. His groans of pleasure spurred me on. His muscular thighs tightened. He was close. And I backed off. Prolonging his release. I peppered kisses from root to tip, then blew a soft breath on his crown. His skin prickled, and he hissed.

"I need to come," he pleaded.

I flashed him a devilish grin, suckled his crown, and then released him with a wet *pop*. I trailed my lip from his tip down to his balls and swirled my tongue over the heavy sacks.

He took in a sharp inhale. "Now you're just teasing me."

I chuckled. Lazarus didn't think it was funny. Before I knew it, he had me on the coffee table and threaded his length into my pussy. He rammed into me; each thrust deep and hard. My nails dug into his thighs as he fucked me. My release crested until I reached the tipping point and fell, taking Lazarus with me.

He crumpled on top of me. Our bodies were covered in sweat.

When we finally caught our breath, Lazarus was bleeding.

"Up, Caveman." I tapped his arm. "Let me tend to your chest."

CHAPTER 59
LAZARUS

AS SHE INSISTED, I sat like a good boy and let Leigh patch me up. It wasn't a big deal. The skin was mostly healed; the worst that could happen was I'd have a wicked scar to add to the many. I owed my survival to Aunt Pol's cryptic message. That small inch to my left—twice—caused the bullet to miss my heart and the coral to glance off the back of my skull. We survived, and that had been the easy part.

When we returned home, Leighton had sat me down for a come to Jesus meeting. I didn't hold back. It was either come clean or lose her forever. And so, I told her every painful, tragic, messy detail of my life. It had been the hardest thing I'd ever done, and the best thing, too. A weight I had been carrying for far too long had been lifted off my chest. My flower understood. She and I both had childhood traumas that we needed to deal with, and we would overcome the ghosts of our pasts together.

She hadn't completely forgiven me for installing cameras in her room, but at least she'd moved in. That was a win. I may have exaggerated being injured far more than I had been. It worked. Sue me.

We'd taken a shower and were now back in bed. Both of us needed some time to recharge the batteries so that we could go at it again. This was the life. I grinned.

"What are you smiling at?" she asked. Her fingernails stroked my scalp while my head rested on her tits, the perfect pillows.

"I'm happy. The past few days have been my version of heaven," I told her.

"Oh." Her voice was hesitant, and her fingers paused in my hair.

"Oh? You disagree?" I tipped my head to look at her beautiful face. "You're not leaving Leighton. This is your home. If you want to live somewhere else, closer to campus or work, we'll find a house for both of us to live in."

She shut me up with a kiss.

"That's not it." She drew away. "I love this life, too. It's uh . . . Catholic Charities called this morning to check in. And . . . I told them I was ready to start work next week. I'd planned to talk to you about it after the doctor left, but we got sidetracked," she continued. "It's time, Lazarus. We have to get back to the real world."

I was milking the whole injured thing. Something I wouldn't have done if she wasn't in my life. I liked having all of Leigh's attention. I was a selfish bastard. Most stalkers were.

I'd been working on what I could from my home office. With Davis out of the picture, there was a lot to do. We did a massive overhaul of our internal security systems, accounts, and personnel. Josiah and Ezekiel took care of most things while I managed incoming projects from home. I'd gotten several contracts for downsizing unwanted partners, ex-partners, competitors, and enemies. People still needed to be killed, and I'd been doing my research and prep. I'd hoped to return to the thick of it in another month, but if Leighton was ready, I couldn't hold her back. Well, I could, but I knew she'd just run away again if I did. The thought made me grind my teeth.

"Next week, huh?" I asked.

She nodded.

One week from now. I didn't like the sound of that, but I kept my trap shut for once.

I buried my face between her breasts and felt her squirm under me. I grinned. She was ready again, and I was hungry.

After feasting on her pussy, Leighton fell fast asleep. Thirty minutes later, an acquaintance of mine arrived.

I covered her up and dragged a chair to her side of the bed.

Rufus set up his equipment as silently as possible. "Are you sure about this?" He whispered.

"Yep." I plunged the needle into her skin, smiling from ear to ear.

A few hours later, Leigh stirred, and I escaped into the kitchen while she freshened up. I busied myself, putting a salad together for her, and set the steaks on the counter. I poured a big glass of wine and set it aside for her. She was going to be hungry and probably pissed. The wine would soften the blow.

Leigh entered the kitchen, her eyes hooded with sleep.

"How long was I out?" she asked.

"Long. It's almost eight." I handed her a glass of water. She gulped it. "More?"

She nodded. I refilled her glass, and she sipped it slowly. "Why'd you let me sleep so long? And are you cooking?"

"You needed the rest, and yes. We haven't eaten since morning," I told her. "Wine?"

"Yes, please." She took the wine glass. "I feel so groggy. And I feel . . ." She looked at her hand. "What the fuck is this?"

Here it comes.

"Lazarus?" She narrowed her eyes and began tugging at the bandage.

"Gently, Flower. Here, let me." I slowly unwrapped her ring finger.

"What did you do, Caveman?" Her tone was tight and controlled.

"Married you." I stepped out of striking distance.

"What are you talking about?" She looked at her hand, tilting her head to read the elegant script running along the front of her ring finger from the cuticle down to her knuckle, and then turned her hand over to read the following set words that wound around her finger from front to back. She gaped. "You can't be serious?! Is this real?" She rubbed the reddened skin and winced.

"Property of Lazarus Ford?" She read the new tattoo out loud. "Oh my fucking god, Caveman! Are you shitting me?! What the hell is wrong with you?!"

She punched my stomach and grimaced. Leighton was a good boxer, but she lacked muscle. It was brutal hit for her delicate hand. I tried not to laugh.

"Now it's official." I grinned.

"No, it isn't." She scowled.

"Yes, it is. You left me, Leighton. I haven't forgotten that. I've forgiven, but not forgotten. This helps with my PTSD."

"You do not have PTSD."

"I do, too! I was devastated without you. Ask Zeke. He'll tell you what a mess I was." I hoisted her on the kitchen counter and stood between her legs. "This makes me feel better."

I leaned in to kiss her, and she gave me her cheek.

"No. I'm pissed at you. How did you do this? Did you drug me?" Her voice was full of fire.

"Yeah, of course. I didn't want you to feel any discomfort, nor did I want to disturb your slumber, my beauty."

"Your boy math skills are fucking epic." She released an exasperated sigh.

"They are. Thanks for noticing. Maybe I'll write a book in my spare time. Do you think I'll make a good author?" I grinned.

"Dammit, Caveman! That wasn't a compliment. And do not change the subject! We need to have a serious discussion about boundaries."

"Oh, yes. We absolutely should. I'll go first." I hooked her chin with my fingers and looked her dead in the eye. "As far as you're concerned. I don't have any."

She inhaled deeply and slowly released it. "I love you, Caveman. I'm sorry I left without talking to you first. Next time—"

"There won't be a next time, Leighton Ford," I interrupted her.

She narrowed her eyes at me. "If you think a fucking tattoo is enough to claim me as your wife, you have a lot to learn, Caveman."

"At least I chose a nice font," I teased.

She laughed. A genuine, I'm-not-mad-at-you laugh. Sure, she was annoyed with my antics, but she wasn't angry.

"Lazarus, we need to . . ."

I covered her lips with mine, swallowing any protests she may have had, and kissed her till she was breathless.

"I love you, Leighton," I whispered against her mouth, got down on one knee, and pulled a ring out of my pocket. "Will you marry me?" I gently slipped the ring on her finger before she could answer.

A big smile spread over her lips. "I love you, too. Yes, I'll marry you. Now come here and kiss me, you big brute."

After a brief kiss, she drew away from me.

"For the record, you could have gone the traditional route, and just proposed with the ring."

I laughed. "Leighton, baby, I'm a hit man and ex-stalker. Traditional isn't in my DNA."

Later that night, I lay awake with Leighton sleeping soundly beside me. She'd said yes. The happiness I'd felt was so foreign, I was almost afraid it was a dream or a too-good-to-be-true scenario. Who would have thought a guy like me deserved love from a woman like her?

Please don't mess it up, Laz. I wouldn't; my sins were on the table . . . or were they? A disturbing thought popped into my head, and I shook Leighton's shoulder. Better get it all out now than wait until the wedding night.

"Leigh, baby. Wake up?" I roused her.

"What's wrong, Caveman?"

"You have to wake up. I have something important to tell you." I pulled her into a seated position.

"Oh my gawd, Caveman. What is it with you and these late-night confessions?" She rubbed her eyes.

"If you're gonna be mean, then fine, go back to sleep," I muttered. Maybe it wasn't the best time.

"Spit it out, Lazarus."

I cleared my throat. "So, um . . . remember when I said I was at your apartment before we met?"

She nodded.

"I, uh, I threw out your vibrator. And the replacement."

She swatted me on the head. And on my shoulder and my chin.

"You woke me in the middle of the night to tell me that?! What is wrong with you?! And my vibrator of all things?! Both of them? You owe me three hundred dollars."

"Owe you?! How do you figure? With all the dick you've been getting, I think you owe me!"

She clocked me on my chin. *Owww.*

"Stop hitting me. This is domestic violence! I'm calling the police." I chuckled.

"I should make you sleep in the fucking guest room for bothering me with this stupid shit."

Guest room. Ah fuck. I may as well get it all out there.

"Okay, so one last thing." I grasped her wrists with one hand. "The guest room is where I . . . um . . . entertained the ladies."

"I'm about to give your man business a field goal-winning kick if you don't get out of this bed and throw that fucking mattress away."

I cupped my junk just as she kicked me in the shin. "Right now? It's two in the morning, snowing outside, and I'm still injured." I tried but failed to hide the laughter in my voice.

She wiggled out of my hold with a huff. "Exactly. You throw out my vibrator. You get to throw out your skank pad at two A.M."

She swatted her pillow angrily and flopped back down on the bed, giving me her back. I snuggled into her side. A minute passed, and I asked, "You still love me, right?"

"You're ridiculous."

"Ridiculously in love," I told her.

"That's cheesy."

"You love my cheese."

She laughed. "Caveman, please go back to sleep."

A few minutes later, Leighton flicked on the lamp and glared at me. "Lazarus, why do I feel like you're withholding something?"

Because I am.

"What did you do?!" She smacked my forehead.

"You're a violent little thing, aren't you?" I chuckled. She smacked me again.

"Fine!" I said. "It was supposed to be a surprise."

Her gaze narrowed.

"I emailed Sister Bernadette at Catholic Charities asking if you could start March first. And she said yes."

Leighton hit me a few times. "Why would you do that?! That's my job!!"

"It was supposed to be a Valentine's Day surprise," I repeated. "We're going on a little vacation for a few days."

"Oh." She calmed down. "Wait. Valentine's Day is tomorrow. Did you clear it with Dr. Hernandez?"

"No, of course not. I'm fine. Besides, we're taking a private jet and we're not leaving the country."

"Where are we going?" she fired off.

"Vegas."

"Why Vegas?"

"To get married."

Ah, shit. That was supposed to be the real surprise . . . sort of. I was prepared to do it caveman-style and drag her down the aisle.

"I'm not getting married in Vegas."

"Why not?"

"Marriages that start out in Vegas don't last."

"That's bullshit. But fine, whatever. We'll get married here with our entire family in attendance. We'll have the ceremony at the Ford family church so no one can say fuck, and everyone will have to be on their best behavior. Your father can walk you down the aisle. Your mother can sit in the front row with her husband. We can invite Dre and his mom. And then we'll have a huge reception at the family estate, liquor up the guests, and watch them tear each other apart. Does that sound better, Flower?"

She laughed. "That sounds fucking awful."

Leighton turned out the light and laid back down. "We're not getting married in Vegas, Lazarus."

"Where then?"

"Anywhere but Vegas or here." She snuggled into my side.

I kissed her forehead and grinned. "It's a good thing; I already have a second option lined up then. We'll have the wedding and honeymoon in St. Thomas."

The End

A NOTE FROM THE AUTHOR

Feedback Request

Thank you for choosing Lazarus and Leighton's story! I hope you enjoyed it. Please leave a review as I'd greatly appreciate your feedback. As a new author I am whole heartedly interested in what my readers have to say. Your feedback helps me hone my craft and publish books you'll enjoy reading. Connect with me on my website at: genaviecastle.com

ALSO BY GENAVIE CASTLE

The Kenzie Chronicles - Series Complete

Fae Magic

Fae Blood

Fae Bonds

Fae Chaos

———

Banished, An Elemental Kingdom Novel

Book Two - Available Winter 2024

———

Chained, A Pure Blood Novel

Book Two - Available Summer 2024

———

Nightmare Girl - Available February 14, 2024

Made in the USA
Columbia, SC
15 October 2024

44248077R00192